PRAISE FOR THE AUTHOR

"He has a gift for dialogue." —*The New York Times*
"Really special." —*Denver Post*
"A crime fiction *rara avis.*" —*Los Angeles Times*
"One of the best writers in the mystery field today." —*Publishers Weekly* (starred)
"Ebullient and irresistible." —*Kirkus Reviews* (starred)
"Complex and genuinely suspenseful." —*Boston Globe*
"Credible and deeply touching. Russell has us in the palm of his hands." —*Chicago Tribune*
"He is enlightening as well as entertaining." —*St. Petersburg Times*
"Enormously enjoyable." —*Ellery Queen Mystery Magazine*
"Russell is spectacular." —*San Diego Union-Tribune*
"This work by Russell has it all." —*Library Journal*
"Grade: A. Russell has written a story to satisfy even the most hard-core thrill junkie." —*The Rocky Mountain News*

OTHER TITLES BY ALAN RUSSELL

No Sign of Murder

The Forest Prime Evil

The Hotel Detective

The Fat Innkeeper

Multiple Wounds

Shame

Exposure

Political Suicide

Burning Man

St. Nick

GUARDIANS OF THE NIGHT

GUARDIANS OF THE NIGHT

ALAN RUSSELL

THOMAS & MERCER

Published by Thomas & Mercer, Seattle

www.apub.com

Amazon, the Amazon logo, and Thomas & Mercer are trademarks of Amazon.com, Inc., or its affiliates.

ISBN-13: 9781477825846
ISBN-10: 1477825843

Cover design by Jason Blackburn

Library of Congress Control Number: 2014939860

Printed in the United States of America

To those out there who are serving as our guardians of the night.

PROLOGUE:

FALLEN ANGEL

Wrong Pauley made sure no one was around before he started down the alleyway toward his burrow. His nightly nesting spot didn't qualify as a Hobbit hole, or even a rabbit hole. It was a hollow in the midst of a strip of ice plant above a cinderblock wall that overlooked an alley. The hollow was in a flat stretch resting near to a scraggly American sweet gum tree. The only sign of Wrong's nest was a concave depression in the greenery, but the bald patch couldn't be seen from below. When Wrong settled into the hollow for the night, he was all but invisible.

Scrambling up the incline, Wrong approached the patch of ice plant from a westerly direction. He always took different routes to his nest for fear of leaving a telltale path in the ice plant. Wrong liked the privacy of his burrow and didn't want to jeopardize it. That's why he always came to his spot late at night and left early in the morning. He was afraid of other homeless people encroaching on his territory. There were offices overlooking the alley, businesses that wouldn't tolerate a shantytown in their midst. He wanted to keep it as his private patch.

As usual, Wrong brought with him only his bedroll and bottle. Before setting out to his burrow, he always stashed his other meager possessions. He was more willing to lose those than his sleeping spot. Wrong always packed in and packed out. His bottle, invariably empty by the morn, went out with him. He also collected any other trash he found in the ice plant. He kept his home, such as it was, neatly maintained.

Keeping low so as to minimize the chance of being seen, Wrong sidled into his space. He unrolled his bedding, an old sleeping bag, and then settled on top of it. A sigh of contentment escaped his mouth, but even that was muted. Wrong was glad he didn't snore, or at least he didn't think he did. When he had shared a bed with his wife, Kim, she always commented on how quiet he was.

"You sleep like the dead," Kim had told him. "You don't move, and you never make a sound."

Of course he hadn't shared a bed with her for ten years now. No, it was closer to fifteen. They had been apart for a lot longer than he and Kim had been married. Like a lot of couples who married young, they had drifted their separate ways, and then Wrong drifted away permanently.

She probably remarried, he thought. *Maybe she's a mom like she always wanted to be.* Wrong was glad they hadn't had any children together. At least he wasn't a deadbeat dad.

He reached for his 7-Up bottle and unscrewed the top. Usually Wrong transferred his vodka into soda bottles. That's what he'd done earlier in the day after putting a good dent into his bottle of Kamchatka. Or was it Popov? He bought whatever was on the bottom shelf and whatever was on sale. Though he knew there was really no point in camouflaging the booze, it was a charade Wrong persisted in. The cops knew what was in his soda bottle, but they turned a blind eye to it. If you kept up appearances, the cops in Venice Beach were mostly cool. You never wanted a cop to get a hard-on for you. When that happened, it was time to get out of Dodge. Before coming to Venice Beach, he had been rousted and sent packing from Glendale and Pasadena.

Venice Beach was more tolerant than most places, but it had plenty of its own dangers. Still, for three years he had made it his home. Or was it four? And what did it matter anyway?

He took a long swallow from his bottle. As the warmth trailed down his throat, he sighed, partly out of contentment, partly out of a sense of loss. Wrong took another drink. In an hour or two everything would be all right.

Wrong stared up at the night sky. Overhead the stars were burning bright, as if to compensate for the waning moon. There had been a time when Wrong had studied many things, including the stars in the sky. That was when he was known as Ron and before he became Wrong.

As he took another drink, his eyes scanned the heavens, and he found familiar constellations and stars. That was another thing he liked about his rabbit hole. The lights in the alleyway didn't intrude on his nest or obscure the stars. Wrong stared up at the cosmos. He didn't want to think about the past, present, or future. He didn't want to feel bad, or feel anything, so he drank some more.

It was an unusually quiet night for Venice Beach. Wrong's nest was a few blocks inland from the boardwalk, but in the stillness he could hear the waves breaking as if they were right on top of him. He was nearing the oblivion he wanted, that place where he wasn't awake, but not quite asleep either. His hand moved in reflexive action, periodically lifting the bottle to his lips with the thoughtless regularity of long practice.

In the back of his closed eyelids, Wrong became aware of flickering lights. He tried to ignore the intrusion, but then he heard a whining as invasive to his ear as a circling mosquito.

His first thought was that an electrical storm was approaching. There were several moving lights in the sky, but they didn't look like lightning, even if he wasn't sure what they did look like.

Around him the humming was growing louder. It wasn't music—not exactly—but Wrong felt as if the sounds were reaching out to him. It was like the Pied Piper was playing; the hair on his head and body began dancing to another's tune. There was this sensation of static electricity running up and down his body. He didn't like being touched that way. It felt like trouble. Wrong had survived on the streets by running from any potential danger. He scrambled to his feet and grabbed his pack and bottle, but before he could flee, a burst of light detonated all around him. It was like a thousand camera flashes going off right in front of his face. He covered his eyes, but it was too late. He couldn't see anything. Everything was black.

Wrong dropped to his knees. "I'm blind!" he screamed.

No one answered.

He began clawing at his eyes, trying to free his face from an obstruction that wasn't there. He pulled at his eyelids and waved his hands in front of his eyes. At first he saw nothing, but then he began seeing kaleidoscopic images of dark circles and stars and shapes exploding. Wrong's breathing steadied. He wasn't completely blind.

As his sight slowly began to come back, Wrong tried to make sense of what had happened. By keeping his mind occupied, Wrong could feel his panic subsiding. Once upon a time he had used his mind and enjoyed making sense of intellectual riddles. Had L.A. experienced a nuclear explosion? Could the burst of light have been the result of a meteorite falling? Or maybe the eruption of light had occurred when a gas line ruptured. *No, no, and no,* he thought. There had been no sound of an explosion. And there was no ready answer for the flashing lights in the sky that preceded the blinding flare.

With his mind occupied, Wrong stopped fixating over his eyesight. He was still puzzling over what happened when he became aware of the stars overhead. The starlight seemed muted, and he suddenly realized the alley was aglow with light. His temporary blindness made him cautious about looking directly at the light, so he did his viewing out of the corners of his eyes. It looked as if there was a spotlighted figure sprawled down in the alley. It was almost as if a piece of the sun was now resting on the asphalt below him.

Wrong recalled all the warnings he'd heard while growing up about the dangers of staring at a solar eclipse with your naked eye. Everyone said you'd go blind if you looked at the darkened sun, but Wrong had never been able to resist a few quick glances, just as he couldn't now.

He raised his hands, opened up slits between his middle and ring fingers, and peeked at the figure. The shock of what he saw caused his hands to drop. Wrong wasn't sure whether he should be terrified or fall on his knees and give praise.

The figure was bathed in light. What he was looking at wasn't ghost-like or wispy or insubstantial. It was ethereal, and it wasn't human.

He was staring at an angel, a fallen angel.

CHAPTER 1:

ZERO FOR HERO

It had been a long, hot afternoon of canvassing, and because of that, I began venting to my partner.

"No good deed goes unpunished," I said.

Even though Sirius was the one with the coat of fur, he was still sympathetic to my whining. My partner doesn't complain, but that didn't mean he wasn't feeling the heat. Dogs don't need words to say a lot, but their humans need to know how to listen to them. I noticed he was slightly panting.

"Water break," I announced.

Sirius wagged his tail. We stopped at a brick planter that extended along the front yard of a house and paralleled the sidewalk. I took a seat on the edge of the planter and used the wrought iron as a backrest. The shrubbery made for a good sun break for the two of us.

I poured water into my partner's collapsible water bowl which was adorned with a display of a paw print and the words "Good Dog." Some marketing director must have thought it would be cute to write the words "Good Dog" like a five-year-old might, with reversed letters and smudges.

"I guess we're supposed to imagine that's how a dog writes," I said. "But who would be silly enough to think they could speak for dogs—or write for one?"

It was a rhetorical question, but I didn't bother to tell that to Sirius. Besides, the question was meant for me. I was the one guilty of impersonating a dog.

"I knew you wouldn't mind my writing back for you," I said. "And it's not like you're a very good typist."

Sirius finished with his drinking and offered my hand a forgiving lick.

"I'll bet you would have thought it was funny," I said. "Too bad the public defender, Francisco 'I-am-going-to-sue-your-ass' Garcia, didn't."

Garcia wasn't the only one who was unamused. Captain Brown had called it a "juvenile act," and Captain Becker had been upset I'd used the official letterhead of her station in my correspondence. Chief Ehrlich had told me he was disappointed, and when the Chief was disappointed, you got assignments like this one. "Our" letter was no doubt the reason we were now doing our canvassing.

I joined Sirius and took a long drink.

"It's a tempest in a teapot," I said, "but Garcia is trying to play it up in the hopes of getting a better deal for his scumbag client."

Garcia was representing a lowlife named Enrique Castro; before his capture the LAPD had called Castro "Robbing Hood" because of the hoodie he always wore when doing his purse snatching.

"Garcia is trying to hoist me by my own petard," I said. "You wouldn't happen to know what a petard is, would you?"

Sirius rolled over and exposed his chest. He might not have known what a petard was, but he did know he liked his tummy scratched.

"If Garcia was stupid enough to send that first letter," I said, "what did he expect?"

Garcia had written to "Officer Sirius" asking him to supply a report detailing his involvement in the arrest of his client Enrique Castro. "Officer Sirius" had written back. Well, that wasn't quite true. I had promoted "Officer Sirius" to "Detective Sirius."

"My father was a patient man," I said. "He was much more patient than I am. But even he had his limits. Once or twice I heard him say: 'That fellow couldn't count his balls and get the same number twice.' I guess Garcia detected a little bit of sarcasm in that letter 'we' wrote."

Sirius nudged my hand. My partner has a better sense of humor than Garcia.

"Lawyers," I said.

My ranting about Garcia was more misplaced than not. It was another lawyer, and the client she represented, who were playing on my mind more than Garcia. Criminal defense lawyer J. Gloria Keller, better known as "J. Glo," was now the mouthpiece for Ellis Haines, a.k.a. "the Weatherman," a.k.a. "the Santa Ana Strangler." Haines was back in L.A. to testify on a case. The city was aflutter with the return of its serial-murdering prodigal son. Sirius and I had apprehended Haines, but not before he shot us. We had captured him in the midst of an inferno; the fire had left its mark on all of us.

J. Glo was working on Haines's appeal. The testimony he was giving was in regards to one of Haines's purported victims. Now the thinking was that someone else had strangled the woman called victim number nine. Haines's return to L.A. meant the circus had come back to town, and J. Glo wanted me to be a part of it. Haines was requesting a face-to-face with me and Sirius during his expected short stay in the downtown L.A. County Jail.

It had been months since I had seen Haines. But that didn't mean I hadn't heard from him. Just the week before, I had received an email that I knew had originated from him. For a man locked behind bars, he seemed remarkably unfettered, with minions only too ready to do his bidding. The subject line on the email read: "The Burning of Los Angeles." The message said,

What sustenance is there for you in a land stripped bare by locusts? Do you cry? If so, you are an optimist, for it was written, "Only those who still have hope can benefit from tears." And I wonder if it is you screaming or if it is a police siren, or if there is even a difference. We can talk of this when you visit.

The tone of the email told me Haines was its author, even if I didn't know what he was talking about. After I googled "the burning of Los Angeles," I was led to Nathanael West's *The Day of the Locust*. It was a book I hadn't read, but it seemed like something Haines would love. West's L.A. consisted of masqueraders and the dispossessed. It was a city on the brink, a city bankrupt in spirit and culture. The synopsis of the book talked of riots and deaths, and spoke of the artist and main character, who dreamed of painting the burning of Los Angeles and all the lost souls contained therein. It wasn't a book I was going to read, but it fit in perfectly with Haines and his apocalyptic visions.

The email was untraceable; the sender had made sure of that. But I knew who the sender was.

For a time I had regularly visited with Haines at San Quentin. Ostensibly, I was helping the FBI's Behavioral Unit, but there was more to it than that, even if I didn't like to admit it. My near-death experience had left scars and scabs that I felt the need to pick.

Of late I had tried to distance myself from Haines. You would think that would be easy, but it wasn't. Even from the confines of a maximum-security prison, he was able to reach out to me. I couldn't shake the feeling that my partner and I were in his crosshairs, and he was just biding his time over squeezing the trigger.

Like it or not, Sirius and I were forever linked to this century's messianic bogeyman. For the second year in a row, the Weatherman's displays were topping the YouTube charts. I had heard that some of his rants had more than a hundred million hits.

I looked around. Even on a hot day I felt a chill. Sirius must have sensed my discomfort, for he turned his head toward me and made a little sound.

"It's all right," I said, scratching him under his chin. "Let's get back to work."

We were going door to door in Culver City in the hopes of getting a lead on the man the media had dubbed "the Reluctant Hero."

"I can understand his reluctance," I said to Sirius. "Being a hero is way overrated."

I was speaking from experience. Three years ago the citizens of Los Angeles had decided Sirius and I were heroes after we caught Ellis Haines.

Culver City is a five-square-mile enclave in West Los Angeles. Most of its neighborhoods are identified by parks. We were working the Blanco Park neighborhood near The Corner Elementary School, the same school where the shooting had occurred and the mystery of our heroic enigma had surfaced. Sirius and I were scheduled to do an appearance at the school in a few days. The goal was to bag the proverbial two birds with one stone—we would do community outreach and use that opportunity to ask questions of students and teachers about that enigma now known as the Reluctant Hero.

The houses on the street had been built in the early fifties but were well maintained. So far our canvas had allowed us good looks at the homes, but not many of the people in them. Either the residents were ignoring the stranger at the door, or they were working. NBH was my shorthand of the day—nobody home. The other popular entry in my notepad was D-SAT, police lingo for those who didn't see a thing.

"If someone doesn't want to be a hero," I said, "what law is it that says he has to be?"

Sirius didn't answer. Chief of Police Andrew Ehrlich wanted us to find the hero, but his strings had been pulled by the mayor. The Chief had deemed it a special case, but I still suspected it was a special punishment because of the "Officer Sirius" letter. Currently, two detectives work LAPD's Special Cases Unit (SCU): me and fur face. We're the ones who get the strange and unusual cases that don't fall into neat categories. And sometimes we get the Chief's shit work, especially if we get on his shit list.

I rang the doorbell on a single-story ranch-style home. The tinted glass wasn't quite dark enough to obscure movement behind it, and it was clear we were being scrutinized through a peephole.

"Smile," I said to Sirius.

The door opened six inches. My partner wagged his tail, and it opened another six inches. He likes the game of open the door and is better at it than I am. I can only offer nods meant to be encouraging. The pronounced scarring on my face from our fire walk with Haines looks even scarier when I smile.

I offered up my wallet badge and my name, and the woman interrupted me: "I thought so."

"Excuse me?"

"You and your dog looked familiar. The two of you caught the Strangler, didn't you?"

I nodded. Suddenly she was all smiles. Her eyes were curious, with a shine I had seen too many times before. Otherwise sensible people are fascinated by Ellis Haines, and through me try to get their secondhand thrills.

"Is the Weatherman as eerie as he seems to be in person? He reminds me of a vampire."

"I'm afraid I don't know any vampires," I said and then added, "Missus?"

She heard the question and saw my raised pen. "I'm Heather Francis," she said. "And it's 'Missus' with an asterisk. I'm divorced."

Her smile and manner were flirtatious, but I kept my professional front. "I am here because of what happened at The Corner Elementary School last week," I said. "If you don't mind, I'd like to ask you a few questions."

"The shooter's in jail isn't he?" she said.

"He's locked up and not going anywhere, but we want to make sure he was acting alone. And we'd like to determine whether the shooting was premeditated. Have you been following the coverage in the local media?"

When she nodded, I asked, "Did the suspect look familiar to you? Had you seen him in the area before?"

Heather shook her head. "Not to my knowledge."

"Have you noticed any unusual characters lingering around The Corner School during the last week or so?"

"I don't recall any, but then I try to avoid the school during drop-off and pickup times. That's when it's a zoo."

What had happened was every parent's nightmare. Two days ago our shooter had entered the playground area, rambling about "changelings" and "demon spawn." He'd brandished his gun and ordered the children to line up at the fence.

The chaos had been captured by a teacher surreptitiously filming with her phone. She was afraid another Sandy Hook was taking place, and wanted the video to be her last will and testament. When a custodian and teacher tried to intervene with the gunman, he emptied his magazine in their direction. Luckily, he wasn't a good shot, and only the custodian sustained minor gunshot wounds. As the shooter was reloading a new magazine, the Reluctant Hero suddenly appeared. He blindsided the suspect with a textbook tackle, and within moments other teachers piled onto him.

Only the side of the Hero's face was apparent in the footage. He was white, had dark hair, a medium build, and appeared to be an inch or two shy of six feet. It was likely he was under thirty; all the onlookers agreed he covered a lot of ground very quickly.

I gave Heather Francis an encouraging nod and continued my fishing expedition by saying, "I'd hate to think what might have happened if the Reluctant Hero hadn't shown up."

"He was a godsend," she said.

"And then he just disappeared without even a backward glance, like he was the Lone Ranger."

That's what intrigued the people of Los Angeles more than anything else. L.A. is the capital of promotion, and self-promotion is epidemic. Trying to get noticed is a full-time pursuit for all too many.

"It's likely the Hero is from around here," I said. "Did he look familiar to you?"

"Who could tell? The film they've been showing looks like one of those Sasquatch sightings. The camera is all shaky, and the images are so grainy, it makes it hard to see what you're looking at."

"It wasn't Sasquatch," I said. "The Hero doesn't have facial hair, and his feet are normal sized."

"So much for my theory," she said.

I closed my notepad but wasn't able to make a clean getaway like the Hero.

"I read that you go and see *him* every month," she said.

The hunger was in Heather's voice and her eyes. Ellis Haines received more mail than any prisoner in the world, most of it from women. Some were curious, some wanted to be his pen pal, and many wanted to marry him. It was a rare day when Haines didn't get at least one proposal of marriage.

I began backing away. "I used to do that to help out the FBI. Their Behavioral Science Unit is interested in the FUBAR minds of serial murders."

"FUBAR?" she asked.

I sanitized the acronym: "Fouled up beyond all recognition. Ellis Haines is a psychopath."

My phone began singing, which gave me the perfect exit cue. I called out my thanks and started toward the sidewalk. My phone is programmed with one special ringtone identifying this particular caller. I interrupted the rendition of "Hail to the Chief."

"Gideon," I said.

"Good afternoon, Detective. This is Dawn from Chief Ehrlich's office. Are you available to talk to the Chief?"

"I'm great at multitasking, Dawn. I'm good to talk and piss him off at the same time."

Dawn had been calling on the Chief's behalf for long enough to expect a sarcastic remark, and I was rewarded with a laugh. She was Ehrlich's much-too-pretty administrative assistant. My administrative assistant has fleas.

A new voice came on the line: "How goes the hunt, Detective?"

"I am afraid that today I am zero for hero."

"Hemingway said, 'As you get older, it is harder to have heroes.'"

Before becoming top cop of L.A., Ehrlich had been an academic. His critics say Ehrlich likes lecturing so much that he should return to the classroom, and the sooner, the better. I didn't know much about Hemingway other than he blew his brains out, so I didn't comment.

"Last night dispatch received an unusual call," Ehrlich said. "A man who identified himself as Ron Pauley reported that he had seen a murder. I want you to handle this . . . situation."

"Why am I getting it instead of Homicide?"

"Did I say a homicide had been committed?"

"You said a man identified himself as being a witness to a murder."

"That's correct. But the legal definition of a homicide is the killing of one person by another, whereas murder has a broader meaning."

I was afraid I was going to get a lecture, but Ehrlich cut to the chase, at least by his standards. "This *situation* is already drawing media scrutiny. I don't want it said that LAPD gives short shrift to any of its citizens, and the media needs to know that we're doing our due diligence. Talk to Pauley and follow up on his story. I understand he's homeless but lives in the vicinity of the Venice Beach boardwalk."

"What's Pauley going to tell me?"

"Last night he claims an angel was murdered in Venice Beach."

CHAPTER 2:

DEATH IN VENICE BEACH

In college I read Thomas Mann's *Death in Venice*, a story about a writer who gets fixated on a young man while vacationing in Venice. The object of his obsession kept him in Venice even as an outbreak of plague fell upon the city. I wasn't anywhere near as enamored as my professor was with the story. He found a lot of symbolism and metaphors in Mann's writing. Some of us divine things that others don't or can't.

If I were an angel, I don't think I'd choose Venice Beach as a place to play my harp. Those in search of L.A.'s best freak show go to Venice Beach. What doesn't fit under the big top, or what's been swept out with the elephant droppings, is there. All sorts of performers flock to the boardwalk to sing, dance, gyrate, and do performance art and comedy. They depend upon the kindness of strangers. There are plenty of nonperformers as well, looking for handouts.

My cell phone rang, but I didn't immediately answer. There were two reasons for that: I was enjoying the musical ringtone of the Peter Gunn theme that my lady friend, Lisbet, had installed, and I could see the caller was Captain Brown, the Chief's main toady. Lisbet had also decided my texts should be announced by the Munchkins. It's a good thing my phone is usually in silent mode and set to vibrate.

I had no choice but to take Brown's call. Like Ellis Haines, Brown has two nicknames, but his are Brownnose and Radar. The former needs no explanation; the latter is for his resemblance in looks and actions to Radar O'Reilly from *M*A*S*H*. The two nickname camps seem evenly divided. I usually go with Radar.

Reluctantly, I shut down Peter Gunn, and from inside the car answered his call hands-free. "I am following up on your earlier conversation with Chief Ehrlich, Detective," Brown said.

"Is it true every time a bell rings, an angel gets its wings, Captain?"

"Let's stay on task, shall we?"

Then again, Brownnose isn't a bad nickname either.

"The witness who reported the crime is Ronald Pauley, who goes by the name of Wrong with a 'W.'"

"Right," I said, "with an 'R.'"

"Mr. Pauley usually roosts in an area known as the Drummers' Circle," Radar said. "He has been panhandling in Venice Beach for a few years and has a criminal record. Because of his fondness for drugs and alcohol, he's been arrested for, among other things, being drunk and disorderly, public intoxication, petty theft, and assault and battery."

"So he's no angel," I said.

"That isn't the point, is it?"

"I'm still having trouble figuring out the point."

"The media has picked up on Mr. Pauley's story. This morning he got a spot on drive time radio, which snowballed into more radio and television interviews. Mr. Pauley is on record as saying the police have not followed up with his reporting a crime. We need to show that is not the case."

"I get the need for a dog and pony show," I said. "What I don't get is why the Venice Beach substation isn't handling this."

"The Chief watched one of Pauley's interviews. For whatever reason, he thinks you're right for the job."

"It must be my angelic face."

Radar sighed. "I expect you to be respectful around Mr. Pauley, especially given the media interest."

"I wouldn't be surprised if Wrong with a 'W' listened to too many tracks of 'Stairway to Heaven.'"

"Facts always work better than supposition. Keep me informed as to the status of your investigation."

Radar hung up on me before I could tell him that Jimmy Page once said, "I'm looking for an angel with a broken wing."

Maybe I would have made captain if I had listened less to Led Zeppelin. "Ooh, it makes me wonder," I sang, trying to hit Robert Plant's high notes.

Sirius nudged me. I guess he thought I was sick.

* * *

On a busy weekend Venice Beach can draw up to half a million people. Inexplicably, it's the second biggest tourist draw in the L.A. area, Mickey Mouse and Company being the first. Luckily, it wasn't a weekend, but there were still plenty of people strolling along the Venice Beach boardwalk.

I decided to take in the steroid route and began my walk at Muscle Beach, but only a few bodybuilders were out pumping iron. There was more action on the outdoor basketball courts; when I was younger I'd had enough game not to disgrace myself and had occasionally played on those courts. I could have parked closer to the Drummers' Circle, but my roundabout route was also a trip down memory lane. Jen and I had spent one of our too few anniversary nights at the Marina Pacific Hotel, which is now the Hotel Erwin. It was an adventure for us, a getaway not that far from our home, yet a world away. When I'd made the reservation, I'd mentioned that it was our anniversary, and the staff had upgraded us to a beautiful ocean-view room. Looking at the hotel now, I could see how it had gentrified in the years since Jen's and my stay, but that still didn't take away from my time-in-a-bottle moment.

Sirius and I paused in our walk to take in the view of Venice Beach's long stretch of sand. The sun was sinking into the west; soon people would be watching for a green flash.

"I wish we could both get off our leashes," I said to my partner.

We started walking again. I was the only one on the boardwalk wearing a blazer and a tie. Everyone knew I was a cop, but no one changed their behavior. A homeless man waved his "I Need Weed" sign my way.

There weren't any other dogs besides Sirius; there's a dog ban along the boardwalk that's in effect from Memorial Day until Labor Day. Still, there was an assortment of animals. One man was wearing a boa, as in *constrictor*, around his neck. Not far from him was a colorfully tattooed woman who paled in comparison to the macaw that graced her shoulder.

The scene at Venice Beach wasn't the ocean life as sung by the Beach Boys. The sun, surf, and sand were there, but so were tarot readers, tattoo artists, and psychics. It was L.A. after all; storefronts advertised the availability of Botox at the beach. There were also storefronts that advertised the doctor was in and ready to see to your medical marijuana card. I didn't see the need. Just walking the boardwalk got you a contact high.

Eventually, we made it past the gauntlet, leaving behind the vendors and panhandlers. The vying music from stores and performers gradually became background noise.

The drumming circle hadn't yet come together, but it was just a matter of time. The players were always well away from the boardwalk and were a scene unto themselves. On weekends more than a hundred performers often gathered. Not everyone was a percussionist, but if you could bang it or clang it, there was a place in the circle for you. The middle of the circle was for the swaying dancers, who often danced to the beat of their own drummers. The circle was known to play for hours and hours without a break. From a distance, the argument was always which could be detected first: the beat of the drummers or the scent of cannabis.

I started asking people who looked like locals where I might find Wrong. Most were noncommittal and walked by me without comment, but a few pointed me toward likely spots.

My inquiries brought me to a homeless man with dreadlocks who was missing his two front teeth. Even before I asked, he said, "You here about the angel?"

At my nod he said, "Give me five dollars and I'll take you to Wrong."

"I'll give you a buck now and a buck when we get there."

"You cops are cheap," he said, but extended his hand anyway. I handed him the dollar, and we started walking.

"Today I'm a tour guide," he said. "Be sure to tip your tour guide. Your dog don't bite, do he?"

"It depends on the tour."

"Third time today I've taken people to Wrong. Got me five dollars from them other folk."

"TV people?" I asked.

He nodded. "They not cheap."

"They not underpaid cops."

"You not doing the job right if you underpaid."

"You're probably right."

"I never seen an angel. But I seen the devil three times."

"Is that all?"

"I wish I never seen him."

"Truth," I agreed. "What's your name?"

"Wish it was Abraham Lincoln," he said.

I offered up "George Washington," which he accepted with undisguised disdain. "This don't count as the buck you owes me, or my tip neither."

Then he said, "Moses Perry."

"Is that your real name?"

He nodded, and I asked him his date of birth. I would have guessed him at seventy, but he said he was forty-eight. Living on the streets, you age fast.

"How long have you known Wrong?"

"It's been awhile," Moses said. "Sometimes we work together gatherin' up cans, but not today. He says he's keepin' village."

"He's keeping village?"

"He's stayin' where the angel died."

"He's keeping vigil?"

"That's it."

Moses turned one eye to Sirius. "What big teeth you gots," he said.

"Don't worry about him. He's a pussycat."

"He look like a wolf."

"He's part French poodle."

Moses laughed. "Poodle," he said. "Shit."

"So other than an angel coming to slum here, has anything unusual been going on?"

"You hang here, you sees about everything."

"Is it Wrong's habit to see things that others don't?"

Moses shrugged. "Lots of folk aroun' here not right in they heads. But Wrong's all right."

"Booze and drugs can make someone hallucinate. Is that what happens when Wrong uses?"

Moses smiled, and his missing teeth made the inside of his mouth look cavernous. "That what you want to hear?"

"If it's the truth."

"You sure you a cop?"

"I passed the cheap test, didn't I?"

Moses laughed at that. "If Wrong was wasted, well, then he sober now, and he still tellin' the same story."

We turned inland from Ocean Front Walk. Moses said, "Wrong used to sleep nights on Third Avenue near Rose, but that before Silicon Beach."

Google had come to Venice and opened a headquarters on Second Avenue, what locals were calling Silicon Beach. Moses laughed at the double meaning. I wasn't sure if cosmetic surgery was offered on the Venice Beach boardwalk, but I wouldn't have been surprised if it was.

We stopped walking when we reached an alleyway with an embankment. Moses gestured to a man leaning against a cinder-block wall. Then he opened his hand, which was the signal for me to open my wallet.

I gave him a dollar, and he said, "What about my tip?"

"Why didn't I just give you five dollars when you first asked?"

"You stubborn and cheap," he said.

"When you're right, you're right," I said, and fished out another dollar. Moses took it without a word and walked away.

As I approached Wrong Pauley, both of us studied each other. He was only fifty-two, but deep wrinkles lined his face, and his posture was bent from the world-weariness he carried.

Even though the day was hot, he was wearing an old corduroy coat and had on at least two shirts.

"Wrong Pauley?" I asked.

When he nodded, I identified myself, but not my four-legged German Shepherd partner. Pauley called me on my breach of etiquette. "What's his name?"

His eyes and words were directed toward Sirius. It's always easy to pick out dog lovers. They look at dogs with the same expression a sumo wrestler has gazing at a sushi buffet.

"Sirius," I said.

"Sirius," he said, still staring at my partner. "The dog star."

I hid my surprise. Some homeless people can't remember their own name.

Without being told, Sirius went to Pauley and rested his head on his lap. Pauley's sudden smile seemed to erase all his wrinkles. He began petting Sirius.

"You are beautiful, aren't you?" he whispered.

It was clear Sirius agreed.

Pauley didn't lose his smile, but as I watched, I saw his eyes water, and he was forced to wipe away a tear with the back of his hand. Although his words were meant for me, he did his talking to Sirius.

"Two years ago I adopted a stray," he said. "She was the sweetest little terrier mix you've ever seen. I called her Ginger because she had this ginger-brown coloring. In the sunlight you could even see the red tints in her wiry fur."

He kept stroking Sirius, lost in the reverie of Ginger.

"What happened to her?" I asked.

For a moment Pauley frowned, but the presence of Sirius comforted him. He made his confession to my partner. That's the way it is with some of us; we have trouble opening up with people, but not with dogs.

"Ginger deserved a better life," he said. "She had some close calls from the gangbangers who would bring their monsters to the boardwalk and not control them."

Pauley shook his head. "One time Ginger had to jump into my arms to escape the jaws of a pit bull. Thank God, I caught her. She would have been a chew toy."

Sirius licked Pauley's hand. "Oh, you are beautiful," he told my partner once again. "Ginger was beautiful too."

As Pauley scratched Sirius's chest, their foreheads touched. "You got to be able to take care of your dog, and I wasn't able to. Ginger wasn't eating right. She never went hungry—I saw to that—but there were days I couldn't get her dog food, and she had to eat bologna or hot dogs. I got no problem treating myself like shit, but I couldn't do that to Ginger.

"So one day we took a long walk over to West Pico, and I made a deal with the people at the shelter. I told them they had to find Ginger a nice family. I made them promise me they wouldn't put her down, and I said I would be visiting every day to make sure of that.

"When I left Ginger there, she raised a ruckus, yipping and crying. Even when they took her away, I could still hear her. It nearly broke my heart."

Pauley stopped talking. He buried his face a little more into Sirius, and I saw his body shake a few times with suppressed sobs. Finally, he began talking to my partner again.

"I went back the next day, and the next and the next," he said. "I never saw Ginger because I didn't want to get her upset, but she always sniffed me out or heard me talking to the people at the desk, and she cried for me to get her out, but I couldn't do that.

"I wanted to, but it wouldn't have been right. You know what I hate more than anything else? I hate it when bums use their dogs like they're an ATM and wave signs that say, 'My Dog is Hungry.' In my experience they're the worst. Their dog is only a prop for getting them drug and booze money. Those are the dogs animal control should be picking up for their own good.

"Bastards," he said.

Pauley didn't say anything for a minute, and I didn't rush him. "On the fourth day, Ginger was gone," he said. "They told me a family came in with two little girls, and the children fell in love with her. That's what I wanted to hear more than anything, but it still hurt. I knew I'd never see my Ginger again. But I'm glad that's how it turned out. Whenever I have a bad day, all I have to do is think about Ginger with her family, and that makes me feel good."

With his confession done, Pauley raised his head and took a deep breath. When my partner likes to tell me that everything is all right, and I don't need to be sad, he offers me his paw. That's what he did with Pauley. Wrong solemnly shook.

"I am very happy to have made your acquaintance, Sirius."

I decided to get in on the conversation. "I heard you saw something unusual last night, Mr. Pauley."

He nodded, but he was still more comfortable speaking to Sirius than to me.

"I think I experienced a miracle. That sounds crazy, I know, but I am not sure what else to call it."

"Tell me what happened."

He took a deep breath. "I was sleeping over there," he said, pointing to the eucalyptus tree resting above the embankment that was surrounded by ice plants. "It's a good spot. My back's protected, and from ground level no one can see me."

I nodded. You don't survive on the streets without being careful. I listened as Pauley talked to my partner about seeing strange lights in the sky, and how the hairs on his body rose up and how he was blinded. When his vision came back, he said, the alley was awash in light.

"And that's when I saw a being of light," he said. "I saw ethereal light, the kind of light you only see in Renaissance paintings, the kind of glow that cannot be contained. Never before had I seen such a light. It was like the nimbus of the moon had come down to rest in my alley. I saw the otherworldly."

"When did this happen?"

"I would guess it was a little after two in the morning. I don't have a watch. Normally, I would have been long asleep, but the lights in the sky still had me up."

"Could it have been an electrical storm?"

Pauley shook his head and turned from Sirius to look at me. "There was a pattern to the light. I suspect some kind of triangulation was occurring."

I must not have hidden my surprise very well. "Once upon a time I was a civil engineer," Pauley said, "but then I became an uncivil engineer."

Pauley seemed to appreciate my laugh and began directing his answers more to me than my partner. "I tried to make sense of the lights," he said. "At first I thought it might be one of those moving spotlights advertising a business. But the dispersal of light wasn't right."

"What do you mean by that?"

"It didn't follow a regular pattern. And the angle of the lights was such that it was clear it wasn't being generated from the ground."

I continued jotting down my notes while trying to hide my surprise. A Cal Tech professor might talk about dispersal of light and the angle from which it was generated, but I didn't expect that explanation from someone who lived on the streets.

"Then the lights drew closer, and the humming became louder," he said. "Before it had been like the annoying whine of a mosquito, or a swarm of mosquitoes, but suddenly it was right on top of me. That's when my hair rose up."

"As in it actually stood up?"

He nodded. "I'm talking head, arms, and legs."

"Mr. Pauley, were you drinking last night?"

"Of course I was," he said, "just as I have every day and night for as long as I can remember, except for today."

"What happened today?"

"I chose not to drink. I have been sober for the last fifteen hours."

There was no sign of delirium tremens or any withdrawal effects. Every time Pauley opened his mouth, I was impressed by his clarity. He surprised me. I was like the audience who pre-judged Susan Boyle before she sang in public for the first time; her voice was not what they expected. Wrong Pauley wasn't what I expected.

"What prompted this newfound sobriety?"

"I wanted to be clearheaded in my testimony. I know it is human nature to discredit what I saw. And the ramblings of a drunk would make such a dismissal that much easier. I don't want naysayers to have that opportunity."

"I'd like to know exactly what it is that you saw."

"I saw an angel murdered."

CHAPTER 3:

ANOTHER RUNNER IN THE NIGHT

"Let's hear about this hark the angel," I said.

"No hark," said Pauley, "no trumpets. But there were lights, lots of lights."

He pointed to a spot about fifty feet down the alley. "The burst of light came from that direction. I would almost call it a detonation of light. Imagine if a magnesium flare went off right in front of your face. I was blinded by the light."

I wasn't sure whether his reference was to Paul of Tarsus or Manfred Mann.

"Bit by bit my vision started coming back," he said. "I conjectured all sorts of possibilities for that light. When I saw the alley lit up, I wondered if a shooting star had landed in Venice. But it was a different kind of heavenly body. I looked upon an angel."

"How can you be sure what you saw was an angel?"

"It was a being of light, a life form of radiance. What else could it have been?"

"I'm not sure. That's why I'm asking questions. What did your angel look like?"

"It had a manlike form, but from it shined a light I could only describe as heavenly. What I saw was not flesh and blood. It was a being of light."

"If what you saw was manlike, was it male?"

"His features looked male."

"Did he have wings?"

"Not so as I noticed. But he was on his side, and I didn't take notice of his back. My attention was on his chest. That's where he was wounded."

"You could see the wound?"

"What I saw was his life force draining out ."

"Can you be more specific?"

"I watched a man bleed out once," Pauley said. "That's what was happening to the angel, but instead of bleeding blood, he was bleeding light. Light kept streaming from out of his chest. It was like his heart was pumping out iridescence."

He choked up and was unable to continue talking. Tears streamed down his face. Sirius sensed his distress and gently nudged him with his muzzle. Pauley seemed grateful for the contact and ran his hands down Sirius's nape.

"It's my job to be skeptical," I said. "I am the cop version of Doubting Thomas. If I can't see the wounds or touch them, I need to ask a lot of questions."

"I understand."

"Could what you have seen been some kind of reflection, maybe some kind of anomaly of light?"

Pauley shook his head. "If you had been in the angel's presence, and seen and felt what I did, you would know that what I was looking at was not the aurora borealis or some kind of diffraction of moonlight, but an actual being."

His articulate testimony made me forget Pauley was homeless. But I couldn't overlook that, or his history of substance abuse. Even if Pauley wasn't using now, and assuming he wasn't mentally ill, he'd still have been drinking heavily for many years. The miracle would be that his brain *wasn't* pickled. At the moment he was more than lucid, but at other times he might not have had command over his thoughts. Some drunks see pink elephants; Pauley saw an angel.

"Are you a religious man, Mr. Pauley?"

He laughed under his hand. "Before yesterday I was more of an agnostic than anything else."

"Were you raised in a religious household?"

"My father described us as members of the C&E Church."

"C and E?"

"Christmas and Easter."

"Have you ever had visions before?"

"If you're asking whether I suffer from schizophrenia, I don't. I've never had visions. And to save you from asking, I've never seen a unicorn, an extraterrestrial, or a mermaid."

"But you saw an angel," I said.

"If you think I wanted to see an angel, you're wrong. I didn't want that kind of responsibility in my life."

"What do you mean?"

"Seeing the angel changed things. It brought me obligations. That's what I've tried to avoid all my life. But because I was witness to the angel, I have to tell others what I saw. To not do that would be an affront to God."

"Do you think there's a reason God would send an angel to you?" I asked.

"Not one I can think of."

"What did you do when you saw the angel?"

"I tried to hide my eyes from it. I wanted to crawl away. I felt exposed in its presence, completely and totally exposed. I have never felt so unworthy in my life."

"You felt the angel was judging you?"

He shook his head. "I was doing the judging. In the angel's light, I could not hide from myself."

"What happened then?"

"I could see the angel was hurt. It was the only thing that kept me from running away. And so, on wobbly legs, I made my way toward him. I was trembling all over. When I was maybe a dozen steps away from him, he turned his head my way. There were no words exchanged between us, but I'm certain he knew I was there to try and help. It seemed to me he extended his hand toward me, and I was touched by his light."

Unaware of what he was doing, Pauley extended out his own hand and for a moment seemed to forget where he was.

"In that moment my life changed," he said. "The angel's light entered into me. I received its last blessing and felt as if I was being given a new life."

Pauley's words could have been offered by any true believer. Someone else might have said, "Amen." I asked another question.

"What happened to the angel?"

"The light kept pouring out of him," said Pauley. "I was afraid he was dying, and I was panicking trying to figure out what to do. Since no one was around, I decided to run to the nearest payphone to call 911. I yelled to the angel that I was going for help and took off at a run. The nearest payphone is about a quarter mile from here. I didn't get very far, though, because just as I was turning the corner, this car pulled up at the opposite end of the alley. My first impulse was to flag it down, but I was afraid. It gave off this bad vibe. Maybe I was anxious because the car didn't have its headlights on. Or maybe it was the way it crawled forward in complete silence, like some kind of stalking animal. Just seeing it scared me."

"What kind of car was it?"

Pauley shook his head. "It sort of looked like one of those fancy sports cars."

"Could it have been a Porsche?"

"It was something like that. The car was a two-seater, a roadster I think."

"What color was it?"

"Black," said Pauley. "It was so dark it blended with the night."

"Could you see the driver?"

"Indistinctly," said Pauley. "The car windows were tinted, but there were glowing lights coming from inside the car."

"What do you mean by 'glowing'?"

"There were flashing lights that lit up the front window."

"Like from a dashboard display?"

"I think it was more than that. There was a colored grid pattern reflecting on the window."

"Could you see the driver?"

"Only indistinctly," Pauley said. "It sort of looked like he was conducting."

"What do you mean?"

"His hands were moving back and forth."

"What other impressions did you get of the driver?"

"I am pretty sure he was white and clean shaven."

"Any guess as to his age?"

"He was young, probably in his mid-thirties."

"How did the angel respond to the presence of the driver?"

Pauley rubbed his hands and looked uncomfortable. "When the car appeared, the angel tried to get up. I got this sense it was desperate to escape. That's why I didn't dare move. That's why I stayed in the shadows. If the angel was scared, that was reason enough for me to be. And then I heard the voice, and as loud as it was, I think my heart was beating louder."

"What voice?"

"The voice of the devil," he said.

Here it comes, I thought. Crazy always has a way of showing itself. "Is that so?"

"That's how it sounded to me. It was cold and terrifying."

"Did you see this devil?"

He shook his head.

"He was invisible?"

"No," said Pauley, "the voice came from above."

I didn't mask my sarcasm: "It was a voice from on high?"

"No, it was a voice that came from an amplified source."

Crazy wasn't showing itself in the way I had expected. "What did this voice say?"

"I'm not sure of the exact wording, but it was something like, 'Don't you know that we judge angels?'"

I tweaked the quote: "'Know you not that we shall judge angels?'"

Pauley visibly started; he moved his head back as if avoiding a fastball. "That's it!" he said. "How did you know?"

I didn't credit or blame my Catholic upbringing, nor did I tell him it was a quote from Corinthians.

"Was there anything distinguishing about the voice? Did it have an accent?"

"No accent," Pauley whispered, "and nothing distinguishing except that it was a prideful voice."

"Prideful?"

"He was gloating. He was proud that the angel was down."

"What happened then?"

Pauley shook his head, not wanting to say anything more.

"I need to know what you saw, Mr. Pauley."

In a voice not much more than a whisper Wrong said, "There was this sound, and it scared me, so I dropped to the ground and covered up. I am pretty sure there was a blast of light, but I was too scared to do anything other than close my eyes. A few minutes passed before I got enough nerve to look around. When I did, the angel was gone."

"So you didn't witness the angel's murder?"

"Isn't it enough to have seen the smoking gun?"

"You think the angel was vaporized?"

He nodded.

I looked around the area. "I don't see any remains."

"Who says angels have remains?"

"I don't have a case if there aren't remains or if there isn't evidence that there was a body. Right now there are no remains, no other witnesses, and a murderer believed to be the devil. Those aren't exactly building blocks to making a case."

"When I said the murderer was the devil," said Pauley, "I only meant he was the devil in human form."

"Was your angel symbolic as well?"

He shook his head. "The angel was only too real."

CHAPTER 4:

GET OFF OF MY CLOUD

Pauley and I walked around the supposed crime scene. Because the buildings overlooking the alley housed commercial tenants, it was unlikely I would be able to find anyone to corroborate Pauley's fantastic story, but that didn't mean I was without witnesses.

"Eyes in the sky," I said to Pauley, and then pointed out the security cameras. "There should be some good alley footage available from last night."

I was studying Pauley's reaction to my announcement, wondering if he'd be unsettled, but the opposite happened; Pauley looked relieved.

"Thank God," he said. "That means others will be able to see what I saw. That will be the proof I need. I can understand why no one believes my story. I know you don't. I get it. I'm no prophet."

"I wouldn't know. I've never met a prophet. But the more we talk, the more you sound like one, which begs the question of how the hell you ended up living on the street."

"That's easy," he said. "I'm a drunk. Until I saw the angel, my only motivation was to get enough money to drink. But now that thirst is gone."

"Maybe that qualifies as a miracle."

I continued to scrutinize the alley, but more from habit than anything else. It wasn't like there were going to be shell casings or blood evidence.

"Where did you last see the angel?" I asked.

"A few feet to your right," said Pauley.

In the old days homicide drew chalk outlines around the body. I thought of where that chalk outline would be and wondered if it would have included wings. I hunched down low. At first glance there wasn't anything to be seen. I touched the asphalt. It was tacky to the feel, and shiny. The shininess extended out to a radius of about ten feet. I stood up and took some pictures with my phone.

"Along with the blinding light, did you experience a blast of heat?" I asked.

Pauley thought about it. "Now that you mention it," he said, "I think I did."

I took a few more pictures and then turned to Pauley and passed him my business card. "Call me if anything comes up. My mobile number will get me night and day."

He thanked me and then asked, "Can we go look at those security tapes now?"

"Heaven is probably going to have to wait until tomorrow," I said. "I'm going to check, but I'm pretty sure all the businesses with security cameras have closed shop for the day."

"Won't their tapes be recorded over?"

I shook my head. "Don't worry about that. These days most surveillance recordings are stored off-site in a cloud server."

"I like the sound of that," said Pauley, suddenly smiling. "My angel is up in the clouds."

I hoped his head wasn't there as well. "I'll see what I can do about bringing your angel down to earth. Tomorrow I'll view the security footage and then have it sent to my laptop, so you can see it as well."

"I'd appreciate that."

I had the impulse to do a little more. "Why don't I bring lunch at the same time?"

"There's no need," said Pauley a little formally. He was a beggar, but on his own terms.

Sirius started wagging his tail. "Don't disappoint my partner. He knows we're talking lunch and doesn't want to miss out. His favorite is a meatball sandwich with marinara sauce."

Pauley scratched under Sirius's ear and went back to speaking to him instead of me. "I love marinara sauce too, but over a plate of pasta."

"I'll make you an offer you can't refuse," I said, doing my best Vito Corleone. "I know a good place nearby that does takeout. You want parmesan cheese on your pasta?"

"No cheese," said Pauley, "but a piece of garlic bread to sop up the marinara sauce. That's my idea of heaven."

"What kind of pasta do you want?"

"What do you mean?"

"Do you want spaghetti, ziti, penne, vermicelli, linguine, or bowtie?"

And then I remembered another kind of pasta: "Or angel hair?"

His face lit up at my last suggestion, and for a moment all his hard years of drink and homelessness seemed to lift.

"I choose to be on the side of angels," he said.

* * *

Before taking my leave of Venice Beach, I made sure all the businesses with security cameras were closed. As I had suspected, they were all locked up tight. If I had been working a homicide, I would have forced the issue and found a way to look at the footage without delay, but this wasn't a homicide case. Truth to tell, I wasn't sure what kind of a case it was. Because I was on the cusp of overtime, I decided to call it a day. LAPD frowns on any overtime involving angels, unicorns, fairies, or Big Foot.

What I wanted was in the cloud, which explains why on the walk back to my car I started whistling "Get Off of My Cloud." It would have been more appropriate had I been whistling a tune from the Doors. Venice Beach is, after all, the birthplace of the Doors, and even today Jim Morrison is remembered in a large mural off Ocean Front Walk. But when a tune gets stuck in your brain, there's nothing to do but go with the flow. And so Sirius heard Mick's words instead of Jim's, and I told him two was a crowd on my cloud.

My singing is borderline animal cruelty, but my partner wisely knew better than to believe a word I was singing.

Hands-free I called Lisbet Keane from the road. When we'd talked the day before, Lisbet hadn't been certain if she would be able to clear her schedule for the night.

"Sirius wants to know if you can come out and play," I said.

"I'm afraid I am looking at an all-nighter," she said. "I'm supposed to have a presentation ready tomorrow that isn't even on the drawing board. Right now I'm getting ready to brew a pot of coffee and settle into my flannel nightgown."

Lisbet is a graphic artist with her own business. She has learned only too well that when you work for yourself you better have a son-of-a-bitch for a boss.

"It doesn't sound like a romantic evening is in the offing."

"Not unless there's something about flannel you find sexy."

"If anyone can pull off that look, you can."

"Did I also mention my granny panties and fuzzy slippers?"

"What color are your granny panties?"

"You're incorrigible."

"You want me to drop off some takeout?"

"I think it would be better if you offered me a rain check for tomorrow night. I know if I don't say good night now, I won't have a good day."

The two of us had been dating for five months. Lisbet came into my life through the death of a little girl named Rose. Out of a terrible occurrence we had come together as a couple.

"Finish your work," I said, "and we'll get together tomorrow night. Seven o'clock work for you?"

"It does."

"I'll bring the food. You bring the granny panties."

She laughed and then said, "You're a shit," before hanging up.

* * *

The drive home to Sherman Oaks was bumper-to-bumper most of the way, which might explain my reaction when I pulled into my driveway and saw my next-door neighbor waving a bottle of Sam Adams from his porch.

"God, yes," I said.

The thought of cold beer prompted my beeline to Seth Mann's front door. Sirius was just as enthusiastic even without the beer. Whenever I'm out of town, Seth looks after my partner and spoils him terribly.

Seth waved us both inside. I didn't pass by him empty-handed. We went to our usual spots; me to an easy chair, Sirius to his hemp doggy bed. From his chair and from mine, Seth and

I extended our bottles and lightly tapped the necks, and then I took a long pull of liquid.

"Nectar of the gods," I said.

"If not quite ambrosia," said Seth, smacking his lips, "close enough."

In addition to being my best friend, Seth is a shaman. Over the years I've loved telling people his line of work just to see their reaction. Invariably they want to know what he "really" does, and I tell them that he really is a shaman. Seth has a long definition for what a shaman is, but doesn't object too much when I say he's a medicine man. He actually takes his craft seriously and spends a good deal of time down in South America working with the "masters." In L.A. he's quite well known in the holistic healing community, and he does guest speaking all over the world. People are drawn to his bonhomie. He looks and acts like the Laughing Buddha, especially when he wears a robe. Seth is short but has a big belly, big ear lobes, and a big smile. He is homely by almost any definition, but that doesn't stop beautiful women from wanting to spend time with him.

Shaman, hell; he's a witch doctor. Either that, or with all his herbal lore he's created Love Potion Number Nine.

"You didn't need much encouragement tonight," Seth said.

"You caught me in a weak moment. To be honest, though, I'm still waiting for my first strong moment."

"Has Sirius eaten?"

"He had some oatmeal this morning."

"Let me guess: you gave him what you didn't want to eat for breakfast."

"He liked it considerably more than I did."

Lisbet and Seth have both been trying to get me to improve my diet; Sirius is the one benefiting from my new health regimen.

"No lunch?"

"We were on the run."

Seth was already up and walking toward his freezer. He's always ready to look after Sirius at a moment's notice and takes his parenting duties very seriously. In preparation of Sirius's visits, he freezes patties of turkey and yam. Escoffier probably wouldn't approve, but Sirius does. He loves his turkey yam burgers.

"Want one?" Seth asked. He was serious.

"Let me see, gobble-gobble orange-colored goo or hops and barley." I tapped my empty bottle.

"Your loss," said Seth. "Sometimes I crumble up the patties for my own dinner. They make great tacos."

"I yam what I yam," I said, and then tapped my bottle again. It got the desired effect of a new brew.

Seth went back to his Chef Boyardee act. He was sautéing green beans and egg in a little olive oil and adding them to the turkey and yam. Sirius was watching the preparations with great approval, much like a diner appreciating the tableside service of cherries jubilee set aflame. The mutt's dinner actually had a beguiling aroma, much as I hated to admit it.

"Are you still in the doghouse?" Seth asked.

"Interesting choice of words," I said.

"I thought you'd like it."

"It's a legal tactic the public defender is using to try and divert everyone from the real issue that he's representing a scumbag."

"Is that so, Officer Sirius?"

"I should be the one suing, and for that very reason. The shyster wrote a letter of inquiry to Officer Sirius instead of Detective Sirius. I like to think Sirius got the same promotion I did."

"Are you ever going to show me the letter you—I mean Officer Sirius—wrote?"

"It's a typical police report except that *Detective* Sirius does reference bunnies a few times. And he goes on and on about a dead squirrel we encountered. And he quotes me when he writes, 'My partner says there is no better game than locking up assholes who deserve it.'"

"You really wrote that?"

"Detective Sirius did."

"Any other gems?"

"I liked the way Detective Sirius ended his report. He wrote something to the effect of, 'All in all, it was a great day. All days are great days, but especially catch-the-scumbag days. I would say it was a perfect day except for the fact that I never got to roll around on that dead squirrel.'"

"And you wonder why the defense attorney took umbrage."

"It was a good arrest," I said.

The two of us had been helping out Valley Division and had done a stakeout where a number of purse snatchings had taken place. Sirius had nailed Robbing Hood red-handed right after he snatched a purse out of the hands of an elderly woman and began riding off on his bicycle. My partner took down Robbing Hood with a perfect tackle.

"I hope that's the end of Officer Sirius's literary career."

I nodded. "I'll let Bob Crais be the dog whisperer. For me, it's tough enough being the human whisperer."

"So what case had the two of you so busy today?" Seth asked.

"Cases," I said. "We spent most of the afternoon trying to hunt down the hero without a name, and we just got back from investigating the death of an angel."

Seth looked away from his skillet toward me. "What did you say?"

"You heard me. A witness claims he was there when an angel was murdered in Venice Beach."

I motioned for Seth to tend to the skillet, which was starting to smoke.

"I want to hear everything," he said.

"Let's make it the grand finale," I said. "First I want to get your thoughts on the Reluctant Hero."

My shaman frowned. His curiosity was piqued, and even heroes pale in the company of angels. "Are you talking about the school shooting hero?"

"One and the same," I said. "Why hasn't he come forward? The city of Los Angeles wants to throw him a ticker-tape parade. He'd be on *The Morning Show, The Afternoon Show*, and *The Tonight Show*. He would be the talk of the nation. And after his book and movie deals, he'd be set for the rest of his life."

Seth removed the skillet from the heat and then added a prohibitively expensive cup of chicken meal and brown rice dry dog food. The kibble Seth buys is so expensive I am surprised it doesn't come with gold leaf. After stirring his gastronomic masterpiece, he put Sirius's dog bowl on the counter to let it cool.

"You need only look in the mirror for insight," he said. "You still hate being a hero. Given a choice, you would have embraced anonymity. Even today you dislike being recognized for what you did."

"I don't like the guilt by association of Ellis Haines."

Seth nodded in a noncommittal fashion. He knew there was more to it than that.

"Besides, there's another big difference between me and the Hero: I was just doing my job."

"Perhaps the hero is like you in that he doesn't think he's a hero."

I laughed. "Flying bullets didn't stop him. They would have stopped me."

Seth tested the dog food with his index finger and decided it had cooled off enough. He put the bowl on the floor and then sat down in the other easy chair.

"The Reluctant Hero might look at his actions differently than most," he said. "It's possible he feels unworthy. I wouldn't be surprised if he feels guilty about something. Perhaps he can't come forward for a compelling reason. Maybe he's a wanted criminal. Or his presence on the scene could implicate him in activities of which he is not proud. All of us have secrets; maybe his compel him to keep his heroic act quiet, especially if that publicity could complicate, or even ruin, his life or that of others."

I was nodding my head to everything Seth was saying. "My gut agrees with what you just said, especially his not wanting to be exposed for fear of harming either himself or others. I have no proof of that, but I'll be surprised if I'm wrong."

"What's his motivation?" asked Seth.

I shook my head.

"Guess," he said. "Tell me the first thing that comes to mind."

"Love," I said.

My own answer surprised me, but it seemed to work for Seth. "Now you just need to find out if it is self-love," he said, "or the love of others."

"Is that all?"

"We know the Hero is a hero. It would surprise me if his behavior isn't, well, heroic."

"You think he doesn't want to hurt someone?"

"It could be more than one person."

"Part of me just wants to let him be. Part of me is damn curious as to why he wants to be anonymous."

"So you're going to continue looking for him?"

"The mayor is anxious to give him the key to the city. And the Chief is anxious to please the mayor. And Sirius is damned nosy."

"I thought your false report had put your anthropomorphic days behind you."

"Don't worry, I learned my lesson. But I wasn't kidding when I said Sirius is damned nosy."

At the mention of his name, Sirius looked up at both of us. His eyes were twinkling and his tail was wagging. He knew he was in on the joke. I would swear to that, but never again would I put it in his writing.

"I want to hear more about the angel," said Seth.

"Is your interest personal or professional?"

"It's both, but my view of angels is not totally in keeping with Judeo-Christian tradition. I believe angels live on a higher plane and act as messengers between our world and the spirit world."

"Then how come we don't see these angels?"

"How come we don't see the air around us?"

"Have you ever seen an angel?"

"I have seen helping spirits who may or may not have been angels."

"And what do those helping spirits look like?"

"They are beings of light. They are human in form, but not flesh or blood. Imagine trying to see the reflection of your face through the reflection of moonlight on a calm lake. Your features emerge through the light. That's akin to the fleeting images I've seen."

I chewed my lip. Wrong Pauley had described his angel in much the same way.

"This afternoon I talked to a homeless man in Venice Beach who claims he saw a fallen angel who was wounded. And then he thinks someone murdered that angel."

I described what Wrong Pauley had told me, including my questions and his answers. It took me a long time to tell the story, but Seth never interrupted, just listened carefully the whole time.

"I'm sure it's all a waste of time," I said. "The security footage will probably show moonlight interpreted by my drunk as an angel."

"I wouldn't be so sure," Seth said. "Some people are able to see what others won't or can't."

"This isn't a production of *Harvey*," I said. "This is supposed to be an investigation."

"In the Bible, Daniel saw an angel with a face like lightning. That's hard to imagine, isn't it? Confronted by such a face, I doubt if most people would even recognize what they were seeing."

"Then maybe it wasn't there. Maybe it was a *figment*. In my work that happens all the time. People let their imaginations go wild, and they fabricate a reality that was never there. I expect that's what happened with my witness."

Seth only smiled. "The path will lead you where the path leads you, but I wouldn't be so sure of your destination before you set out. Cicero said 'So near is falsehood to truth that a wise man would do well not to trust himself on the narrow edge.'"

"You think you're the only one who can quote an ancient philosopher? Plato said: 'He was a wise man who invented beer.'"

"Does that mean you're ready for another?"

"Far be it from me to contradict Plato."

* * *

The magic of good, unhurried conversation, complemented by beer, sent me home happy. A late night snack seemed in order, so in my own kitchen I made an open-faced sandwich of turkey breast, romaine, and heirloom tomato, along with a smidge of brown mustard, olive oil, and balsamic vinegar. I munched away while watching the late local news. Some of my general contentment eroded during the weather segment. I wondered if I was being overly sensitive or if the weatherman really was an Ellis Haines clone. Like Haines, he enjoyed winking for the camera and acting as if everything was a big joke. His gestures were also a lot like those Haines used: a swirling index finger for a coastal eddy; spread hands to signal a blanket of fog. All the weatherman was missing was a garrote.

I had probably just watched too much footage of Haines at work, and now saw him even when he wasn't there. The good news, or at least weather, was that it was going to be nice in L.A. for the next few days. I tried to think about that, and not the Weatherman, so naturally Ellis Haines kept intruding into my thoughts.

SAD, I thought. Not the condition of Seasonal Affective Disorder, but the state of the law and J. Glo's tactics.

I pulled the bedcovers back and settled in. Sirius took up his spot on the carpeting right next to the bed. I wondered if my presence comforted him as much as his did mine. Every night I faced sleep with some apprehension. My fire dream came with less frequency now—only about once every four nights—but it had been a week since its last visit. A flare-up was overdue.

I call it a dream, but that isn't accurate. Whenever my vision occurs, I return to hell, feel the flames and inhale the smoke, and experience in exact detail the events of that night. Doing it once was bad enough. Doing it time and again is torture.

Pass me by tonight, I thought. It was the kind of prayer you might make to the angel of death.

I fell asleep and awakened in hell.

Sirius stood over his prisoner, ignoring his gunshot wound.

He wagged his tail at my praise even as his blood poured out of him. The red flow was far too fast. That scared me even more than the searing flames all around us.

It was the end of the world, but my partner was still wagging his tail.

The Santa Ana Strangler was babbling to me, trying to tell me he was a fireman. "Shut up," I said, cutting short his lies.

My index finger was white from its grip on the trigger. It was on the edge, just a whisper away from delivering death.

The Strangler knew death when he heard it and stopped talking.

I ripped off my LAPD windbreaker and tried wrapping it around Sirius's chest to stanch the blood. It didn't work. Sirius was getting wobbly and starting to tremble. But he was still wagging his tail. I had to get him to safety.

I had put him in this position. I had given him the orders. I had sacrificed him in order to catch a piece of shit who had killed too many people and had now killed my partner.

No, not yet.

I thought about Jen. I had failed her just like I had my partner. She'd had the flu, for Christ's sake. It wasn't like she had come down with the Ebola virus. When you have the flu, you're supposed to drink liquids, get plenty of rest, and take aspirin. And you're supposed to get better. But Jenny never got better. She died.

I should have insisted that she take it easier. I should have taken time off from work and made sure she stayed in bed. I should have looked after her like she always looked after me.

The flames were all around us; smoke was everywhere.

"We're going to carry my partner out of here," I told the Strangler.

As he opened his mouth to object I said, "If he doesn't live, I am going to empty my gun into you."

And then I heard this voice in my mind, and it said, "Why wait?"

* * *

I gasped like you do when you jump into icy water. My system went into its customary shock. As usual, Sirius was trying to ease my return with his calming presence, his muzzle nudging my face.

He's alive, I thought, and relief overwhelmed me.

I'm alive, I thought, and even felt pretty good about that. There had been a time when I hadn't.

My skin was hot to the touch, but at least this time there were no heat blisters I could see. As inexplicable as it might seem, the fire was still able to burn me.

My breathing became more regular, and with my return came the *moment after.* I still don't have an explanation for this strange window into a consciousness beyond my understanding. It isn't a psychic connection, or at least not exactly. Sometimes a hidden insight reveals itself. Sometimes I see things that were unseen before. Sometimes the gods whisper revelations into my ear, although I always have to pay Charon the toll for receiving my otherworldly insights.

"I'm glad we had our chance to talk about the angel," said Wrong Pauley. *"It came to me just in time."*

Pauley looked different. He looked at peace.

"I am going to follow the angel now," said Pauley. *"You're going to have to follow it as well, but in a different way."*

Pauley smiled, but it was a Cheshire cat kind of smile. It was obvious he wasn't all there.

"Give Sirius a hug for me," he said, and then added, *"It's too bad we didn't get to have that pasta."*

That's when I awakened fully. What I called my shake and bake was done. As usual, reliving the fire and experiencing the moment after left me spent. In the morning I would think about my vision and what it meant. But now I needed my sleep.

As I drifted off, I thought about Jenny. Until tonight I had forgotten she'd been on my mind during the fire. The trauma of my partner's shooting had brought all my feelings of helplessness to the fore.

I fell asleep, but it wasn't the alarm that awakened me. My cell phone was playing my Peter Gunn ringtone. I answered it before the sax players really went to town.

"Detective Gideon?"

I looked at the time. It wasn't quite four in the morning.

"Yeah," I said.

"I'm sorry to bother you, Detective. This is Officer Casey Nance. I'm calling from Venice Beach. I wouldn't be disturbing you at this hour except that we just came upon a body of a man carrying your business card."

"Where are you?" I asked, and Nance told me.

"I'll be there in thirty minutes," I said.

CHAPTER 5:

FADE TO BLACK

"So what was he doing with your business card, sir?"

Patrol Officer Nance was handling the case log. The officer was young and gung ho. His short haircut and straight posture made it a sure bet he had come to the LAPD from the military.

Nance was shadowing my movements. He wasn't the only one interested in what I was doing. Sirius was waiting in front of my parked car where I'd told him to *sitzen und bleiben* (sit and stay).

Instead of answering the officer's question, I continued my walk-through of the area. The discovery of a body invariably attracts a crowd, but Wrong Pauley's death had caused barely a stir. When it comes to the homeless, people are as likely to look away in death as they are in life. Besides Nance and me, there were now only two others at the scene: a coroner's investigator and a detective from the West Bureau. The last loose end to be tied up, removing the body, would soon be addressed by a rolling gurney.

"Who discovered the body?" I asked.

"I spotted him while on patrol," Nance said. "If not for the moonlight shining down on him, I would have driven right by."

"Did his halo give him away?"

"Excuse me, sir?"

"Forget it. What time did you spot him?"

Nance looked at the notes he was carrying: "It was just after oh-three-hundred. At first I thought he was just dead drunk. I lowered my window and yelled at him to get the hell out of the street. When he didn't respond, I got out of the squad car and checked to see if he was breathing. Then I called the paramedics."

"How long before they arrived?"

"About twenty minutes," he said, and then checked his notes. "Twenty-three minutes," he said.

"Where was the body?"

"Pretty much where it is now," he said. "I've got a sketch of its location and position if you want to see it."

"In a minute," I said. "Did you know the victim?"

"I knew him by sight," said Nance. "I've been working patrol here the last nine months, and I'd seen him around. Usually his hands were wrapped around a bottle, and he was half in the bag."

Soon he'd be all in the bag, but I didn't say that. I continued studying the body from different angles, and my interest in the dead man began to unsettle Nance.

"Everyone says he died of natural causes."

Instead of responding I continued looking around. The crime scene tape had been peeled away in preparation for the body's removal. As far as everyone was concerned, this was no crime scene.

I thought about how Pauley and his angel had died in the same alleyway.

Nance tried to get me talking again. "You knew him?" he asked.

I nodded.

"The paramedics said he probably had a heart attack."

My eyes went up the incline to where Pauley had said he roosted most nights. There was a trail in the ice plant where it looked like Pauley had either slipped or rolled down to the alleyway. There were no other trails in the ice plant, nothing to suggest that anyone besides Pauley had made a path in the foliage.

There were no criminalists on the scene. Without any sign of a struggle, without any visible wounds on the victim, everyone was happy to call it a natural death.

"I'm surprised the paramedics didn't say he drank himself to death."

"They kind of did."

"Did they also say he's a bum and that's reason enough to bag him and tag him?"

Nance didn't respond for a few moments, but then he asked, "Is there something about this guy I should know, sir?"

The officer had done his job. There was no reason for me to be acting like a prick.

"I interviewed him about ten hours ago," I said. "That's why he had my business card. In this same alley he said he saw an angel being murdered."

Nance nodded. "I heard something about that."

"It was a big joke for the media."

"He got his fifteen minutes of fame just in time."

I shrugged.

"Was he nuts?"

I was slow to answer. How do you explain a man who loved a little dog so much that he was willing to give her up for her own good? Wrong Pauley was a drunk, but he had somehow managed to hold on to his humanity in circumstances where it would be all too easy to shed it.

Pauley had offered up most of his confessions to the sympathetic ears of Sirius. I make most of my own confessions in just such a manner.

"Nuts?" I asked. "I don't know. But you're going to think I am."

"Why is that?"

"Watch and see."

The coroner's investigator had finished talking with the detective and was now wheeling the gurney toward Pauley. I stepped in its path and shook my head.

"I'm taking over," I said. "The body's not moving until after the Crime Lab sends someone to work the scene."

Alvarez, the detective from West Bureau, turned on his heels. "What?" he said.

"You heard me."

He came at me fast and furious. Alvarez is a big guy who's used to throwing around his weight. He put his face right in my grill. "What the hell?"

His show of bluster didn't bother me, but the same couldn't be said for my partner. Alvarez was fast on his feet, but my partner was a lot faster. He had come up silently, but now he made his presence known. Sirius's growl was more than a warning: the death rattle of a rattlesnake couldn't have been any more threatening.

The growl was like a fist to Alvarez's stomach. He stepped back so fast he almost fell. His eyes were wide with fright and his face drained of color to cadaver white.

With raised hands he continued backing away. He stared at my transformed partner. A little earlier Sirius had been wagging his tail and acting like an affection hound; now he was a hellhound. His hackles were raised, his teeth exposed, and his ears back.

I said, *"Lass das sein!"* In German that means "Don't do that." Speaking in German makes everything sound more serious than it is. The Californian version would have been, "Cool it, dude."

Sirius stopped his growling.

Alvarez got control of his voice and his trembling. He didn't like the way his fright response had taken over and decided to overcompensate.

"If your dog comes at me again I'll shoot him," he said.

My growl might not have been as good as Sirius's, but it wasn't far behind: "You reach for your gun, and I'll be the one going for your throat.

"With my teeth," I added.

Nance stepped between us. "Do you want me to call the Crime Lab, Detective?"

"I'll call them," I said.

"Really?" said Alvarez, injecting about as much sarcasm as possible into the word.

"That's the plan."

"No, that's bullshit."

Alvarez turned around and started walking away. With his back to us, he flipped us the bird.

"Woof!" I said, doing a passable imitation of a big, threatening dog.

Alvarez jumped, and his head whipped back. Nance and the coroner's investigator tried covering up their laughter. I wasn't as diplomatic.

"Asshole," said Alvarez, but he kept walking.

"He's probably a cat lover," I said to my partner. "It might be he's related to the Wicked Witch of the West."

I did my best Margaret Hamilton imitation: "I'll get you, my pretty, and your little dog too."

My witch imitation didn't scare my partner. He wagged his tail.

* * *

Cop shows love to play up the excitement of a crime scene investigation. They show criminalists performing all sorts of high-tech experiments. Anyone who has worked a crime scene knows how tedious it really is. The entire process is designed to err on the side of caution and is painstakingly slow.

Having quickly exhausted my usefulness at the scene, I vacated it at my first opportunity to look at surveillance footage from nearby businesses. The idea was to get answers, not more questions, but that's not how it was working out.

"No luck?"

Adrienne Kahn must have heard my groaning. Earlier, she had given me a demonstration with the security system, showing me how to retrieve footage from the remote server. I had been left alone until now to do my looking.

"Lots of it," I said, "but all bad."

Adrienne was a paralegal who worked for the legal offices of a lawyer who still hadn't made it in to work. My guess was that she pretty much ran the show. She was a pleasant woman somewhere between forty and fifty. At first glance she looked homely, but she had a beguiling smile that changed her features and gave her an exotic attractiveness whenever her lips folded upward.

While showing me how to work the system, Adrienne had quietly commented on how glad she was to see that Sirius and I had recovered from our encounter with the Weatherman. That kind of compassion and interest I can live with. Any conversation that doesn't belabor Ellis Haines is a good conversation.

"You ever see anything like this?" I asked.

I lined up the footage, and we both stared at a monitor showing the alley shrouded in darkness. In the midst of the ice plant was an upraised patch that I was pretty sure was the figure of Wrong Pauley. There were no cars in the alley, and no pedestrians. Then the darkness was pierced by what looked to be a long flash of lightning. Immediately afterward it was as if some director yelled, "Fade to black," because that was all there was: darkness.

"It goes on like that for almost an hour," I said, advancing the digital frames for her. "Everything remains dark until the picture finally comes back into view."

Adrienne shook her head. "That's strange."

"Two other offices in this building have security cameras looking out to the alley. The same thing happened with their systems."

"That doesn't sound like a coincidence."

"I don't think there's been a more suspicious gap since Nixon's Watergate tapes."

The paralegal politely smiled. It wasn't clear whether she knew what I was talking about. The famous eighteen-and-a-half-minute gap had happened in a 1972 audiotape conversation between White House Chief of Staff H. R. Haldeman and President Richard Nixon. Nixon's secretary, Rosemary Woods, had tried to claim she was responsible for part of the apparent erasure, but few believed her.

Watergate had happened before I was born, but I'd heard it rehashed many times between my parents. My mother was a Nixon supporter; my father not so much. He called him "Tricky Dick." My mother thought Miss Woods accidentally erased the tape; my father was sure Nixon had erased incriminating evidence so as to save himself from being brought up on charges of treason.

Rosemary Woods and Nixon were long dead, so that ruled them out as suspects. I had to figure out who or what was responsible for the mysterious gap on the tape. The flash and outage hadn't only happened during the time Pauley died; it had also happened during the time the angel was supposed to have made its earthly appearance and then departure.

"The same thing happened the night before," I said.

From the cloud I retrieved footage from the time when Wrong Pauley had claimed to see an angel. Once again there was a flash of light and then darkness.

"May I?" asked Adrienne.

I moved out of the chair and let her work the controls. The view on the monitor didn't change.

"I don't know what to tell you," she said. "As far as I know, the system has been operating perfectly."

That seemed to be the general consensus of all the businesses with security systems.

I thanked her for trying to help. And then I excused myself to try and figure out what the hell had occurred.

* * *

When I returned to the scene, Officer Nance was still there. I looked at his case log and saw that on paper very little had happened in my absence.

The Forensic Field Unit was about ready to call it a day. I went and chatted up Gina Frost, a vivacious Filipina I had known for some time. Even at a crime scene, Gina usually has a big smile on her face. Gina describes herself as a "mail-order bride." As far as I know, she is serious about that. Her husband is twenty-five years older than she is and probably never knew what hit him when she landed on the shores of California. After getting here, she discovered cop shows, particularly those featuring criminalists and forensic evidence. With her eyes on the prize, she went to school and got her degree in biology with a minor in forensic science. She definitely doesn't fit the mold of most criminalists.

"You gone for so long," she said in her accented English. "What, you no love me anymore?"

"You know I'm crazy about you, Gina."

"Good thing you leave handsome officer here," she said, flirting with Nance. "He no run off like you."

"You're making me jealous."

"That a good thing. I no like being taken for granted. My husband do that. He sit in his chair all day, and when I get home, he say, 'I'm hungry.' I tell him if he want Blue Plate special, then get out of his chair and make dinner. He say, 'I should divorce you.' I say, 'You do that, old man.' But he too scared to do that. He call me angel of death. He think I know how to kill him and make it look like natural death. And he right about that!"

"Speaking of which," I said, "did you find anything unusual about this death?"

"Nothing stand out," Gina said. "Maybe toxicology report show he swallow a bag of Skittles, but don't hold your breath."

Gina always liked to use American slang, and the more the better. A bag of Skittles referred to pills. As for not holding my breath, it would probably be a minimum of five weeks before a toxicology report would be sent my way.

"What did the security footage show, sir?" asked Nance.

"I saw a lot of light," I said, "but not the kind that illuminates."

My cryptic explanation didn't work on Nance. "What do you mean, sir?"

I explained about what I had seen—or, more accurately, not seen—on the security footage. Nance chewed his lips for a moment and said, "That sounds military."

"What do you mean?"

"I was a surveillance radar technician, sir. My job required me to know about jamming and blocking. Before our guys would do a recon in areas that were hot, we sometimes used blockers to disable digital imaging devices."

"What are blockers and how do they work?"

"There are different kinds. One system fires a beam of light that puts spy cams out of action. Or it might be that dazzlers were used."

My nodding encouraged him to continue.

"A dazzler is a directed energy weapon, or what's called a DEW. Directed energy weapons can be used to overwhelm optical systems. Dazzlers can also blind people, at least temporarily. But it's against international law to deploy permanently blinding laser weapons."

"So these dazzlers would be able to take out security cameras?"

"That would be a piece of cake, Detective."

"What kind of range do these dazzlers have?"

He shook his head. "I couldn't say for sure. That wasn't my field, sir."

"Whose field was it?"

"More often than not," he said, "it was the black ops guys."

CHAPTER 6:

GREEN MACHINE, DARK MACHINATIONS

"It's a great day so far," I said to Sirius. "We made a departmental enemy, there's no physical evidence to suggest that Wrong Pauley was murdered, and the only thing we have to go on are my field notes of a dead man who said he was touched by an angel. Apparently that didn't do him much good, did it?"

Sirius wagged his tail, and I scratched the back of his head. My partner is definitely a glass half full kind of guy, and for that I am eternally grateful.

"All right," I said. "Let's go for a late lunch. How about In-N-Out? I'll get you a Protein Style."

A Protein Style is secret code for a burger without the bun. Normally the burgers are all cooked medium well, but my partner is usually able to sweet-talk his way into getting it very rare. We were a few miles away from the nearest In-N-Out, and the traffic made it a fifteen-minute drive, but when we got within a block, Sirius started pacing the back seat, his tail wagging. He definitely knew what the plan was, and approved.

After getting our food, I pulled into a parking spot and fired up the laptop. I kept one of my hands grease-free and used it to read and scroll. Occasionally a hairy muzzle rested itself on my shoulder, which was my signal to pass over a fry. It's taken years, but my partner almost has me trained.

When the fries ran out, Sirius decided it was a good time to take a nap. While he snored, I kept working. When I reread Wrong Pauley's description of the stealth car, it made me sit up a little straighter. If the car in question truly was noiseless, it either had to be an electric car or a hybrid vehicle in electric mode. Luckily, Pauley's description seemed to preclude popular models like the Prius or Fusion. If Pauley was right about the car's having only two doors and looking like a sports car, that limited the possibilities. Still, I soon learned there was no shortage of electric and hybrid cars now being offered.

I tweaked a few search engines, ruling out the Smart Electric, Mitsubishi, Chevrolet Spark EV, Ford C-Max, and the Nissan Leaf. Since the Fisker Karma and Porsche Panamera both had four doors, they didn't make my short list.

Pauley had said the car looked like "one of those German sports cars." I was pretty sure his reference had been to a Porsche Boxster, and so I wrote down its dimensions, including wheelbase, length, width, and height. Then I did my visual test drives of a Honda CR-Z, Cadillac ELR, BMW i8, and Tesla Roadster. I ruled out the Honda because it was a coupe, and the Cadillac dropped out of consideration because it didn't look like a Porsche.

Sometimes when you're following a lead, you forget what started you on that road, and it suddenly occurred to me I was spending a lot of time pursuing anything but a sure bet.

"There's something . . . incongruous about this search," I announced.

My partner opened one bloodshot eye. He looked skeptical.

"Yeah," I agreed, "there's also something incongruous about me using the word 'incongruous,' but here I am trying to track down a car based on the eyewitness account of the same eyewitness who saw an angel."

My partner closed his eye. I am sure it was merely coincidence, but he chose that moment to pass wind.

"No more In-N-Out for you," I threatened.

He didn't open his eye a second time; I opened a window.

* * *

As needles in the haystack go, I had found an interesting one. Fewer than two thousand Tesla Roadsters had been sold in the United States during its four years of production ending in 2012. Having a price tag of more than a hundred thousand dollars might have had something to do with that.

I was lucky that the number of cars sold was so low, but if there is an epicenter for Tesla Roadsters, it can be found in Los Angeles. The cachet of an electric vehicle in a Lotus Elite body had attracted its share of wealthy owners, including actors, producers, and movers and shakers. You could be green and still go from zero to sixty miles per hour in 3.7 seconds. If cost wasn't an option, you could have your cake and eat it with Ed Begley Jr.

I knew I was getting ahead of myself, but without any other potential leads I did a records search on owners of Tesla Roadsters in the L.A. area. After printing out a list, I eyeballed registered owners in Venice Beach as well as the neighboring communities of Santa Monica, Marina del Rey, Mar Vista, and Culver City. It was a limited pool of fewer than a hundred names, but that still promised to be time consuming.

Before starting down that road, I wondered if I would be better served by getting the video recordings from other surveillance cameras in the area. Just because the footage in Wrong Pauley's alley had been compromised, that didn't mean nearby cameras hadn't captured the car's comings and goings. It would help, though, if I could be certain the car I wanted was a Tesla Roadster.

My eyes returned to my printout. I didn't expect anything to stand out among the vehicle records. In fact, nothing should have stood out. It wasn't like I was looking for a particular name. And yet what the patrol officer had said about "black ops" was still fresh in my mind, something that made me start when I saw the name Orion-Zenith.

Orion-Zenith—called OZ by most—is a defense contractor. I didn't know much about the company, but did find it curious that OZ had a Tesla Roadster as a company car.

The Tesla was registered to the OZ offices in El Segundo, an area known as the South Bay of Los Angeles because of its location on Santa Monica Bay. There were a number of other aviation companies in El Segundo, including Boeing, Raytheon, Lockheed-Martin, Northrop Grumman, and the Aerospace Corporation. According to what I read, OZ was one of the fastest-growing companies in the world because of its success in UAV (unmanned aerial vehicles) research and development.

OZ made drones.

When you're a civil servant, time is on your side, or at least that's what I always tell myself. Slowly but surely, I was working my way up the OZ food chain. When my phone call was transferred for the third time, I was hoping that was a charm. I had said the same thing to three different employees: "This is Detective Michael Gideon of the Los Angeles Police Department. I'm wondering if I could talk to Mr. Corde about the Tesla Roadster he drives. We would like to know if it was at the scene of a mishap two nights ago."

"Mishap" is not a word you'll find in the California Civil Code. It's an imprecise word, which is why I was using it.

The "Mr. Corde" I was trying to talk to was Drew "Rip" Corde, the founder and CEO of OZ. The OZ articles I had skimmed through had all mentioned the flamboyant Corde. I was pretty sure Corde had never met a camera he didn't like. In a few of those pictures, he'd been posing in front of a black Tesla Roadster.

The elevator music was playing again. "You know what Lily Tomlin once said?" Sirius pretended to be interested in what Lily and I had to say. "'I worry that the person who thought up Muzak may be thinking up something else.'"

Sirius rolled on his back in order to be scratched. I think it's the price he demands for being my audience.

"Detective Gideon?"

It was a human voice, a friendly voice, a very feminine voice.

"Guilty," I said.

She laughed a little, and I stopped scratching Sirius. I had found an audience who didn't demand payment.

"I understand you are trying to talk to Mr. Corde, Detective—is that correct?"

"Two for two," I said, and she laughed again.

"And you wish to speak to him about his Tesla Roadster and an incident that occurred two nights ago?"

I hadn't used the word "incident," but since we were getting along so famously I let it slide. "That's right," I said.

"I hope you don't mind my asking, but are you the same Detective Gideon who captured the Weatherman?"

Before I could answer, she whispered, "That's not something I would be asking except that Mr. Corde wanted me to find out."

Her tone made it clear it was a question she would have preferred not asking. "It's a dubious distinction," I admitted, "but it is mine."

"Thank you," she said. "Mr. Corde is tied up with meetings right now, but he says if you would like to talk later, he is available."

"Great," I said. "I'll give you my mobile number so he can call me when he's free."

I heard the uncertainty in her voice again. "Mr. Corde would prefer a face-to-face meeting, and he's hoping you would be amenable to doing it at his residence."

"What day is today?" I asked. "I only jump through hoops on Tuesday and Thursday."

"I am—"

I cut off her apology. "I'm just kidding. I don't shoot the messenger, especially when she has a boss who loves to posture more than a bodybuilder. When and where does he want to meet?"

She gave me an address on Mandeville Canyon Road and said, "Mr. Corde will be available to talk at seven o'clock."

"Yeah, but will he be available to listen?"

I got a last laugh out of her, and we said our good-byes.

* * *

Mandeville Canyon road runs for five miles, starting at Sunset Boulevard and ending just short of Mulholland Drive. Because the two roads don't meet up, Mandeville Canyon is said to be the longest paved dead-end road in L.A. Even with darkness about an hour off, the road was full of bicyclists.

Corde's house was in Brentwood. Even though it's been almost twenty years since O.J. Simpson was accused of murdering his wife, people still associate Brentwood with O.J. For a time his 360 North Rockingham home was a huge tourist draw, much to the displeasure of Brentwood residents. When the house was bulldozed in 1998, O.J.'s former neighbors were delighted. As the crow flies, Corde's house was about a mile from where O.J.'s had been.

A security gate controlled admittance. There was no guard on duty, but the signage didn't welcome the curious. Potential trespassers were told they were facing armed response, dog patrols, and prosecution if they survived their intrusion.

"Liens and snipers and scares, oh my," I told Sirius.

I pushed an intercom button; at least it wasn't labeled DEFCON 1. There were several cameras trained on me. I waved to the nearest one and flashed my badge.

A woman's voice responded. Even over the tinny speaker, her voice sounded clear and beguiling: "May I help you?"

"Detective Michael Gideon here to see Mr. Corde," I said.

The gate opened, and we passed through. In Los Angeles, multimillion-dollar properties are often situated on post-age-stamp lots. Expansive driveways are rare, but I drove at least a quarter of a mile before pulling up to Corde's colonial house. Away from the home was a tennis court and what looked to be an Olympic-sized pool. In the distance I could see a barn as well as a horse paddock. The house was on a canyon, with walking and riding trails leading into the chaparral.

There was a four-car garage separate from the house, but apparently that didn't suffice. Parked next to it was a silver Honda Odyssey with tinted windows. The sunroof was cracked open, but it was impossible to tell if anyone was in the car.

I brushed the dog hairs off my coat and took a stab at fixing my tie, before deciding to hell with that. Corde had arranged for me to visit him at a time and place of his choosing, and I suspected he wanted me to be witness to his affluence and power.

He was used to having others jump to his tune, but cops don't do subordinate very well. It's the reason we became cops. I loosened my tie and decided it was a good time to make a phone call. Lisbet and I had been playing phone tag all day.

Caller ID identified me, prompting Lisbet to answer the phone with, "How come there's never a cop around when you need one?"

"Maybe you should move closer to a doughnut shop."

"It was a rhetorical question."

"You mean like, 'Why do Kamikaze pilots wear helmets?'"

"That question is more ridiculous than rhetorical."

"How about this, then; the cop in me wants to know: 'If a kid refuses to take a nap, is he guilty of resisting a rest?'"

"That's a terrible pun, not a rhetorical question," she said. "Where did we get so off-track?"

"Now that's a rhetorical question."

"Here's a regular old question then: Are you coming by tonight?"

"If you're okay with a late-night visitor, I'll be there with bells on."

"I don't know about you and bells."

"How about if Sirius wears the bells, and I bring the food?"

My partner's ears perked up, and he opened his mouth into what I think of as his smile. He enjoys being acknowledged and responds to that particular note in my voice when I am attempting humor. Best thing of all, he doesn't heckle.

"That works for me. I have no doubt but that Sirius can pull off the bell look better than you."

"What if I told you my nickname is Pavlov?"

My partner's head swiveled, and I followed his gaze. A man wearing jeans, boots, and a form-fitting madras shirt walked out to the porch. His look was designed to be casual—at about a thousand-dollar price tag. The casual unkempt look extended to his facial hair and tousled locks, but I was willing to bet he tended to his stubble and goatee with the kind of care you should only give to a Bonsai.

When Drew Corde pointedly looked at his watch, I turned my head away and continued talking with Lisbet. My exaggerated smiles and hand gestures made it clear to him I wasn't having a business conversation.

"What kind of food are you in the mood for?" I asked.

"Surprise me."

"Eye of newt it is."

From the corner of my eye, I could see Corde approaching my window, but I pretended he was in my blind spot.

"I'm on an amphibian-free diet," Lisbet said.

"I suppose that means no toe of frog either?"

Corde knocked on my window. My partner is not a fan of people who do that. Sirius snarled and showed his teeth. I didn't say, "Good dog," but I did run a hand through his raised hackles. It was clear Sirius didn't like the vibe that Corde was giving off, or maybe he was just picking up on how I was feeling.

I lowered the window an inch and stared at Corde. "I'm a bit pressed for time, Detective Gideon," he said.

My partner growled. I couldn't have said it better. I held up a "just a minute" index finger and went back to Lisbet.

Speaking just loud enough for Corde to hear, I said, "It's a shame some people don't exercise their right to remain silent. Now where were we?"

"I was just about to rule out toe of frog for dinner."

"You really make things difficult, but I'll do my best to find something pleasing to your palate."

"In that case, I might greet you in something other than my flannel nightgown and granny panties."

"Are we talking about an evening of 'Vicars and Tarts'?"

"Not unless you're bringing the priests and the pastries."

I decided Corde had cooled his heels for long enough. "I hope to see you before too long," I said, and she replied, "Make it faster, pastor," and clicked off.

I was still getting used to Lisbet always having the last word. That had been my domain.

I cracked all the windows open to allow for adequate ventilation and told Sirius to stay. My partner made a plaintive noise, which translated to, "Oh, come on."

"Cool your jets and chill," I said.

He exhaled an aggrieved compliance and then grumpily settled into the seat. Apparently I wasn't going to get the last word with anyone.

Corde didn't hide his annoyance at having been kept waiting. In person he reminded me of a fighter pilot: the cock of the walk, with a confident swagger.

"Hope I didn't rush you," he said. His smile only added to his sarcasm.

"You didn't," I said.

"Company and dinner are both due to arrive within the hour. Your meter's running."

"I'd hate to get a ticket," I said. "Lead on."

CHAPTER 7:

TYGER TYGER, BURNING BRIGHT

Corde turned around and looked at me when we entered what he referred to as the great room. Most hunters probably would have called it a trophy room, but monstrosity room might have better described it. Corde continued to study me, but he wasn't alone; there were at least a dozen other sets of eyes following me. As I made my way further into the room, all the eyes seemed to be tracking my movements. Art aficionados marvel at the way the Mona Lisa's gaze follows them. These eyes seemed to be doing the same, and it gave me the creeps.

"Why don't we get comfortable?" said Corde.

I doubted that was possible. Maybe a serial murderer would have found the room cozy. One display—and two of the eyes—featured a male lion with a huge mane. And in the middle of the room, a tiger was staring out from behind a bamboo curtain, its green-yellow eyes sizing me up.

Corde was still watching me. His eyes didn't seem very different from the glass eyes of the predators appraising me. We sat down on dark leather sofas perpendicular to one another.

"Few people enter my inner sanctum," he said, "but I thought it would be a good place to talk to a fellow hunter."

"I am not a hunter."

"Of course you are. You bagged the Weatherman. There is no bigger game."

"That was my job."

"We all choose our vocation—and avocation."

"It's not always a choice. Sometimes people just fall into certain situations."

"I've always wondered why you didn't just kill him. No one would have known."

"I would have."

"If anyone ever deserved death, don't you think the Weatherman did?"

"I'm glad those kinds of decisions are way above my pay grade."

"From what I've read of him, he's still laughing at your mercy. He finds it amusing playing the system. That's why he's in town now, isn't it?"

"It wouldn't surprise me."

"So, you do wish you'd killed him?"

I shook my head. "If I had, my partner would have died. I needed Haines to help carry him out."

"It's been my experience that no good deed goes unpunished."

"I'll take my chances."

My tone made it clear I had no interest in continuing the conversation, and that clearly disappointed Corde. I hadn't come to talk about Ellis Haines. Since Corde seemed to prefer me seated, I decided to get up and walk around the room. I was betting there were more dead animals on display than there were in most hunting lodges. In addition to the tiger and lion, there were a Cape buffalo, leopard, bull elephant, rhinoceros, and grizzly bear. Lining one wall were mounted trophy fish that included a marlin, a swordfish, a great white shark, and a hammerhead shark.

"You killed all these animals?"

"I did."

"Aren't some of your—victims—endangered?"

"You can still hunt the big five in Africa, even though it's becoming more difficult to bag rhinos."

"I thought it was illegal to hunt tigers."

"It is, but the animal you are looking at was deemed a nuisance, and special arrangements were made."

His expression told me that his special arrangements meant a lot of payola. "That sounds expensive."

"Oh, it was."

"You ever consider taking up photography?"

"Hunting is in my DNA. It is my passion. I can happily spend hours talking about guns and rifles, tracking game, and how to deliver the best kill shot. I shot my first duck when I was four and my first deer when I was five. Most hunters going after deer settle for a shot to what's called the 'boiler room,' the heart and lungs. That wasn't good enough for me. I put a bullet in the deer's brain."

He sounded overly proud.

"Are you the one who nailed Bambi's mother?" I asked. "I'm still trying to overcome my childhood trauma."

"You don't approve of the right to bear arms?"

"I would rather we armed bears."

"If you watched the DVD of my bear hunt, you would see the bear in question was already amply armed."

He gestured toward his ursine victim. "Imagine a ten-foot, thousand-pound giant with five-inch incisors and three-inch claws charging you at a speed of forty miles an hour. That's what happened to me."

"Were you backed up by the First Infantry?"

"There was no second rifle waiting to bail me out. I took the bear in one shot. Watch the DVD if you don't believe me."

I could tell he was about to give me all the particulars of the hunt, but I didn't care to hear about conditions, the rifle he used, the type of bullet, or how he delivered his kill shot, so I interrupted with another question.

"Do you tape all of your hunts?"

Corde nodded and gave me an insinuating smile. "They are very well documented."

Our conversation was interrupted by knocking, and then a door opening. A head showed itself, revealing eyes that reminded me of the blue you only see in certain icebergs. The permafrost orbs took me in, and there was no thawing in them. The visitor had a pronounced cleft in his chin, the kind usually seen in animated superheroes. He turned his gaze toward Corde and nodded.

"Excuse me," said Corde, and exited the room.

In his absence I decided to go on a self-tour and began examining the framed photographs lining the walls of the trophy room. Corde and his kills were featured in the majority of shots. Some of the photos had clearly been taken from a high vantage point. As Corde had implied, it didn't look as if he believed in large hunting parties. In many of the shots there was only one other person, the same man who had just shown himself at the door.

When Corde reentered the room, I was still looking at his hunting pictures.

"Trouble?" I asked.

"Only an annoyance," he said.

"I think I recognized your visitor in some of these pictures."

"You probably did."

"So who is your hunting companion?"

"He is Orion Zenith's director of security. I suppose he thinks it's his job to make sure I come back from my hunts alive."

"Does your Man Friday have a name?"

"Rick Novak," he said.

"Let me guess: you can beat him in a footrace."

"Why do you say that?"

"Two hunters are tracking a huge bear," I said, "and suddenly they realize the bear is tracking them, so the first hunter changes out of his boots into running shoes. The second hunter says, 'You don't think you can outrun that bear, do you?' And the first hunter said, 'No, but I know I can outrun you.'"

"As long as whatever I'm hunting can't outrun a bullet, I won't be packing running shoes."

"I'm surprised you can spend so much time away from work going on hunting expeditions," I said.

"Why would you think I spend that much time away?"

I gestured to the room.

"I hunt smart," said Corde. "I know everything about my game before I go in. It always helps to have insider information."

"And how do you get that insider information?"

"I believe in scouting out the object you're targeting. And I know where to go, and when to go, and what to do once I get there. I am usually in and out before anyone even knows it."

"That sort of sounds like someone describing a sniper."

"That sort of describes what I am."

I studied another of his hunting pictures. A dead lion was stretched out in the grass, its massive head listing to one side. I wondered if it was the same lion in the room. Corde's right leg was planted atop the lion's back. Wrong Pauley had said the angel killer had exhibited an unforgettable arrogance and postured in much the same way.

Next to the lion's picture was a black and white sea shot of a large yacht. I could just make out the lettering *Wizard of OZ*. The running lights on the yacht could be seen, as could the lights on deck. Corde was visible, along with Novak and another man. Their features were illuminated by the monitor they were staring into. Removed from the threesome was a woman seated on the deck.

"Night shot?" I asked.

"Helped by the light of a full moon," he said.

"That's quite the clarity."

"I have friends in high places," he said, sounding entirely too smug.

I turned to face him. "Did you take your Tesla out for a drive the night before last?"

"Why do you want to know?"

"It's a police inquiry. Did you, or someone you know, drive your Tesla in the vicinity of Venice Beach at about three in the morning?"

"I am sure, as a matter of course, my lawyer would advise me to say nothing."

"I thought you didn't need backup."

"Why don't you tell me what this is all about?"

"A witness said he saw a murder. It's possible a black Tesla roadster might have been in the vicinity at the same time as that murder."

"I don't remember hearing about a homicide in Venice Beach the day before yesterday."

I was certain Corde was playing me, and just as certain he knew I was holding a bust hand.

"It wasn't a homicide per se."

"What was it?"

"An incident occurred that we're investigating."

"I thought you said a witness saw a murder."

"He saw what he thought was a murder."

Corde looked amused. "You're talking about that crazy homeless man, aren't you? You're talking about that drunk I saw on the news who said he saw an angel being murdered, right?"

"The mental state of the witness is not in question here. I'm still waiting to hear from you if you were driving in Venice Beach the night before last."

"Are you really telling me that's why you're here?"

"That's one of the reasons."

"What's the other? Are you investigating how many angels can dance on the head of a pin?"

I wondered if his analogy was coincidental and decided it wasn't. "Please answer my question."

"What difference does it make if I was driving the Tesla? Let's say the witness is of sound mind and saw me off the angel. Is that a crime?"

I didn't answer.

"I didn't think so," he said. "There's no statute prohibiting the hunting of angels in Los Angeles, is there, Detective?"

"Negligent discharge of a firearm is against the California Penal Code."

"I doubt whether you'd go angel hunting with a handgun, or even an assault weapon. You'd probably need a special weapon. And it's quite possible that kind of specialized high-tech weaponry wouldn't violate any ordinances. If that's so, hunting angels wouldn't be illegal, would it?"

I shrugged, and did my best to not look bothered by Corde's smirk. "Were you driving your Tesla in Venice Beach the night before last?"

"Venice Beach?" he said, and acted as if he was trying to remember.

"I'm sure we can find some surveillance tapes in areas outlying Venice Beach. From those I would be able to determine whether you were driving your Tesla Roadster on the night in question."

"That might be entirely possible," said Corde, "but I'm curious as to whether you have surveillance tape of the Tesla being in the proximity of your witness in Venice Beach?"

He looked at me. All the animals he had killed looked at me. The interview wasn't going as I had hoped.

"I do believe I was driving the Tesla two nights ago," said Corde, "but I can't recall if I ended up in Venice Beach. Sometimes I go out driving to clear my head."

"Did you go out driving last night?"

He shook his head. "Why do you ask? Was another angel murdered?"

"Our witness died last night. We're investigating that death as well."

The door to the trophy room opened, and half a face showed itself. This half-face looked considerably more attractive than all of Rick Novak's.

"Do you or your guest need anything?" a woman asked.

"Good timing, my dear," said Corde. "The detective was giving me the third degree, and I am hoping he won't be bringing out rubber hoses and bright lights. Do come in."

The trophy girlfriend, or so I assumed, walked into the trophy room. She looked to be in her mid-to-late twenties, with ginger hair and a peaches-and-cream complexion. Dangling from her neck was a small golden ankh. She didn't look comfortable in the killing room and kept her eyes averted from the dead animals. There was something familiar about her, I thought, and remembered the picture of the woman on the yacht. She certainly resembled the woman in the photo.

"Elle Barrett Browning," Corde said, "I'd like you to meet Detective Gideon."

She extended a hand, and as we shook, both of us said it was nice to meet the other.

"The detective was just about to get around to asking me if I had an alibi for my whereabouts last night. Would you mind telling him?"

"Drew and I were both here all night," she said.

"You left out the prurient details," Corde said. "I'm sure the detective would love to hear those."

It looked as if Elle blushed, but the room's shadows made it difficult to tell.

"Actually, I wouldn't," I said.

"I am glad one of you is a gentleman." She faced Corde and said, "I thought I'd retire early. I have to be on the set at five."

Belatedly, I made the connection of why she looked familiar. Elle Barrett Browning was a film actress. Her claim to fame was primarily romantic comedies, which might have been why I was slow on making the connection. I am not the demographic for those kinds of films and am beginning to think I am no longer the demographic for any movies. Damn talkies.

"But dinner will be arriving any minute now," Corde said.

"I'm not hungry. And that will leave all the more for the Attack Pack. They're coming over, aren't they?"

"They are indeed."

Corde turned to me. "OZ had its roots in video games, and we still have an interactive gaming division. When the old guard gets together, we can honestly say we're working late while playing video games."

"Sometimes they're down in the Bunker all night," Elle said.

Whenever I hear the word *bunker* or *hunker*, I think of Adolf Hitler and Eva Braun, and I imagine the Allied bombs shaking them in their underground chambers. My grandfather fought in World War II, and I suspect my association comes from stories he told me about Hitler and Braun being hunkered in their bunker.

"Bunker?"

"That's what we call our underground compound," Corde said.

"Imagine the Pentagon war room," said Elle, "with huge monitors and radar screens and tracking devices."

"I find it's a perfect screening room to watch your movies," said Corde. "Even you agreed there was no better place to watch you in your remake of *The Philadelphia Story*."

His words were offered with a smile, but it seemed to me they came with an edge.

"It would make a wonderful screening room," she said, "if that was all it was used for."

"'The time to make your mind up about people is never,'" I said.

They were words I lived by, but my remembering Katherine Hepburn's line from the movie got me two blank stares. For a moment I wondered if I had quoted from the wrong film, but then figured the line had been lost in the remake. Hollywood is known to throw out the baby with the bathwater.

"Where is this bunker?" I asked.

"It's actually not very far from the house," said Corde. "You just take a path down the hill. Unless you're looking for it, you wouldn't know it's there. I had it built into the hillside."

"And that's where the—Attack Pack—meets?"

"It's an ideal gaming spot," he said.

"Does everyone in your group work at OZ?"

He nodded. "We just went from one kind of joystick to another."

"The difference between men and boys is the size of their toys," said Elle.

"I thought you were *retiring*," said Corde. "I thought you needed your beauty sleep. You don't want to look bad on film, do you, and disappoint all those fans of yours?"

"No, I don't want that," she said.

I got the impression Elle wasn't answering his comment as much as she was responding to the undercurrents of another conversation.

"It was nice meeting you, Detective," she said, and took her leave of the room with a lowered head, once more avoiding looking at the taxidermy.

As the door closed behind her, I resumed my questioning: "OZ builds cutting edge drones . . ."

"Not drones," he said, interrupting. "They are UAVs, as in 'unmanned aerial vehicles.'"

"How many different types of UAVs does OZ make?"

"What's your security clearance?"

"My dry cleaner lets me run a tab."

"You wouldn't want me to violate the law, would you, Detective? I am bound by national security not to discuss the particulars of our SUAVE division—that is the Special Unmanned Aerial Vehicle Enterprises. Unless you've gone through an SSBI—Single Scope Background Investigation—or the director of National Intelligence has vetted you to receive sensitive compartmental information, or the secretary of defense has authorized you for a special access program, there isn't much I can say to you."

"Between Google searches and your annual shareholder's report, there seems to be plenty of information out there on OZ."

"That's yesterday's news, and in the war business old intelligence means defeat. OZ is tomorrow's news."

"What can you tell me about your UAVs that doesn't violate confidentiality?"

"They are the new paradigm in weaponry," he said. "Every generation has its game changer, from the atlatl to catapults, to fighter jets. It was radar that won the Battle of Britain. Atomic bombs ended the Second World War. You can't fight the next war using the weapons of the last war."

"Is Dumbledore the next war?" I asked.

It was common knowledge that OZ was developing a new series of microdrones, what they called the "Dumbledore."

Corde smiled. "Who is to say Dumbledore won't prevent the next war?"

"I thought atomic weapons were supposed to be the great deterrent. That doesn't seem to have worked out."

"Maybe the Chinese won't be so quick to act if their numerical advantage can be countered by swarm drones."

"The Maginot line was supposed to be the ultimate deterrent to the Nazis. It didn't work out that way. Whenever I hear about new wizardry, I always think of the Mickey Mouse character in *The Sorcerer's Apprentice.*"

"A lot of people think I named Dumbledore after the wizard in *Harry Potter*," said Corde.

"Didn't you?"

"The science fiction author Arthur C. Clarke once claimed it was impossible to distinguish advanced technology from magic. The average person has no idea what UAVs can and will do. A magic wand is nothing compared to the power I can wield. At this time it takes up to two hundred people to support a single UAV strike. Some of those personnel are at Creech Air Force Base in Nevada, while others might be in Langley, Virginia, and still others nearer to where the drone was deployed. With the Dumbledore all you'll need is one pilot controlling multiple UAVs. In time, that single pilot might even be able to be in charge of a swarm of UAVs, what most call 'nano drones.' But to get back to your question, I actually did not name Dumbledore after a wizard. A dumbledore is merely another name for a busy bee."

"That's not exactly a name that strikes fear in the heart."

"I didn't want a name like 'Predator' or 'Reaper.' That isn't what Dumbledore is about. The name is just what it means. The Dumbledore is small. But it's much more than a humble bumble. Those allergic to bee stings know Dumbledore to be a killer. And when it comes down to it, all of us are allergic to bee stings. It's only a matter of degree. There's nothing that scatters people—or an army—faster than a swarm.

"How do you combat a swarm? How do you go up against hundreds of tiny killers that are able to come together and disperse in a moment's notice? How do you safeguard against something so small but potentially so deadly? Isn't there always a chink in the armor just waiting to be exploited? Killer bees will take on a whole new meaning."

"What's the range of a Dumbledore?"

"That's classified."

"What's its surveillance capacity?"

"That's also classified. It's no secret, though, that it has EO/IR/SARS capabilities."

"And what's that mean?"

"It has electro-optical, infrared, and synthetic aperture radar sensors."

"Does it play a mean pinball?"

Corde answered the question he wanted me to ask, and not the remark I had made. "There are UAV programs doing all sorts of things you could never imagine. They're monitoring terrorists. They're watching borders. They're patrolling pipelines. And maybe you should worry about being outsourced, Detective, because they're also doing police work. UAVs fly more than a million combat missions every year, and these days the Air Force produces more drone pilots than fighter and bomber pilots combined. Remotely piloted aircraft are becoming more the rule than the exception."

"Why don't I find that reassuring?"

"Maybe you sense an end of an era."

"Do you ever pilot your drones?"

"There are few things I like doing better. I am afforded God's eye view."

"If that's the case, the Almighty might need to have His vision checked."

Corde ignored me. He was still experiencing his God's eye view. "I always feel a letdown when I step away from the controls. The world around me feels one-dimensional."

"Maybe if you were on the ground and had an all too mortal view of a drone strike you wouldn't be as enamored with the process."

"I'm sure you are right, but I don't feel bad about that. I want terrorists to be on edge. On the ground people can often hear UAVs patrolling overhead. In Pakistan and Afghanistan they call them 'mosquitoes.' That's the whine they hear. That's how we keep potential insurgents in check. They know we're there. They know they can run, but they can't hide."

"Have you personally performed military operations with your UAVs?"

"Officially, that's classified."

"What about unofficially?"

He smiled but didn't comment directly. "There is nothing quite like being in the ghost world. Though you might be thirty thousand feet or higher, you can clearly see moving images below you. Then you bring down your UAV and do your looking from a sight line just a few hundred feet above the ground, which gives you an overhead shot like a bird. You move in and out, the crosshairs going with you, and with each movement you have the power to rain death. And it's quiet where you are looking, and peaceful. There is no sound. You feel removed; you feel as if you are hovering above that ghost world. As death is dispatched, you watch the victims run, but there's no place for them to hide. Those who run for cover are called 'squirters.' They are like cockroaches when a light's turned on, scurrying and scrabbling. At the last moment their eyes bulge out, and their last word is invariably a curse, not a prayer, even from the devout. Usually they say some variant of 'shit.' Isn't that curious?"

"I don't think I share your fascination."

"I would guess you're in the minority. Do you know that you can go to YouTube and watch UAV strikes? The last I heard there have been over twenty million hits. There's even a term for those who can't seem to get enough of that kind of viewing: drone porn."

"I never thought I'd be glad that Grumpy Cat went viral, but it's nice to know more people are watching her than drone porn."

I didn't mention that Ellis Haines had more views than did drone strikes and Grumpy Cat combined; Corde probably would have liked that analogy better.

Gesturing to Corde's room of kills, I asked, "Have you used your UAVs in your personal hunts?"

"No comment."

"Why is that?"

"There are certain archaic laws limiting UAV access to a particular airspace. I am not about to admit I violated those laws."

"So if you decided to go on an angel hunt using UAVs, it would be illegal?"

"Not necessarily. There is a difference between flying hobby UAVs and flying military UAVs."

"Hypothetically, if someone were to hunt angels, how would they go about doing that?"

"*Hypothetically,*" said Corde, emphasizing the word with a smile, "that would require several new and unique technologies, or so I would imagine."

"What kind of technologies?"

"Let's start from the premise that angels can't be seen with the naked eye. Given that, you would need new imaging platforms and detection systems."

"Are you talking about enhanced radar?"

He waved his hand as if to say I was at least in the ballpark of understanding, which was probably as much as a troglodyte like me could be expected to comprehend.

"Our witness said he saw the angel. If angels are invisible, as you say, how would that be possible?"

Corde offered another shrug. "It might be nothing more than making the invisible visible by applying a kind of particulate matter in the air."

"What do you mean?"

"The easiest example I can offer is how smoke reveals laser beams you wouldn't know were there without the vapor."

"So you've got your advanced radar along with your ability to make the invisible visible. How do you shoot down an angel?"

"I can't imagine it would be easy. You'd need two or three pilots controlling the latest technology in UAVs to channel the prey."

"You'd hunt in a pack," I said.

"Yes, and you'd need special digital weapons."

"Why is that?"

"I am thinking conventional weapons wouldn't bring down an angel." His knowing smile seemed to take up most of his face.

"My best guess is you would need to hunt them with a new kind of DEW."

I remembered the acronym from Officer Nance. "You're talking about a directed energy weapon?" I said.

Corde looked surprised. "Yes," he said. "I imagine you would need the type of weapon that could aim energy without a projectile."

"Does that mean some kind of laser?"

"That could be one type of DEW. But there are many others. What would be best is a mobile DEW with an energy source to tap into."

"So what that translates to is hunting angels with ray guns."

"You sound skeptical. More than a hundred years ago, Nikola Tesla envisioned a directed energy weapon. He even wrote papers on his particle-beam weapon, his death ray. The science has long been there. It has only lacked the proper application.

"It would be ironic, wouldn't it, to be hunting in a Tesla with a weapon imagined by Tesla?"

"'Ironic' is one word for it."

Corde looked pointedly at his space-age watch. It was a less than subtle hint that I should be going, but I acted oblivious to the hint and his expensive timepiece.

"We've all heard about drone strikes on terrorists," I said, "but what about targeted assassinations?"

"I wouldn't be able to comment on that."

"You *can't* comment, or you *won't* comment?"

"The end result is the same, isn't it?"

"The Dumbledore must have been commissioned with certain tasks in mind."

"You're welcome to speculate."

"Is it true that the latest incarnation of the Dumbledore is roughly sparrow sized?"

"I can't comment."

"Does your Dumbledore come with a stinger?"

"Do bumblebees have stingers?"

Corde reached for his phone and took a look at the display. Whatever was texted seemed to please him.

"Are we done here, Detective?"

"I wouldn't want to keep you from your games," I said.

CHAPTER 8:

ANGEL OF THE MORNING

Corde walked me out to my car. Our voices roused Sirius, and I saw the back window of the car was steamed up. My partner had been doing some heavy breathing. Sirius's opinion of Corde hadn't changed during our absence. On seeing him, he began growling.

"No," I said, but not very forcefully.

I got the sense Corde wanted me to be on my way, which was reason enough to linger. "How many acres do you have here?" I asked.

"Thousands," he said, "but I only own fourteen of them. That's the good thing about being on the canyon. No one can develop the land all around me, so it's just like it's mine, without the necessity of paying property taxes."

Several rabbits were warily munching on a lawn that was a stone's throw away from us. Corde raised his hand like a gun and pointed their way.

"Rabbit stew," he said.

"I better warn Harvey not to show up around here. I wouldn't want him to end up in your collection of stuffed animals."

Corde's lips pursed. The big bwana didn't like being mocked. "Maybe I should have a second trophy room. I could display Harvey and an angel or two. And let's not forget Tinker Bell."

"I never do."

"You'd be surprised at all the wildlife around here," Corde said. "In making hiking trails, all I had to do was expand on the existing game trails. The wildlife follows canyon corridors that connect all the way to the Santa Monica Mountains. I monitor what travels along those corridors. I haven't seen a mountain lion yet, but there are plenty of coyotes, bobcats, raccoons, and foxes, not to mention eagles, owls, and hawks."

"How are you able to do your monitoring?"

"Oh, camera traps, infrared, and the like," he said waving his hand and grinning. The subtext, I was certain, was that he flew UAVs along the trails.

Corde's phone made a noise. He studied the display and then pressed a button.

"Dinner," he announced. "I have four of the best chefs in L.A. on retainer. Every night is a gourmet experience. Such a shame you won't be partaking."

I thought about Wrong Pauley and the meal we never got a chance to have.

"Usually I go with what the chef recommends," he said, "but tonight I had a hankering for a particular appetizer and called it in. You ever have 'angels on horseback'?"

His smile was meant to goad me. "I can't recall," I said. "Did you ever have 'spotted dick'?"

Unfortunately, he knew the dish. "I don't like pudding," Corde said, "but I do like angels on horseback. And when you have a craving, you know, you just have to satisfy it."

* * *

I had a craving too. As I approached the oncoming vehicle, I signaled for it to stop.

A white kid was driving a banger. He turned down his stereo when I got out of my car and approached him. "You got the order?" I asked. "My boss wanted me to be sure you didn't forget the angels on horseback."

The kid checked the order. "Yeah, they're here," he said.

"I'm supposed to pick up the food. The boss wants to have a picnic."

The kid started handing over the packages. These weren't paper bags and to-go wrappers, but containers with fitted lids that were ready to be reheated or even frozen. I'd had plenty of Christmas presents that weren't as nicely wrapped.

"It's on the tab, right?" I asked.

The kid nodded but then was emboldened to add, "My tip's not on the tab, though."

I pulled two twenties from my wallet and handed them over. "That work for you?"

He took the money without complaint, made a U-turn, and drove away. I looked around and smiled wide. You never know when you're on camera, and I kind of hoped Corde was monitoring my face at that very moment. I was going to recite Gloria Swanson's old chestnut about being ready for my close-up, but at the moment I was feeling more like Elwood P. Dowd.

"I've never heard Harvey say a word against Akron," I said, quoting from the film, and then got back into my car where my not-so-invisible friend nudged me with his muzzle.

"Do you think Harvey would be as charitable about L.A.?" I asked.

Sirius wagged his tail. Who needs a pooka when you have a dog?

* * *

As it turned out, angels on horseback consists of freshly shucked oysters wrapped in smoked bacon, with a drizzle of lemon juice. Lisbet made more happy sounds. They bordered on Meg Ryan's dining scene in *When Harry Met Sally.*

"Where did you get this food?" she asked for the third time.

I hadn't wanted to tell her until we finished. As Lisbet speared a last morsel, I decided it was time to 'fess up.

"Funny thing about this dinner," I said, and then told her my abbreviated hunting and gathering story.

My story didn't settle with her as well as the meal. "I thought after you got in trouble for that letter to the public defender, you weren't going to do anything silly that might cause problems."

"This won't be a problem," I said.

"How can you be so sure? Can't this man say you stole his dinner? Can't he prove you stole his dinner?"

"He wouldn't do that."

"Are you certain? I seem to recall how you said that public defender couldn't possibly take offense when you wrote him the Sirius letter."

"This is different. Corde is someone who wants everyone to know he's the smartest guy in the room. His ego wouldn't allow this story to get out. He wouldn't be able to stand the idea of people laughing at him, knowing I ate his dinner."

Lisbet was shaking her head. "Even if you're right, I just don't understand men and their pissing contests."

I turned to Sirius. "Explain it to her, would you?"

It was possible Lisbet was reacting as she was because I hadn't yet told her about Wrong Pauley and his angel and his death. Because of that, she also hadn't heard the complete Drew Corde story.

"If this man is the egotist you say he is," she said, "do you think he is just going to turn the other cheek at what you did?"

"You've convinced me. I'll send him a thank-you note for a wonderful meal."

She gave me an exasperated look.

"I'll even include a postscript saying how much you enjoyed the food, and close by asking him for the name of the chef."

Despite her misgivings, Lisbet was having trouble fighting off a smile.

"And let's not forget my P.P.S. of, 'The angels on horseback were to die for.'"

Lisbet started laughing. "You really are an incorrigible shit."

"I love it when you talk dirty to me."

* * *

Sirius's barking didn't come at a good time. When I went to see what was wrong, I told him, "I am about to change your name to coitus inter-*pup*tus. What's up with you?"

My partner went to a window and barked once. I went to where he was standing and cracked open the curtains.

"There's nothing there," I said.

Sirius looked for himself and then stared at me expectantly.

"What?" I asked.

I went back to Lisbet's bedroom. "Now where were we?" I asked.

Without a word, with only a helping hand, she showed me exactly where we'd been. Maybe two minutes passed before Sirius started barking again.

"You've got to be kidding."

He continued barking.

"Maybe it's your high notes," I said.

She slapped my chest and said, "Go see what's wrong."

I went out to the living room. It was clear Sirius was trying to tell me something, but I was too dumb to figure out what was bothering him. When I returned to the bedroom, I said, "Third time's a charm?"

This time we finished our lovemaking undisturbed. Lisbet and I had reached the point in our relationship where once or twice a week we slept over at each other's place. It hadn't been easy for me to agree to this because it had meant telling Lisbet about my burning dreams. I made my confession when the dreams became more infrequent. To date, Lisbet has only been at my side a few times when I've had furnace blasts from the past. She didn't seem to have a problem with my nocturnal inferno; I was the one who was ashamed. I didn't like feeling weak or vulnerable; the dreams turned me into jello.

With Lisbet's head resting on my chest and my arm cradled around her, I told her about Wrong Pauley and then gave her the full Drew Corde story. She listened, letting me tell the stories in my own way, and saved her questions and comments until I finished.

"I don't know if I've ever heard such an incredible story," she said. "Right now I'm feeling numb. How terrible it must have been for Mr. Pauley, watching an angel die."

"It wasn't an angel," I said. "Pauley only thought it was an angel."

"How do you know?"

"I haven't heard of any other angel sightings."

"Maybe that's something most people would keep to themselves."

"The angel Pauley thought he saw could have been—anything. Maybe it was a light reflecting off something. Or maybe it was a new OZ gizmo."

"If that's the case, why didn't Corde just admit it?"

"Imagine the repercussions of a defense contractor admitting that he was illegally flying drones in the city of Los Angeles. That's the kind of thing that could potentially derail his governmental gravy train."

"It still doesn't explain the death of Mr. Pauley."

"Everyone seems to think he died of natural causes."

"Including you?" Lisbet asked.

"I'd be foolish not to take into account the hard life he's led and the damage it must have taken on his body and liver. But what I don't like is that the surveillance systems in the area conveniently went black at the time of his death. Those are the same systems that also malfunctioned at the time Pauley saw the angel."

"I think God has chosen you in this matter, Michael."

Lisbet has faith that I lack. I admire her assuredness of a benevolent God, and her piety. She believes. I test my faith by tossing pebbles at stained glass windows and hoping they don't break.

"I sure hope God has more than me on the side of the angels."

* * *

I was spared the fire dream, but that's not to say I had a good night's sleep. My cell phone and Peter Gunn awakened me from a deep slumber, but I didn't get to it in time, and no message was left. A few minutes later Peter Gunn began playing again. My display showed *Private Name, Private Number,* which meant caller ID was blocked. I picked up anyway with a groggy, "Hello."

At first the sounds on the line were unintelligible, but through the static and distortions I suddenly realized that I was hearing the sound of a couple's lovemaking. And then I heard a dog barking, and in the background was the laughter of three or four men.

The caller clicked off, and I stared at my phone. "Son of a bitch," I whispered.

"What's wrong?" said Lisbet.

"Nothing," I said. "Go back to sleep. It was a wrong number."

Her head dropped back down on her pillow, and her steady breathing resumed, punctuated every so often by a little snore.

I did a slow burn. There was no doubt in my mind that Drew Corde was responsible for the recording. It hadn't taken him long to exact a measure of revenge. Somehow he had found where Lisbet lived and had gotten the number of my cell. Corde must have followed me to Lisbet's place with one of his eyes in the sky. I had brought the evil upon us.

Cops are used to trying to help victims. We're not good at being victims. Corde's violating the privacy of our bedroom shamed me. I could feel the heat in my face. Under the sheets I clenched and unclenched my fists. I wanted to go outside and look at anything suspicious, even if it was the moon. I wanted to take a shower. I wanted to go rattle one particular man's cage.

After an hour of stewing, I soundlessly exited the bed and bedroom. Sirius was resting near the window where he'd heard the strange sounds. I had a feeling he had placed himself there so as to be in a position to protect us.

At my approach he raised his head and his tail thumped once. I got down to his eye level, scratched him, and quietly said, "Sorry I'm deaf. Sorry I was too dumb to realize you were doing your job. You're a better partner than I, Gunga Din."

Sirius took that opportunity to slip me a kiss. Because Lisbet was sleeping, I couldn't scream like Lucy, but I could whisper her outrage when Snoopy planted one on her: "'I have dog germs. Get hot water! Get some disinfectant! Get some iodine!'"

My partner had heard it all before and knew my protesting was most false. I went over to the sofa and stretched out, and surprised myself by falling asleep. Later, I awakened to a figure creeping around in the shadows.

"You'd make a bad burglar," I said.

She came over, leaned down, and kissed my forehead. "Did you have a dream?"

I shook my head. "I was having trouble sleeping and didn't want to disturb you."

Lisbet took a read of my face. She had a talent for knowing when I wasn't telling her the full story, and I suspect she was able to see that was the case.

I attempted innocence: "What?"

"What do you want for breakfast?"

"Coffee would be good, thanks."

"It's already brewing. I'm talking about real food."

I wasn't sure I wanted to spend any time dining, and it probably showed. A wagging-tailed extortionist joined us. He knew Lisbet was talking about breakfast.

"Don't worry, Sirius," she said. "I'll make sure *you* get a good breakfast."

"What about me?"

"You ought to learn to ask nicely like Sirius," she said, and went to the kitchen.

"I hate it when you make me look bad," I told him.

I shaved and showered, and then put on a fresh shirt. Lisbet's and my relationship had reached the point where each of us had toiletries and a few items of clothing at the other's place.

Lisbet was just finishing making breakfast when I took a seat at the breakfast nook. She was singing to the radio as she plated scrambled eggs, hash browns, and sections of cantaloupe onto three plates. I carried our plates over to the table. Sirius was finished with his plate even before we took our seats.

"Did he learn his eating manners from you, or vice versa?" asked Lisbet.

"I'm not sure."

I took a big bite of food, and then a second, before belatedly getting Lisbet's point. The night before the two of us had talked about having a leisurely breakfast together, but I had forgotten about that. Somewhat guiltily, I put my fork down.

Lisbet smiled at my attempt to be mannerly. "So where are you so anxious to be off to this morning?"

"Corde's girlfriend is an actress," I said. "Last night I heard her say she had to be on the set this morning at five. I'm hoping I can question her there."

"What actress?"

"Elle Barrett Browning," I said. "That's some stage name, huh?"

"Actually, I remember reading in *People* it's her real name. I think they revealed that in the issue where she was named one of the sexiest women in the world."

Lisbet sounded a little bit jealous, so I said, "Is that the issue where you're on the cover?"

"You're not totally hopeless."

"I suppose those kinds of articles are what passes for hard-hitting journalism these days. Who says investigative reporting is dead?"

"Tell me about her."

"Corde likes his trophies. I suspect that's what brought them together. But he prefers his trophies mounted and silent. She's not like that."

I recollected what had been said and how the conversation between the two of them had seemed a bit strained. I was hoping they were on the outs and that could be exploited.

But what was really on my mind was the raucous laughter I'd heard on the recording. I felt as if I'd let Lisbet down, and it didn't feel like the right time to tell her what had happened. Being tight-lipped didn't mean I wasn't making good use of my mouth. My plate was now empty.

"You don't have to linger, Michael," said Lisbet. "I know you have important work you need to get to."

Juice Newton started singing "Angel of the Morning." Even over the radio Juice's voice sounded good. It had been years since I'd heard that tune.

"She's playing our song," said Lisbet wistfully.

"What do you mean?"

Lisbet backtracked a little. "Aren't you investigating angels?"

"I am, but I don't think that's what you meant."

"I think it's best if we save this discussion for another time."

It didn't matter that I had already made that same decision on another subject; this was different, or so I rationalized. "I don't want to do that if it means something is festering."

"Nothing is festering. It's just that I'm feeling unsure in our relationship."

"In what way are you feeling unsure?"

"The song is about an affair. I realize you've been through a lot, Michael. I know you can only give so much of yourself at this time. I'm not sure if that will change, or whether it's even fair for me to hope it might change. I think a part of you still clings to your wife. I wouldn't have you deny that love, but I'm hoping you can also find room in your heart for our love."

Juice Newton kept singing. I'm glad one of us had something to say. It took me several moments to figure out a response.

"If Jennifer were still alive, I'm sure she'd tell you I have always been romantically challenged."

"But she knew, unequivocally, you were in love with her."

I shrugged and was once more at a loss for what to say.

"We'll talk later," said Lisbet, "and please don't feel bad. I suppose I've wanted to have this discussion for a few weeks now."

"We're a lot more than an affair," I said.

And then I listened to Juice tell me to call her an angel.

* * *

Ten minutes later Sirius and I were driving away. I hadn't left Lisbet's apartment on a bad note, but it still felt as if things were unsettled between us. She had insisted that we'd talk when both of us had the time, and that I needed to pursue my case.

"Angels need you," she had asserted.

Her faith was her strength; I didn't have any, so I borrowed some of hers for the day ahead.

When I took my leave of her, we kissed each other good-bye, but our lips were more perfunctory than passionate, and reflected our uncertainty. I didn't like disappointing Lisbet, but I wasn't sure it could be avoided. The person I was, I was afraid, might not be enough for her.

I spoke to Sirius: "Don't be like me. Don't you be like me."

Melvin Udall had said the same thing to Verdell the dog in the movie *As Good as it Gets*. A confused man was quoting to his dog from a neurotic character who had also lectured his dog; it was a shame Melvin's words felt so right.

CHAPTER 9:

SILENT MOVIE

I made some calls to try and figure out where Elle Barrett Browning was doing her shoot. The LAPD has long been accused of having a too-cozy relationship with the movie industry. There was a time when LAPD was essentially private security to the stars, and special treatment was doled out. These days it's not nearly as easy for filmmakers to get favors from the police. Retired cops are now prohibited from wearing their old LAPD uniforms, which they used to do regularly at film locations. Filmmakers could count on the uniforms to act with impunity; cops rarely get questioned. It's not the same with rent-a-cops.

There is a price tag associated with off-studio shoots, especially if LAPD has to close a street, or provide a police presence. The film industry usually goes through LAPD's Contract Services Section (CSS), or its Special Events Permit Unit (SEPU), or both. From search engine hits I learned Elle was shooting a film with the working title *Tomorrow Too Soon*. It was a thriller, not her usual romantic comedy. Through LAPD I was able to learn that for the next two days filming was taking place in a vacant wing of the St. Vincent Medical Center.

The hospital was located in the center of Los Angeles in a district known by mapmakers as Westlake, although few of its residents know it by that name. Most people in the area identify themselves as living in the MacArthur Park district. White flight had occurred in the area long before I was born. The MacArthur Park neighborhood is comprised mostly of Hispanics, with its latest influx of residents coming from Guatemala and El Salvador. There are also a number of Koreans living there, courtesy of the expanding eastern boundaries of Koreatown.

An accident forced a detour that pushed traffic over to Wilshire Boulevard. As I turned on Alvarado, I caught a glimpse of MacArthur Park Lake. The English actor Richard Harris's rendition of the song "MacArthur Park" was a huge hit in the late sixties.

The songwriter Jimmy Webb had been inspired to write the verses after losing his true love to another. Webb and his love had picnicked in MacArthur Park, and fed the ducks, and done the paddleboat rides back when the lake used to have paddleboats for rent.

I took a look at the passing park, and so did Sirius. What I saw wouldn't motivate me to write a song.

"Another song was inspired by this place," I told Sirius. "Anthony Kiedis of the Red Hot Chili Peppers wrote about making a drug buy under that bridge over there. That's one of the reasons he titled the song 'Under the Bridge.' It's a good song, but I'll take Richard Harris's melodrama over it any day."

Sirius defers to my choice of music, although when we worked Metro K-9 he did seem to like the song "Who Let the Dogs Out?"

Thinking about Richard Harris made me remember that before his death he had been the original Dumbledore in the

Harry Potter films. I was thinking that Corde had used a Dumbledore, or another one of his UAVs, to intrude on my private life. I wasn't scared of wizards, but modern wizardry scares the hell out of me. Drones are a slippery martial slope. Video game wars make it too easy to kill and too hard for anyone to be held accountable.

I had never been to the St. Vincent Medical Center before but knew its claim to fame was being L.A.'s oldest hospital. The hospital was named after St. Vincent de Paul; I did know a thing or two about him, courtesy of Catholic school. What I remembered most—even more than his acts of charity—was that St. Vincent de Paul was captured by Barbary pirates as a young man and was actually enslaved for a time. As a boy, pirate stories generally grabbed my interest much more than the deeds of saints.

"Arrrghhh," I said to Sirius.

Somehow he took that as an invitation to give me a kiss, prompting me to fake umbrage.

"What kind of a scurvy dog are you? Kiss me again and I'll keelhaul you, then make you walk the plank, and finally feed you to the fish, you festering, flea-bitten swabbie."

My bucko must have thought all of that sounded pretty good because he wagged his tail enthusiastically. After parking, I opened all the windows a few inches and then left my seadog to dream of hidden treasure. Of course his dream wouldn't be about the treasure itself, but the fun in kicking up all that sand. Humans might have created the term "restless leg syndrome"; dogs live it.

I flashed my badge at reception and was directed toward where the filming was taking place. Movie shoots always attract crowds, but the vacant wing was far enough from the goings-on of the hospital that most visitors appeared unaware of what was occurring in their midst.

The moviemaking was supposed to be taking place on a closed set, but a break in the action gave me the opportunity to make my way halfway through the wing before finally being challenged by a Goth-looking production assistant.

"Only crew is supposed to be here," she said, speaking loudly enough to get the attention of a security guard who was helping himself to some pastry that catering had left out.

I displayed my wallet shield to the Goth and then to the late-arriving cavalry. "Detective Gideon here to see Ms. Browning," I said.

The guard took over sentry duty. "Are you on the visitor's list?" he asked, waving a clipboard.

"I am not visiting," I said. "I am working."

I handed him my business card, the one with the LAPD logo that says "Detective Michael Gideon, Special Cases Unit." The guard looked at it and then excused himself.

"You're a cop?" asked the Goth.

"I am."

"I would offer you a doughnut, but they're all gone."

I shook my head. "I'm sorry, but doughnut jokes don't go with your Morticia Addams look. That's why there are no Goth comics. You can only get so many belly laughs out of nihilism and the price of black eyeliner."

She laughed, and I shook my finger at her. "There's no laughing in the *Twilight* world," I said. "That goes against all the rules of angst. It's like invoking Ra."

"I'll try and remember that," she said. "I'd hate to have my dream of being a crypt writer dashed."

I had to give her the laugh she deserved. It was likely she was an aspiring comedian or comedy writer and used people like me to try out material. In L.A. it seems as if everyone has dreams of working at something other than what they do. Even those who make it to the top of their profession want to be something else. Comedians want to be actors; actors want to be singers; singers want to be performers.

I was happy just being a cop, and managed to do my job even while talking with the receptionist. The guard made his way onto the set and then came to a stop, facing a woman seated in a chair. Elle looked up from the screenplay she was studying, and with a bowed head the guard passed her my card. I couldn't hear what, if anything, was said, but I could read body language. Elle's back stiffened when she saw my name on the card, and she pulled at her lower lip. Her fingers nervously traced a pattern up and down the screenplay's spine as she considered what to do.

While the guard awaited her answer, a man carrying a teapot and cup came up to Elle. He was tall and thin, looked to be around thirty, and could have come straight out of central casting as a model of what a Hollywood personal assistant looked and acted like. The man noticed how preoccupied Elle was, and his body language showed his own concern. He bent down and must have asked if she was all right. She waved off his question and with a few words dismissed the guard with her thanks. As the guard trudged away, the second man spoke to her again. Whatever Elle said caused both of them to look my way and take notice of my scrutiny. Elle quickly put on a different face, offering me a smile. Her personal assistant wasn't as charitable. It was clear he wanted to run interference, but Elle shook her head and with a point of her finger gave him directions to do something else. Whatever it was didn't seem to please him, and with an unhappy shake of his head he took his leave, but not before giving me the skunk eye. Elle motioned for me to come and see her, gesturing that I was to follow after her.

"I have been summoned," I told the receptionist, but then added with an Arnold accent, 'I'll be back.'"

Deadpan, she said, "I see dead people."

I wasn't sure if she was imitating Haley Joel Osment or just sharing information. Some matters are best left alone.

When I caught up with Elle, she raised her index finger to her lips before I had a chance to say anything. I played along with her, saying nothing while she led me past a former nurse's station into an unoccupied room.

She signaled to me that our Quaker meeting was not yet concluded, and on the back of her script wrote, *No talking. Let's text instead. What's your telephone number?*

I took my pen, wrote my number down, and Elle wrote hers. She started texting using both thumbs. I don't like phones for talking, and I hate them for texting. Call me quaint, but I don't think the genus *Homo* and our opposable thumbs came about for the purpose of texting.

I don't want our conversation overheard, she wrote.

I hunt-and-pecked my answer: *Overheard by whom?*

She wrote *paparazzi.* I didn't have to write *bullshit*; my expression said as much.

I typed, *OVERHEARD as in what happened last night at my girlfriend's? Someone recorded our lovemaking and then called and woke me up, so I would hear the replay of it.*

Trying to text was frustrating me. My inexpert typing and inability to vent only compounded my annoyance. But even without hearing my story, Elle could see the anger in my expression—and hear it as I pounded at my cell phone.

When Elle read my text, she didn't immediately write back. Finally she wrote, *Sorry.*

I took a few deep breaths. Just thinking about last night's call—and the laughter I heard in the background—made my pulse race. I wanted to spit out questions at her, but instead had to slowly tap away. That quickly tried my patience. Exasperated, I put away my phone and reached for her script. With my pen I scrawled: *This silent movie isn't working for me. We need to talk for real.*

As she shook her head I wrote, *Yes,* and underlined it three times.

Elle could see I was about to start talking. She took back the script and wrote: *I have an apartment with an underground entrance and a private elevator that goes directly to my unit. I can give you a key and we can meet there at six.*

I nodded, and she wrote down her address on Wilshire Boulevard, along with instructions on how to get into her place. As a final touch, she drew a little map. Then she ripped the page out of the script and handed it to me, along with a key.

I decided to ask her one last question and wrote, *I notice you're wearing an ankh. Are you religious?*

Her lips pursed in thought, and she wrote, *I am spiritual.*

I wrote, *Do you believe in angels?*

Elle shut her eyes the way people do when they are in pain or when they just can't bear to see what's in front of them, and then she walked out of the room without answering my question.

* * *

On the walk back to my car I wondered how I would have answered my angel question. I probably would have waffled by saying cops are trained to deal in evidence, which makes belief or disbelief a moot point. Whatever I might have said or done, I wouldn't have responded as Elle did. My honest answer would have been that, despite twelve years of Catholic school, I knew very little about angels. Skeptic or not, it was time to get a belated education.

Cell phones have eliminated the need to memorize telephone numbers, but I dialed a number that had been locked into my brain for many years.

"Do you have half an hour for your prodigal son?" I asked.

* * *

It was a five-mile drive to the place of my birth. I had come into this world in the parking lot of the Blessed Sacrament Church on Sunset Boulevard. If it hadn't been for the acute hearing of a then young priest, I would have died as an abandoned throwaway baby.

Father Patrick Garrity—known by his parishioners as Father Pat—saved my life. Father Pat credits my existence to divine intervention. He saw to my placement with the perfect adoptive family, and over the years has remained involved in my life. In many ways I am the son he could never have, and he has almost a filial pride as to all the goings-on in my life. When I married Jennifer, Father Pat conducted the service; when she died, he helped put me back together.

Sirius led the charge to Father Pat's office, knowing a bag of duck treats was there waiting for him. To get around the rule of no pets being allowed in the church, Father Pat always refers to Sirius as my "seeing-eye dog." According to him, it's not much of a stretch of the truth.

My partner was munching away when I entered Father Pat's office.

"Did you make him say grace first?" I asked.

Father Pat opened his arms, and we hugged one another. He looked up at me, his bright blue eyes magnified behind the thick lenses of his glasses. He's more than a head smaller than I am, but I always feel like a child in his presence.

"It's been too long, Mikey," he said.

No one else besides Father Pat has ever called me Mikey.

"Mea culpa," I said.

That wasn't the smartest response to offer up to a diocesan priest who had majored in classics. *"Beatus homo qui invenit sapientiam,"* he said.

I nodded as if I understood what he was saying, and we both sat down. Sirius stayed at his side. His head was bowed, and it looked like he was praying for another treat.

"No, I did not make Sirius say grace," Father Pat said.

He reached out and patted his head. "But that's not to say his manners weren't impeccable. He took the duck jerky as gently as a penitent does the Host."

In priest-talk the Host is the communion wafer. "The body of Donald and Daffy," I intoned.

Father Pat smiled, but not at my irreverence. "That's one," he said. "The church thanks you for being a sponsor of the Assumption of St. Mary banquet we'll be having."

Whenever I cross an ecclesiastical line, Father Pat imposes a one-hundred-dollar fine on me. I still don't know how I ever agreed to the arrangement, but it does cut down on my irreverence. I never complain, because I owe Father Pat my life, but his fines do seem arbitrary. I suspect they are levied commensurately with the success, or lack of it, of various fundraising campaigns.

"I hope you'll be serving duck at the banquet," I said, and then held my breath for a moment, afraid of being held accountable for another Benjamin.

"It will be mostly potluck."

Father Pat pulled out another small strip of duck from the bag. He looked at me, daring me to say anything, and then raised it above Sirius's snout. While I kept my silence, Sirius gently relieved the priest of the treat.

"Lest you think the only thing that brings me here is to enrich the church coffers," I said, "I am actually here on a case. I need to know more about angels."

"Not that I'm complaining, mind you," said Father Pat, "but why is a representative of the LAPD interested in angels?"

I told him the story of what Wrong Pauley had seen. When I finished, Father Pat rubbed his forefingers up and down on his chin. His lips were pursed and he looked to be deep in thought.

"Do you believe he saw an angel?" he asked.

"I believe *he* believed he saw an angel."

Father Pat nodded and thought for a moment about what to say. "I am not sure what to tell you. I cannot speak for what this man saw or did not see. I can only tell you what the Bible says of angels, which is a very different thing than what you might have learned from Hollywood or Hallmark cards or popular music."

The Padre gave me a knowing look; that pretty much summed up my limited knowledge of angels.

"The Bible tells us that angels are bodiless, immortal spirits," he said. "However, scripture also makes it clear that they can take visible form."

"Immortal?" I asked.

Father Pat nodded. "I know you said this man believed he witnessed the murder of an angel, but scripture tells us this can't be. In Luke it is written that believers who go to heaven can no longer die, for they are like angels. God gave mankind souls; angels are spirits. And spirits cannot die."

"So you think it's likely my witness was mistaken, or maybe deluded?"

He shook his head. "I am afraid I don't have enough information to even speculate. Your witness never said he saw an angel being murdered. That was his conclusion. Wrong Pauley was looking away when he believes the angel was vaporized. He said he assumed the angel was murdered, but he didn't witness it. In the Bible there are a number of accounts of angels fighting demons. The Archangel Michael had to fight a demon for twenty-one days."

"My witness said he saw the angel's life force spilling out from him. He likened it to someone who was severely wounded bleeding out."

"In that analogy, he made the mistake of comparing humans and angels. One is flesh, the other is spirit."

"He called the angel a 'being of light.' Is that in keeping with scripture?"

Father Pat nodded.

"I can't rule out the possibility that he was having an alcohol-related psychosis. By his own admission he would have been legally intoxicated at the time of his sighting. And he admitted to a long history of drug and alcohol abuse. If any testimony could easily be discredited, it would be his. Plain and simple, he's not a reliable witness."

"And yet you believe what he told you?"

I nodded and then added, "That's not to say I haven't had eyewitnesses offer sworn testimony that was ultimately proven to be wrong beyond any shadow of a doubt. And those eyewitnesses weren't even drinking. Sometimes our eyes deceive us."

"What aren't you telling me?"

"My witness is dead," I said, and I told him about the death of Wrong Pauley and my subsequent interview with Drew Corde. When I finished, Father Pat folded and unfolded his fingers and appeared at a loss of what to say.

"In my work I hear many unusual stories, Michael," he said, "but your story is certainly the most unusual I have heard in some time."

"My witness was drunk," I said. "He saw something unusual and then watched a man get out of his car and proclaim how we shall judge angels. I am wondering if his hearing convinced him he was looking at an angel."

"I suspect he wasn't a man who was easily influenced," said Father Pat. "His description of the angel did not include its having a halo or wings. Most people expect their angels to have those things, even though they are not Biblically based. Your story would be far less bothersome to me if your witness had claimed to have seen a fat, little cherub, with rosy cheeks, who looked like a flying toddler."

"I wish he'd had the chance to talk to you," I said, "and not me. All he got from me was Doubting Thomas. Seeing what he thought was a wounded angel wasn't easy for him. And he was shaken by hearing our mystery man make his pronouncement of judging angels."

Father Pat sighed. "I am afraid when I heard your story it had much the same effect on me. I will be sure to offer up a prayer for him."

"And I will try and figure out what he really might have seen and what happened to him. Maybe he was witness to some kind of imaginary and illegal game. Maybe drones were being used to hunt down a new kind of target. Those involved clearly didn't want anyone to know of their activities. That would explain why all the surveillance footage was disabled."

"But what it wouldn't explain," said Father Pat, "is why anyone would want to hunt angels, even the imaginary kind."

I thought of Corde's trophy room. Given an opportunity to bag an angel, I knew he would be first in line. I didn't say that to Father Pat, but he seemed to be thinking the same thing.

"There's something about your story that reminds me of the hubris of Nimrod," he said. "You might remember that Nimrod was a king, and the mightiest of all hunters. His power was unequaled among men, as was his pride. It was Nimrod who ordered the Tower of Babel to be built."

He made his stairway to heaven to display his power. Nimrod did it because he could. I was willing to bet Nimrod was also the kind of guy who would have hunted angels.

"I believe angels are all around us," Father Pat said, "but we are unable to see them. There are passages in the Bible where God has suddenly revealed his host of angels, and His opening that curtain allowed human eyes to see what was there all along. But as reassuring as it would be to look upon that heavenly host, I have to admit that I do not like the idea of mankind having angel radar. I would be frightened as to how we would put to use such optics. It is better to remain blind to some things."

"You don't need to worry about angel radar."

"And why is that?"

"Because I have devil radar," I said. "I'll find our bad guy, or bad guys."

"As always, you will be in my prayers."

"I count on that. I know I don't need to tell you this, but let's put the confessional seal on what we discussed, okay?"

"In that case," said Father Pat, "I'd like to hear your Act of Contrition."

It had been a long time since I'd said those words, but I managed to stumble through them. I half-expected Father Pat to fine me another Benjamin for my slip-ups, but instead he offered me absolution.

CHAPTER 10:

A WHALE OF A TALE

In the parking lot I caught up with my missed messages. J. Gloria Keller had called three times. Each message was more pointed than the last, with her last one close to outright blackmail.

"My client says if you don't agree to meet with him forthwith, he will supply me with information with which we can revisit the legality of his arrest. I expect to hear from you today."

J. Glo was a publicity hound, but she was also said to be the worst kind of legal beagle: smart, tenacious, and unrelenting.

"Crime doesn't pay," I said to Sirius, "unless you're a lawyer."

Having one lawyer threatening to tie me up was bad enough, but now I had two. Maybe, I thought, I could put an end to being tag-teamed. It would mean getting J. Glo to do something I couldn't. I called her number and she surprised me by picking up herself.

"So what does Ellis Haines have on you?" she asked.

"You're the queen of nuisance suits, so your guess would be better than mine."

Actually, it wouldn't. I had arrested Haines without ever reading him his Miranda rights, but under oath I swore that I had. It is the only time I ever knowingly lied under oath, and not a day has gone by when I haven't felt a twinge of regret. I justified my lie in the knowledge that it kept a monster locked up. Somehow that monster had divined how my lie ate at me.

"Nuisance suits?" she said. "You've got the wrong lawyer. My clients pay me six hundred dollars an hour not to do nuisance suits."

"It must be that I have nuisance suits on my mind," I said, and explained the letter written to Officer Sirius and the one that had been written back to Francisco Garcia. "That's why I didn't get right back to you, and that's why I'm jumping through hoops now. I'm working two priority cases, and with a potential lawsuit hanging over my head, I'm not sure I can clear the time to see your client."

"That's your best attempt at poor, poor, pitiful me?"

"I was thinking of another Warren Zevon song: 'Lawyers, Guns, and Money.'"

J. Glo wasn't exactly sympathetic. "If you'd sent me that letter, Detective, I would have also played gong with your man tonsils."

"Let's agree to never play marbles then."

"All the public defender is doing is using your note as leverage to get his client off."

"Garcia is also threatening a civil suit against me for what he termed were 'emotional injuries' he claims were caused by the false and slanderous allegations submitted to an officer of the court."

"That's the usual sound and fury," she said. "Is that what's got your panties in a twist?"

"Boxers," I said, "or is that TMI?"

"Are we doing this dance because you want me to do a reach-around with the other lawyer?"

"I am not quite sure how to answer that."

Lawyers like to hit under the belt. J. Glo liked to describe under the belt.

"You want me to make this situation go away, and if I do, you'll see my client, right?"

"I don't remember saying that."

"I am not trying to entrap you into asking me how much for a happy ending, Detective. We're just doing a little quid pro quo. So, if I make your life easier, are you going to do the same for me?"

I decided to reward her for completing a sentence without referencing genitalia: "Yes."

"Ellis Haines will begin testifying later this week. You'll meet with him at a time of our choosing in the next two days?"

"Why don't I just visit with him in the Q when he's sent back?"

Haines was imprisoned in San Quentin. The FBI's Behavioral Science Unit had been disappointed when I put an end to my monthly visits to see him, but there came a point when even I realized just how toxic those meetings were to me.

"Mr. Haines insists that the three of you have your *reunion* in Los Angeles."

"It will be just like old times," I said. "Should I bring matches and tinder as well?"

"The only thing you need to do is free up your calendar."

"I'll do that, assuming that other encumbrance we talked about no longer has its talons in me."

"You and Officer Sirius need have no more worries on that account."

"Detective Sirius," I said.

"No wonder people are threatening to sue your ass."

* * *

Because J. Glo was in the top pantheon of criminal defense lawyers, it stood to reason that she could exert a lot of influence on her peers. Having Haines for a client gave her the kind of exposure money couldn't buy, which was a pretty sad state of affairs if you asked me. Career advice in this modern world: hitch your wagon to a notorious murderer if you want to get ahead.

Although Sirius and I aren't assigned to any division, world headquarters for LAPD's Special Cases Unit (SCU) is a cubicle at the Central Bureau on East 6th Street. That's the same location where Officer Sirius received his fateful letter from Public Defender Francisco Garcia.

We drove along Interstate 101. It had been two days since my last appearance at Central, and the watch commander took note of our entrance. Sergeant Perez has a loud voice, perfect for his job.

"How are you, Detective Snoop Dogg? And you too, Sirius."

Every time Perez sees me, he uses a different dog nickname. I'm not officially one of the Central troops, but Perez likes to ignore that fact. He also likes to refer to SCU as the "Strange Cases Unit," not Special Cases Unit.

"Mail has been piling up for you, Slumdog Millionaire. Do you think I'm a carrier terrier?"

"Now that you mention it," I said, "everyone has been wondering about your habit of saying 'hello' by sniffing asses."

Perez started scratching his nose with his middle finger. That was about as subtle as he got. Sirius followed me over to an open cubicle and dropped down for forty winks. While I sorted through paperwork, he snored. He was still snoring when I began answering my emails. The Chief had forwarded several letters directed to his office. On each was his same designation: *Special case?* I punted on two of them.

The third wasn't as easy to put aside and certainly qualified as a special case. The National Oceanic and Atmospheric Administration (NOAA), and the National Marine Fisheries Service (NMFS), were requesting assistance from LAPD and the Los Angeles Port Police. They wanted us to be on the lookout for whale parts that might have been harvested from a blue whale. The agencies were investigating what they termed a "suspicious cetacean death" about fifteen miles off the coast of Los Angeles. Although foul play was not a certainty, the early forensic tests on remains found seemed to indicate an unnatural death. The letter went on to say that there were only two thousand blue whales in existence and that they were the largest animals ever to have lived on earth—*ever.*

"As in they are bigger than the biggest dinosaurs that ever walked, swam, or crawled," I said to Sirius.

My partner didn't react, but then he'd never gnawed on a brontosaurus bone.

The letter concluded by stating that even if the blue whale had died a natural death, the trafficking of any of its parts was illegal under the Marine Mammal Protection Act. We were advised that one item that might turn up on the black market was the whale's eight- to ten-foot penis.

"Hello, Moby Dick," I said.

Every year, migrating gray whales travel along our coastline. Blue whales don't usually frequent Southern California waters, but this year an abundance of krill had brought them close to shore. For the last month whale-watching firms hadn't been able to keep up with all those hoping to get a glimpse of the extremely rare leviathans.

Since the NOAA-NMFS investigation was still in its preliminary stages, I wrote back and identified myself as their LAPD departmental contact and asked to be kept in the loop. In a separate email to the Chief, I wrote that I didn't think it would serve our purposes at this time to put a BOLO out on a ten-foot penis, especially as foul play hadn't been definitively established, and it wasn't even clear if any harvesting had taken place.

"Detective Alfred Kinsey at your service," I mumbled.

Organizing my case notes took another hour. Most of that time was spent detailing my Wrong Pauley findings. There wasn't much to write about the Reluctant Hero. In the middle of a piece of blank paper, I entered a question mark and then circled it. Then I inked in The Corner School and drew an arrow from the question mark to the school. I suspected the Reluctant Hero had some unknown connection to The Corner School. I went back to reviewing my notes, hoping to find something I might have overlooked.

My doodles didn't make anything jump out at me. Maybe something would surface when Sirius and I visited the school. The principal of The Corner School had jumped at the idea of our visit.

In between making some calls, I did computer searches. I spent part of the afternoon learning what I could about Elle Browning and Drew Corde. Elle was tight-lipped about her private life; Corde less so. There were several pictures of Corde with a possessive arm around Elle. The two had been an item for six months. Neither had ever been married. Judging by all the other pretty women Corde had been pictured with, he seemed to be a player, although Elle was the first actress he'd dated. From what I could determine, Corde was Elle's first live-in relationship.

My other searches had me looking at Orion Zenith, IMDb, unmanned aerial vehicles, angels, undetectable poisons, surveillance, spy toys, and modern weaponry. If the NSA were monitoring suspicious searches, mine would have been at the top of the list.

I twisted and tweaked my angel search, and stumbled on the Howard Fast short story "The General Zapped an Angel." Fast's tale was set during the Vietnam War and revolved around a twenty-foot angel shot down by American forces. Since no one in the army seemed to know what to do with the angel's body, it was stored in a helicopter hangar. The situation resolved itself when the angel everyone believed was dead suddenly awakened and flew away. The angel looked none too pleased with the military.

It was a strange tale, I thought, but I suppose it had a happy ending. Wrong Pauley's story didn't.

The writer Howard Fast is remembered mostly for his novel *Spartacus*. Kirk Douglas, in arguably his best role, played Spartacus in a movie with the same name. Over two thousand years ago Spartacus led a slave revolt against the Roman army, but things didn't work out for him. It isn't easy taking on the world's supreme military force.

At the moment, I was feeling like Spartacus.

"I'm Spartacus!" I said to Sirius.

He wagged his tail. I guess he was Spartacus too.

"Want to go catch some rare air, Spartacus?"

Sirius jumped up. He knew what that meant, and couldn't wait.

* * *

In Los Angeles County all dogs are supposed to be leashed. Violation of the county code can result in a fine north of two hundred dollars. Normally, Sirius and I adhere to the law, but when it comes to playing with discs, Sirius and I are scofflaws.

Dogs and discs originated in Los Angeles. In 1974 college student Alex Stein smuggled his dog Ashley Whippet into a nationally televised baseball game between the Dodgers and the Cincinnati Reds. During the eighth inning Stein and Ashley jumped the fence and went onto the playing field, and for eight minutes the two of them entertained the crowd. The spectators weren't the only ones enthralled; announcer Joe Garagiola gave a play-by-play of Ashley's thrilling catches to the nation. At Chavez Ravine, and on television sets across the country, spectators were introduced to the sport of discs and dogs. Judging by the crowd, the acrobatics of Ashley Whippet were much more appreciated than the game itself, but finally Stein was escorted from the field and arrested.

Sirius and I have never done our tossing and catching in Dodger Stadium, but in the tradition of Stein and Ashley we have illegally ventured on many other fields around the county. For the fifteen or twenty minutes we play, Sirius is unleashed. When the two of us worked Metropolitan K-9, we spent countless hours scouting out potential play sites. We were always looking for that spot where we could play with our discs, relatively undisturbed.

For Sirius, playing with discs was love at first bite. He enjoys retrieving balls or sticks, but it's clear they're only pleasant diversions. Discs are another matter. Before I toss that first disc, he actually trembles with anticipation.

A favorite spot of ours was an elementary school only a few miles from where I was going to be meeting with Elle. One of its attractions was the back entrance that allowed for speedy departures. I don't like having to play the cop card to other cops. It's better to just not get caught.

I gave Sirius a flexible disc to hold in his mouth during our drive there. He looked and acted like a kid on Christmas morning. We parked on the street but still had to walk by several signs informing us that unauthorized visitors weren't allowed, dogs weren't permitted, and playing on the fields was prohibited.

Other people apparently obeyed the signs, as the school fields were deserted. I walked the grass, looking for gopher holes, foxtails, glass, or anything else that could harm Sirius. As usual, we did a short warm-up. I had four discs, all different sizes and weights. They each had their own purpose, much in the way different golf clubs do; I had my "driver" disc for long-distance throws, my "wedge" disc for maximum loft time, my "putter" for accuracy, and my utility disc for all around play. My favorite picture of Sirius shows him proudly holding all four discs in his mouth.

Sirius and I have developed our own vocabulary when it comes to our disc routines. "Rare air" is when I really let one fly; "track" is when I am going for a boomerang toss, and he expects it to hang in the air and then come back; "fast" is when I toss all four discs in rapid succession, and he has to make a series of catch and drops so as to catch all four; and finally there's "ninja," which is our wild-card toss and catch. When ninja is declared, Sirius doesn't know where I am throwing the disc, and he's further handicapped by having his back turned to the action. Ninja means Sirius has to be ready for anything and react instantly. When ninja is called, Sirius is expected to think and act on his own.

One day I am going to get a vet to explain to me how dogs can catch discs as well as they do despite their visual acuity not being anywhere near that of a human's. A typical dog has 20/75 vision, which means what a human can clearly see at seventy-five feet dogs can only see at twenty feet. I do know dogs detect motion much better than humans do, so maybe that allows them to see the big Frisbee picture better. They also have a wider view of the world than do humans, as their eyes are at the sides of their head. However they do it, some dogs are great at catching discs. Most retrievers take to it easily, but disc catching doesn't seem breed specific. One of the best disc dogs I have ever seen was a Boston terrier.

We started with a few easy tosses. Hip dysplasia is common among German shepherds, but Sirius seems to have missed that bullet. He also seems to have missed the memo that he's no longer a spring chicken. Sirius loves it when I toss the disc sixty or seventy yards and he catches it on the fly.

"Rare air," I said, and he started running.

I stepped into the throw; it didn't wobble, but flew true. The tracking missile began its pursuit. Sirius ran hard, his strides growing longer and longer. Just before gravity claimed the disc, my partner launched himself. His timing was perfect; like a classic outfielder scaling a fence, he went higher and higher to make the play. When he caught the disc, I cheered, and Sirius began his long lope back. He pretended to be nonchalant about the whole thing, but his wagging tail gave him away.

"Track," I announced and turned to face the wind.

Like a discus thrower—or maybe a whirling dervish—I started in on my rotation. The idea was for me to release the disc into the wind. I finished my spinning and whirled the disc into the unseen current. The Frisbee went higher and higher; for a moment it looked as if it was suspended in air, but then it started coming back toward us. As it dropped, the disc picked up speed. Someone adept at tossing discs can confidently throw into the wind and wait for the disc to return like a boomerang, right back to the throwing hand. My throw was off, and the wind was showing the errors of my way. The disc was going to overshoot us by at least twenty feet, but Sirius was already moving. Displaying the footwork of an athlete, demonstrating perfect timing, he leaped into the air and landed his prize. All the proud papa could do was cheer.

"Gravity is overrated!" I yelled.

It's a phrase disc players like to use, and I was most definitely in the presence of a disc player.

Usually Sirius and I play disc at dusk. It's cooler then, and it's also a time when parks and schools are likeliest to be deserted. Sirius was panting from the hot day, and I didn't want him overheating. Since the plastic discs can conveniently serve as water bowls, I filled two of them up. Sirius humored me by drinking, although his posture was saying, "Come on, throw the thing."

There were at least two more hours of light left in the day, but even when we play in the near-darkness, that doesn't bother Sirius. Dogs have much better night vision than humans.

I hadn't officially announced ninja yet, so I did a few short tosses. One thing about ninja is that anything goes; Sirius had to be ready for anything and make the play before the disc hit the ground. I sent him long, and Sirius didn't disappoint. He loped back to me and couldn't resist showing off at the end, tossing the disc into the air. It landed a few steps from my feet.

"Quit getting cocky," I said. "It's time for ninja."

There were no trees near the field and not much to hinder Sirius's line of vision. I positioned him facing away from me, his hindquarters touching an upright soccer post.

"Ninja!" I yelled, faking one way and then throwing the other.

My misdirection froze him for a moment, and he was slow on picking up the direction the disc was heading, but the instant he got his bearings, Sirius went into overdrive. Despite a valiant effort, his slow start doomed him, and Sirius failed to make the play.

The boobirds came out, or at least one did. My partner pretended to ignore the peanut gallery. He retrieved the disc and brought it back to me. Without being told, he repositioned himself behind the soccer upright and waited on my command. He would be blind to where the disc was first tossed.

I chose my disc carefully: I was going for maximum time aloft. When the disc did return to earth, it would be coming fast and at a sweeping angle.

Once more I went into my whirling dervish routine. Even without looking at me, Sirius could hear what I was up to. As I released the disc I shouted, "Track ninja!"

It was up to my partner now. He had to track the disc and then be ready to make the play. Past experience cued him into the fact that I was going for maximum time aloft with a boomerang return. The disc went skyward, climbing and climbing. I was already backpedaling, knowing it would come down at least twenty-five yards from where I was standing. I began running with my head turned back toward the descending object, and it seemed as if the disc was in hot pursuit. Just as contact was imminent, Sirius leapt into the air and caught the disc only inches from my neck.

"Good dog!" I yelled.

Disc in mouth, he circled back toward me. I mussed up his fur, and made a fuss over him. Like Oliver asking for more, he dropped the disc atop my right foot. I had to disappoint him.

"Sorry," I said. "It's time for us to reach the unreachable star."

Don Quixote was nothing without his Sancho Panza; it was the same with me.

CHAPTER 11:

A STAR IS TORN

Elle's building was only a few blocks from Central Westwood; to the west was the UCLA campus, and to the east was Beverly Hills. The Residences, as it was called, spanned twenty-four stories but had fewer than eighty condos. The least expensive units started at three million dollars.

I followed Elle's printed directions and found the underground entrance in the back of the building. There was a manned security booth, but Elle had called in and put me on the approved visitor list. I was directed to pull into one of the temporary parking spaces. As I parked, Sirius began to pace in the backseat.

"Chill," I said. "I am going to meet with a woman I saw pictured holding some kind of exotic pet like a chinchilla or kinkajou or hedgehog. Or maybe it was one of those hairless cats. So you're going to stay here so as to avoid any untoward encounter."

With a grunt, Sirius settled into familiar real estate.

I had made a point of arriving fifteen minutes early. That would be enough time, I hoped, to stop sweating and make myself somewhat presentable. Despite my intentions to treat Elle

Barrett Browning like everyone else, I found myself doing more tidying up than usual. I keep a toiletry kit in my car, and I commenced with dabbing on some aftershave. Then I started crunching on some breath mints.

In the hours since my morning meeting with Elle, I'd had time to rethink our silent conversation on both a personal and professional level. My anger, combined with the texting and note writing, had thrown me off my game. Despite that, Elle hadn't seemed surprised when I'd told her that someone had recorded Lisbet's and my lovemaking. I also found it interesting that Elle never defended her boyfriend against my not-so-veiled accusations. Of course she had blamed the paparazzi for forcing us to communicate through texts and notes, but I wasn't buying that.

I decided to turn on the AC for a minute; even though I wouldn't leave Sirius without cracking open all the windows, the subterranean garage had retained much of the heat of the day. Besides, I could use the chill myself; I was still sweaty from our disc diversion.

Another car entered the garage during our cool down. The black Tesla Model S sedan silently pulled up to the elevators. The driver's door opened, and I saw Elle Browning's personal assistant get out of the car. He came around the side of the car and opened up the passenger door, extending a hand to help Elle out of the car. Then he stepped over to the elevator and pressed the up button. Maybe he was protective and didn't want Elle to break a nail, or maybe she insisted on the star treatment. Elle spoke to him as she stepped inside the elevator; whatever she said made him smile.

He returned to the car and then parked a short distance away in a charging station for electric cars. I studied him as he hooked up the charger to the Tesla. Maybe he heard my engine running, or it's possible he felt my eyes on him. He turned around and we made eye contact. What he saw made him scowl and then turn his back on me.

There's no better way to get a cop's attention than by ignoring him. The car was now cool enough for Sirius to be comfortable. I exited my vehicle, and my footsteps announced my approach, but Elle's assistant still didn't acknowledge me.

"How long does it take to charge the car?" I asked him.

Without facing me he tersely said, "About half an hour."

"So this must be one of those superchargers?"

He minimally tilted his head in agreement.

"I think I saw you at the hospital this morning. Are you Elle's chauffeur?"

"I'm her assistant."

"That must be interesting work."

He didn't answer.

"I'm Detective Gideon," I said. "And you are?"

Since I hadn't conveniently disappeared in the face of his ignoring me, he turned and faced me. "My name is Joe Valentine, and I hope you won't think I'm rude, but if you have any questions about Ms. Browning and her business I'm not at liberty to comment."

"And why is that?"

"I signed a nondisclosure agreement when I took the job as her assistant, and it specifically prohibits me from discussing my employment or anything that has to do with Ms. Browning."

The words were right, but the vibe wasn't. Valentine couldn't mask his disapproval of me.

"In that case I'll ask you something that doesn't have anything to do with your boss," I said. "You seemed bothered when I showed up at the hospital this morning. And you kind of seem bothered now."

"It's my job to run interference for Ms. Browning."

"It seems like you wear a lot of hats. You bring tea, you're the driver, and you act as security. You do windows too?"

He shrugged and said nothing. Maybe he thought answering would violate his NDA. But I thought it was more likely he just didn't want to talk to me.

* * *

I stepped into the elevator and used the key that Elle had provided me. It began an almost soundless ascent and came to a stop one floor from the penthouse. I wondered who had those digs. The elevator opened into a private hallway, and I entered the foyer of a residence whose front door was open.

"Hello?"

Out of sight, a voice called, "Come in."

I followed the sound of the voice. Elle was sitting on a sofa in the living room, and behind her was the L.A. skyline. From up high, the city looked clean and new. Distances can be deceptive.

Elle was wearing the same clothing she'd had on that morning. It was probably dinnertime on the set, and it was likely she would have to return to work. She was holding a wineglass, but I wasn't sure if she was drinking wine or water. The liquid was clear, whatever it was.

"Can I get you something to eat or drink?"

I shook my head and said, "I'm good."

I pretended not to be nervous in her presence. I guess there was more than one actor in the room. Cops like to act as if we're incapable of being starstruck and that being in the presence of celebrity isn't any big deal. But cops are as human as anyone. I tried not to touch my scarred face, but I couldn't help but be mindful of my deformity, especially in the presence of her beauty. I practiced a trick a cop at Metro had taught me:

to avoid being influenced by a beautiful woman, he said you should always stare at the bridge of her nose. In that way, he said, she thinks you're making eye contact with her but despite that are impervious to her charms. Most of the time I appeared to be looking at Elle, I was actually acquainting myself with the bridge of her nose.

Big name actors are well insulated from the world at large. Access to the star is limited by publicists, agents, lawyers, and managers. That Praetorian Guard restricts entry to their charge. This kind of contact was very unusual.

"Thank you for seeing me," I said. "I'm not very good with Quaker meetings. Since you're not holding a phone or pad, I'm assuming we can talk freely."

"The Residences caters to public figures. This is a security building especially designed to keep wannabe intruders at bay."

"How does it do that?"

She pointed to the windows. "The windows have been treated so that we can look out, but no one can look in. That treatment also prevents cameras from being able to take pictures of anyone inside. If someone were to try and snap a picture of us now, we wouldn't even be a blur."

"What if someone wanted to record what we were saying?"

"Most of the actors, athletes, and entertainers who live here have the noise generator package, which prevents even the best surveillance systems from being able to eavesdrop. Those noise generators make the spoken word unintelligible on recording devices."

"I generally don't need a noise generator to be unintelligible," I said.

That got me a polite smile.

"How long have you lived here?"

"I bought this unit three months ago," she said.

"Where did you live before?"

"I still have a beach house in Malibu. That's my main residence. And most nights I'm at Drew's place."

"Why did you buy this?"

"It's my downtown getaway. Why do you ask?"

"I wondered if the privacy afforded here had anything to do with your purchasing it. After what happened to me last night, I could understand why someone would want their privacy safeguarded."

"I bought here because it fit my needs," she said, and didn't elaborate.

"When we talked this morning—or should I say when we wrote our texts and notes—you didn't act surprised when I told you someone managed to make an audiotape of what should have been private time between me and my girlfriend."

"I wasn't sure how to react. It was clear you were upset. I didn't want to make matters worse."

"Three or four men were laughing in the background while the tape was playing. It was dirty laughter, the kind where everyone knows they're doing something wrong, but they're still clearly reveling in the wallow."

Elle looked down at her wineglass and refused to meet my gaze.

"I don't think it's a coincidence that the Attack Pack came over last night. I suspect they were the ones I heard laughing in the background."

"I went to bed early," she said, still not looking at me.

"Do you know the regulars of this Attack Pack?"

"You should ask Drew."

"Speaking of Drew, did the two of you discuss the reason for my visit yesterday?"

Elle shook her head.

"I'm investigating the death of a man who died two nights ago. Twenty-four hours before he died, this man said he was witness to the murder of an angel."

Elle involuntarily reached for the ankh tucked under her shirt.

"This witness saw a Tesla Roadster pull up to what he said was the downed angel. As he described it, the angel was bleeding out or, more accurately, was losing its light. He said a man got out of his Tesla and stood over this angel just like a big game hunter."

I waited for her to react. After a few seconds she asked, "What happened then?"

"My witness was terrified. He was cowering behind shrubbery, afraid of being seen. When he finally got nerve enough to look, the angel was gone. And the Tesla was silently being driven away."

Elle was a good enough actor to be able to control her expression, and even her eyes, but her complexion had grown noticeably paler.

"Have you ever heard your boyfriend talk about angels?"

"I'm not sure I should be discussing that," she said hesitantly, "or anything at all with you."

"Why is that?"

"It might compromise Drew's special security clearance. He's impressed upon me the fact that he deals with very sensitive material and that I'm not allowed to talk about anything I might have seen or heard. He said that's a violation of national security."

"Angels are a violation of national security?"

"I don't know what is or isn't."

"Your boyfriend is a hunter. Have you ever gone hunting with him?"

Elle looked even more uncomfortable. "I don't see the point of your question."

"I want to know if you've been in his presence when he's hunted something."

"I am not going to answer that question because of my concerns about national security."

I thought about that. Hunting rabbits with a .22 wouldn't raise national security issues; hunting them with a drone and a death ray would.

"It seems like no one wants to comment about anything. I just finished talking with your Man Friday downstairs, and he was tight-lipped about everything. I don't think he would have even ventured an opinion about the weather."

"I'm glad to hear that. The media loves to take innocuous remarks and blow them up into something they aren't."

"I am not the media, and I don't want a headline, but I do want a few answers. Have you seen one of your boyfriend's drones in action?"

She nodded. "It's no secret that I visited the OZ facilities in Palmdale and Rancho Bernardo and watched some of the drones being tested. I even participated in company publicity shots."

"And that's the only time you've seen your boyfriend's drones in action?"

"I didn't say that. As I told you, I'm uncomfortable about saying much at all."

"Does Corde bring his work home with him?"

"What do you mean by that?"

"I think you know exactly what I mean by that."

"I need to get back to *my* work, Detective."

"My angel witness died only a day after trying to tell the world what he saw. I don't know if that's a coincidence or not, but I'm investigating it. What I don't think is a coincidence is that after I had a run-in with your boyfriend, five hours later there was an unauthorized recording of me making love to my girlfriend."

"I am sorry, but I don't know anything about that."

"I'm sure that's true, but I think there's a lot you do know and aren't saying."

"I'm afraid I have to get back to work."

"When J. Edgar Hoover was running the FBI, he thought he was above the law. Hoover wiretapped Martin Luther King and recorded him having sex with women other than his wife. Afterward, Hoover enjoyed playing those tapes to other listeners. It's hard to imagine that kind of abuse of power. Or is it?"

The room was preternaturally quiet. We were alone in a city of almost four million people.

Elle broke the silence by asking, "Have you told your girlfriend about what you heard?"

The unexpectedness of her question put me at a loss for words. Finally I said, "There wasn't a good time today."

It was a lame answer, and I knew it, so I kept talking. "When she learns, it's going to upset her. And I am the one responsible. I brought this upon her."

"It's not your fault."

"I wish I believed that. The FBI sent King a copy of their sex tape. The hope was that he would resign his position. Some say the powers-that-be wanted him to commit suicide. The collateral damage was that Coretta King stumbled onto her husband's sex tape. She was the one who suffered more than anyone."

"It's good that you don't like disappointing your girlfriend," Elle said, "but you still need to tell her."

"Lately it seems all I'm doing is disappointing her. But she still persists in thinking I'm on the side of angels."

"Maybe she's right."

"I need you to tell me the names of the Attack Pack. I need to question someone who was at the house last night."

"As I told you, I retired for the night. I don't know who was there."

"But you do know the usual suspects."

"I've already explained I can't comment because I'm not sure what would constitute a violation of national security."

"Playing video games has nothing to do with national security. That's what the Attack Pack does, isn't it? The least you can do is to give me one name. I'll take it from there."

She thought about it, sighed, and gave me a name.

CHAPTER 12:

FLIGHT OF THE BUMBLEBEE

Before driving home, I called Lisbet. Our conversation was brief, and though we both tried to be upbeat, there was underlying tension. We hadn't made any plans for the evening, and Lisbet didn't demur when I told her I was tired and going home. Confession might be good for the soul, but I still didn't tell her about the cause of my previous night's insomnia. That was yet another conversation I was putting off for another time. I got the sense I wasn't the only one putting off conversations. Despite that, or maybe because of it, I felt the need to talk, even if not to Lisbet.

"Call Shaman," I told my phone. For once it listened to me. When Seth answered, I said, "Do you have the yam special available tonight?"

"Do you have a reservation, sir?"

Sirius started wagging his tail when he heard Seth's voice.

"Look under the name Sirius. Or it might be under the last name of Dog Star."

"Ah, yes, there it is. We'll be expecting you at eight o'clock, party of two. Would you like to hear tonight's specials?"

"I think the only thing I'll want to hear is the clink of ice cubes."

"That can be arranged, sir."

Everyone needs a best friend. I am lucky that mine lives right next door. Since Jenny's death I had spent many evenings with Seth. I am still not sure what would have happened to me had he not been there.

He met us at the door, swept his arm to welcome us in, and said, *"Senores, bienvenidos."*

His Spanish accent is flawless; mine isn't. But I knew how to ask for a drink. *"Quiero beber alcohol."*

"Por supuesto," Seth said.

Sirius's dinner and our drinks were already waiting. Sirius was served first, but I was used to that.

Seth brought my drink with his. He extended his glass toward mine and said, "To the angel's share." I repeated his toast and then drank. The extra dozen seconds of aging made my bourbon taste just perfect, and after a long sip that bordered on a gulp, I sighed gratefully.

Before sitting down, Seth brought over an ice bucket, tongs, and a bottle. Seth would have been able to make both Emily Post and Doc Holliday happy.

My second sip was more restrained. "Angel's share," I mused.

"Based on our last discussion," Seth said, "and our current imbibing, it seemed an appropriate toast."

Seth likes his toasts. "Probably more appropriate than you even know," I said.

The angel's share is what distillers refer to as the evaporation loss of spirits during aging.

"You know my witness who saw the fallen angel?"

Seth nodded.

"He's dead."

I thought about Wrong Pauley and his dog Ginger and his sad and too short life. Without saying anything, I extended my glass, and Seth lightly met it with his. Then I related my investigation into Wrong's death and my encounter with Drew "Rip" Corde.

"It might be my own bias," I said, "but when I found myself looking at all those dead animals in his great room, it felt like I was in the presence of a serial murderer."

Most people are lucky enough to have never been in the presence of a serial murderer. Too much of my life had already been spent in the company of Ellis Haines.

"Why is that?" Seth asked.

"A lot of serial murderers like their trophies. Haines was one of those. He kept items from his victims, and though he didn't admit it, I'm sure those tokens allowed him to relive his awful crimes. Corde's killing room was like that, but he didn't even have to hide his handiwork. Everything was on display.

"What struck me most was his tiger. My eyes kept returning to it. I know it was my imagination, but it felt alive. It was beautiful, and it was terrible, but both those descriptions fail to describe its magnificence."

Seth nodded, and then he started reciting, his voice at first not much more than a whisper, but then growing louder and more assertive:

Tyger tyger, burning bright,
In the forests of the night;
What immortal hand or eye,
Could frame thy fearful symmetry?

In what distant deeps or skies,
Burnt the fire of thine eyes?

On what wings dare he aspire?
What the hand, dare seize the fire?

. . .

When the stars threw down their spears
And water'd heaven with their tears:
Did he smile his work to see?
Did he who made the Lamb make thee?

I felt numb, and not from the drink. The words had drawn me in and continued to resonate with me.

"I skipped some stanzas," Seth confessed. "Shame on me. There was a time I could recite Blake's 'Tyger' in my sleep."

"You mean your nightmares?"

"That is the greatness of Blake."

"As striking as the images are, I'm not sure I know what the poem means."

"You're not alone. There are many interpretations. Some say it's about God creating evil. Others say it is Satan who in the darkness of Hell created his Frankenstein-like creatures."

"What did that line about the stars throwing down spears mean?"

"What did it mean to you?"

"I couldn't help but think about drones."

Seth smiled. "I don't think Blake was thinking about drones. It's likely he was influenced by Milton's *Paradise Lost*, where the angels defending heaven threw down their spears and wept when their brethren who fought with Satan were cast from heaven."

I nodded at his explanation; Seth decided he wanted one of his own. "Why were you thinking about drones?"

As dispassionately as I could, I told Seth about what had happened the previous night. When I finished, he said, "So how do you feel about what occurred?"

"I didn't know how unattractive my heavy breathing was. I sounded like an asthmatic wildebeest."

"My guess is that isn't very high on your list of concerns."

"I should have listened to Sirius. He kept alerting me with his barking. Sirius was hearing something. He was telling me to watch out. I was the one who ignored him. I won't make that mistake again."

My partner lifted his head at the mention of his name. Seth thought Sirius was my spirit guide. I guess that was another way of saying he was my guardian angel.

"OZ produces several models of UAVs," I said. "Their latest UAV is the Dumbledore, a miniaturized spy drone. Ten years ago if you'd said the word 'drone' everyone would have thought you were talking about a male bee."

"If I remember correctly," said Seth, "bee drones have no stingers."

"I suspect the Dumbledore drone does and that the sting is lethal."

"And what makes you think that?"

"Wrong Pauley," I said, "and the progression of UAV technology. Today I spent some time researching drones. Back in 2008, the US Air Force showed off prototypes of bug-sized drones called micro-air vehicles, or MAVs. Even then defense experts were talking about these bugbots having the capacity to emit chemicals or poisons. Since that time MAVs have come a long way. I can't imagine spying or swarming would be their only capability. I suspect one of the unspoken features of a Dumbledore is that it could easily be used as an assassination vehicle."

"'Death, where is thy stinger?'" said Seth.

I nodded. "What if poison was injected that mimicked a mosquito bite? No pathologist is going to take notice of a mosquito bite, but something as innocuous as that could mark the spot where a lethal toxin was injected."

"And you think that's what happened to the homeless man?"

"He was a witness, even if I'm not sure to what. And then he died."

"When I was a boy, I saw my sister have a bad anaphylactic reaction to a bee sting," said Seth. "I was afraid she was going to die. If we hadn't had epinephrine, I think she would have. Her throat closed up, and she could barely breathe. It wasn't until she had her second shot of epi that her breathing regulated."

I thought about Wrong Pauley again and Dumbledore. He might have died just such a death. What if the microdrone was equipped with a stinger that caused anaphylaxis? Even an autopsy might not be able to reveal how he died.

"How's your hunt going for the Reluctant Hero?" Seth asked.

I was glad we were off the subject of drones and death. "It's been on the backburner, but tomorrow Sirius and I are going to The Corner School. After we do our little PR program, I'll be talking to some of the kids and teachers."

"I'd love to see you and Sirius in action."

"He's the action part. I'm the window dressing."

We sipped our drinks in companionable silence. I was the one who finally felt the need to talk.

"It looks like the Officer Sirius situation has finally been put to bed. Or at least that was the message I received while driving home."

"You don't make it sound like that's good news."

"It involved quid pro quo, and I'm not sure if I got the better of the deal. In order to make that nonsense go away, I agreed to meet with Ellis Haines the day after tomorrow."

"You made a deal with the devil."

"It didn't involve my soul, or at least I don't think it did."

"I'd advise not signing anything in blood."

"I hate the sight of blood, especially my own."

Seth stood up. I thought he was refreshing his drink, but instead he went over to his vinyl collection and began going through his albums.

"I think we need the right music," he said.

Seth stores his large vinyl collection in drawers he had specially constructed. He also has a vast CD collection, but he claims the vinyl sound is better. Being practically tone deaf, those nuances are lost on me. He finally found the album he was looking for.

There is something almost sacramental in the way Seth prepares albums for playing. Before playing the record, he checks the turntable and needle for dust. In his examination he uses everything but white gloves. His albums are housed vertically in acid-free plastic sleeves from which he carefully removes the records, making sure not to touch them with his fingers so as not to leave oil on the vinyl. Seth has a carbon-fiber record-cleaning brush as well as a cleaning mitt. He uses either, or both, to make sure the album is spotless. This time he cleaned with the mitt, rubbing in a circular motion from inside to outside.

As Seth prepared the vinyl for playing, he offered up some background as to what we would be hearing. "Rimsky-Korsakov created this piece from a Russian folktale. At the onset of the story, the youngest of three sisters marries the czar and bears him a son. The jealous older sisters have the mother and her newborn prince thrown into the sea, but the mother and her child are saved by a magical swan. The czar does not know what happened to his wife and son, but fears they are dead. As the prince grows up, he desires to see his father, but they are separated by a great distance. Once more the magical swan is able to help, changing the prince into a flying insect so that he can undertake the long flight home."

Seth lowered the needle, and the familiar music began to play. It is a great gift to be able to laugh at what bedevils you, and Seth gave me that gift.

Together the two of us listened to "Flight of the Bumblebee." When the last furious note ended, Seth went back to the turntable and carefully lifted the needle.

"So the prince was turned into a bumblebee?" I asked.

"His visit home was quite eventful," said Seth. "Even though he couldn't reveal his true presence to his father, the bumblebee prince managed to sting both of the evil sisters, blind the primary usurper, and escape capture."

"I'm hoping the prince prevailed and lived happily ever after."

Seth nodded. "He not only returned home to his father but even married the magical swan that turned out to be a princess who had been transformed into a bird."

"I hate it when that happens."

Seth's hand was still hovering over the turntable. "Again?" he asked.

"By all means."

Once more we listened to the frenetic flight of the bumblebee. In my mind's eye I could see the bumblebee stinging the twisted sisters, blinding the bad guy, and ultimately winning the day.

The music was even better the second time around.

CHAPTER 13:

GAMES WITHOUT FRONTIERS, WARS WITHOUT TEARS

In the aftermath of catching Ellis Haines, Sirius and I were the most popular PR tools of the LAPD. For a time, it seemed as if everyone in L.A. wanted a piece of us. I limited our appearances, citing the need for intensive physical therapy. That was true enough, but my reluctance was more a result of my feeling like a fraud. I was no hero; I had put my partner in harm's way and in trying to save his life had saved my own. I was messed up big time before going into the fire, and more messed up afterward. My walk through the flames permanently scarred my face, but it was the hidden scars that disabled me even more than the obvious ones.

Going out in public on behalf of the LAPD earned me brownie points. Early on I had thought to parlay those points into a detective's job at Robbery-Homicide, but ultimately I was given something even better. Sirius and I work our special cases and have autonomy unheard of in the department. Of course, no job is perfect. At least once a month Chief Ehrlich expects Sirius and me to do a PR appearance on behalf of the department, what I call the "Dog and Phony Show."

At our appearances I never mention the Weatherman or what happened in the fire. I know those questions will come in the Q&A afterward. I am usually able to quickly dispense with the more common inquiries, offering up pat answers that don't require thought. My brief talk centers around police work and community outreach. The real star of the show is Sirius. We've developed a routine that shows a trained K-9 in action, along with a few tricks of our own that we've developed. It's perfect for my ham of a partner. His performance might not be French poodle cute, with music and conga lines of dancing canines, but it's a fun routine. Best of all, Sirius does most of the work and gets just about all of the attention. That's how I like it.

Our scheduled appearance at The Corner School wasn't on orders of the Office of the Chief of Police (COP), but had been arranged by me. In a looser atmosphere I was hoping to hear things about the Reluctant Hero that I might not otherwise.

We arrived at the school half an hour early and were cleared to proceed by a security guard. The presence of security was something new to the school since the shooting. I was directed to check in at the administrative offices, and after doing so was offered a tour.

Dawn Barry was the assistant principal of the school, and identified herself as "Doctor Dawn." Apparently our visit fell under Dr. Dawn's purview. She was small and blond. My mother, I am sure, would have described her as "spunky," but my mother is one of the last people in North America who uses the word "spunky." Dr. Dawn was our tour guide.

Because my Reluctant Hero case was on life support, I took the tour as an opportunity to ask lots of questions about the shooting. My goal for the morning was to shake branches and hope something might drop.

The first stop on the tour was the school garden, where both Sirius and I sampled some snow peas, lettuce, and green beans.

Between mouthfuls I said, "You can tell the children that you witnessed police officers eating their vegetables."

"You can be sure I'll do that," said a laughing Dr. Dawn.

"Maybe you ought to take some pictures," I said. "People would believe Sirius ate his vegetables; they'll need proof that I did."

Dr. Dawn snapped some photos with her phone. As we posed and she clicked away, I asked, "How are the students doing?"

I didn't need to add the words "post-shooting."

"There's a lot of lingering anxiety," said Dr. Dawn. "We have daily talk sessions where we encourage the students to express what they're feeling. And for those reluctant to talk, we have also been doing a lot of journaling."

"I imagine those journals have been revealing."

"They've told us a lot of things," she said, "but mostly we've learned the children are still afraid."

"What do they say about the Reluctant Hero?"

"Some of the children are convinced he was a spirit or an angel. They say that explains how he disappeared."

"Maybe they're right. No one has come forward yet. Did you get a good look at him?"

She shook her head. "At the time I was mostly in shock. What I remember more than anything is how I tried to keep my own fears in check long enough to herd some children behind me. That's what had my attention just as everything was happening."

"I kind of expected the Reluctant Hero would turn out to be a dad just too shy to come forward."

"I pride myself on knowing the parents of our students," Dr. Dawn said. "And I am sure I never saw this man before."

"Is that how it was with all the children?"

"Pretty much."

"Pretty much?"

"One or two of the kids thought the Reluctant Hero was the father of one of our third-graders, but he only had a passing resemblance to him."

"I think I heard about that," I said, although I definitely hadn't heard about it. I threw out a common name, hoping to get her to respond. "That was Mark's dad, wasn't it?"

My stab in the dark proved to be close enough. "Matthew," she said, "Matthew Pullman."

I acted as if the name were familiar to me. "And you've personally seen Matthew's father?"

She nodded. "He isn't our Reluctant Hero. Mr. Pullman is heavier and less . . ." It took her a moment to find the word for which she was searching: ". . . vigorous."

"Will Matthew be attending our group session?" I asked.

The school's administration had arranged for a group of students from each of the grades to meet with me and Sirius after our presentation.

"I'm not sure," she said.

"If at all possible, I'd like him there."

"I'll have that arranged," said Dr. Dawn, and she paused to make a note of it. I was glad she didn't ask me why I wanted him there.

Even the best elementary school in the world doesn't have that much for tour guides to work with. We walked down a long hallway with art projects on display and spent time in an unoccupied science lab looking at the student science exhibits. Class was in session, but those students we encountered went wide-eyed when they spotted Sirius.

Our last stop was the playground where the assembly was going to be convened. There were two classes doing physical education; one was on the blacktop, the other on the field. The blacktop group was playing a game where they were trying to keep a few beach balls aloft; the students on the grass were lined up, head to feet, handing off balls over their heads without looking.

"We've tried to move away from traditional games like basketball and dodgeball," she said. "In these games there are no winners and losers, and the children need to act cooperatively."

"Any of the kids die of boredom yet?" I asked.

"PE might not be as exciting to the athletes, but with this setup there are fewer children dreading it. Our games preclude the trauma of being picked last for a team or the pressure of being the scapegoat when a team loses."

"In elementary school my favorite part of the day was PE, but I went to one of those unenlightened schools where we kept score and tried to kill the opposing team."

"Did you like school, Detective?"

"I took my role there very seriously."

"And what role was that?"

"Class clown," I said.

A bell rang—apparently school bells have not yet been deemed traumatic—and students began to assemble outside. Sirius knew the students were there to see him and posed accordingly.

"It's a police dog," I heard a lot of the kids say.

The makeshift stage was roped off so that I wouldn't worry about too many grasping hands trying to pet Sirius. I wasn't worried about my partner, but didn't want him to have to deal with the crunch of kids. Sirius is particularly gentle with little ones.

If you raise them right from the time they are young, they're no threat. I am talking about children, of course.

Dr. Dawn introduced the two of us. Usually Sirius and I get our names linked with the Weatherman during any introduction, but thankfully there was no mention of Ellis Haines. If the kids were lucky, they had never heard of him. The children had already had their own encounter with crazy and didn't need to learn about another nut job.

After Dr. Dawn passed the baton to me—that is, the handheld microphone—we shook hands. She forgot to extend that courtesy to Sirius, who called her on it by extending a paw as she walked by. All the children called out to Dr. Dawn, and she did an about-face and returned to shake with Sirius. That had all the kids buzzing.

Almost all eyes were on Sirius as I began my talk. I told the children that unfortunately bad things sometimes happened to good people, and to good kids, but I reminded them that there were a lot more good people in the world than bad people, people like the Reluctant Hero and their parents and their teachers. I told them that it was okay to be afraid, but that there were many people ready to help, such as firefighters, social workers, school staff, and the police. I commended them for responding so well during their own emergency. And then to lighten up the mood, I told the kids it was important to have a good diet, which should include fruit and vegetables.

"Do you think Sirius likes fruit and veggies?" I asked.

"No," shouted most of the kids. I was heartened by their skepticism.

"Well, he does. Today we were snacking in your school garden. Dr. Dawn even took pictures."

The kids demanded proof and then squealed with laughter at the pictures of Sirius sucking down green beans like he would strands of spaghetti. My partner loves to pose for pictures.

"Do you like fruit and vegetables?" I asked.

My question got a mixed reaction. "Well, they're good for kids and dogs. Sirius eats them every day. His favorite fruits are apples, bananas, cantaloupe, and mango, and his favorite vegetables are steamed carrots, broccoli, and pumpkin."

The kids thought my partner's diet was pretty funny and started yelling out their favorite fruits and vegetables.

"There are some fruits and vegetables you should never give to dogs," I warned, and then named some of the chief culprits like onions, garlic, avocados, grapes, and raisins.

Small but serious heads nodded back.

"Do any of you have dogs?"

If the teachers were hoping to keep their charges quiet, it was now a lost cause. All sorts of names and breeds were shouted out.

"Make sure you keep chocolate, candy, and gum out of the reach of your dogs. Those can be poisonous. You wouldn't want them to get sick, would you?"

"No!" they all chorused.

"That's real important to remember, and I know you will. Okay, now we get to the good part of my talk because it's time to introduce my partner. The two of us have worked together for five years, and I couldn't ask for a better friend or partner. Give a nice welcome to Sirius!"

Sirius bounded over to me. "High five," I said, and he raised his paw high. In my lowest voice I said, "Low five," and he raised his paw just a little. "Shake," I said, and he shook. And then I said, "Shake your booty." His tail wagging had the crowd cheering.

"Some of you might have recognized the name Sirius," I said. "My partner was named after the brightest star in the night sky. That bright star is called Sirius, which is also known as the Dog Star.

"My Sirius is a working dog," I said. "All sorts of breeds of dogs are used in countless ways. They herd and protect and guide.

And because dogs have such a keen sense of smell, they are used to sniff out all sorts of things ranging from bedbugs to truffles.

"A dog's sense of smell is more than a thousand times better than a human's, and in some dog breeds their sense of smell is millions of times better. That's why dogs are so good at tracking, or detecting all kinds of scents."

I called for Dr. Dawn to join us and asked if she wouldn't mind taking a walk and hiding Sirius's Frisbees along her route. As she set out, I told Sirius, "No peeking," and he responded by burying his eyes in his paws. Judging by the reaction of the kids, Sirius should have won the Oscar.

When I sent Sirius to find his discs, he rounded them up in record time. His reward was getting a few minutes of disc play where his every catch was loudly cheered by the children.

It was nice to hear the laughter and see kids being kids. I hoped they'd be lucky and never have to encounter violence again. At the end of our presentation, Sirius and I were ushered into the teachers' dining room, where we met with the student representatives, a few teachers, and Dr. Dawn. The kids were looking all around; there really wasn't much to see, but they seemed tickled to be allowed into the teachers' clubroom.

"We won't be here for long," I promised. "I am sorry all of you had a frightening experience, but the LAPD hopes we can learn from what happened so we'll be able to better deal with trouble in the future."

I asked the children to introduce themselves and took note of Matthew Pullman. He was maybe nine years old and carried himself like a jock, a look accentuated by his L.A. Lakers garb. After their introductions, I asked the children to tell me what they had seen and experienced when the intruder came to their school. Before long the Reluctant Hero became a topic. There was agreement as to the direction he came running from, but not so much agreement as to what he looked like.

The gunman had appeared at The Corner School shortly after eleven thirty. First lunch had just begun, which meant first-, second-, and third-graders were eating. Second lunch was for the older children. Because it was a pleasant day, everyone was outside. The children who had brought their lunch were already seated; those who hadn't brought lunch were waiting in line to get it.

Matthew Pullman told me he was one of those who had brought his lunch and had been outside with his friends. Because of that, they were among those who had been the closest to the gunman.

I tried to get more of the story but went about it in a round-about way by taking note of what Matthew was wearing.

"You like the Lakers?" I asked.

He gave an enthusiastic nod.

"What about the Clippers?"

"They stink," he said.

A few of his neighbors disagreed. Despite playing basketball in the same arena and same city, L.A. fans are adamant about favoring one team over the other.

"What do you think of your PE classes here at school?" I asked.

Even with Dr. Dawn present, Matthew signaled thumbs down.

"I know the intruder appeared just after first lunch started," I said, "but I'm wondering if anyone noticed him before he trespassed on the school grounds."

One of the boys sitting next to Matthew raised his hand, and after learning his name was Jacob, I asked, "What did you see?"

"I saw a man walking back and forth along the fence."

The fence in question separated the playing fields from the street.

"Was there anything in particular that made you notice this man?"

The boy scrunched up his mouth before saying, "He looked angry."

"And when did you notice him?"

"During gym class," he said.

"What time was that?"

Matthew answered instead of Jacob: "Right before lunch."

"Both of you had PE right before lunch?"

The boys nodded.

* * *

On my drive to El Segundo, I discussed what I had learned at The Corner School. Sirius is a great sounding board. He's a careful listener and allows me to go off on tangents without interrupting.

"The shooter and the Reluctant Hero were both seen coming from the same direction," I said. "Fewer than fifteen seconds separated their appearances. If Jacob was right, and the shooter was acting strange, my guess is that the Reluctant Hero observed this—which would explain how quickly he was on the scene. But what it doesn't explain is why he was at The Corner School in the first place."

I considered the time sequence. "Gym class started at 10:40, and concluded at 11:25. Our witness says the shooter was pacing outside the school fence during that time. At approximately 11:32 shots were fired. No more than fifteen seconds after those first shots were fired the shooter was tackled and no longer a threat. If the Reluctant Hero was watching the suspect and reacted that quickly, he had to be parked near the school. No one noticed him, though—at least not on that day."

The freeway traffic was stop and go, which allowed me time to do a drumroll on the steering wheel.

"We know why the shooter was there. He was having a psychotic episode, and his voices were telling him the children were demons. But why was the Reluctant Hero parked there?"

It's a suspicious world, and being a cop made me that much more suspicious. Sometimes in order to catch bad people, you have to think like one. Could the Reluctant Hero be a pedophile? That would explain why he hadn't come forward. If he were a convicted pedophile, he would be banned from being anywhere near a school. Watching students would have been grounds for his arrest.

Perhaps he was a pedophile who hadn't acted on his urges. If that were the case, he still would have wanted to leave without being questioned. His shame might have made him run away. A life of quiet desperation might be better than having his desires exposed.

"No," I said. "My gut tells me that's not what we're looking at."

The only problem is that my gut *wasn't* telling me what we were looking at.

"Let's assume the Reluctant Hero was there to watch the gym class. Both of us know those games the kids play are not exactly spectator sports."

Sirius draped his head over my shoulder. He concurred with my speculation.

"If he didn't care about the game, his interest must have been in one of the children. But why would you be surreptitiously watching a kid?"

I did another steering-wheel drumroll.

"He could be an estranged parent. It might be his spouse has sole custody over the child. And maybe there's a restraining order keeping him away. If it was a rancorous divorce, it's possible he's been out of his child's life for years."

It seemed a stretch. Even a long-absent parent would likely be recognized by his child.

"What if he was there scouting out the school for another reason?"

I tried to come up with any other reason, but couldn't. It wasn't like the school was a jewelry store or bank, and the location needed casing.

"What if he was plotting something illegal, though," I said, "like child abduction?"

Now I was really stretching the plausible. The Corner School wasn't a cult. Its students wouldn't need to be deprogrammed.

"He was watching someone," I said. "And for some reason he had to do it from the shadows. And he didn't want this someone to be exposed. He acted in order to protect a child from a madman and then disappeared to protect that child from any collateral damage."

That felt right to me. I was still a long ways from an explanation, but I found myself nodding. Sirius must have been encouraged as well. He gave my ear a little kiss.

* * *

My smart phone is synched to my car stereo. I have downloaded at least a thousand songs on my phone, and I offered up my choice as a voice command. My tune selection was repeated and moments later Peter Gabriel's "Games Without Frontiers" started playing. I listened to its opening as the wonderful Kate Bush sang (and mispronounced) "Jeux sans frontieres." Most listeners think she's singing the words "She's so popular."

I'd watched children playing games that morning, and now I was traveling to the adult version. Peter Gabriel started whistling, and I joined him. Sirius's ears popped up. Our noise sounded interesting to him.

The OZ offices in El Segundo were spread out over several business parks, and we searched out the building we were looking for. The subtitle of the song I was listening to was "War Without Tears," the very kind of war OZ was pretending we could have.

It was evident that Orion Zenith's business had grown so quickly it had outstripped all its original space. The business, it appeared, was busting out at the seams. We drove by the corporate offices, a six-story building that stood like a watchtower among all the OZ edifices. Neal Bass didn't have an office in that castle, which was probably a good thing for my purposes. Being somewhat removed from their headquarters might make it easier for us to talk. Elle Barrett Browning had identified Bass as being a member in good standing of the Attack Pack.

I found the address I wanted, a three-story building that was close enough to be able to see the watchtower but far enough away to have its own space. The last words before I turned off the ignition were Gabriel's: "If looks could kill, they probably will."

"That's next," I said to Sirius. "We won't even need UAVs. We'll just give a nasty look and that will be it."

I hoped I wouldn't live to see that day.

In the midst of the industrial park were some islands of green. Sirius got to do some sniffing and watering at one of those islands before I returned him to the car. I opened all the windows for him, gave him some water, and said, "Pleasant dreams."

As hard as it was to imagine, I was standing in the middle of a war zone. War was being plotted and waged inside of these buildings. In President Eisenhower's Farewell Address to the Nation in 1961, he'd warned about the growing influence of the military-industrial complex. Ike could say those kinds of things because he was a five-star general and World War II hero. Only the extremists of the John Birch Society could question his patriotism.

It was almost as if Ike had been looking into a crystal ball. In the years since his address, the military-industrial complex had grown exponentially, and the world certainly didn't feel safer because of it.

A middle-aged receptionist with a nametag of "Cheryl" acted as the gatekeeper into the building. I approached Cheryl's desk and said that I was there to see Neal Bass.

Unsmiling, she asked, "Do you have an appointment?"

I placed my badge wallet on the counter and said, "Please tell Mr. Bass that Detective Gideon needs to talk to him."

The sight of my shield seemed to improve Cheryl's mood. I sensed she didn't think much of Neal Bass.

She wrote down my shield number and then pointed to a notebook and said, "Please sign in, Detective."

When I finished, I was directed to take a seat. While I waited, Cheryl buzzed other employees in, took calls, and texted. I suspected one of those texts involved my presence, because a minute or two into my wait she told me, "Mr. Bass will be down to see you in a few minutes."

It was closer to fifteen minutes before Neal Bass appeared. He was probably in his early forties but looked older because he was mostly bald and had a paunch his loose Polo shirt couldn't quite hide.

Bass passed through the security door by the reception desk and started talking to me even before we were close enough to shake hands. "I'm not sure what you are here about, Detective, but I'm afraid I really don't have time to talk to you without an appointment. Besides, if this is about a charitable contribution for the Police Athletic League, you'll need to talk to Investor Relations, and they're in another building."

I was sure he had been rehearsing that speech for the last five minutes. I was sure he'd looked into a mirror and practiced his "too busy to talk" demeanor. I was sure he was ready to put off my request to talk now by repeating how his schedule was jam-packed.

As he extended his hand to me, I said, "Do you recognize me with my clothes on?"

That wasn't what Bass was expecting to hear. That wasn't what Cheryl was expecting to hear. But it sure did interest her.

"Oh, wait," I said. "Unless you had one of those infrared things doing the recording, there would have only been an audio feed and no video, right?"

Bass's hand was still hanging in the air in expectation of our handshake and my dismissal. Now he didn't seem to know what to do with it, or with me.

"Are you sure you don't recognize me?" I asked. "You need some heavy breathing as a reminder?"

I smiled for Bass. At the reception desk I could hear the buzzing sound of incoming calls, but Cheryl was making no move to pick them up. This was too interesting.

Bass looked down and seemed surprised to see that his hand was still extended outward. He dropped it to his side.

"Come with me," he said.

Cheryl buzzed us through.

* * *

Bass said nothing as he led me down a hallway. I guess he was once more rehearsing what he was going to say. When we came to a stop at an unoccupied office, he threw the door open and said, "I don't know what your game is, but I only have a minute to talk."

"The law is very specific when it comes to homicides," I said. "You can be convicted of being a coconspirator to a murder merely by having knowledge of it, or being in the presence of the murderer when it was committed, and not coming forward to report the crime."

Bass backtracked several steps and dropped down into a chair. "What are you talking about?"

"I was acquainting you with the law."

"You must have me mistaken for someone else. I don't know you, and I have no idea what you're talking about."

"You and your Attack Pack cronies gathered at Drew Corde's house on the night before last."

"So what? We've been playing video games one night a week for the last dozen years."

"You should have stuck to playing video games. But instead of doing that, you were listening to a tape of a couple making love. That's how you know me. I was half of that couple."

"I don't—"

I cut him off: "Don't make it harder on yourself than is necessary. Don't lie. The last thing you want to do is paint yourself into a corner and not leave any way out. You're looking at some serious charges."

Bass was sweating. He looked uncomfortable in the same way that Elle Browning had, his head turning one way and then the other as if afraid someone was listening.

Finally he stammered out, "You got the wrong guy."

I shook my head. "I probably don't need to tell you that voiceprints are like fingerprints. Our guys in the lab are great at matching up these sound waves, or whatever they're called. It looks like a lot of squiggly lines to me, but they know their stuff.

And let's face it, Neal, I'm betting you've got quite the distinctive laugh. You strike me as a nice guy, but that laughter wasn't nice. It sounded nasty and mocking. "

I looked at his ringless finger, the hairs sprouting around his ears, and his unkempt appearance. Bass could have used a woman's touch, something I was betting was absent from his life.

"When I heard you laughing, Neal, it felt like I was in a high school locker room again. You made what was beautiful feel dirty. I don't know if we can nail everyone from the Attack Pack with the voiceprints from that recording, but I have no doubt we'll be able to nail you."

"I didn't have anything to do with it," he said. His mouth was open to say more, but he suddenly reconsidered whatever he was going to say.

I raised my hands, as if to show how helpless I was in this matter. "Remember what I said about being a coconspirator, Neal. Your presence makes you guilty. I'm just hoping you didn't have any knowledge of or involvement in Wrong Pauley's death. That could be the difference between a slap on the wrist and life in prison."

"What are you talking about?"

"Wrong Pauley was a homeless man who was in the wrong place at the wrong time. I guess his nickname was the story of his life and death: wrong spelled W-r-o-n-g. Anyway, he was the one who witnessed what happened in Venice Beach. I'd like to hear your version of events."

Bass looked confused, but it might have been part of his act.

"Pauley went to the press with his story," I said. "He told the world he witnessed an angel being murdered. It was only a day later that Pauley was dead. I think he was murdered."

"I know nothing about angels or murder," Bass said. "Not a damn thing!"

His eyes met mine; he wanted me to see how adamant he was.

"How long has the Attack Pack been flying UAVs instead of playing video games?"

Bass didn't answer. What he had heard made him afraid. I wish I could have taken credit for scaring him, but I had the feeling the thought of someone else frightened him a lot more than I did.

He asked, "I am under no obligation to answer any of your questions, am I?"

I tried to calm him down and keep him talking. "If you cooperate, I'll cooperate. If you come clean with what you know, we'll work out a deal you like, and I'll be in your corner."

It was a roundabout way of saying "no," and Bass knew it. Flight mode kicked in. He jumped up from the chair and hurried out of the room.

CHAPTER 14:

MATCHMAKER, MATCHMAKER, MAKE ME A MATCH

On my drive home I once more journeyed into the past with my musical time machine. Earlier I had heard Kate Bush's voice and decided to dial in her song "Running Up That Hill." While Kate sang about making a deal with God, I thought about my deal with the devil. In the morning I would be meeting with Ellis Haines.

Knowing my partner would also be meeting with him, I told Sirius, "I'm glad your rabies shots are up to date."

I thought about potential next moves. It was likely Neal Bass would contact Drew Corde. Maybe I was already in the cross-hairs of the military industrial complex. Paranoia made me want to know as much as possible about OZ and their UAVs.

Everyone should have a nerd for a friend, especially if you're technologically challenged. Peter Burns had been my go-to nerd for twenty years, ever since the two of us were undergrads at Cal State Northridge. It was Peter who helped me pass calculus and physical chemistry. When I bought my first personal computer,

Peter was there, holding my hand. I doubt whether I ever would have figured out my large-screen TV and its surround sound without Peter doing the installation. I am not sure what I bring to our friendship; maybe Peter just pities minds like mine that aren't digitally friendly. To keep him on retainer, I occasionally take him out to lunch or dinner.

I instructed my hands-free phone (come to think of it, he tutored me on the phone as well) to "Call Peter Burns."

He picked up on the second ring. "What's not working now?"

"Did it ever occur to you I might just be calling to chat?"

"That would be a first."

"Enough with our chat," I said. "I need to pick your brain on drones and Orion-Zenith."

"Why would I know anything about either?"

"You're an engineer."

"I am a mechanical engineer who works on the development of medical devices. You'd be better served by talking to an aerospace or aeronautical engineer."

"Do you know one?"

"You think engineers are some kind of Masonic club?"

"Maybe without the secret handshakes," I said.

"If I ever have a meter maid question, I'll be sure to call you. After all, they're members of the law force community, aren't they?"

"They're actually the backbone of it, and I'll tell you whatever I know about them, but I probably know more about lovely Rita, meter maid."

Peter sighed. "As it so happens, you are in luck. Dr. Dante Inferno knows just about everything about drones."

"Is that a real name?"

"It's a real stage name. I know him as Isaac Siegel, but he likes to be called Dr. Inferno now. The two of us actually took bar mitzvah classes together."

"And how does Dr. Dante know UAVs?"

"It's what he did in San Diego for the last decade until he resigned his day job six months ago. The whole time I've known him, Isaac has been a performer, but he finally decided to quit his engineering job to pursue his dream of being a full-time entertainer. We actually caught up together earlier this week after his show."

"What kind of show?"

"I think he calls it blaze wizardry, but he's a magician. This week he's headlining at the Magic Castle."

* * *

Peter called me back ten minutes later. He'd talked to Isaac Siegel—a.k.a. Dr. Dante Inferno—who had agreed to see me within the hour. I was cautioned not to be late because Dr. Inferno would be performing on stage in the Palace of Mystery at eight thirty.

I knew I was getting close to the Magic Castle when I started seeing the sidewalk stars appear along Hollywood Boulevard's Walk of Fame. As usual, TCL Chinese Theatre (which everyone still calls Grauman's Chinese Theatre) was ground zero for a cluster of tourists, street performers, panhandlers, and crazies. Celebrity look-alikes, identifiable more by costumes and props than their supposed resemblance to the stars, were staked out along the block. All were willing to pose with tourists, for a fee. I could see multiple Marilyn Monroe and Elvis look-alikes, a few costumed superheroes, and a Charlie Chaplin. I think there was also a Bogart as well, but I wasn't looking at him, kid, but making my turn.

As I drove up the hill, I had a good view of the Victorian mansion now known as the Magic Castle. Like most grand old houses in SoCal, it had gone through several incarnations before its present use, but for the last half century magicians had been casting their spells at the Castle. The edifice might not exactly be Hogwarts, but by L.A. standards the old house is unique, and I've always liked the way it's framed by the backdrop of the Hollywood Hills. Like so many things inside of it, the Magic Castle itself is an illusion. As large as it looks from the outside, it's three times bigger inside, with much of the building underground.

The wind was pushing at the palm trees lining Franklin Avenue. It was a hot late afternoon, with the mercury in the low eighties. There was a yellow tint to the air, probably a combination of smog or soot from a fire. The Magic Castle always looks better after sundown. The same grounds that look faded in daylight beguile in the evening. At night the property is lit up, and its colorful Victorian cupolas seem to offer up an invitation to the past. I wasn't here for the illusion, though.

The Magic Castle refers to itself as a club. It is the home of the Academy of Magical Arts, and in order to visit the club, you must be invited by one of its members. My first invitation had come courtesy of Russ Donnelly, a cop who performs there whenever they let him.

I drove up the steep drive to the valet stand and flashed my shield to a waiting valet. LAPD accounting tends to frown on ten-dollar valet service, so I asked where to park and was directed down the hill.

There's much about the Magic Castle that screams tourist trap, but in an innocent way. The building speaks to a time when kitsch was good fun, and part of that fun was the understood wink that came with the kitsch. As I approached the entrance, I could hear the sounds of old-time music drifting out of the building. Visitors to the castle find themselves in a waiting room with no obvious door through which to proceed. Encircling the waiting room is a faux bookcase that doesn't even pretend to be the real thing.

A young blond woman standing behind the reception desk said, "Welcome to the Magic Castle."

I approached her and said, "I am Detective Gideon, here to see Dr. Inferno."

The hostess pointed to an owl perched above the fake books and said, "You can gain entry . . ."

"Thanks," I said. "I've been here before."

I stepped over to the bookcase and said, "Abracadabra."

The owl didn't stir and the hidden passage didn't open. I turned to the hostess, frowned, but raised my index finger to my lips to ward off any hints.

I took in a lungful of air and tried another spell, confidently announcing, "Hocus-pocus."

Once again, nothing happened. There wasn't even a "who" from the owl. I gave a side-glance to the hostess, demonstrated that there was nothing up my sleeves, and signaled the need for one more attempt.

On the third try I did my best Ali Baba and said, "Open sesame." This time the owl's eyes flashed red, and the passageway opened.

Every kid in the world wants a house with a secret passageway. Adults want them too, but they usually settle for a walk-in closet or a kitchen with an island.

"I was just testing the bird," I said to the hostess, who was pretending to look interested.

I followed the red carpeting forward and was beckoned inside by piano music. The pianist was said to be Irma, a ghost who likes tickling the ivories. Irma has kept up with the times; her repertoire includes modern selections, but at the moment she was doing ragtime. This time I didn't stop in Irma's Room to call out a request or sit down for a cold one at the antique bar that formerly served a London pub, but continued walking. Posters and playbills lined the walls, showcasing magicians of the past. Judging from the old photographs, bad makeup isn't a recent invention.

Having never visited the Houdini See Room, I looked for signs pointing out the way. That's when I became aware of all the eyes peering at me. Owls of all shapes, sizes, and materials are perched throughout the Magic Castle. I am okay with owls, but I could have used less in the way of *who*, and more in the way of *where* to find the meeting spot.

As it turned out, the Houdini See Room was on the second floor. Since I was a few minutes early, I had time to tour the unoccupied room. The area wasn't large, maybe five hundred square feet, which explained why it wasn't used for everyday shows. Along the walls were exhibits that offered a look back at the life of Harry Houdini. The displays showed handcuffs, straightjackets, shackles, and pictures of Houdini's death-defying escapes. Even Harry wasn't perfect, though, as the room also had on display the only set of handcuffs ever said to have foiled the legendary escape artist.

"Detective Gideon?"

The voice was overloud; a stage voice. Most people aren't able to sneak up on me. I turned around and saw a man in a black shirt and suit who wasn't Johnny Cash. His dyed ebony hair made it difficult to gauge his age, but he was at least forty.

"Dr. Inferno, I presume? Or do you prefer Isaac?"

"Please call me Dante, or better yet, Dr. Inferno. It's a name that pleases my mother to no end. Nowadays she goes around saying, 'My son, the doctor.'"

The line, I was sure, was part of his act. He seemed to acknowledge that by saying, "If you don't mind, I will be practicing different parts of my performance as we speak."

"Fine by me," I said.

If I'd been smart, I might have asked him about that performance before agreeing to be audience to it.

"I'm a bit of a Houdini buff," he said, "so I thought this would be a good place for us to talk."

He gestured to a green felt table, the kind where cards are dealt, and we both sat down.

"They use this room for small dinner parties where they occasionally have séances," he said. "One of Houdini's great passions was debunking mediums. He pursued it vigorously. Some might even say fanatically."

"Why? Was it personal for him?"

With a nod, Dr. Inferno said, "I think it was. In Houdini's day spiritualism was very popular, and every city had its mediums who claimed to be able to contact the dead. Some of those mediums were quite the celebrities. Houdini probably didn't like that. He was never one to want to share the limelight. But it was the death of his mother that caused him to take a close look at spiritualists. Being a bit of a mama's boy, Houdini hoped to be able to communicate with his mother in the great beyond, but he didn't let his grief get in the way of his judgment. When he realized that mediums were merely preying on the vulnerable and that their supposed communication with the dead was nothing more than parlor tricks, Houdini became an avenging angel and began exposing the tricks of their trade."

"Houdini probably would have been a good detective."

"As they say, it takes a thief. You might even argue that Houdini had a criminal mind, as he loved tricking people. He would have made a great mastermind in one of those locked door mysteries."

Dr. Inferno pointed to a display. "At the New York Hippodrome in 1918, Houdini made a five-ton elephant named

Jennie disappear in front of thousands of people. Of course Houdini claimed it was a ten-ton elephant."

"What are a few tons among friends?"

"Mere peanuts," he agreed.

"Care to tell me how Harry did it?"

"Let's ask him, shall we?"

"Are we going to hold a séance?"

"More of a channeling," he said.

A magician's wand suddenly appeared in Dr. Inferno's hand. I was okay with his sleight of hand, but not with what happened next. A ball of flame shot out of his wand and went at least ten feet into the air. I jumped about that high myself and almost overturned the table.

Dr. Inferno wasn't done with playing with fire. He was juggling a fireball from one hand to the other. Not content to keep the exhibition outside of his body, he appeared to move the ball of fire through his stomach and then out his back, and then reversed the route. With a final hard yank, he pulled the flame out of his chest. There was a loud bang and a bright flash, and the fire was extinguished.

"If you were a beautiful young woman," the magician told me, "I would have turned the ball of fire into a rose and presented it to you with the words 'I'm carrying a torch for you.'"

"I came close to presenting you with something as well, but not a rose."

He caught my drift—so to speak—but wasn't quite penitent about it. "Distractions are part of every illusion, Detective. They are but one of the elephants in the room."

"What are some of the others?"

"Illusionists utilize a variety of techniques. To achieve their goals, they use optical, mechanical, and psychological means.

Magicians exploit deficits in our vision and brain. Our everyday perception employs all sorts of shortcuts, and the performer knows how to produce a temporary blindness, if you will. Cognitive illusion can be induced by misdirection, distraction, and sleight of hand. A flash of light—my favorite technique—is a perfect way to distract. My comedy is also a distraction. A laughing audience is inattentive to many things. And you can never forget about the man in the audience."

"What man?"

"The stooge, the shill, the plant," he said. "The person in plain sight, or in the wings, whom no one recognizes for what he is; the man sitting in the audience who might be gathering information for the performer, or who makes you look one way when you should be looking another."

"There are lots of things to look for."

"Too many," said Dr. Inferno. "That's what the illusionist counts on."

"Speaking of the Wizard of Oz," I said, "what can you tell me about Drew Corde?"

"That's not his only nickname. In the defense industry some also call him the Prince of Darkness."

"Do you know Corde?"

The doctor shook his head and said, "Not personally, but I know those who have worked with him and dealt with him."

"What's the scuttlebutt?"

"He's brilliant. He's arrogant. He's a genius. He's an evil genius. He's ruthless. He plays to win. He thinks he's smarter than everyone else and he might be right in that. The defense industry is the perfect business for him because he believes that business is war and you should take no prisoners."

"You wouldn't be surprised if he used unethical means to procure governmental contracts?"

"I would be surprised if he didn't."

"Do you think illegally monitoring conversations and conducting surveillances would be among his bag of tricks?"

"OZ has both a public product line, and a not-so-public one. Those who are in the spycraft business do not exactly advertise their trade."

"I know their public product line features two different UAVs," I said, "the Dumbledore and the WWW, the Wasp Warhead Weapon."

"The rumor is that the WWW was originally called the Wicked Witch of the West, but sales came up with the acceptable acronym of the Wasp Warhead Weapon."

"I'm surprised they didn't call it the Flying Monkey."

"OZ marketed the WWW as a cheaper alternative to the Predator and the Hellfire Missiles it fires. At a cost of only thirty thousand dollars apiece, the Wasp Missiles are half the price of a Hellfire."

"What a bargain," I said. "You mentioned the not-so-public offerings of OZ. What else do they make?"

"For years there's been talk about a drone mostly referred to as the Specter."

"What's special about it?"

"The word on the street is that it has stealth capabilities; it's a UAV undetectable to radar."

"It sounds like the perfect tool for spies and voyeurs," I said. "Maybe that's what was used on me."

I told him about the recording made of Lisbet and me; the doctor wasn't convinced it was the smoking gun that I made it out to be.

"The Specter might be a good tracking instrument, as are so many drones, but making that kind of recording would be problematic. Drones aren't designed for close-up monitoring. Their optical systems allow for great camera surveillance, but they make too much noise to provide good audio."

I wondered if the Specter had found a way to muffle its sounds. The recording of Lisbet and me might not have been acoustically perfect, but no one was going to mistake what was going on.

"You can be your own Q these days," said Dr. Inferno, referencing the eccentric scientist in the 007 films. "Just go to any hobby store. There are plenty of UAVs you can buy off the shelf. Add a Smartphone as a camera, and control your flight patterns with a notebook or tablet, and you can be Bond, James Bond."

Dr. Inferno began to shuffle cards. From the way he manipulated the deck, I knew I wouldn't want to play poker with him. "I've always been what they call a comic magician. My act is interspersed with one-liners. Around five years ago I started playing with fire."

"Didn't your mother warn you not to play with matches?"

"I guess I had a burning ambition to perform."

On cue, a card flared up. I tried not to react like the Scarecrow. Dr. Inferno displayed the flaming card, and then made it disappear.

"It's my job to amaze the audiences, and make them laugh."

"That's the same thing I try and do."

"Detective," he said, "you're so boring you can't even entertain a doubt."

It was a line he probably used on hecklers. I tried to think up a rejoinder, but the doctor was already on a roll. "Detective, you're nobody's fool, but don't give up hope. Perhaps someone will adopt you."

I did the best rim shot possible with my fingers and then tried to steer him away from his act.

"I am working a case where there was a witness to some unusual goings-on," I said. "My witness noticed moving lights in the sky and speculated there was some kind of triangulation going on involving the tracking of an object. While observing this, my witness said there was this huge burst of light that caused all the hair on his body to stand up."

"A hair-raising experience," said the doctor.

"Got anything besides a bad pun?"

"If his hair really did stand up, that suggests some kind of electrical weapon was brought into play."

"Are you talking about a directed energy weapon?"

He shrugged. "It's possible. Or it could have been something else entirely. What kind of flash of light are we talking about?"

"He described it as a detonation. It was of a magnitude that he was blinded for a minute or two. When his eyesight returned, he saw what he thought was an angel bleeding out light on an alleyway below where he was."

Dr. Inferno stared at me. His finger scratched at the table, signaling me as if I were a blackjack dealer: *Hit me.*

"Three surveillance cameras were aimed at the alley where he said he saw the angel. During the time in question, all of the footage on those cameras was somehow disabled. Someone suggested a dazzler might have been used to accomplish this."

The doctor shook his head. "It's more likely the surveillance optics of the cameras were overloaded by mechanical and electronic jamming."

"You have a scientific explanation for the angel as well?"

He shrugged. "It's possible your witness was looking at a bogey."

"I assume you're not talking golf."

"Fighter pilots refer to unidentified aircraft or objects as bogeys. Our angel might have been a specialized image being tracked down by UAVs."

"You're saying the angel could have been a projection?"

"Think of it in these terms: your witness might have seen the end result of a military-sized version of laser tag. The projection, or hologram, might have been equipped with an electronic kill target."

"Have you heard of such a thing?"

"Not specifically," he said, "but there is a long history of drones being sent off to dispatch specific targets. Various versions of the Chukar, which was named after a partridge, have been around for a long time. The Chukar was designed as an aerial target and is used in missile training exercises. When a drone brings down a Chukar, the pilots like to say they've bagged their bird."

"You think the angel was part of a very elaborate video game?"

"It wouldn't surprise me if that were the case. The military hasn't had an easy time retaining drone pilots. Their quit rate is three times that of manned pilots. Would you rather be a fighter jock experiencing the thrill of ten g's, or a drone pilot staring at a computer screen and moving around a joystick on a twelve-hour surveillance mission? Drone work, for the most part, is dull. But if you can attract gamers and make drone piloting feel more like a game, you might be able to retain those pilots."

"And you think this angel might have been part of their gaming?"

"It's possible."

"Why wouldn't Corde have said anything about that?"

"Companies like to keep their secrets. Maybe OZ is planning on putting out a UAV simulation. Or maybe that's the kind of program that's not politically correct, and they'd be worried about a corporate black eye."

"Are there any rumors about OZ drones being designed to perform assassinations?"

"I haven't heard that kind of talk," he said, "but I wouldn't be surprised at all if that were the case."

"Brave new world," I said.

"You can't imagine how happy I was going from the war business to show business," he said.

Dr. Inferno stretched forward slightly, opened his hands, and showed me a cigarette and a box of matches. "Do you mind?"

"They're your lungs."

"I don't smoke, except in my act."

He did imaginary scales with his cigarette hand, and the cancer stick vanished from sight. Then he lit a match, and it disappeared in front of my eyes.

"Up your sleeves," I said.

He took up his black jacket, rolled up his dark sleeves, and lit another match, which also vanished.

"It's in your hand somewhere."

He extended his hand my way and let me see that nothing was there, then stretched that hand behind my ear and came away with both flaming matches. I tried to mask my discomfort as Dr. Inferno continued playing with fire. He inhaled the matches, which seemed to extinguish them, but then he exhaled a stream of fire and they were alight again.

With a voice I hoped didn't reveal how I was feeling, I said, "I'm afraid I didn't bring marshmallows."

"What a shame."

I didn't clap, afraid that it might encourage him. I didn't clap, afraid that he might see my trembling hands.

And then someone started talking, but it wasn't either Dr. Inferno or me. It took both of us a moment to realize what we were hearing. One of the attractions in the room was a facsimile of Thomas Edison's wax cylinder recording device that had captured Houdini's voice. It was Houdini who was talking.

"Interesting," said Dr. Inferno. "I think our séance worked. Houdini told his wife that he would try to contact her after his death, but that was one feat with which he apparently didn't meet with success."

"It would have been a hell of an encore."

"Whenever I perform at the Magic Castle, I usually walk over and visit Houdini's star on the Hollywood Walk of Fame."

"I didn't know he had one."

"Houdini did several films."

"The special effects must have been great."

"Surprisingly not," he said. "Houdini believed in doing his own stunts. In those old, silent films, Houdini really performed his own wing walking on a flying airplane, as well as other death-defying acts. The public wasn't very impressed. They preferred the fantasy and drama of special effects as opposed to the sweat and blood of the real thing."

"I wish I was surprised by that."

I thanked Dr. Inferno for his help and reached out to shake his hand. I suppose I should have expected to find something palmed in his hand. The object was transferred over to me. The box of matches displayed a picture of Dr. Inferno tossing a fireball; on the back of the box were his telephone number, his Facebook page, and his website.

"I perform at just about every kind of occasion."

"You do funerals?"

"I'm especially good at cremations."

I decided to leave before the good doctor got it in his mind to give me a hotfoot.

"You've been a great audience," he said.

CHAPTER 15:

BURNING DOWN THE HOUSE

Once I reached the safety of my car, I started taking in deep breaths, but it still felt as if no oxygen was reaching my lungs. My hyperventilating made me dizzy, and my body temperature went from hot to cold, and I started shivering. I suppose I was undergoing mild shock, but I was aware enough to feel my partner pawing at me. His nails raked my side and my legs, and felt enough like tickling to make me laugh.

"Okay," I said, "okay."

Sirius still wasn't convinced I was all right. He nudged my neck a few times with his muzzle, and I reached back and ran my hand along the side of his head.

"Thanks," I said at the comforting touch and concern of an old friend.

I hadn't been ready for my old friend PTSD, and if I'd had half a brain, I should have told Dr. Inferno I wasn't comfortable with his performance, but pride had kept me quiet. I hadn't wanted him to know just how scared I was of his fire act.

I took a deep breath. My burn counselor would have described what had happened as a "hiccup" or "slight misstep." That's how they talk in rehab. It had been almost three years since Sirius and I had taken our fire walk. Somehow the fire still managed to surface, and to burn.

Another breath, another confession: "That's why I stopped seeing Haines," I said, admitting it to Sirius. "I wanted to put the fire behind me. But we have to visit with him tomorrow, and I've got that pit-in-the-stomach feeling. He's the one who should be feeling that way, not me. He's the one behind bars; he's the one sentenced to death. So why am I the one who feels tied up in knots?"

I thought about Lisbet. She wanted more from our relationship. She wanted more from me. It was clear that I hadn't committed, that I wasn't "all in." Why was it I could tell Sirius secrets that I kept from her? Wrong Pauley came to mind again. He had opened up to Sirius and allowed me to be an eavesdropper to their conversation. And his most unselfish act had been to give up his beloved Ginger, who had loved him for all his faults.

Maybe I was scared to let Lisbet see me afraid. It was easier not to say anything, easier not to open up. But secrets came with a weight. And it was hard for relationships to support that kind of weight.

I had opened up to her about some things, but more because I had to than because I had wanted to. Because we sometimes shared a bed, she knew about my PTSD and that I occasionally had night terrors. But if our relationship was to go to the next level, I needed to get past one day at a time. I either needed to fish or cut bait. Lisbet was probably more right than wrong in saying our relationship felt like an affair. When one partner has a lot of secrets, how could it help but feel like anything else?

"Call Lisbet," I told my phone.

She answered on the first ring. "I was just thinking about you."

"And you still picked up?"

"You sound tired."

"I guess I am. It's been a long day. Sirius and I started the day at the elementary school where that shooting took place. Sirius got a standing ovation, while I played second fiddle."

Sirius's ears perked up at the mention of his name.

"I'll bet the kids loved you."

"I'm glad they got a kick out of our dog and phony show. They've been through enough."

"Any leads on the Reluctant Hero?"

"They might not be exactly leads, but at least I now have a few things to look at."

"I prayed for you today," Lisbet said. "I asked for angels to watch over you."

"Thanks," I said, "but I thought I was the one who was supposed to be helping the angels."

"Symbiotic relationships are the best."

"I'll try and remember that."

"Where are you now?"

"I'm out at the parking lot of the Magic Castle."

"Really?"

"Cross my heart."

"What are you doing there?"

"I came and interviewed one of the performers. Up until recently he was an engineer working full time in the drone industry."

"But now he's a magician?"

"He's a fire performer," I said. My tone changed, becoming more personal and more honest. "While I was talking with him, he was fooling around and doing some of his performance.

He scared the hell out of me, but I didn't let him see how afraid I was."

"So you just suffered in silence?"

"What doesn't destroy me makes me stronger."

"And pride goeth before a fall."

"I fall before your big proverbial guns. You had me at 'goeth.'"

"I'm glad."

"Sometimes being scared isn't so bad, though. The first time you came over to my place, I decided to get a romantic fire going in the fireplace. It took all my nerve to start that fire, and the only thing that got me near the fireplace was cuddling with you. But it was worth it."

"Next time let me start the fire."

"That's a deal."

"You need to get a good night's sleep."

"I'll try."

"You're going to see him tomorrow, aren't you?"

Lisbet knew about my appointment with Ellis Haines. "Yes."

"I'll pray for you again."

"That will be my secret weapon."

"Yes, it will."

I wish I had her faith. I didn't, but I was still glad her faith was on my side.

"Will I see you tomorrow?" she asked.

"I sure hope so."

"Me too," she said. "Good night."

"Don't let the bedbugs bite."

I knew Lisbet would have preferred ending our conversation with each of us saying, "I love you." But she didn't say it, to spare me. I wasn't good at declaring my love. Maybe I didn't like feeling that vulnerable or exposed. I did love Lisbet, but it was easier for me to offer up some rhyme or funny line.

The dial tone told me she wasn't there. "I love you," I said.

* * *

We made it home a little before eight. There was a familiar foreign sports car in Seth's driveway that I'd seen a few times. If memory served me, the car belonged to a redhead I'd glimpsed on early mornings when both of us were leaving for work.

"I'm afraid you'll have to put up with my cooking tonight," I told Sirius.

Since fruit and veggies had been a big part of my talk, I heated up a little olive oil, added a few florets of broccoli, a third of a cut-up carrot, and some green beans. Between my sautéing, I added cooked chicken breast and scooped out a cup of kibble. Then I mixed everything together.

"Dinner is zerved," I said, speaking with a French accent.

Sirius sniffed my concoction, decided it was probably edible, and started eating.

I opened my refrigerator door and poked around a little before giving up. There weren't even any fishes and loaves. I opened the pantry closet door and debated between canned chili and canned ravioli. Chef Boyardee won. While the ravioli was being nuked, I poured two fingers of bourbon.

"Corn, rye, and barley, children," I said, and took a sip.

I carried my drink and ravioli over to the easy chair and got comfortable. After a few sips of bourbon, the ravioli started tasting better. I picked up the remote, turned on the TV, and did some channel surfing. Even the bourbon didn't help me find anything I wanted to watch. Eventually I settled on a cooking show. It seemed ironic that my evening's repast had come from a can, and now I was watching chicken cacciatore being prepared.

Sirius came and joined me. Maybe he was hoping I'd be inspired to do some real cooking.

"I don't think I've ever had chicken cacciatore," I said. "What about you?"

It was the kind of thing his Uncle Seth might have cooked for him, but without the white wine or garlic.

"The secret," said the chef, offering up a smile that showed every one of her too white teeth, "is the capers."

"Remember that, will you?" I said to Sirius. "The capers are the secret."

It was a secret that would have to keep. There were no capers in the pantry, and I was pretty sure there never had been.

My eyes started getting heavy about the time the chicken thighs were being smothered in diced tomatoes. I don't think I made it to the shot of the chef taking that first bite and then faking a culinary orgasm.

The smoke was everywhere. It was a black, strangling snake. It pressed on my throat, and constricted my insides. It was a poisonous snake, and there was no getting away from its poison. It burned my insides. My lungs were on fire.

I began coughing and couldn't stop. My chest felt as if it were being hit by a hammer. It was all I could do to keep standing. Flames reached for me. I tried to shield my partner from their reach even as I coughed up lava. That's what it felt like. Inside and outside I was on fire.

My paralysis didn't go unnoticed. The Strangler was fighting the snake as well, but he didn't have a bullet in his leg. And his partner wasn't bleeding out. I knew what he was thinking. It was almost like his thoughts were in my head. He was going to drop my partner and run into the smoke. He would hide in its black embrace.

I shifted Sirius in my arms and raised my gun. Through my coughing I managed to croak, "Try it."

"Try what?" the Strangler asked.

"Make a run for it."

The voice didn't sound like mine. It sounded like the rasp of some deadly creature, of something wild.

"No," said the Strangler, afraid of my invitation. The killer was afraid of me.

"This way." I motioned with my head, and we continued carrying Sirius through the flames, continued our march to hell.

As usual, I awakened with a gasp, sucking in as much air as I could. It didn't matter that I'd relived my fire walk more than a hundred times; each time I felt the pain anew, and there was no building up any tolerance. My clothing was soaked from my night sweats, my flesh was hot, my pulse racing.

Sirius was there at my side. He always eased my landing. I suspect he had hastened the conclusion of my revisiting hell by nudging me and making noises.

"I'm okay," I croaked, my throat still tight and sore from my remembrance of smoke inhalation past or somehow experiencing it again.

And then the relief swept over me. The closest I ever came to becoming a junkie was after the fire; I wouldn't have survived if not for the pain meds. The momentary relief from pain, doled out just often enough to offer a memory of normality, kept me going. As the burning in my body and mind receded, I experienced my moment after. Seth said it was an opening of my third eye and a vision from the spirit world. It was my dream within a dream, my oracle who spoke to me, even if I often had trouble divining what it said. The insights my moment after afforded me came with a price: they only came after revisiting my fire walk with Ellis Haines.

At first it felt like I was looking at a Hitchcock film. Someone kept closing doors, windows, curtains, and shades.

"Keep out," said Elle Barrett Browning. She wasn't talking to me, but to someone I couldn't see. "This is my home, and you're trespassing."

She closed more drapes, but to no avail. The flash of cameras kept going off.

And then a man ran to her side. "We have to leave," he said. His coat covered up his face, and he raised it to shield her features.

He was hiding in plain sight; he was the Reluctant Hero. I identified him, but I didn't know who he was. Or did I? And then I became part of the vision. I was walking along the sand, but something was wrong. There was this sound . . . this buzz. Angry bees were coming my way. I turned my head and saw the swarm. It looked like a twister was coming at me. There was only one possible escape, and I took it, throwing myself into the ocean.

I dove deep and didn't come up for air for a very long time. When I broke the surface there was no sign of the swarm, but there was no sign of land either. It seemed as if I was in the middle of the ocean.

"I am going to drown," I said, "unless I find an island."

And then the waters around me roiled, and a whale sounded right next to me. An island had found me. The whale opened its mouth, and like Jonah I was swallowed up, and around me was blackness.

Insistent barking interrupted my vision. It was loud and serious, and demanded my attention. I opened my eyes. Sirius wasn't letting up. This was his I-mean-business barking.

I jumped up to see what was bothering him. That's when I saw the orange glow. This wasn't my fire dream. This was a real fire. There were flames coming from the roof. I took a breath, steadied myself enough to face my fiery unresolved demons, and then ran for my phone.

I was a body in motion while making my 911 call. I raced outside and worked both hose and phone. While telling the dispatcher the nature of my emergency and where I lived, I sprayed my roof with water. The fire hissed its hatred as I continued the stream, aiming at its heart.

When I finished talking to the dispatcher, I yelled into my smartphone, "Call Shaman."

I have a one-story ranch house. If it had been a two-story house, I might not have been able to save it. After being burned by fire, I had made sure my house had plenty of outside water pressure. The fire was getting the full force of the hose, which slowed its advance.

A sleepy voice spoke into my ear, "It's late even for someone having a mid-life crisis."

"There's a fire on my roof!"

"I'm on it!"

Seth made it over in fifteen seconds. I wouldn't have minded had he taken another five seconds to put on underwear, but I didn't tell him that.

"There's another hose on the side of the house!"

For a heavy guy, Seth moved very quickly. Moments later the spray from the second hose was raining down on the flames. Bit by bit the fire began retreating, but not without sounding like an enraged wildcat. It spat and hissed and batted at the spray, and its noises tugged at my short hairs. Sirius didn't like it either and responded with growls.

It must not have been more than five minutes from the time I called 911 when approaching sirens could be heard. The fire was still putting up a fight, but the house was no longer in danger of going up in flames. I was lucky my roof had asphalt shingles, and not wooden shake shingles. The wood shingles look better, but they're just kindling to a fire. Choosing function over aesthetics might have saved my life.

The fire crew took over, and while the flames were being extinguished, it sounded to me as if they were voicing the threat of "We're not finissssshed."

"Are you all right?"

Seth was the one asking the question. A naked man who looked like the Laughing Buddha was concerned about my well-being.

"I am going to feel real bad if you get arrested for public indecency, Seth," I said.

At that moment Seth's redheaded lady friend appeared. She was wearing a Batik kimono robe that somehow looked wonderful on her even at two in the morning.

"Michael," he said, "I don't think you've met Tiffany."

We shook hands, and I said to her, "Please take your naked hero home."

Tiffany covered her mouth and giggled. And then she took her naked hero home.

CHAPTER 16:

BEWARE THE JABBERWOCK

The fever that came with being burned was upon me. I felt light-headed and reckless. I was supposed to be living proof of the saying "Once burned, twice shy." I needed to keep my distance from the burning infection of the past. Surviving fire had scarred me inside and out. After burn therapy, slathering on sunscreen and avoiding prolonged exposure to sunlight became part of my daily regimen. On those days I neglected to do this, I paid for my negligence. It wasn't only getting burned; it was like being touched with madness.

There were plenty of choices for my morning music. Bruce Springsteen's "I'm on Fire" almost got the nod. And I couldn't have gone wrong choosing either The Doors' "Light My Fire" or Johnny Cash's "Ring of Fire." But there really was only one choice: I called out my musical choice and then cranked up "Burning Down the House" by Talking Heads.

"Let's burn rubber," I told Sirius.

In the backseat it looked like he was grinning.

Caffeine and music were going to get me through this day. I hadn't slept since being awakened by the flames. In the light of day, the roof looked like a dragon had done some heavy breathing on it. To the visible eye you could no longer see the smoke, but it clung to the house and would for days to come. When I'd changed into what I thought were fresh clothes I quickly realized I smelled like a chimney.

The firefighters had admitted to me that my fire looked "suspicious." Firemen are like cops; they are supposed to follow protocol and offer few opinions.

Captain Lance Redding had punted when it came to official comment. An inspection team would be going over my roof during the light of the day, he informed me. Unofficially, though, he admitted that it was obvious some kind of accelerant had been used to set the blaze.

He didn't speculate as to how the accelerant had gotten up on the roof. I speculated plenty. I knew drones had the ability to drop and ignite accelerant. Fire has long been a part of every martial arsenal. My first Watch Sergeant had always lectured his charges to "Know thy enemy," a quote he lifted from Sun Tzu's *The Art of War*. I am not sure if he ever read Sun Tzu's book, but he did love to quote from it.

After almost being consumed by fire, I decided to learn more about my enemy. Both my Watch Sergeant and Sun Tzu might have had a problem with me identifying fire as my enemy, but it was the demon I was still struggling to overcome. I had hoped studying fire would help me overcome my pyrophobia and lessen my PTSD. It's a good thing that of late no one had bothered to ask, "How's that working out for you?"

If you had to define the Vietnam War in one terrible picture, Nick Ut's black and white Pulitzer Prize–winning photo would be it. The picture showed a naked nine-year-old Kim Phuc fleeing with other villagers down Highway 1 in South Vietnam near the Cambodian border. Napalm had already melted Kim's clothes and left almost a third of her body covered with third-degree burns. No viewer of Ut's photo could look away from the horror etched on a little girl's face. That single picture helped end a war. When I see Kim's open mouth, I can hear her screams, or maybe I just remember my own screams. Her picture was taken more than forty years ago; miraculously, she survived. It is a photo that once seen is never forgotten.

For thousands of years fire and war have been synonymous. Nazi Germany thought it could bring England to its knees by using incendiaries and firebombs.

Greek fire was developed some fifteen hundred years ago. The accelerant was delivered on ships through the use of catapults and tubes, and resisted even dousing with seawater. At the prow of warships were huge carved heads of ferocious beasts, and inside those fearsome heads were tubes designed to squirt out their terrible spray. It was said when the Greek fire was unleashed, the beasts looked as if they were vomiting flames. Who needed the help of dragons when you could make your own dragons?

Drew Corde knew about my fire walk, and I was sure Neal Bass had told him about my visit and how I'd sweated him. I was betting Corde had decided to return that favor. Maybe he had intuited my fear of fire; he had to know that, at a minimum, I would have a healthy respect for it.

I sniffed the air. Showering and lots of deodorant hadn't masked the smell of smoke. It was on my clothes; it was on me. I looked at my face in the rearview mirror. Most people would assume the redness in my features was from too much sun. Dark circles dominated my face. Maybe they hid the fear I felt, and the fever. Corde seemed to know all my Achilles heels. He'd targeted the woman I loved by pulling back the curtain on our love life, and he had brought fire to my house. I wasn't sure if he had hunted down angels, but I knew if that were the case, it was only because he hadn't had the opportunity.

That Corde would go after an officer of the law, especially in a city like Los Angeles, spoke to his assuredness. There are more than ten thousand police officers attached to the LAPD. If you have that many brothers and sisters, you can be assured no one is going to pick a fight with you, but Corde didn't seem to be afraid of that army. Either he thought he was above the law, or he was counting on his own "big brother"—the US government. OZ had close ties with the CIA and other military and governmental organizations. His team was potentially bigger and badder than my team.

"Yeah, but you're on my team," I told Sirius.

I turned up the tune. David Byrne was warning me about nasty weather, which made me laugh. Sirius and I were on our way to see the Weatherman. That was the kind of thing Ellis Haines would say.

Talking Heads said I needed to fight fire with fire. It sounded like good advice, but it might have been my fever talking to me.

* * *

The Los Angeles County Central Jail has been in operation for more than fifty years. There is no shortage of people who think it should have been shuttered long ago in favor of a new facility, but the price tag of up to two billion dollars for a new jail is what has kept the old one operational.

Ellis Haines was Central's new celebrity inmate. He had been transported from San Quentin Prison and was being housed in

Central so that he could appear as a witness in a trial being held in the nearby L.A. County Superior Court. Evidence suggested that one of the murders Haines had been convicted for might have been committed by a copycat. Haines had admitted his guilt as a whole but had never offered specifics on any of the homicides. Supposedly he was going to disavow this murder.

Haines was being held in "Celebrity Row," a special wing of the jail where celebrities or defendants in notorious cases were housed. The cells aren't any better there, but from a control booth deputies can easily monitor the inmate, with video cameras able to track every move. Because the wing is off by itself, prisoners on Celebrity Row are isolated from the six thousand other inmates housed in the jail. According to media reports, despite the jail's overcrowding Haines was currently the only inmate in what deputies called "the Penthouse."

The jail is centrally located in L.A.'s downtown in the triangle that is north of the 101, east of the 110, and west of Interstate 5. It isn't far from Chinatown, a spot that invariably disappoints tourists, who find it small, dirty, and dingy, at least when compared to San Francisco's Chinatown or New York's. It might not be a great Chinatown, but it's still been featured in many films, the best of which was Roman Polanski's *Chinatown*. My proximity to it was some kind of conduit to the film, and images of the movie along with snippets of dialogue played in my head. I had this sense my brain was trying to make some connection that I couldn't quite hold on to, but maybe it was only my fever doing the talking. I thought of Robert Towne's larger than life characters of Jake Gittes, Evelyn Mulwray, and Noah Cross. It was Cross who said that at the right time and right place, people are capable of anything. I always wondered why he hadn't said that at the *wrong* time and *wrong* place people are capable of anything.

"Two Wongs don't make a right," I said aloud, and then added, "Forget it, Sirius. It's Chinatown."

I could see my partner studying me with his big brown eyes. There was no doubt in his eyes. I didn't want to look at my own bloodshot eyes to see what they were saying.

* * *

J. Glo had cleared the way for Sirius to accompany me into the jail. My partner's being an official LAPD K-9 made his entry easier, but Men's Central Jail was also used to dogs being processed in and out. Drug dogs were frequently called on to do their sniffing of cells and inmates, and the jail had a Custody Canine Program where select inmates were taught to train and care for rescued dogs. Despite that, I wouldn't have brought Sirius with me if not for Ellis Haines insisting on a "reunion" of the three fire survivors. It would serve him right if Sirius bit him. Haines had shot my partner and almost killed him.

J. Gloria Keller was waiting for us in visitor processing. She was actually a petite woman but managed to look and come across as large. J. Glo had an expansive blond perm that added inches to her face and frame. She wore platform shoes and liked tropical colors. Her voice was feminine when she wanted it to be, intimidating when she didn't. Today her outfit was tamer than usual, and I was guessing she had dressed in the jail-appropriate garb of a conservative pants suit as opposed to her usual short dress and form-fitting (in other words, tight) blouse. L.A. has a history of high-profile female defense lawyers, including Gloria Allred, Leslie Abramson, and Shawn Holley Chapman. J. Glo was now at the top of her class and knew it.

I was running a little late, but I'd phoned earlier to tell Ms. Keller that I had been delayed by a fire. She had sounded skeptical at the time, and looked relieved at my approach.

"I was afraid you weren't going to show up," she said, "and I know my client would have been most unhappy at that."

"I'm happy to be able to accommodate you," I lied, "especially now that there are no more legal swords hanging over my head."

"Funny how things work out," she said.

"I hope you've learned your lesson," I told Sirius. Bending down, I ran a hand along his nape. "Impersonating a human is a serious crime."

I should know. It was something I had been doing for years.

It didn't take long to get processed. I had to give up my gun; so did J. Glo. She had a Springfield XD three-inch sub-compact that fit very nicely in her purse.

I don't like jails or prisons. Sirius picked up on my vibe and pressed into my left leg. It was nice not to have to say anything and still be so understood.

We were accompanied inside by a deputy who made no attempt to engage us in conversation. J. Glo told me we were going to a special meeting room she called "O.J.'s Crib."

"O.J. spent thousands of dollars having the meeting room converted so that it could accommodate his legal dream team," she said. "When O.J. would meet with his four lawyers, they wanted to be sure there was ample room for them to spread out their legal papers."

Luckily for us, O.J.'s Crib didn't require much of a walk, and we avoided some of the more unsightly areas of the jail. Still, there was no scenic route, and ending up in O.J.'s Crib hardly made the journey worthwhile. Space is at a premium in jails, and this "special" meeting room wasn't even the size of a small hotel conference room. The area was just big enough to fit an eight-foot-by-four-foot rectangular table.

J. Glo and I took seats on opposite sides of the table. Its surface was some kind of laminate. Perspiration from lots of sweaty palms had somehow managed to soak into the plastic, resulting in a tired gray color. I looked around, hoping to see an "O.J. was here" carved into the table, but there was no sign of graffiti.

Sirius took the opportunity to sniff his way around the room. When he paused too long at one spot, I said, "No peeing." Unlike most of the jail, the room was thankfully devoid of the odor of urine.

The sheriff's deputy maintained his position just outside the door. I wasn't used to such special treatment and wouldn't have gotten it had I been there on a normal visit. Ellis Haines changed the regular equation.

"My client speaks very fondly of you," said J. Glo.

I wasn't very interested in talking to a defense lawyer who was said to be working hard on an appeal of Haines's conviction, but common courtesy demanded some kind of answer, even if it wasn't something she wanted to hear.

"Your client is a murdering, narcissistic socio-psychopath who tried to kill me and my partner," I said. "A week ago he sent me an email that referenced the burning of Los Angeles. It's our misfortune that for some reason we continue to enter into his grandiose fantasies."

"You should know that he refers to you as his 'friend.'"

"Beware the Jabberwock."

"What?"

"It's a line from Lewis Carroll's poem 'Jabberwocky.' When I was growing up, my father always told me to beware the Jabberwock. I think he meant I shouldn't believe what I know isn't true. That was the monstrosity of the Jabberwock and why it was to be feared, or so my father thought."

For a poem that is supposedly nonsensical, much in the way of symbolism and meaning has been found in "Jabberwocky." I don't believe my father ever knew that in Carroll's personal life, he was suspected of being a pedophile. If he had, I am sure that would have colored my father's impression of his writing, and he wouldn't have enjoyed reading Carroll as much as he did.

"You don't think my client considers you his friend?"

"As much a friend," I said, "as the walrus and the carpenter thought of the oysters they *befriended*. And *we* know what happened to them."

Apparently *we* didn't know. At her look of incomprehension I said, "More Lewis Carroll."

"You're not like most cops, are you?"

"For the sake of my profession, I hope not."

We stopped talking when we heard someone singing. It wasn't as good a rendition as Sam Cooke's, but Ellis Haines can carry a tune far better than most. As he came closer, the lyrics from "Chain Gang," and the sounds of his chains, could be heard that much more clearly. The man known as the Santa Ana Strangler, and also known as the Weatherman, was making his entrance.

He already had enough nicknames; I decided to not refer to him ever again as the Jabberwock. But that said, I still knew to beware of him.

Three sheriff's deputies accompanied him. If Haines was hoping for them to join in a doo-wop chorus, it wasn't happening. The three men didn't look amused by their charge's singing. It's possible they were jealous. Haines pulled off his *a capella* performance with the assurance of a seasoned professional. I am sure his millions of Facebook fans would have loved it, but when he finished, no one clapped.

He had on handcuffs and leg manacles. The county provided his wardrobe: blue shirt and blue pants. The only thing differentiating him from other inmates was a red wristband, which I suppose identified his special status.

We watched as the guards removed his handcuffs. When they came off, Haines asked, "What about the leg irons?"

The sheriff's deputy, who was apparently in charge, shook his head. J. Glo spoke up, "I am respectfully requesting you remove the leg manacles of my client."

The shackles weren't mandatory, but were put on or taken off at the discretion of the guards. The head deputy thought about J. Glo's request and then gave the barest nod. A few moments later the rest of his chains came off.

"Thank you," said Haines, entering the room. "Now I can practice my Electric Slide."

The deputies offered no comment other than to lock the door behind them. The same guard remained standing outside the door while the other three walked away.

Haines did a little soft shoe on his way to shake hands with J. Glo, or maybe he really was doing the Electric Slide. It's a dance I'm not acquainted with, but then I'm acquainted with very few. I remained seated, and when Haines turned my way, I didn't offer a hand or a smile. That seemed to amuse him.

"Didn't I tell you I would get out of San Quentin at a time of my choosing?"

"You call this getting out?" It was my turn to look amused. "You went from one shithole to another."

"I was getting a bit weary of the cold and fog in the Bay Area. This is my little vacation in sunny L.A."

"The weather's here," I said. "Wish you were fine."

He took a step closer to me, and Sirius growled. It was one of those guttural growls that come from deep down in the throat. A leveled gun wouldn't have said, "Proceed at your own peril" as much as that growl did, and it stopped Haines in his tracks.

"I mean him no harm, Sirius," Haines said. "I merely wanted to get a better look at Detective Gideon's coloring. And isn't that smoke I smell on him?"

"Detective Gideon had to deal with a fire," said J. Glo. "Despite that, he made it here to see you."

Haines looked to me for an explanation. For a moment I wondered if he might have been the one behind the arson. His followers—his "extended family"—were deluded sorts who thought Haines had great insights into the impending Armageddon. Some were crazy enough to think he was some kind of messianic voice. Those kinds of followers would have thought nothing of torching my house. But his interest didn't seem to be feigned.

"I'm your Venus, I'm your fire," he mused, quoting from the Shocking Blue song "Venus."

I hate it when Haines quotes from songs and movies, because I'm always doing the same. I don't like it when I see anything of him in me.

"It was Mars, not Venus," I said. "I was in the war zone, or maybe it was more like the war drone."

Sirius continued his growling, but it was a syncopated threat. His throaty pauses made me think of a time bomb.

"It's all right," I told Sirius. "Settle."

He growled a little more and I said, *"Pfui."*

Phooey is not much of a threat in English. It's the kind of oath—"Oh, phooey"—you'd expect from Rebecca of Sunnybrook Farm. Give it a Teutonic accent, though, and the warning sounds positively barbaric. If I were German, I wouldn't use my native tongue to say "I love you," for fear the object of my affections might mistake the tone of my voice to think I wanted to make schnitzel out of her. Advice to German romantics: do your professing of love in French or Italian. Advice to dog handlers: German is a great tongue to make your point in a forceful manner.

Sirius stopped growling, but his hackles were still up. I've often wished I had hackles.

"I guess he remembers you," I said.

Haines smiled and then turned away from Sirius and me, to his lawyer. Nothing was said, but J. Glo rose at what must have been a prearranged signal.

"I need to make a call," she said. Before going off to make that call, she warned Haines, "Remember, whatever you say to the detective is not privileged."

She asked the guard to unlock the door, but he refused to comply until Haines seated himself in the chair that J. Glo had vacated, the seat right across from us. Sirius lifted his head so that it rested on the table, and the two of us stared at Haines.

Speaking in a voice that the deputy couldn't hear, Haines said, "Tell me about the fire."

"You didn't arrange for me to be here to talk about a fire."

"And yet wouldn't you say it is—ironic—that we who were brought together by fire now find it has reared its head again?"

Both of our faces had keloid scarring from the fire, mine on the right and his on the left. We had been carrying Sirius, and during our walk experienced such intense heat, the sides of our faces closest to the fire began burning away. I touched my keloid involuntarily; his hand mirrored the motion and touched his.

"The fire occurred at your house," he said, "didn't it?"

"Why do you think that?"

"Your clothes smell of smoke."

"My roof," I admitted.

"Someone was sending you a message, weren't they?"

"The fire is being investigated."

"But you already know who set the fire, don't you?"

I shrugged.

"It is the rare individual who would be so audacious as to challenge one of L.A.'s finest."

I didn't say anything, but that didn't stop him from trying to read my features.

"You mentioned something about a war zone and a drone."

"I am a poet."

"It must be a very powerful individual," he said, "someone who is quite confident of his position in society and quite certain he is above the law."

"Sort of sounds like you, doesn't he?"

"Or you?"

"How can I be above the law when I'm part of it?"

"When we were walking in the fire, any notion of morality was burned away," Haines said. "The only thing that separated the two of us from being murderers was the tiniest bit of pressure withheld on your part. I know how close you came to emptying your gun into me. On two occasions, I remember, I feared to breathe, afraid if I even twitched under your gaze it would mean my life. I've thought about those moments many times. You were ready to murder me. I've wondered what prevented you, and the only thing I can think of was that you needed a fellow Sherpa to carry Sirius. Had he died, I have not a doubt but that you would have murdered me."

Sirius's ears were up, responding to Haines using his name. I stared at Haines but said nothing. He was right, but I wasn't going to tell him that.

"I hope you remember your lessons from that night. Your survival might depend on it. If your enemy dares to set your house on fire, do you think he'll hesitate in harming you in any way that he can? The morality of right and wrong serves no purpose to a dead man. You need to *reach out* to him."

Haines wasn't telling me to reach out. He was telling me to murder.

"I'd be afraid of doing that," I said. "I'd be scared of being put into a cell adjoining yours."

"All you have to do is whissss-per a name to me," Haines whissss-pered.

I found myself leaning closer to him, hanging on to his words.

"There will be no blowback," he said. "You will be untouchable in this matter. And you can take comfort in your belief that your enemy's transgressions warrant his death. You need not worry about him using his power to hurt you, or those close to you. You would not want societal constraints and the narrow window offered by your badge to result in your death. And you cannot let his position dictate to you. Alexander the Great and his groom by death were brought to the same state."

I was sure Haines was citing some classical reference in talking about Alexander the Great, but all of that was window dressing. He was offering to put an untraceable hit on Drew Corde. There was a time when I would have taken great umbrage at such a proposal, but I stopped thinking in absolutes long ago. I am not saying I was tempted to whissss-per Corde's name, but imagining his death was a pleasant enough way of passing the time.

"I appreciate the offer, but I'll pass."

"I hope your righteousness doesn't kill you. Do you resist doing this because you are worried about your immortal soul?"

I made the sounds of sniffing. "The smell of sulfur does tend to get me thinking about it."

"I've missed our visits. Why is it that you stopped seeing me?"

If I had told Haines that seeing him wasn't good for my immortal soul, it would have been close to the truth. Instead I said, "You weren't providing me with the kind of information deemed useful by the FBI and their Behavioral Science Unit, and I got tired of wasting my time."

"What if on your next visit I promise to answer all the tedious questions contrived by their small minds?"

I thought about it. He'd snared me nicely. "Then I guess the two of us will soon be making the Quantico headshrinkers very happy."

"My L.A. vacation will probably last only the one week," he said. "I'm hoping you can visit at the onset of fall."

"I can't wait: falling leaves, changing colors, and doing trick-or-treat with a serial killer."

"Seasonal affective disorder killer," he said.

"Are you and J. Glo still working on that scam?"

During one of my last visits to San Quentin, Haines had confided in me that he and his mouthpiece were working on a legal appeal based on SAD—seasonal affective disorder. The claim was that he had strangled all his victims during severe Santa Ana winds. The devil hadn't made him do it, he was asserting, but the winds had.

"The deleterious effect of gusting winds on the human psyche is well documented," he said.

"Most people go out and fly a kite, not commit a murder."

"You should know that I am doing my best not to involve you in my appeal," he said.

"Why would I be part of your appeal?"

"I have often wondered if you would lie again on the witness stand. Imagine this scenario: moments after raising your right hand and making your oath to God, my counsel would be asking you, 'Detective Gideon, did you ever read my client his Miranda rights?' If you lied again, wouldn't that constitute a mortal sin? Wouldn't that condemn you to hell?"

"You seem awfully concerned with my spiritual well-being."

"As I said, I am trying to save you from what I am sure would be a terrible dilemma. That's one of the reasons I am testifying in this trial. What I say should prove useful for my appeal."

"Why is that?"

"I was convicted of a murder I did not commit. That fact helped to paint my guilt. And it also brings into play fruit of the poisonous tree."

"During your trial, you admitted your guilt."

"I said I was guilty, but I never provided specifics."

"I heard through the grapevine that you're not only here because of the trial. The word is that you've been providing investigators information about other unsolved homicides of which you supposedly have insider knowledge."

"Ever watch a dog drool over a steak? That's how subtle your comrades-in-arms have been. While I've been discussing how practice makes perfect and how experience shows you the way, your Keystone friends have been oh so very interested in hearing about my early performances. All I need do is mention a detail or two, and that starts the drooling."

Haines turned his gaze to my partner. "I beg your pardon, Sirius. I didn't mean any offense at the dog and drooling remark."

Sirius growled. I really couldn't blame him, and he heard no "phooey"—or "pfui"—from me.

"So all this is just a show," I said, "and when the time comes to admitting further guilt, the only thing you'll offer up is a performance of you playing the detectives."

"I wouldn't go so far as to say that. I will testify truthfully. I did not murder the woman that the court identified as victim number nine. The inept use of the garrote on her should have made it clear to everyone that her death was the work of a copycat and an amateur. They know who killed her now, and they know it wasn't me."

It was believed that Haines had strangled eleven women, but statements he'd made recently put the number of his victims at more than fifteen and hinted that manual strangulation had not been his early MO. One of the cryptic comments he'd offered to the investigators was that the answers to his early crimes "were blowing in the wind." This had led them to identifying half a dozen other potential homicide victims who had died in the middle of raging Santa Ana winds prior to his strangulation murders. All the women had suffered severe lacerations that had likely been inflicted by a machete.

"It's all a game to you, isn't it?"

"I wish it was. During one of my interviews I told one of the gendarmes that I grew up at Camp Crystal Lake and my favorite childhood activity was playing hockey. Can you imagine me playing hockey? It took them a week to figure out what I was saying."

Haines had referenced the villain from the *Friday the 13th* movies, a villain who wore a hockey mask and liked using a machete on his victims.

"Are we done here?" I asked.

"We are not even close to done, but if you so choose, we are finished for now."

I called out to the sheriff's deputy that I was ready to leave. J. Glo must have been nearby, because she reappeared at the door. When I stood up, Haines remained seated.

He spoke so that only I could hear: "To whom should I give your regards?"

Saying the name would be like sending off a UAV to kill. I could take out Drew Corde long distance. I want to say it wasn't tempting, but it was. I want to say I didn't think about offering up his name, but I did.

"Broadway," I answered, and it was my turn to soft-shoe my way out of the room.

CHAPTER 17:

THE TELL-TALE HEART

The house was at the end of a quiet cul-de-sac. Even though most of the homes were more than half a century old, they were well kept, and their add-ons and sprucing made them appear more contemporary than their years. All the houses had small yards; the majority had been built up with an added second floor. The house I was visiting had that upper-story addition. Judging from the basketball hoops, soccer nets, and chalk art on the driveways and street, it was a neighborhood with a lot of young families. Because it was a school day, those children weren't anywhere to be seen.

A Camry with a fresly applied bumper sticker of "Corner School Proud" was parked in the driveway. Since the shooting, many of The Corner School parents were making that pronouncement in a variety of forms. The bumper sticker gave me hope that Mrs. Pullman was home.

I went up the walkway to the front door and rang the bell. A dozen seconds elapsed before I heard a woman's voice asking from behind the closed door, "Yes?"

I held up my wallet badge to the peephole. "I'm Detective Michael Gideon," I said. "Yesterday I visited The Corner School along with my K-9 partner Sirius. The two of us did a little show for the kids, and then I had the pleasure of meeting up with some of the students afterward. Matthew Pullman was one of those students. Am I talking to his mother?"

The door opened, and I was greeted by a big smile that seemed to cast light on the attractive face of a woman whose ancestors had to have hailed from Ireland. "I'm Kelley Pullman," she said, extending her hand, "Matt's mom. All he could talk about yesterday was you and your dog."

She leaned forward, making sure her hand extended beyond her protruding stomach. Kelley Pullman looked to be well along in her pregnancy. She was wearing a sleeveless maternity dress that was stylish even with her large baby bump. Topping out at around five foot two, her frame, when not pregnant, would have been petite, but now she was busting out at the seams. Her russet hair was slightly up, and her bangs were down.

"I came bearing gifts," I said. "I happen to have a shirt that's too small for me, but after yesterday I knew just the right person for it."

I showed her what was in my hands. The yellow Lakers jersey was the real thing, with the exception that, instead of a player's name and number on the back, there was the designation "MVP" and below that the number "1." After Sirius and I had survived our encounter with Haines, the Lakers organization had sent us some gifts. The shirt actually wasn't too small for me, but I couldn't bring myself to walk around in a jersey that proclaimed me as their most valuable player. At the same time it wasn't something I could part with easily as it had been signed by the Lakers team.

That's what Kelley noticed. "It's autographed!" she said.

"The jersey is a few years old," I explained, "and most of the players who signed it are no longer even on the team."

"Still, it's a collectible. I'm sure it's valuable. I'd consider buying it from you, but I couldn't accept it. That would be too much."

"My work prohibits me from taking money for it, and the truth is that I'll never wear it, so I really do want Matthew to have it. The jersey's not doing me any good gathering dust in a drawer."

I extended it to her, and she reluctantly took it from me. "Matt is going to go crazy for this."

Then she opened the door wider. "The house is a mess, but please come in, Detective—I'm sorry I don't remember your name."

"Detective Gideon," I said.

I followed her into the house. By my standards it looked clean, but she began apologizing again. "I meant to start tidying up after taking Matt to school, but then I went and nodded off. It seems like all I do is nap these days. I was just about to get a cup of coffee. Would you like one?"

"I definitely would," I said. "I'm operating on vapors. Last night there was a small fire at my house, and as a result I barely slept."

"That's terrible!" she said. "What happened?"

"The fire department is looking into it, but I wouldn't be surprised if it was an electrical fire."

Actually that would surprise the hell out of me, but that was the easiest explanation to offer.

"You'll have to do the sniff test on the jersey," I said. "It might have picked up some of the smoke smell."

"I can't imagine after dealing with a fire you're not home recovering. And to think you actually made a special trip here to deliver the jersey."

I was getting tired of hearing what a nice and thoughtful person I was. I was the wolf in sheep's clothing—or at least the Lakers jersey. "I do better when I'm working," I said.

And working was what I was doing. I had no idea what I was looking for, but with glances I hoped weren't obvious I was trying to take in as much as I could. Off the entry door was a small living room full of familial bric-a-brac.

"Let me get that coffee," she said. "Why don't you grab a seat in the living room?"

As Kelley went to the kitchen, I looked around the living room. There were lots of family pictures. Matthew was the star of most of the shots. Even though he was only a third-grader, there were pictures of Matthew with soccer, football, baseball, and basketball teams. Youth sports seemed to be his life.

Kelley's voice came from the kitchen: "What do you take in your coffee?"

"I'll take cream and sugar, if you have it."

It wasn't my usual order, but I hoped it would take longer to prepare and give me more time to look around.

"I'm afraid we only have milk," she shouted.

"Beggars can't be choosers."

From the kitchen I could hear the microwave heating up our coffee. I went from picture to picture and started seeing some older photos that showed life before Matthew. There were a number of pictures of Kelley with a man I assumed was her husband. I had seen the blurred images of the Reluctant Hero taken on the camera phone, and there was a resemblance. Both men had short, dark hair with intense brown eyes and an olive complexion, and looked to be around five foot ten. But The Corner School assistant principal was right in her description of Mr. Pullman as being heavier and less "vigorous" than the Hero. While he wasn't fat, his more recent pictures showed him with a slight gut and a face that was becoming jowly.

I continued scrutinizing pictures. There were several wedding shots. It looked like theirs had been a large wedding, as the picture showed six bridesmaids and six groomsmen. All the groomsmen were wearing tuxes except for the best man, who was outfitted in his military dress uniform. He had on a tan beret and a uniform of green. There was no question as to the familial resemblance; the best man had to be brother to the groom.

Everyone in the wedding party shot was smiling except for the best man. There was something of the thousand-yard stare in his expression. I wondered if he had come from war or knew he would soon be returning to it. His lost expression set him apart from the other faces, especially his radiant brother's. I've known too many grooms who, in their nuptial photos, looked as if they were going to the gallows instead of their wedding. That wasn't the case with Matthew's father. This was his moment of triumph. His bride didn't look as ebullient. Weddings are stressful, and Kelley's smile couldn't quite mask her anxiety.

"I'm surprised you didn't drop off the jersey at the school," yelled Kelley from the kitchen.

There wasn't a good answer, but I tried to offer a plausible explanation.

"I wanted to make sure you were okay with accepting it for Matthew, and I was in the neighborhood anyway."

I was afraid her next question would be to ask how I had learned where Matthew lived, so I kept up my patter while continuing to study the pictures.

"I should be the one making coffee. I'm sure these days it's hard being on your feet."

"I'm glad to have something to do," she said.

I could hear her putting coffee cups on a tray, and that was my signal to move away from the wedding photos back to the sports pictures. As Kelley entered the living room, I turned to her and said, "Let me help."

"No need," she said, placing the tray on a table and then handing me my cup. "Here's your blonde with sand."

"My what?"

"I worked in a diner while going to college. One of the old-time waitresses used to always call coffee with cream and sugar 'a blonde with sand.'"

"I've eaten too many meals in too many diners, but I've never heard it called that. Of course usually I just order it black."

"Shirley called that 'high and dry.'"

"It sounds like you learned as much at that diner as you did in college."

She laughed. "That might be true. When people ask where I met my husband, I'm never sure whether to tell them it happened on the job or at college."

"Which was it?"

"Both." Kelley smiled. "I was a freshman at Cal Poly, San Luis Obispo, when D.C. was a senior. D.C. was in the computer engineering program, and I was studying business. I worked nights at the diner, and he always came in to get his coffee fix, or at least that's what he led me to believe. Only after we started going out did D.C. admit he didn't really even like coffee. It was the cheapest thing on the menu, and it gave him something to linger over, but mostly it gave him an excuse to see me."

"How long did it take him to ask you out?"

"D.C. didn't exactly sweep me off my feet. We knew each other for almost a year before he finally asked me out. From what he told me, he practiced his speech for weeks. Of course I found that hard to believe because all I remember was his asking me if I was doing anything special for the weekend."

"As a whole, men aren't the smooth operators we think we are. Most of us barely bumble and stumble along. Just ask my girlfriend."

I sipped my coffee. "Do you know the sex of your child?"

"It's a girl!" Kelley beamed.

"I wonder if she'll be a jock like her brother."

"I'm hoping she'll be a little less frenetic than Matt."

"Did you and your husband play sports?"

"To a certain extent we did, but I wouldn't call either of us overly athletic. We each have jock siblings, though. My sister played field hockey and soccer, and my brother-in-law lettered in just about everything. I was told he was all this and all that."

"I think I saw him in your wedding pictures. He was the one wearing his military dress uniform, right?"

"That's Caine," she said.

"As in Abel and Cain?"

"Sort of," she said, "but it's spelled with an 'e,' and it's his middle name. I guess Caine is a family surname on the mother's side. Neither D.C. nor Caine liked their first names, so they both sort of lost them."

"I couldn't help but notice Caine's outfit and beret," I said. "Only Special Forces get to wear those, right?"

Kelley nodded. "He's with the Seventy-Fifth Ranger Regiment."

I whistled. "Those guys are the real deal."

She looked into her coffee and remembered to nod.

"Is he the older or younger brother?"

"Younger," said Kelley. "He's three months older than I am."

She wasn't smiling now, but tried to pretend that everything was fine, which only accentuated her melancholy.

"Is he in the thick of it now?"

Kelley thought about that and finally said, "He soon will be." Then she looked at me and faked a smile.

She put down her coffee cup and reached for the jersey. It was a good way for her to change the subject. "I'm afraid that once Matt puts this on, he'll probably never want to take it off."

I finished my cup of coffee. I had come on a fishing expedition but hadn't really expected to land a fish. At the moment, I was half-wishing it had been the one that got away.

"I do have to run," I said. "Thanks so much for the coffee. And good luck with your bundle of joy."

Despite my encouraging her not to get up, Kelley walked me to the door. When I arrived at my car, she was still standing in the doorway and offered me a little wave.

I waved back. She thought I was one of the good guys.

"Let's get out of here," I said to Sirius.

CHAPTER 18:

DRIVERS EDUCATION

When Sirius and I walked into Central Police Station, Sergeant Perez began singing, "My dog has fleas."

As far as I know, Perez doesn't play the ukulele or guitar, but I guess he knows someone who does. Guitarists and uke players sing that song to help them tune their instruments. Perez sings it to annoy me.

"My dog has fleas," he sang again. Being off-key didn't help his song.

"Your wife has crabs," I sang, hitting the tune just right. Maybe that's why Perez flipped me the bird. He was jealous of my singing.

I spent a few minutes sorting through messages and mail. My position in the LAPD is unlike that of any other detective anywhere. The myth of being a detective is that you have autonomy on the job; the truth is you are part of a bureaucracy and have to spend a lot of time dotting *i*'s and crossing *t*'s. Most law enforcement bureaucracies breed mushroom management. I didn't have to do that kind of shoveling and was spared most of the day-to-day headaches that other investigators have. As police work goes, I've won the lottery, other than my obligatory PR appearances. As long as Sirius and I are still remembered for bringing in the Santa Ana Strangler, LAPD will use us to curry favor. With Ellis Haines now in town, the media was all atwitter. Media Relations had fielded several requests for me to be interviewed and was trying to pin me down for a date and time. I had reluctantly agreed to sit down with the media on the day Haines was scheduled to testify in court.

From across the room Perez was exaggeratedly sniffing. Even more exaggerated was the disgusted expression on his face. He smelled the smoke and knew it came from me. Instead of explaining what had happened, I turned my back to Perez and pulled a business card from my wallet. Captain Redding had told me he'd be working the scene with arson investigators. I dialed his mobile number.

"Redding," said a raspy voice.

"Misery loves company," I said. "This is Gideon. You sound as tired as I am."

"Arsonists don't keep banker's hours. I wish they did."

"Are you at my house?"

"I am. It's nice to see a front lawn with more weeds than mine."

"'A weed is just a plant whose virtues have not yet been discovered.'"

"As I live and breathe," he said, "who would ever have thunk it—a cop philosopher."

I didn't bother telling him that it was a favorite quotation of Seth's, who attributed it to Thoreau, or Emerson, or some transcendental witch doctor.

"It's a line that gives me a handy excuse to avoid weeding."

"Yeah, I'll try it on my wife and see how it works on her."

"So what's the light of day tell you other than that my lawn has weeds?"

"It's looking more and more like naphtha."

"Which is what exactly?"

"It's a distillation of petroleum. You might have heard it called white gas. You get naphtha from a particular mixture of hydrocarbon molecules."

"And how does one acquire white gas?"

"You go to a sporting goods store and buy that flammable stuff used in camping stoves and lanterns."

"And how did it end up on my roof?"

"Evidence suggests a balloon."

"You mean someone tossed a water balloon on my roof?"

"That's possible. But based on the extent of the spray, it's more likely that someone used a balloon launcher."

"Are you talking about a catapult?"

"That would work, but so would a wrist launcher. If you know how to use one of those, they're quite accurate. A balloon filled with accelerant could have been delivered from across the street or even farther away."

"Low tech," I said.

"You sound surprised."

I guess I was. I had assumed my hellfire had been delivered courtesy of a drone.

"I guess I'm more pissed than anything," I said.

"I hear weeding is supposed to be therapeutic and a stress reliever."

"Is that what your wife tells you?"

"How'd you guess?"

* * *

I texted Elle's private number with the message: *We need to meet ASAP.* When I didn't get a response, I couldn't be sure if Elle was ducking me or busy on the set. I gave her the benefit of the doubt and spent a few minutes learning what I could about Neal Bass. In my hunting and gathering of data, one thing jumped out: Bass was lucky to still have a driver's license. A few months back he'd had to go to court to get a reckless driving charge reduced from a misdemeanor to a traffic violation. Over the past four years he'd been cited multiple times for speeding, tailgating, a rolling stop, careless driving, and unsafe lane changes. During that time he'd attended traffic school twice and wasn't eligible to attend for another six months. Another ticket might result in the revocation of his license.

Bass's cherry-red Porsche Boxster wasn't exactly an inconspicuous car. It was a vehicle designed to get noticed. To traffic cops and the CHP, it might as well have come with a sign that read, "Ticket me."

I leaned back in my chair and considered my next gambit. Corde had targeted my Achilles heel; I gave some consideration to his.

Elle still hadn't responded to my text, so I sent her another: *When and where are we meeting?* While waiting for her to respond, I researched Caine Pullman. It took a little digging to get his real first name, which was Todd. If I'd been named Todd, I probably would have gone with my middle name as well.

Caine's regiment was based in Fort Benning, Georgia, but home seemed to be the hot spot du jour. He had served in Iraq and Afghanistan. Through social media I saw that yesterday Caine had posted from "the happiest place on earth." He had visited Disneyland.

Donald Calvin Pullman was my next search engine target. D.C. was the director of information systems of a local wireless company. My search for background information on him was made easier because Pullman wasn't an overly common name.

I called D.C.'s workplace, and after getting his voicemail, hung up. When I called back, I was able to get a human being who identified herself as D.C.'s administrative assistant. According to her, D.C. was in a meeting and wouldn't be back until late afternoon. I asked if she could do me a favor, and she did.

* * *

The bright red Porsche was in a reserved parking spot in front of the building. There was a prominent sign warning scofflaws that unauthorized vehicles would be towed at the owner's expense.

I was sitting in a parking lot down the street, where the rest of the hoi polloi parked their cars. It was 12:30 p.m., and over the last half hour I'd seen a slow but steady lunch exodus take place from the building I was watching. There were several delis in the industrial park, and some of the workers were combining a walk with lunch. I was hoping Bass hadn't brown-bagged it, or wasn't one of those who believed in walking to lunch.

I used my stakeout time to text and make calls. *Still waiting* was my message to Elle.

With our mobile population, and cell phones on the constant move, you never know where you're calling. The area code I punched in was 706, a Georgia designation. D.C. Pullman's administrative assistant had supplied me with Caine Pullman's cell phone number. Kelley had said that Caine would soon be back in the thick of it. His trip the day before to Disneyland gave me hope he was still in California.

My call immediately went to voice mail. A deep voice said, "Leave a message. If I know you, I might call back."

At the beep I said, "You don't know me, but you do need to call me back. This is Detective Michael Gideon of the Los Angeles Police Department. I'll be expecting your call."

I left the number of my cell and repeated the number a second time before hanging up.

At a little before one, Neal Bass left the building and approached his Porsche. As he pulled out, I fell in behind him. All the tickets hadn't improved his driving. It only took him five seconds to be going fifteen miles an hour over the speed limit. As he approached a stop sign, Bass paid little heed to the octagonal reproach. He applied his brakes for maybe a nanosecond and then swept by. That's when I put on the light show, swinging the dual-deck light bar atop the hood and unleashing a flashing red beacon.

Bass's body jerked at the sight of the lights, and then he pulled over to the side of the road. I parked behind him but kept the lights rotating. Bass was none too gently hitting his forehead on the steering wheel as I approached.

"License and registration, please," I said.

At the sound of my voice, Bass's head pivoted my way. "You," he said.

"Me," I agreed.

"You set me up."

"I made you drive through the stop sign?"

"What do you want?"

"Like I told you, I want your driver's license and registration."

"We don't have to go there, do we? I thought you wanted to talk."

"That was yesterday."

"Why do you want to mess with my life? You already got Rip all over my ass."

Drew Corde liked others to call him "Rip." It was a good reason not to call him that.

"And how did I do that?"

"You tell me."

I had assumed Bass had contacted Corde about my visit, and that had resulted in my roof fire, but if I was to believe what he was saying, that wasn't the case.

"All right, let's talk. Follow me."

We drove forward a short distance and then turned right on a street that dead-ended at a storage facility. Most of the parking spaces in the lot were unoccupied, and I signaled for Bass to pull up next to me in a quiet spot under an overhang of eucalyptus trees. We lowered our windows and carried on a conversation from inside our cars.

"What's this about Corde chewing you out?"

That got an aggrieved nod. "He called me maybe an hour after we talked. Rip really laid into me. I'm taking a chance even talking to you now. You're not going to give me a ticket, right?"

"You're saying Corde knew I came to see you?"

Bass nodded. "He told me if you ever called or came around again, I should refer you to our company lawyers."

"How did he know I came to your office?"

"You're not the one I should be thanking for that?"

I shook my head and Bass shrugged. "Maybe Cheryl dropped a dime on me. She's a real bitch. Or maybe one of us is being monitored. I don't even want to guess. I'm already paranoid enough as it is."

"Is there a reason for your paranoia?"

Bass didn't respond.

"Three nights ago you were at Corde's house. Is that right?"

"That depends. You're not giving me a ticket, are you?"

"Not if you answer my questions."

"Yeah, I was there."

"Who else was there?"

"It was just Austin Delaney, me, and Rip."

"Who is Delaney?"

"He's an OZ old-timer who goes back to when we were making video games."

"Does he still work for OZ?"

Bass nodded.

"Wasn't Novak there as well?"

"He arrived later, when the gaming was all but done."

"It's my understanding that there are four or five Attack Pack regulars."

"Armand Goldberg's wife is expecting—Armand's another OZ gamer from way back—so he couldn't make it."

"What time did Novak show up?"

"It was after midnight."

"Do you always game that late?"

He nodded.

"Tell me about Novak."

"He's the security director of OZ, but more than that he's Rip's right-hand man. Usually you don't have to look any farther than Rip's shadow to find him."

"What's his first name?"

"I think it's Rick, or Eric, but no one calls him that. He's the kind of guy who doesn't have a first name, or need one."

"How so?"

"It's like those *Men in Black* movies. The agents don't have names. They're letters, like 'A' or 'K.' Novak should be 'N.'"

"Is Novak a former spook?"

"That's my understanding."

"What's a former spy doing playing video games with your group?"

"The rest of us play. When Novak gets his hands on a joy stick, he becomes a killing machine."

"Does the Attack Pack only play with video games?"

Bass's confused look made me clarify: "Has your group operated drones from inside the Bunker?"

"I'm not going to answer that question."

"You just did."

"Can I go?"

"Soon," I said. "Three nights ago were you and the Attack Pack playing with drones?"

He shook his head.

"That's odd," I said. "You still haven't explained how it is that I heard your laughter in the background when someone called me and played back a recording of what should have been private time between my girlfriend and me."

"If I answer, can it be off the record? I'm talking no attribution to me now or down the road. And what I say stays between us. I don't want it repeated or put in a report. I'm afraid of it coming back to me, and when I say 'afraid,' that's what I mean."

"I'm okay with off the record."

"Hypothetically, let's say a certain someone played a recording of two people screwing. There was no explanation, just the sounds of a couple going at it. That's all I know about that subject."

I thought about the phone call to my cell and the recording that I'd heard, and wondered how the recording had been made.

"I got to get moving," said Bass. "If we linger here, it will catch the attention of some eye in the sky."

"What can you tell me about the angel?" I asked.

His puzzlement couldn't be faked. He wrinkled his brow and shook his head. "When you asked me about angels the last time, I didn't know what the hell you were talking about, and I still don't."

"Did Corde ever talk about angels?"

"Never."

"Did you ever participate in a UAV hunt that targeted an angel simulation?"

"Like I already told you, I'm not going to admit to being part of any UAV hunt."

"Let's make it a hypothetical situation. Have you ever heard of an angel simulation being used as part of a drone targeting game?"

"No, I have not."

"And you never heard the name Wrong Pauley, and know nothing about his death?"

"The only time I heard his name was when you brought it up."

"Did you ever go hunting with Corde?"

"Not really," he said.

"What kind of answer is that?"

"It's the kind of answer you give when you don't want to comment."

I searched my memory. Something was there. And then I remembered the picture taken on Corde's yacht. The features of three men could just be made out in the darkness. The light coming off a monitor had illuminated Corde and Novak. I was pretty sure Bass was the third man.

"You're in that photo hanging in Corde's trophy room, aren't you? You were on his yacht."

"What about it?" Bass wasn't looking very happy.

"All the other pictures had to do with one hunt or another."

"We were fishing," he mumbled. "What's the difference?"

"It looked like a recent shot."

"A few weeks ago," he said. "I can't tell you much about the outing because I don't remember much. I drank too much, and I got seasick, and by the end of the night I was puking my guts out."

I opened my mouth to ask another question, but before I could speak, Bass started his engine. It was loud; it roared. And the roar made me think of Corde's trophy room, and the lion, and especially the tiger.

Bass's eyes met mine. He was anxious to take his leave of me. When I didn't tell him to stay put, Bass hit reverse hard and then punched down on the accelerator. As he patched out, he left heavy tire treads behind.

He wasn't a good driver. And I doubted he was a good liar. I was confident he'd told me no lies, but also knew he'd only told me part of the story.

CHAPTER 19:

HEROIC FAILURE

Normally I keep my cell phone in silent mode and feel a buzz when there's a text or phone call. I guess that's why I still wasn't used to Munchkins singing my text alerts.

"Ding dong! The witch is dead."

Elle Barrett Browning had finally gotten back to me. Her text was brief: *C U Mulholland Scenic Overlook west of the 405 just off Mulholland at 10 p.m. I M driving black Tesla Model S. Let's meet near fire road at top of trail.*

I texted back: *I'll be there.*

I wondered at Elle's choice of spots. In some ways it made sense. The Mulholland Overlook offered a way of hiding in plain sight, at least at night. The overlook was convenient to the interstate, and as L.A. goes, it was a secluded spot. I wondered if Elle knew her proposed meeting place had the reputation of being a lover's lane. Officially, it was closed at nine in the evening, but with both the Mountain Recreation Conservation Authority and LAPD stretched thin, it was rarely patrolled.

The theme song from *Peter Gunn* with its wailing brass interrupted my thoughts. I stilled the trumpets by taking the call.

"This is Gideon."

A gravelly voice said, "You called me."

Even though the caller didn't identify himself, I knew who was on the other line. "Thanks for getting back to me, Caine. Is it all right if I call you 'Caine'?"

"Is it all right if I call you 'asshole'?" he asked, his words slightly slurred.

"Call me whatever you want, Mr. Pullman."

"I'm fucking with you. You can call me anything but 'Mr. Pullman.' That's my father's name—and my brother's."

He took a deep breath and then let out an even deeper sigh. "You're the cop Kelley said came by with that Lakers shirt, right?"

"I am."

"You're the fucking Trojan horse."

"Did you tell Kelley that's what I was?"

Caine sighed again; it was longer than his last sigh, and sadder. "In case you hadn't noticed, Kelley's pregnant and ready to pop. She's also an innocent. I spared her the turd in the punchbowl. She would have worried about *le turd*.

"Excuse my French," he said. "That's what comes of spending an afternoon of drinking at the Bar Marmont. They got lots of drinks with fancy French names. You ever been there?"

The Chateau Marmont is on Sunset Boulevard. The hotel is a favorite haunt of the stars. It's also where John Belushi died of a drug overdose.

"I've been there on police business, but I've never dined or eaten there. It's on my bucket list."

"It was on mine too. It was supposed to be the ultimate watering hole, but next time I'll go to a titty bar instead that doesn't have names for its drinks."

"What were you drinking?"

"The Jalapeno," he said. "That doesn't sound French, does it? It's a margarita made from jalapeno tequila."

"My best friend likes to drink a mescal that comes with worms."

"The Bar Marmont probably charges extra for those."

"Have you eaten dinner? I'd like to meet with you. It would be my treat."

"Those kinds of meals are always the most expensive."

"We need a face-to-face. We need to talk."

"Do we? Did I mention I got memory issues? It's a blast injury thing. That's what happens when you're in the vicinity of too many IEDs. You get deficit awareness and PTSD."

"Are you sure you're not just suffering from selective memory loss?"

"Fuck you."

"I'm not your enemy. Meet me for dinner. I'll prove it."

"Fine," he said. "Let's have dinner at Kabul Fried Chicken. I'll be back there in two weeks. Their chicken might not be finger-lickin' good, but if you leave with all your limbs intact, you got to think it was a good meal."

"Why don't you pick somewhere in L.A., and why don't we meet tonight?"

He didn't answer right away but finally said, "You ever eat at the Musso & Frank Grill?"

"I've been there a few times."

"It's supposed to be a Hollywood landmark."

"It is, and the food's good. How about we meet there in an hour? I'd be glad to pay for your cab and your meal."

The silence was even longer this time. When I was just about ready to ask if he was still there, Pullman whispered, "Fine."

* * *

Before setting out for the restaurant, I pulled over at a neighbor-hood park and found a spot that gave me a good vantage point. As far as I could determine, there was no vehicle tailing me and no one observing my movements. My watchfulness wasn't limited to ground activity. I scanned the skies. It was probably wishful looking more than anything else. Military drones could do their spying from as high as ten miles up. It was possible I was being spied on and with my naked eye couldn't even see the vehicle doing the spying. But that, I was thinking, had been my mistake. I had been so fixated on drones that I had overlooked the obvious.

Dr. Inferno had told me that UAVs weren't good at audio sur-veillance. He had said that picking up conversations was diffi-cult because of the noise produced by the drones. Being "eyes in the skies" was one thing; being ears on the ground was another. Drones were not yet capable of being the fly on the wall.

I hadn't processed much of what Dr. Inferno said because his playing with fire had scared the shit out of me. It had taken me until now to remember what he had told me about creating an illusion, or an effect. He had spoken about misdirection and how it could keep you from seeing what was there. There was also expectation, with the magician setting you up into believing you were seeing what wasn't there. But he'd also warned me to "watch out for the man in the audience." I had forgotten to look for the plant, the shill.

Performers have used shills since time immemorial. The man or woman in the audience or crowd is planted there to facili-tate the performer and performance, whether by laughing loudly or testifying or bidding up an item or being the apparent ran-dom everyman called upon. Sometimes shills cross the line from facilitating to aiding and abetting. Professional gamblers have been known to use plants to team up against the unsuspecting.

I took Sirius for a short walk and made sure no one was monitoring us, at least by conventional means. When we got back to the car, I placed Sirius's water bowl on the ground, and then on hands and knees began my search.

It took me fewer than five minutes to find the black box taped in the back wheel well. It wasn't obvious, and I wouldn't have seen it if I hadn't been looking for it. You never see the man in the audience either, unless you're looking for him. And even then, you sometimes don't see him.

I was fairly certain the GPS tracker had been planted during my visit to Drew Corde's house, and I was also fairly certain who had done the planting. There had been that knowing look that passed between Corde and his director of security, the enigmatic Mr. Novak. According to Bass, Novak had arrived late to the Bunker. I suspected he had been occupied that evening. He had put the GPS tracker in my vehicle and used it to follow me to Lisbet's house. When I had returned to my car after talking with Corde, I hadn't paid close enough attention to its fogged-up state and Sirius's agitated condition. My partner's presence had prevented entry into the vehicle and kept Novak from splicing into the electrical system or hiding the bug inside the console of the car. If that had occurred, the tracker would have been impossible to find. Instead, Novak had been forced to use a passive tracker with its own battery pack. Sirius's slobber, the timely text to Corde telling him the task was done, and the foggy back windows were all clues I had overlooked. While I had been trying to get a bead on Corde, Novak had been getting the bead on me.

* * *

Sirius and I cruised down Hollywood Boulevard. Over the years L.A. has spent a lot of money trying to revitalize the area so that it doesn't look like blight. You don't want the tourists to be iffy about their tourist traps. Through good times and bad, Musso & Frank's has endured and been an anchor of what's called "Old Hollywood."

I parked in the back, making sure Sirius had everything he needed, and then walked out front. I did a little weaving, but not because I'd been drinking. Hollywood Boulevard is home to lots of stars in the sidewalk, and I avoided stepping on them. Whenever I'm a pedestrian in the area, I remember the rhymes of childhood: *Step on a crack, break your mother's back. Step on a line, break your father's spine.* I don't know if there is a rhyme about stepping on stars, but I try to skirt them anyway. In front of the restaurant, I sidestepped Aaron Spelling, John Barrymore, and Gene Autry. The Marg Helgenberger star was a new one to me. I'd watched her show *CSI* once or twice, and wished that catching crooks through science was as easy as television made it seem. Most cops wait months to get results back from the police lab. Without any toxicology report yet available on Wrong Pauley, I still couldn't be sure if I was dealing with a homicide or not.

I was early, and I remembered that during my recent visit to the Magic Castle, I'd been told about Houdini's star. I gave some thought to trying to hunt it down but decided not to even try. Locating a particular star isn't as difficult as finding a needle in a haystack, but without a star guide map it's not easy. The Hollywood Walk of Fame now has more than two thousand stars. There's probably not a bigger monument to oversized egos, if you exclude the pyramids. It does give me a bit of satisfaction, though, knowing that a mythical amphibian like Kermit the Frog has his own star. That green reality has to bring some of the A-list egos down to earth.

Nothing looked different inside Musso & Frank's, and that was the point. Patrons wanted the good old good old. A few of the waiters working at the restaurant looked as if they had been there when the place opened in 1919. The servers wore old-time red tuxedo jackets that reminded me of the deep red bellhop uniform I'd seen on vintage film clips of Philip Morris Johnny. It had been almost half a century since Johnny's "call for Philip Morris," but had his doppelganger appeared in the restaurant, I wouldn't have been surprised.

I was seated in a worn leather booth with a view toward the reservation stand. After my conversation with Pullman, I couldn't be sure he would even show. A Hispanic waiter who looked to be in his mid-sixties came to my table. I told him I was waiting for a friend, and he asked if he could get me a drink while I waited. If you should order a martini anywhere, it's at Musso & Frank's, but I violated tradition and went with an iced tea. My waiter took the order without comment. Had I ordered that martini, I'm sure I would have gotten a nod of approval instead of his silence.

The menu looked much the same as I remembered. Where else in Los Angeles can you get chicken à la king, Welsh rarebit, and grilled lamb kidneys with bacon? If the copy in the menu could be believed, the kidneys were Charlie Chaplin's favorite. I wondered if Chaplin had ever come from the set for his kidneys with his Little Tramp greasepaint mustache still painted on. Apparently Chaplin had been such a regular that the restaurant had kept the table nearest the street reserved for him. To this day it's still called the Charlie Chaplin table. If memory served me, Chaplin's star was a block away, located outside the Hollywood Wax Museum. At least it was near his table.

Time passed, and I began to fear that Pullman was going to be a no-show. My waiter seemed to perk up a little bit when he revisited the table a second time and I put in an order for a baby iceberg wedge. These days even iceberg lettuce seems to be a thing of the past, replaced by microgreens, arugula, and endive. My wedge arrived before Pullman did, and I started eating. With the generous amounts of bacon, chives, and blue cheese, all I was missing was the potato. It wasn't what you'd call a healthy salad, but it was tasty.

I was just finishing up the salad when a face I'd seen in the Pullman wedding photos entered the restaurant. In the years since the wedding, Caine Pullman had noticeably aged. He wasn't wearing his uniform, but anyone with eyes could tell in a glance he was military. It wasn't only his haircut; you could see it in his posture and bearing.

As I started to rise, his head turned my way. He motioned with a hand for me to sit and then marched toward the booth. His handshake was about what I would have expected; it didn't quite break bones.

"Michael," I said.

"I thought we'd agreed I could call you 'asshole.'"

He faked a smile while taking a seat in the booth. I was glad he remembered our earlier conversation after drinking so many jalapeno margaritas. Too many drinkers talk and don't hear. Judging by his clear eyes and quick movements, he had put his afternoon of drinking well behind him.

"They don't have your jalapeno margaritas here," I said, "but they do have world-class martinis. I'm hoping you're not drinking, though, and not just because it will save me a dozen bucks a pop. I'm working a case, and I could use your help on it. If you agree, I'll need you to have a clear head."

The last thing Pullman was expecting was for me to ask for his help. He had come ready to argue and lie, and maybe even to fight. His surprise showed in his expression and voice.

"What do you have in mind?"

"I need someone watching my back. The people who might be targeting me already know about my partner, but they wouldn't expect you."

Our waiter chose that moment to swoop in. He delivered another menu and asked Pullman, "What can I get you to drink?"

My Ranger considered his options and said, "How about a coke, but served in one of your martini glasses?"

The waiter didn't bat an eye. "Would you like olives or a cocktail onion with your coke?"

"Olives," said Pullman.

The waiter left and Pullman said to me, "At least it will feel like a martini."

"Maybe I'll do the same with my next round of ice tea."

Caine took a moment to study my face. "So, are you bullshitting me, or do you really need my help?"

"It's legit. I can use another set of eyes. I'm hoping you'll just be along as insurance, and you won't have to involve yourself in any other capacity than observing. Normally, I would never consider involving a civilian, but you're not exactly that, are you?"

"*Sua sponte.*"

"You'll have to translate."

"It's a Ranger motto, and means 'of my own accord.' When you're a Ranger, you volunteer three times: for the Army, for the Airborne School, and for the Ranger Regiment. We do what needs to be done on our own accord."

"Are you willing to volunteer for a fourth time?"

"What's the mission?"

I told him about Wrong Pauley and the angel he claimed to have seen, the sex tape, the GPS tracker on my car, and the fire set on my roof. He heard about my meeting later that night and how drones might be part of the overall equation. I finished my story at the same time his coke arrived in the requested martini glass. Three olives speared by a toothpick sat in his drink.

Pullman raised his glass, and with a nod once more said, "*Sua sponte.*"

I clicked glasses with him, and our waiter asked, "Are you gentlemen ready to order?"

* * *

Pullman took a last satisfied bite of his rib eye in béarnaise sauce. I had gone with the fettuccini alfredo. Supposedly the genesis of my pasta came from a recipe supplied by Douglas Fairbanks and Mary Pickford. Neither was alive to confirm this. And since they were known for their silent movies, maybe they wouldn't have commented anyway. I was glad the two old stars had supplied their recipe. Some things shouldn't be tampered with, and chief among them was the fettuccini alfredo.

With the meal finished it was time to address the elephant at the table. Rather than dance around it any longer, I said, "How is it that your nephew didn't recognize you?"

Caine scowled at me. "What if I said I don't know what you're talking about?"

"Then you would be lying."

He scowled a little more before finally saying, "Anything I say is just conjecture. Everything I say is off the record. Can we proceed that way?"

"It works for me."

"Matthew has never met me. I'm his mystery uncle who is always fighting in one war or another and is forever in some shithole location."

"The two of us can talk hypothetically," I said, "but you are still going to have to come clean about this Reluctant Hero thing."

Pullman stiffened, but I continued talking without giving him a chance to speak.

"It's the only way we can keep it quiet. I'm not the only one who has been trying to find your identity. The *Times* is on it, and so are two or three of the gossip rags. It wouldn't surprise me if they identified you in the next week or two.

"That's why we have to beat them to the punch. That's why I want to arrange a private ceremony with the mayor giving you the key to the city, along with controlled media coverage. Those media outlets at the ceremony will have to agree not to release your name for the reason that you are a member of an elite military unit and because the nature of your sensitive missions requires anonymity. I'll see that they don't even identify you as a Ranger. That way no one will be able to know if you're a Ranger, a SEAL, or Delta, or Recon. We'll make sure they pixelate your image and electronically disguise your voice. As for print media, photographers will have to sign a release agreeing to no face shots. At the ceremony, you won't give a speech and won't take any questions. LAPD Media Relations will read a prepared statement saying that you were taking R&R in Los Angeles and just happened to be in the right place at the right time.

"If we don't do this preemptive move, it will just be a matter of time before you're found out. Doing it this way will secure your privacy. I can guarantee you that even the scandal sheets won't reveal your identity because of the umbrella of national security, as well as not wanting to violate the Patriot Act."

While talking, I'd kept my eyes on Pullman's face and watched his expression change from anger to doubt, to hope.

"You really think that will work?" he asked.

"I'm sure of it. And it's the only way of controlling the media and getting ahead of the situation. Enough details will be provided for them to have their story while at the same time protecting your identity. What's best is that the story we'll be feeding to the media is completely true, even if it's short some details."

"You'll be in charge of all this?"

"I will."

Pullman sat there thinking about it. I could sense a huge weight lifting from his shoulders. If I didn't know better, I would have said his eyes teared up, but Rangers don't cry.

"Everyone's still going to think I'm some kind of hero," he said. "That's a lie."

I nodded. "I understand your embarrassment. I felt the same thing when everyone was trying to make me the toast of the town, and the whole world was told I was this brave guy, all of which just made me feel like that much more of a fraud."

Pullman was nodding. "All I did . . ."

He stopped talking, so I finished the sentence for him: "Was what any father would do."

Pullman took a deep breath. He looked tired. "What else you got figured out?"

"You're a good man trying to make the best of a difficult situation."

"You're wrong. I'm not a good man."

"You're in love with Kelley," I said. "I suspect you've been in love with her from the moment you first met her. I saw how miserable you looked in the wedding photos. She was haunted as well. My guess is you both fell in love days before the wedding. The last thing either one of you wanted to do was betray your brother. And yet you couldn't deny your love for one another. After the wedding, going to war probably felt like a relief from that impossible situation."

Pullman nodded but said nothing.

"Matthew is your biological son," I said. "Your brother doesn't suspect, but you and Kelley know. I imagine you've been surreptitiously monitoring him ever since he was born. You've had to do that because all this time you've avoided seeing him in your brother's presence. And it's also too hard for you to be around Kelley. You're afraid of what you might reveal. That's why you were at The Corner School. You were watching from a vantage point where Matthew couldn't see you. You're good at observing without being seen. It's fortunate you've also been trained to recognize danger and react to it."

Pullman looked down at the table, his chin supported by his hands.

"My unit thinks I'm—kind of crazy—even for a Ranger. What others think is fearlessness is really my not giving a shit whether I live or die. I can't have the woman I love, and I can't have a family, so in the back of my mind I've accepted that it would be easier to die on a battleground far away. It seems to me that would be the best way to tidy up the mess that's my life."

"Does your brother know you're in L.A. now?"

He nodded. "The other day we got together for lunch. You guessed right about me. I can't do the family get-together thing. So I told him I'm in town with a few other Rangers and that we're busy running around raising hell. I've even done some social media posting to make that seem true."

"But what you've really been doing is spending your leave watching Matthew and Kelley."

He shrugged. "It's better for them not knowing I'm around. And it doesn't hurt as much seeing them from a distance. It would be torture if I had to be in their presence. They've never noticed me spying on them."

"You said you spoke with Kelley about the Lakers jersey."

He nodded. "I've talked with her every day I've been in L.A. Supposedly we're going to get together for breakfast or lunch, but it's not going to happen. It would hurt too much, even after all this time."

"Does Kelley know you're the Reluctant Hero?"

He shook his head. "I don't think she's made the connection. Maybe she knows better than to speculate. So far we've kept our secret without hurting D.C. and messing up Matthew's life. I'm really glad Kelley's pregnant, and I'm not just saying that. This time she can have a baby without all the turmoil that came with Matt."

"He's a great kid."

Pullman smiled. It was almost the smile of a proud father.

CHAPTER 20:

THE K-9 PRAYER

As we walked to my car, I again made sure Pullman was helping me of his own volition.

"Before this goes any further, I need to know you're good with this. It's not like I'm deputizing you. This is all unofficial, and like it or not, in this operation your capacity is that of a civilian observer. But that doesn't mean things might not get dangerous. And if you're volunteering because you think you're obligated to me or have this idea that you need to give to get, you need to think again. You don't owe me anything."

"You're doing me the favor," said Pullman.

"How so?"

"The whole time I've been in L.A. I've been jonesing like the dude in that 'Nam film with Brando."

"*Apocalypse Now*," I said.

The Sheen character of Captain Willard needed his mission. Apparently Pullman did as well.

"You know things aren't right in your life when you look forward to going back to war," he said. "With this hero thing hanging over my head, I kept thinking about bugging out, but I was afraid if the shit hit the fan and I wasn't around, Kelley and Matthew would be thrown under the bus."

"When are you being deployed again?"

"Two weeks," he said.

He was used to going into the heart of darkness, I thought. Unfortunately, so was I.

* * *

Pullman had brought with him what he called his "AWOL bag." It was lucky for me that he seemed to think it was his duty to always be ready for combat. Only after Pullman met my partner did he begin to loosen up. Humans can try to forge connections for hours that dogs can establish in mere moments.

"You got yourself your own war dog," he said. "War dogs kept me sane over there, or at least close enough for government work."

For the first time since I'd met Pullman, there was a relaxed smile on his face. He scratched just under Sirius's ears and seemed to know the spots to apply magic fingers.

"On one aerial insert we were up in a Hercules transport, about to be dropped into another goddamned hot spot," he said, "and who should be jumping with us but a handler and a soldier dog. We were doing a HAHO—a high altitude high opening—way up, and the dog was wearing his own oxygen mask. I remember he looked cool as a cucumber. I *know* he was a lot less nervous than I was. He was strapped to his handler, and the two of them didn't slow up the line for even a second. One moment they were there, and the next they were out the chute with an open parachute. I never thought I'd see a sight like that. I kept my eye out for them as I was dropping. What I saw will always stay with me. The dog's fur was being blown back, and he looked as pleased as if he were in an open convertible, cruising down the blacktop with his fur flying."

The image Pullman painted made me laugh. One of the things Sirius loves best is sticking his head out an open window.

"I didn't know the dog's name at the time, but later I learned it was 'Astro.' Hell of a name, eh?"

"It's a good one."

"In the Army most of the handlers say their dogs outrank them. The handlers tell everyone they're the grunts, and their dog is the NCO."

I nodded. "It's the same way with this partnership. I tell everyone that Sirius outranks me. The toughest thing for me is when I have to send him out knowing I'm putting his life on the line."

I added a confessional of my own: "A few years ago he got shot and burned because I told him to go into a fire after a bad guy."

"Is that how you got your scar?"

My hand moved to my face, and I nodded. "I got shot too, but my wound wasn't life threatening. His was."

"That comes with the territory when you're a war dog. They go where they're told, even if it's to the gates of hell. When SEAL Team Six got Bin Laden, they took a war dog on the mission."

"I didn't know that."

The lovefest between Pullman and Sirius continued while I drove; the Ranger scratched, and my partner happily received.

"I probably would have died over there if not for the soldier dogs," Pullman said. "I've watched them sniff out dozens of IEDs. And there's no better early warning system when you're on patrol."

"You'll get no argument here. This one might have saved my life last night."

"You got two of us watching your back tonight," he said.

"I hope that's enough."

"You ever hear the poem 'Guardians of the Night'?" he asked.

I nodded. "Most cops I know call it the K-9 prayer."

"Last month we had a memorial for an explosives dog named Ruger. His handler just missed buying the farm and blamed himself for Ruger's death. He said he missed Ruger's signaling an IED and kept walking. Ruger ran forward and put himself between the handler and the IED. The handler said Ruger died to save him. Talk about raw grief."

"I wouldn't want to be that handler for anything."

"There's no good bag and tag, but this was one of the worst I've seen. The handler tried reciting the poem, but he couldn't, so we all took turns reading it. There wasn't a dry eye at the ceremony, and we're talking about a group of guys that would sooner lose a nut than be seen bawling."

"Been there, done that," I said. And then I recited:

Trust in me, my friend, for I am your comrade.
I will protect you with my last breath.
When all others have left you and the loneliness of the night
closes in,
I will be at your side.

Pullman nodded and said, "Go on."

"It's a long poem," I said, "and I only know parts of it."

"It's the ending that always gets to me. Do you remember that part?"

I gave it a little thought, and the words came to me:

And when our time together is done,
And you move on in the world,
Remember me with kind thoughts and tales.

For a time we were unbeatable,
Nothing passed among us undetected.

If we should meet again on another street,
I will gladly take up your fight,
I am a Police Working Dog,
And we are the guardians of the night.

Pullman was nodding. "That's it," he said, "except I've always heard it recited as 'A Military Working Dog.'"

"The author is unknown, so I don't know if he worked with police dogs or military dogs, but when you're out there, and that loneliness of the night closes in like he wrote about, I don't think there's a dime's worth of difference."

"Guardians of the night," said Pullman.

The Reluctant Hero got the poem as few others would. For a minute or two we drove in companionable silence. I don't think either one of us trusted our voices.

* * *

Mulholland Drive is one of the most famous streets in Los Angeles. Movies, songs, and books have incorporated the name. It is part of the L.A. lore. In one form or another, Mulholland stretches from the Pacific Coast Highway into Hollywood. For the most part the road follows the ridgeline of the Santa Monica Mountains and the Hollywood Hills.

We exited the 405 and headed west. Elle's suggested meet-up spot was in the Encino Hills, and I played the tour guide with Pullman.

"I'll be parking next to an area known as Dirt Mulholland," I said. "It's an eight-mile-long unpaved fire road that winds above the western San Fernando Valley. Because the overlook and Dirt Mulholland are officially closed at night, expect it to be dark."

"It's a good thing I ate my carrots," said Pullman.

I could see his head moving to the right and the left as we traveled up the winding road. As close as we were to L.A., it still felt as if we were out in the country. The road followed along a canyon that was for the most part undeveloped, probably because of the steep drop-off. On the other side of the road was a high embankment. Up on the ridge, but not within sight of the road, were some McMansions.

It was fewer than two miles from the freeway turnoff to the overlook, but it felt longer.

"If we continued on the paved road, it would take us to suburbia," I said.

I turned left and started up the dirt road. We went slowly out of necessity. The road was rutted, and it was even darker than I had thought it would be.

"I've been up on the fire road a few times," I said, "but I haven't hiked its length. It lets out in Woodland Hills. You can drive from there to the 101. If the bridge there looks familiar to you, that's where the opening to the original *Invasion of the Body Snatchers* was filmed. It was there that Kevin McCarthy went running around screaming, 'You're next!'"

"Sometimes I wonder if the pod people didn't already take over," said Pullman.

"You have any doubts?"

We drove by a few scofflaws violating curfew who were parked on the side of the road.

"During the day this is mountain-bike Mecca," I said. "It's also popular for the dog set. I'm surprised Sirius hasn't gotten me to take him for a hike around here. If you want to get a glimpse of what the Cold War looked like, you can take the fire road to San

Vicente Mountain Park and see an old Nike missile command post. In the fifties there was a whole defense system ringing Los Angeles. Those missiles were supposed to keep the city safe from the Soviets."

"Been there, done that," said Pullman.

We reached the top of the road. To our right and left were barriers preventing vehicles from traveling along the fire road.

"This will be where I end up parking," I said.

"I'll need to take a quick look around," said Pullman.

Before I could reply, he exited the car and disappeared from view. Sirius wanted to go with him, but the two of us had to wait. He reappeared a few minutes later.

"Drive back down to the paved road, so I can get the lay of the land," Pullman said.

There was still plenty of time before I was supposed to meet with Elle, so I did as he asked. While Pullman studied the streets and the terrain, I advised him of potential targets he should be aware of.

"I'm fairly certain the GPS tracker on my car was put there by a man named Novak who is the security director for OZ. If the stories about him are true, Novak's previous employment was in intelligence, and more specifically black ops. He shouldn't be underestimated. It is possible Novak was involved in a potential homicide I'm investigating. I also suspect he set the fire on my roof.

"I expect the GPS tracker he attached to my car might bring him to us. I want you to spot the spotter and see what he's up to. Be on the lookout for a white male, around five eleven and very fit. If you get close enough to see him, he has salt-and-pepper hair, blue eyes, and a Dudley Do Right cleft in his chin."

"Who?" said Pullman.

"Just look for a chin dimple," I said, and dug my index finger into my chin.

"So you're kind of dangling yourself as bait?"

"It's more like I'm hoping to bring him out into the open," I said.

I had given a lot of thought as to how I had been set up. Novak had put the tracking device on my car while I was visiting with Corde. After reconstructing my visit, I had remembered the silver minivan parked next to the garage. That wasn't a vehicle Corde or Elle would ever drive, but it was the perfect surveillance vehicle. It was anonymous, the kind of car you wouldn't look at twice, with tinted windows that made it difficult for anyone to see inside. You could store lots of electronics inside. And with the sunroof open, you could do things without ever leaving your vehicle—like use a wrist launcher to send balloons filled with accelerant atop my roof.

"You might want to keep your eyes open for a silver Honda Odyssey with tinted windows," I said. "I think there's a good chance that's what our suspect will be driving. To help with your surveillance, I brought you some thermal imaging binoculars."

Pullman shook his head and patted his pack. "Why do you think my AWOL bag goes everywhere with me? I've got everything but my pickle suit inside, including my own CSS scope."

"What's a CSS scope?"

"Can't see shit," he said. "Now why don't you find a quiet spot for me to change?"

In the darkness Pullman pulled on black sweats and dark hiking shoes he called his "go fasters." He lifted up what I assumed was his CSS scope and looked out of it into the darkness.

"This is usually attached to my Black Widow rifle," he said. "It's going to be strange going after your secret squirrel without some firepower, but at least there won't be any battle rattle to give me away."

He reached into his bag and pulled out a black Ka-Bar knife with a wicked-looking blade. After cutting a few hairs from the top of his hand, he sheathed the blade and stored it in his sweats.

"You're a civilian, remember?"

"Even if I were just going to church, the knife would be coming with me."

"I've always wondered if nuns packed heat."

"I'll see you when I see you," he said, "even if you don't see me."

"You sure you want to get out here? We're more than a mile from where I'll be parking."

"'You better be willing to hump, if you don't want the enemy to get the jump.' Those are words I live by. I got your six. But I got it even better by getting a feel for what's around us. When you go into dark territory, it's nice to know what you're stepping into. You think your secret squirrel will be gunning for you tonight?"

Matters had escalated. My house had almost burned down. If I was right about Wrong Pauley being murdered, I had to believe I was the next target.

"I'm not sure. All I know is that Corde and Novak are high-tech hunters who have taken down a lot of big game. And I'd be wise to be expecting anything from ray guns to drones."

"If a drone gets sent your way, I won't be able to stop you from becoming bug splat."

"Thanks for your reassurance."

He shrugged. "You never want to go into battle with a pucker factor of anything less than a ten."

"I'm about there already."

"I'll alert you with a text or call if I see anything interesting. And if you don't hear anything from me, we'll rendezvous here."

"You're going to be doing a lot of walking."

"Then I better beat feet," he said.

He gave Sirius a last scratch and then was gone. One moment he was there; the next I couldn't see him.

My pucker factor ratcheted up to an eleven.

CHAPTER 21:

STARGAZING

From where paved Mulholland ends, it's about a quarter mile drive up to the fire road. With all the ruts and washboard dirt with gravel, you feel every inch of it. I passed two parked cars on the side of the overlook, but there was no one parked up at the top. I had expected to find at least one teenaged couple, and wondered if parking at make-out spots was a thing of the past. Maybe the Phantom Killer, the Zodiac Killer, the Son of Sam, and the Lover's Lane Killer, have dissuaded couples from steaming up their cars in secluded spots.

It was just as well there were no lovers out this late. It saved me from having to feel like a voyeur without a date. With no one to romance, I had nothing else to do but look out the front windshield. Because I was parked far enough away from the lights of downtown L.A., I was able to take in all the stars overhead. The night was aglow with their twinkling. My gaze fell on the three stars that make up Orion the Hunter's belt. Tonight I wasn't sure if I was the hunter or the hunted.

The outside temperature was June pleasant, in the high sixties. For most of the month L.A. had been spared "June gloom"—coastal clouds that sometimes extended into the Southland—allowing me to see the night sky. Sirius the star wasn't visible. In summer it doesn't show itself as it does in the winter.

It was Jenny who gave Sirius his name, and after anointing him she'd led me by the hand outside, where she had pointed out the Dog Star for me to see. I smiled at the memory. It was good to now be able to do that. Instead of ruminating about Jenny's death and the void it left in my life, I could remember her now with a smile.

My partner appeared to be looking at the stars with me, so I told him, "The Greeks thought Sirius was the cause of the fiery weather in the summer, and because of that they were the ones who coined the term *dog days of summer*. They also used to sacrifice some poor red dog every year so as to bribe the gods into not burning up their crops."

As if to comment, my phone sang, "Ding dong! The witch is dead!"

I checked the text. Elle had written: *b there in 5*. She was one of those texters who abbreviated words like *am, be, you, are*, and *see* with letters like *m, b, u, r,* and *c*. Not to be outdone, I texted back the letter *k*.

The night was unexpectedly still, and during my wait there hadn't been any coming and going of cars. That made the approach of headlights all the more noticeable. It was too dark to get a good look at the car, but the distinctive headlights of the Model S announced Elle's arrival.

"Showtime," I said, and rubbed my hands.

Elle was either looking for privacy or didn't notice my parked car. She chose a spot opposite of where I was, pulling up next to the west fire gate. When she turned off her headlights, her black car disappeared from sight.

We were at the south fire gate, separated by about seventy-five yards. Sirius and I walked in the direction where she had parked. Either there was no moon, or it was hiding behind clouds. Starlight was our guide. I didn't walk quickly; the asphalt was uneven, and the potholes were almost as prohibitive as landmines. The thought of landmines made me think of my Ranger. Somewhere out there he was watching me.

A light showed itself, and I followed it. The illumination came from a cell phone. Elle was texting someone. After Elle's text I had set my phone to vibrate, not wanting any more Munchkins announcing the Wicked Witch was dead. As it turned out, they wouldn't have been singing anyway. My phone didn't vibrate; Elle was texting someone else.

The light on her cell extinguished before we reached her car. Rather than startle Elle, I hit my phone flashlight app and held the strobe toward her before turning it off.

Her window opened a crack. "Detective Gideon?"

"Right here," I said. "Why don't you unlock the passenger door?"

I heard a click, took a moment to tell Sirius to *Sitz* (sit), *Bleib* (stay), and *Pass auf*! (pay attention). With my partner on alert, I opened the passenger door.

"Was that a dog I saw?" asked Elle.

"It was."

"He can come inside and sit on the backseat if you want."

"He's fine out there."

She touched her cheeks and said apologetically, "I'm still wearing makeup. It's a good thing it's so dark. I must look like a mess."

If she was expecting me to remonstrate, I didn't. "Thanks for seeing me," I said.

"Your texts made me think it must be important."

"There have been some developments. Last night someone set fire to the roof of my house."

"That's awful," she said. "What time did it happen?"

"Around two in the morning."

"It couldn't have been Drew," she said. "I was with him from nine on at his house. We were together the entire time, and he didn't go out."

"That doesn't surprise me. I've had a bit of an epiphany about your boyfriend. He is the wizard of OZ after all. And you know every great wizard has his apprentice. Tell me about Novak."

"What do you want to know?"

"He drives a silver Odyssey, doesn't he?"

"I suppose he does."

"Did you talk with him?"

She shook her head. "He often bypasses the main house and goes directly to the Bunker."

"You mentioned the Bunker has a lot of monitors. Is that where the house's security system is located?"

"That's not my area of expertise. But, yes, I suppose it is."

"I noticed a lot of cameras around the property, both inside and outside. Let's assume Novak was in the Bunker. Would he have been able to monitor my movements and listen in to my conversation with Corde?"

"I don't doubt but that's possible. Why do you ask?"

"Novak is there for all your boyfriend's hunts. They're a team. In the trophy room there are a lot of pictures of Corde and his kills that I suspect were taken by Novak. There are also photographs with both men in the same shot, usually with a kill. There was something different about those pictures, but I was slow to make the connection. What I should have asked was who took those pictures and how they were taken. Your boyfriend led me to believe that most of the time he and Novak hunt by themselves. But there had to be someone else there to take their pictures, right?"

"The camera could have been put on a timer," she said.

"That's possible, but some of the photos were clearly taken from above. You can see this in the angle and wide expanse. That made me realize what I should have seen from the first: some of those pictures were taken with a drone camera."

"I don't understand what all that has to do with me."

"You were in one of those pictures taken from above. You were on the *Wizard of OZ* yacht. Did you know about the eye in the sky?"

She thought for a moment. "I don't think I was privy to that information, no."

"And yet you bought into a security building that prevents just that kind of surveillance."

"I bought into a security building that keeps the paparazzi at bay."

"When we met at St. Vincent's, you refused to talk. We had to resort to passing notes back and forth."

"You don't know how ingenious the paparazzi are."

"Is it the paparazzi you're worried about, or is it Novak?"

"What are you talking about?"

"How did you and Corde meet?"

"We were set up by a friend."

"What friend?"

Elle took a sharp breath and then said, "I think we're done here."

"The animals have already escaped the barn, Elle. Closing the door won't help you, and neither will your shutting me out."

"That's your best barnyard philosophy?"

"Corde has something on you, doesn't he? When the two of you were in the same room, I had this sense of underlying innuendo and threats."

"You must have imagined that."

"I don't think so. My guess is that the two of you only came together as a couple after he targeted you. Of course it's possible he was secretly testing one of his drones in the Malibu area, or maybe he and Novak were hunting something, and he happened to come across you. But I doubt that. I'm thinking he was a high-tech stalker and managed to invade your privacy in ways you couldn't have imagined. Whatever he filmed apparently compromised you, and he's used that blackmail to keep you under his thumb."

"I don't have to listen to your wild conjecture."

"Corde loves his trophies. I think it's a sickness he shares with others who have that same compulsion to revel in their kills. It's almost like a junkie needing a fix. What I need from you is to find evidence of his having violated the law."

"And you're trying to tell me it's in my best interests to bring that evidence to you?"

"It's your chance to be free of him."

"Do you really think he'd go quietly off to jail? If I help implicate him, do you think Rip Corde would forgive and forget?"

"You need to get out from under Corde's thumb. And it's not his forgiveness that's important. Your fans would forgive you for just about anything. But it's possible it wouldn't even come to that. As I keep turning up the heat on Corde, he's probably going to start gathering anything that might incriminate him, with the intent of getting rid of it. It's possible he'll even destroy whatever he has on you, assuming it was illegally obtained."

"I am not admitting to anything."

"You wouldn't be with him otherwise."

"How can you be sure of that?" She didn't sound quite as defensive; the tone of her voice was softer.

"I can't, but my gut tells me I'm right. When I first met you standing in the great room, I could see how it bothered you to look at Corde's kills. And when I told you about Wrong Pauley's death, you were upset. But I think you were the most upset when I asked if you knew anything about Corde's hunting angels. At the time you refused to talk about it."

She turned her face away from me, and when she spoke, her words were directed to the window. I could barely make out her whisper: "Don't expect me to say anything now."

"Corde told me all his hunts were well documented. He's no different from some murderers I've put away in that they kept mementos of their victims. Corde has some of his kills on display. I think he has other items he can't display but keeps handy for his own satisfaction. Does he have a safe?"

"Two," she said.

"Where are they?"

"One is in his office. He keeps valuables and sensitive work papers in it. And the other is in the Bunker. You wouldn't know it's there. It's hidden behind a false wall."

"Do you have access to it?"

Her head still wasn't facing me, but at least she was no longer staring out the window. Now she was looking straight ahead. "I don't know the combination if that's what you mean. And I heard him brag that not even the world's greatest safecracker could open it."

"If he gets worried that I'm going to drop a search warrant on him, you need to watch him closely to see if he starts removing items from the safe. If he's planning a bonfire, you might get a chance to swoop in and remove things without him knowing."

She didn't nod or agree, but Elle didn't voice any objections either.

"Do you go down to the Bunker often?"

"Rarely," she said.

"The next time you know Corde is going to be away, I would like you to search through it. It's possible he hasn't locked up everything, but just hidden it. If he has the kind of sickness I suspect, he'd want immediate access to it."

"I don't think there are any angel harps down there."

"You're probably right. But the devil is in the details."

"I'm cold," she said.

"Take my coat," I said, and despite her objections I removed it. "You'll have to excuse its smoky smell."

I helped drape it around her shoulders, and Elle whispered, "Thank you."

"I'm going to need to have all my clothes laundered."

She took a deep breath, smiled, and said, "It's actually a pleasant smell, like a beach bonfire. I'm just sorry to hear your house was set on fire. Was there much damage?"

"It was mostly confined to the roof, even though there was a lot of smoke."

"And the fire department is sure it was arson?"

"They've got the what and the how."

"And you think you have the who and the why."

"Mr. Novak is a person of interest."

"Was your girlfriend home when the fire started?"

I shook my head. "It was just my four-legged partner and me. He was the one who sounded the alarm. I think he saved my bacon."

Sirius had actually awakened me from two fires—my dream and the burning roof—but that wasn't something I told her.

"At a minimum," I added, "a lot more than the roof would have burned had he not gotten me up."

"When I first met you, I didn't realize that it was you who caught the Weatherman. I remember reading all the stories about your rehabilitation. I know it was painful and long, but anyone seeing you now wouldn't realize how severely you were burned."

"You haven't seen me with my clothes off."

"Not yet," she said.

We both laughed, but it was my turn to avert my eyes from her gaze.

Elle asked, "Have you talked to your girlfriend yet about the recording?"

I shook my head. "I've been too busy to see her."

"Sometimes I think my busy schedule is an excuse not to face up to certain things in my life."

"When the two of us do catch up, we'll need to deal with a lot of deferred discussions."

"Trouble in paradise?" There was a flirtatious quality to her teasing voice.

"The troubles, and the problems, are all on me."

"Oh, no," she said.

"What?"

"It sounds like you're about to drop the 'I love you, but I'm not in love with you' line."

"That's not my plan. But she might be better off if it were."

"That sounds virtuous. It sounds as if she'll be hearing, 'It's me, not you.'"

"I'm not an actor. I don't rehearse my lines."

"Touché," she said. "But it does sound like both of us are in need of a great escape."

She reached out and touched my arm. I wasn't sure how to respond to her flirtation and wondered if I was reading her signals wrong. It made no sense for someone like Elle Barrett Browning to be flirting with me unless it was something she did with everyone.

"Cops have always been my personal heroes," she said. "I had a tough upbringing. My mother was schizophrenic, but at the time most people just called her nuts. The police were always getting called out to our house. They were the good guys. As a girl I knew I wanted to end up with a good guy."

"That's not Drew Corde, is it?"

"No, it's not. Are you a good guy, Michael Gideon?"

"I don't know, but like the bumper sticker says, 'One day I hope to be the person my dog thinks I am.'"

Elle laughed, and squeezed my arm with her hand. "You're funny, and I think you are a good guy. Are you really going to be there for me?"

She left her hand on my arm. I wondered if she knew how much heat her touch was generating. And if she knew how uncomfortable it made me feel.

"Cross my heart," I said.

"And hope to die?"

"Preferably not."

Her fingers pressed into my arm. "Let's just say, for argument's sake, that you're right about Drew's hunting me down and in the process gathering damaging information. What could you do about that?"

"If he gathered that information illegally, it couldn't be used against you in court."

"What about the court of public opinion?"

"I'd do whatever I could do to protect your privacy within the law."

It must not have been the answer she wanted to hear because her fingers stopped massaging my arm.

CHAPTER 22:

THE SKY IS FALLING

With Sirius at my side, I watched the Model S drive off. I still wasn't sure if Elle was going to cooperate with me. She claimed that, other than Corde's talking about "gaming" and "hunting" with UAVs from inside the Bunker, she didn't have any definitive proof that he was engaged in illegal activities. Elle reiterated that she had been with Corde the night Wrong Pauley died, and could offer little more than her own "suspicions" when it came to the angel Pauley claimed to have witnessed.

It wasn't until I vacated her car, and was saying good-night at the opened driver's side window, that she offered up to me, "Seraph's last tariff."

"What's that supposed to mean?"

"Just a few nights ago I heard Drew laughing and talking with Novak. And I'm almost certain he said, "'Let's see to a seraph's last tariff', or something like that.

"I wished I'd heard more," she added, and reached out and touched my hand by way of apology.

And then her black car silently disappeared into the night.

I stood there, still feeling the warmth imparted by her hand. She must have gotten over being cold.

"Jenny used to always have cold hands," I told Sirius. "And when I'd mention that they felt like icicles, she would say, 'Cold hands, warm heart.'"

If Jenny was right, I wondered if the reverse was true.

I was aware enough to know that Elle's reaching out to me was likely nothing more than her stroking my male ego. The logical part of my mind knew she was manipulating me for her own purposes. And yet there was a part of me that wanted to believe she wasn't just giving lip service about wanting to settle down with a good guy and how I fit that bill to a T.

"But this isn't a romantic comedy," I told Sirius.

My partner wagged his tail. "Exactly," I said. "It's a buddy film."

As I carefully walked to my car, I found myself whistling "As Time Goes By." I wondered if I was whistling in the dark, or thinking about a kiss, or contemplating a sigh.

"Play it, Sam," I said.

If my Ranger was monitoring us, he probably wondered what I was doing talking to myself. Then again, he'd done enough of his own talking with Sirius. I thought about his story of the war dog parachuting down to earth tethered to his handler and looking like it was just another breezy ride along the PCH with the top down.

I looked around. If Pullman was somewhere out there, he couldn't be seen. It felt strange thinking I was under surveillance. My every movement began feeling contrived, and I was glad to get into my car. I checked my cell phone. My Reluctant Hero hadn't called or texted, and I was hoping no news was good news.

I felt the urge to call Lisbet and wondered if that was prompted by guilt. "Call Lisbet," I told my phone, but the expected female android response of "Calling Lisbet" didn't materialize. I wondered if there was no cell signal, but after checking, I found three bars. I tried manually dialing Lisbet's number but had no better luck. Another inspection of my phone showed that it had plenty of juice.

Maybe it was one of those atmospheric things. There had been a few times in the past when cell phones in the Southland had been impacted by sunspot activity. I started up the car and began driving. Two minutes into the drive, I became aware of a thwacking sound coming from the back of my vehicle. I lowered a window and slowed down, listening more closely. One of the tires must have picked up a rock or stick. That wasn't surprising, given the state of the unpaved road. I tried to convince myself the impediment could wait until I found an open gas station, but as I listened, the sounds got worse. At the same time my car began to feel sluggish, as if the gas wasn't reaching the engine. A sudden shaking overtook the car. There was a coughing sound, as if strangling hands had wrapped themselves around the engine's throat, and my car came to a shuddering stop. The only thing I could do was steer it toward the side of the road.

When I tried starting the car again, the engine wouldn't turn over. My best guess was that I had traveled about a quarter mile from the scenic overlook. That meant my meet-up point with Pullman was another half mile down the road.

The night and day difference of this section of Mulholland Drive could be seen all around me. L.A. seemed like it was a world away. It was dark and quiet. There were few residential lights to be seen; they were almost like distant stars. Road traffic, at least for the moment, was nonexistent.

I reached for the handheld that I carry in the car, but only got static when I hit the transmit button. Clicking on different police frequencies didn't help. *Forget sunspots,* I thought. This was something else. It was easy to be paranoid. I thought about Wrong Pauley and the security cameras in his alley. The electronics had been jammed.

In the quiet of my stationary car, I heard a hissing sound. The noise was coming from outside. My cell phone couldn't call out, but it wasn't completely disabled. I turned on its flashlight app and then exited the car to follow the sound of what had to be escaping air. Up close I could see one of my rear tires was going flat. It had been pierced in multiple spots by a flattened piece of twisted metal. Both tires had picked up pieces of metal. The flat tires could have been caused by Dirt Mulholland. I had noticed the tread on my tires was low; there was no way I should have been off-roading.

Stay or go? I thought. If I stayed with the car, Pullman would eventually meet up with me. Right now I couldn't be sure if he was down the road waiting at our meeting spot or on his way from the overlook. If someone was targeting me, by waiting for Pullman I'd be a sitting duck. If Novak had disabled my car and jammed my communications devices, he'd be looking for a broken-down car, but even more likely he'd be looking for its occupant. Abandoning the vehicle seemed the better choice.

Before setting out, I drew a few arrows on my dusty car to show the direction I was heading. I wanted Pullman to know which way I was going. I decided not to leave the hazard lights on. The car was far enough into the brush not to be a danger to passing vehicles.

Sirius thought that our taking a walk was a wonderful idea. If I'd had his night vision, I might have been more enthused. Dogs have large pupils and lenses adapted for low-light vision, and there wasn't much more than starlight to guide us. Behind their retinas dogs have something called a tapetum, which acts like a mirror. That's why we can see light reflect from a dog's eye at night. It also bounces back light, giving photoreceptors a second opportunity to capture light, even the kind of light only offered up by stars. I let my partner be my seeing-eye dog.

On the drive in I hadn't noticed the lack of streetlights. My headlights had made me unaware of the long stretches without illumination. Now I had to navigate those patches of darkness.

"Dark territory," I said to Sirius.

That was one of the Ranger's expressions. From what I gathered, it meant going into war.

We walked for five minutes and didn't encounter any cars traveling along the road. If we had, I wasn't sure whether I would have chanced flagging one down or moved out of sight among the weeds beyond the shoulder of the road. In the midst of my uncertainty, I became aware of the buzzing.

It sounded like someone was mowing their lawn in the far distance, but no one does yard work at eleven o'clock at night. Besides, the nearest lawn was probably a mile away.

The surrounding canyon took up the sounds. It wasn't a loud buzz, but more of a reverberation. The humming sound seemed to be moving. It annoyed as a flying mosquito would. Hadn't Wrong Pauley said something about that?

And with that realization, the hairs on my neck rose.

Corde had said the people in Pakistan and Afghanistan called UAVs "mosquitoes." Though the drones flew too high to be seen, when conditions were right they could be heard. They were that distant buzz that reminded everyone they were being watched. They whispered of death.

In the past few days, I had wrongfully blamed drones for violating Lisbet's and my privacy and for setting my roof afire. Like the boy who cried wolf, I had cried drone twice. But that didn't mean I was wrong this time. The hairs on my neck were telling me I was right, even though I didn't want to be.

I started running. What had Corde called those who fled? "Squirters," he had said. I was a squirter.

Sirius ran with me. He thought it was a game. The buzz sounded louder and closer, but I wasn't sure what direction it was coming from.

Before he had disappeared, Pullman had joked about a drone being sent my way, or at least I had thought he was joking. He said he wouldn't be able to prevent me from being bug splat if that happened. Those were the kinds of drones he was used to; when a Hellfire Missile hits, there's not much in the way of remains. I doubted that was the kind of drone I was facing. A missile strike in the greater Los Angeles area would be noticed. A "nano" drone was another matter entirely, even though drone killer bees weren't yet a reality. A swarm wasn't coming my way. The Dumbledore was said to be the size of a small bird, not a bumblebee. That was the stinger I was worried about.

My eyes had adjusted as much as they could to the darkness. I looked around. I wanted to see possibilities, even if I wasn't sure what that looked like. There were no trees to be seen and nothing in the way of shelter. I was in an ideal spot to be ambushed. On one side of me was a canyon, and on the other was an embankment too steep to be traversed. I thought about trying to find a hiding spot but quickly rejected that idea. If a drone was coming after me, it would have infrared viewing. My body heat would be a giveaway; maybe a *dead* giveaway.

The mosquito sounds were definitely louder. I tried to track the noise. The lawnmower sounded as if it was directly overhead, but in the darkness I couldn't see more than a few dozen feet in any direction. I was in one of those dark patches between streetlamps. As I ran, I tried to think, tried not to panic, but my head was doing a Linda Blair. Even if I couldn't see my enemies, I knew they were coming for me.

As I drew nearer to the streetlamp, its light allowed me to better see the surrounding area. Unfortunately, there was no refuge to be seen. If I could get down into the canyon, I might find a stand of thick shrubbery, but the path was steep, and the odds were more in favor of my breaking a leg than finding shelter. If I stayed near the road, it was likely a car would come along, and I could flag it down. It might provide shelter enough from what was above, assuming it wasn't a Hellfire missile. This was supposed to be fucking L.A. But what if a car didn't come along?

I ducked my head, spooked by a shadow. Or maybe I was just jumping at shadows. The mosquito buzzing was filling my ears. I wondered how fast the drone could fly and how maneuverable it was. I looked up and around and wondered if whoever was operating the drone was staring at the whites of my eyes.

My breath was ragged. It wasn't like I could outrun a drone anyway.

I stopped running about fifty yards away from the streetlamp. I was tired of being a squirter. The attack would come soon, I was sure. I thought about firing a couple of rounds into the air. The gunshots would be noticed by someone. Maybe they'd bring my Ranger. But if an attack was imminent, that help wouldn't come in time.

An idea came to me, prompted by desperation. It was crazy, with little to no chance of success. But what else was there?

"Ninja," I said to Sirius.

My partner went on alert, ready to track down the disc. He didn't need for me to show him the disc; with ninja he had to be ready for a surprise, ready for anything. Or so I hoped.

"Ninja," I said again, and positioned him so that he was staring at me, following my every movement. Then I walked off a dozen steps, putting some distance between us.

Sirius's ears were up, and his body was tensed. It was Hail Mary time. I needed him for a miracle. Ever since our fire walk with Ellis Haines, I hadn't put in the time training Sirius that I should have. The average handler spends sixteen hours a month doing maintenance training with his charge. When we'd been with Metropolitan K-9, the two of us had regularly put in twenty-five hours of training in any given month. In K-9 parlance, I hadn't wanted to be a thirty-miles-per-hour trainer with a ninety-miles-per-hour dog. Sirius had always been exceptional; he needed an exceptional handler.

Post–fire walk, I should have been coaching him on tactical tracking, smoke deployment, building searches, suspect tests, and obedience. To get Sirius ready for the unknown, I should have been deploying him in different terrain and weather.

Now I was hoping that our playing with discs might save my life.

The buzzing came at me, and I began to run. "Ninja," I shouted.

I wondered if that would be the last word I ever spoke. It was better than saying "shit," I supposed—what Corde had said was the famous last word of most drone targets.

Even as the buzzing filled my ears, I heard another sound: breaking glass. My ears were playing tricks on me. I didn't know if the noise came from up the road or down the road. And then I sensed a shadow flying at me, and I was sure it was the drone. But I was wrong. The shadow belonged to my partner. Sirius had thrown himself into the air. On those occasions when Dr. J. and Michael Jordan flew fifteen feet through the air, their efforts were forever etched into the minds of spectators. Sirius's vault put them to shame. By my calculations he went almost twenty feet before his flight was cut short. I was the reason for that. Sirius's leap ended on my back. The impact of one hundred pounds of flying dog sent me airborne, and I came down hard at the side of the road.

That's when I felt the hot air of machinery too close, and my face was stung by pebbles shot up by shifting tires swerving on asphalt. A dark shadow—a black car—roared by, passing within inches. I had expected the attack to come from above, but it had come from the ground.

Sirius was on top of me, growling back at the threat and ready to protect me against anything. The breath was knocked out of me. I couldn't say anything, let alone growl. As I struggled for air, I shifted, and Sirius moved from my back to my side. His hackles were raised, and he was on the alert.

When I finally had breath enough to talk, I said, *"So ist brav,"* and gave him a hug. "You're the best boy in the world."

He liked the sound of that and started to furiously wag his tail. He must have thought I was okay too, because I got a big lick. This time I didn't do my Lucy speech about germs.

Once again the thought of a drone had put my head in the clouds, and I had been oblivious to what had been a more imminent threat. The drone had been the spotter. It was the car that was supposed to have killed me.

I slowly got to my feet. I was scraped all over and could feel seeping blood on my upper chest and face, but nothing was broken.

"You play a mean game of tackle," I told Sirius.

I had only gotten the briefest glance of the passing car; it had been accelerating along the straightaway with no lights and had come straight at me.

I listened for the mosquito sound; it wasn't to be heard. As I looked around, I could make out a distant glow I hadn't seen before. Somewhere down the road something was on fire. Flames were reaching for the sky. Normally, the sight of a raging fire would have scared the hell out of me, but for some reason I found it reassuring.

My cell phone, on silent mode, suddenly did its shake and bake.

"You alive?" asked a voice on the other line.

"Barely," I said to my Ranger. "I thought you had my six or seven or whatever the hell that number is that means you're covering my ass."

"It seems as if a lot of people wanted you dead, and there was only one of me. But don't go anywhere. I'm less than a click away from you. See you in five."

"You and your damn numbers," I said, but he'd already hung up.

CHAPTER 23:

GAMBLING IN CASABLANCA?

While I waited for Pullman, I could hear sirens sounding in the distance. There was a nearby fire station at the bottom of Mulholland, I remembered. It sounded as if everyone was converging on the fire. Sirius and I waited, well off the side of the road. A few cars passed by, but they meant us no harm. With all the activity it no longer felt as if my partner and I were the only ones living in L.A.

It was only because I felt Sirius tense that I turned. Despite Pullman's running at a fast clip, I had neither heard nor seen him.

"It's okay," I told Sirius, and he left my side and ran to Pullman.

When the Ranger reached me, I said, "So what the hell happened?"

"I was kind of hoping you could tell me," he said.

The light from the streetlamp was enough for him to see my scrapes. "I didn't think the driver would still be coming for you after I took out his windshield and forced his hand."

"I'd be dead if it weren't for Sirius."

"I got to get me a war dog."

"So who was it who tried to run me down?"

"That I don't know. But I'm pretty sure he was getting his orders from Novak. And I'd bet the farm that he's a pro who's done more than a tour or two with the CIA. Next time you have me watch your back, I'll need a program to sort out all the bad guys."

"What's that supposed to mean?"

"There were lots of players, Gideon. I spotted the minivan you told me to watch for. It was too dark to positively make out who the driver was, but it had to be our secret squirrel. He cruised up and down the road a few times, looking like some kind of a hungry shark trying to scare up a meal. But that was only the first player."

"How many players are there?"

"I count at least three, but there might be more. You almost got an up-close-and-personal introduction to our friend in the black Charger. And there was the third invitee who paid a visit to your parked car. But what say we talk while we walk?"

"Lead the way."

"Let's follow the sirens. I'm betting we're going to find your friend Novak."

"What makes you think that?"

"Because right after I threw two rock fastballs at the windshield of the Charger, a few things happened that I don't think were coincidental. First, I heard the noise of twisting metal caused by impact. And suddenly that lawnmower sound was no more. About that same time I noticed flames lighting up the sky down the road. Something must have happened to Novak and his car. He sent up his drone to spy on you and give directions to the driver of the Charger. Death by drone would have had every LAPD detective looking into your killing. Death by a hit-and-run on a crazy winding road after your car broke down would be one of those tragedies no one looks into very carefully."

"So you think something happened to Novak while he was operating the drone?"

"The timing of the fire suggests that. One moment the drone was aloft, and the next it wasn't. I didn't hear any explosion, but with most car fires there isn't one. Whatever the case, a fire doesn't combust like that without a lot of help."

"I'll take your word on the sequence of events," I said. "I was a bit preoccupied by a car trying to run me down."

"My bad," said Pullman, "but next time you send me into dark territory, at least give me something to fight with. Sticks and stones aren't my preferred weapons."

"And drones aren't mine."

He looked at me. "You well enough to run?"

When I nodded, he said, "Let's do it."

* * *

I got to hear most of Pullman's story while we ran. He hadn't been idle while scouting my parked car.

"The guy on the scooter was your first visitor," Pullman said.

This was beginning to sound like a Fellini film. "What guy on the scooter?"

"The guy who came along a little while after you got in the car with the star. He parked down the hill, and at first I thought he was just out for a little stroll. He walked by your car and went a little way up the fire road. I thought he was looking for a place to piss, but I guess he was just making sure no one was around. After he turned around and started walking back, he stopped by your car and bent down. I assumed he was tying the laces to his running shoes. But what he was doing was sabotaging your car."

"Describe him for me," I said.

"He was tall and thin. I'd put him at six one or so, and not much more than a buck fifty. He had his helmet on the entire time, but he moved like someone south of thirty."

That meant it wasn't Corde. And it wasn't Neal Bass.

"It's another shill in the audience," I said.

"What do you mean?"

"I'm not even sure. It's a gut feeling. Go on."

"I couldn't help but wonder if there might be something hinky about scooter guy, so I followed him down the hill. I expected he would head toward the 405, but instead he went the opposite way. From the dirt road above, I used my CSS scope and watched him pull up to our black Charger. Scooter guy nodded to whoever was sitting in the Charger, and then he reversed his route.

"This wasn't the first time I'd seen that Dodge Charger, by the way. It seemed odd to me that the driver just sat there waiting.

"I decided there wasn't much I could do besides join our mystery driver in his waiting game. When you finished with your silver screening—and I must say that from what I observed the two of you looked cozy together—I tried to call you to tell you what was going on. That's when I discovered my cell phone transmission was being jammed. I assumed Novak was lining you up in his crosshairs, so I decided the only thing I could do was to beat feet and try to get to our meet-up spot as quickly as I could.

"I made it to your abandoned car, and saw the directions you left for me. At about the same time, I heard the sounds of an approaching vehicle. Because I was operating under rules of engagement, I kept out of sight, which is why the driver of our curious Charger never saw me.

"From behind some brush I watched him insert some kind of pronged device up your tailpipe, and with two separate thrusts he pulled out the cause of your car's failure. I could actually smell the potatoes from where I was observing."

"Potatoes?"

"I'm pretty sure they were russets, and probably from Idaho. It was those potatoes that caused your engine to shut down. When the cylinder head fills with compressed exhaust, it cuts off the fuel. And without fuel the engine essentially runs out of gas."

"You want fries with that?" I muttered. "I didn't know about the potatoes. But I did notice both back tires impaled with metal wiring."

"For thousands of years caltrops have been used in war. That's why the driver of the Charger pulled out his pliers. I watched him remove the evidence of someone tampering with your car. That way, when your body was found down the road, everyone would assume it was just one of those unfortunate accidents of a driver leaving his broken vehicle and getting killed by a hit-and-run."

"What's our Mr. Potato Head look like?"

"He's a white guy, maybe forty, five foot nine and very fit. He moved like someone who knew what he was doing. After he finished covering up the tampering with your car, he drove down the road but didn't go all that far. I caught up with him and observed him for a minute. At first I couldn't understand why he was just sitting in his car and waiting, but then I heard the buzzing sound moving back and forth overhead, and it suddenly struck me that the eye in the sky was tracking you. And then I realized that Novak wasn't planning on sending a missile your way. That would have been a tad obvious. But what if he dispatched a different kind of missile? What if he was herding you to just the right spot on the road where a car could run you down? From his vantage point above, Novak would know when the coast was clear and when to dispatch his four-wheeled missile.

"I went a little ways down the canyon so that the driver wouldn't see me, and after skirting by him, I ran as hard as I could. I wanted to reach you before the Charger was given the green light, but I was too late. When the Charger came my way, I did what I could, but the two stones I threw only slowed it down. My hope was that the shattered windshield would cause your hit to be called off. No hit man wants anything to make him stand out. But I guess it wasn't deterrent enough. Thank God for your war dog."

"Amen," I said.

*　*　*

The fire was out before we arrived on the scene, but half a dozen emergency vehicles were still on the scene. Novak's Odyssey was gutted.

"It looks like a bomb hit it," I said.

"Or a drone," said Pullman.

"You mind keeping a low profile while I check on this?"

My Ranger pointed to a spot off the road. "I'll be sleeping over there."

*　*　*

The black Charger with the broken windshield was found the next morning in a Target parking lot in Burbank. The car had been stolen and was wiped clean of fingerprints.

As for the man on the scooter, that was a nonstarter. There are tens of thousands of wannabe hipsters living in the L.A. area, and it seemed as if every one of them drove a scooter.

In the two and a half days since almost being run down, I had been spinning my wheels in lots of directions but had come up with nothing. Everyone involved, or potentially involved, was stonewalling.

On advice of his team of lawyers, Drew Corde hadn't commented on what had happened other than to have one of his mouthpieces read a statement purportedly written by him that threw his erstwhile best friend to the wolves. According to his statement, "Longtime employee Rick Novak, of his own volition, engaged in questionable activities that resulted in his unfortunate death."

Corde's lawyer had gone so far as to say that Novak "had apparently and regrettably gone rogue for his own uncertain purposes."

OZ and Corde had put as much distance between themselves and Novak as possible. Their strategy seemed to be working; it's hard to connect dots when you're going against a legal team with lots of erasers.

That's why I was surprised to see Corde's name come up on my cell phone display.

"Detective Gideon?" he said. His usual bravado sounded noticeably absent.

"I'm glad you decided to return one of my many calls, Mr. Corde."

"As you undoubtedly know, I was being advised by my lawyers not to comment on this matter."

"And so why are you calling me now?"

"I thought it was time we had a chat, although I'm sure my lawyers would be apoplectic at the thought of such."

To my knowledge, Corde was the first person I had ever heard use the word "apoplectic" in a sentence.

"Here's to apoplexy," I said.

"Before I continue with this conversation, I need you to confirm that this call isn't being recorded and that no one but you is listening to me speak."

"You've got my ears only."

"I will take you at your word, with the understanding that a lie on your part would be entrapment."

"I already told you that this is between us. If you need it signed in blood, then let's arrange a face-to-face."

"I don't believe at this point such is necessary. At this juncture what I'm doing is sending up a trial balloon."

"And here I thought you only sent up drones."

He ignored my comment. "I think we both have things the other wants, Detective Gideon, but with the lawyers involved we are likely to be left wanting."

"So you want to cut a deal?"

"I want to come to an understanding."

"I'm not the only one working the case now. LAPD has investigators from SID, SIS, RHD, and Counter-Terrorism turning over rocks."

The acronyms were short for Scientific Investigations Division, the Special Investigation Section, and Robbery-Homicide Department.

"And that's just the homeboys," I said. "The Feds are also actively investigating."

"And what everyone is going to discover is that Rick Novak crossed the line. They are going to agree he must have been unbalanced to do what he did."

Corde was reminding me of the Claude Rains character of Captain Louis Renault in *Casablanca*. He knew he was lying, and I knew he was lying, but he had to play his part in the charade.

"'I'm shocked,'" I said, "'shocked to find that gambling is going on in here.'"

I didn't quote the next line, when the croupier showed up and handed Louis money, saying, "Your winnings, sir." I had seen *Casablanca* so many times that I could probably quote the entire film.

"From what I understand," said Corde, "there's been a lot of evidence uncovered that suggests Novak went rogue."

"Is that right? The way I see it, he didn't blow his nose without you knowing."

"That won't be the conclusion of others."

"Phone records show he talked to you minutes before he jammed communications."

"We spoke on an unrelated matter."

"What about his drone?"

"Please," said Corde. "What Novak was flying was more of a remote-controlled flyer than it was a UAV. From what I understand, it wasn't a commercial UAV, but something an experienced hobbyist could have built. If there was some tie-in with OZ, or with me, why wouldn't he have used a Dumbledore or a Wasp to attack you?"

"The answer is simple: you wanted plausible deniability in case anything went wrong."

"Your time would probably be better spent looking at Novak's erstwhile employment than his present job," said Corde.

"I suppose it was the CIA who got to Novak's house and computer and wiped everything clean?"

"Doesn't that sound like something they would do? And wouldn't Novak's training with them, and his contacts, also explain how he was able to obtain state-of-the-art jamming equipment?"

"Did you call me for any other reason than to try and spin an international conspiracy theory?"

"As I said, I might be able to supply you with information that I know you are most anxious to hear."

"So talk to me."

"I might know something about your mysterious man on the scooter."

"If you are as innocent as you say, then it would be to your advantage to tell me what you know."

"This is supposed to be quid pro quo. But I will tell you something for free: the man on the scooter didn't kill Rick Novak."

While Rick Novak had been trying to kill me with a drone, someone had taken him out with a Molotov cocktail. Two bottles filled with flammable material had been tossed into the sunroof of his minivan. For good measure, a third Molotov cocktail had been thrown at the driver's window and had shattered on impact. Both the inside and outside of the car had been ablaze within moments. Novak had died of smoke inhalation and burns.

"Then who did?"

"I don't know."

"If that's true, what good is your information?"

"You need to look for another murderer. I had nothing to do with Novak's death."

"Novak isn't my priority. And his homicide isn't my case. Even if it was, my top priority is Wrong Pauley. That's my interest."

"But what's your real interest?"

"I just told you."

"No, you didn't. You know to what I am referring. Or do you want me to pretend surprise and proclaim, 'Gambling in Casablanca?'"

So he did know my reference, just as I knew his.

"The trail has gone cold, Detective. You might think you have smoking guns, but all you have is smoke. And that's all you will have. I've been doing some overdue spring-cleaning. And though I am not admitting to any guilt, I am confident there is nothing that can tie me in to the attempt on your life."

"Then why are we talking?"

"You might be able to prove that I illegally deployed UAVs, but even that's no sure bet. I want to put everything behind me."

"I would think illegally deployed UAVs would be the least of your worries. Why is that important to you?"

"Isn't it obvious? OZ depends on its government contracts. If I were prosecuted for illegally operating a UAV, the government would likely be punitive. Even the cloud of illegality might cause the government to take its business elsewhere."

"Let's say I stopped looking at illegally operated drones. What do I get in return?"

"You'd get what you wouldn't otherwise, what with my spring-cleaning. There's no longer a trail for you to follow. Everything is gone now, do you understand? The only way you'll know is through me. And I think you'd give just about anything to know, wouldn't you?"

I didn't answer. I was glad he couldn't hear how loud my heart was beating or see my hungry expression.

"If you want to know the truth about angels, Detective, if you want to know the full story, we'll need to come to an understanding."

CHAPTER 24:

PRISONERS AND CONUNDRUMS

I tried to stall Corde. I wanted to believe I could get answers without him, but he knew my game and tactic and said he needed to hear from me in the next forty-eight hours. If we didn't come to some understanding by that time, he warned me, "You'll forever be in the dark." And then he added, "You don't want your angels to fly away, do you?"

Because I'd put my personal life on hold for so long, I allowed myself an evening for recess with Lisbet. Absence had made our hearts grow fonder, and for the time at least, our recent tiff seemed to be forgotten.

When Lisbet pulled up in my driveway, Sirius and I came out to greet her. Mouths and tongues came at Lisbet from all directions, and her laughter was contagious. When she disentangled herself from us, I gathered up the grocery bags. Tonight was going to be a treat: Lisbet had insisted on making dinner.

As we made our way up the walkway, Lisbet had her arm draped over my shoulder, and I had my arms around the groceries. My partner did a lot of tail wagging. I set the groceries on the kitchen counter and then took a seat on a barstool at that same counter. The only job Lisbet had assigned me was to get two bottles of wine and to make sure her glass didn't run dry while she made the meal.

"I took my task very seriously," I told Lisbet. "Earlier today I went to Mission Wine on Burbank Boulevard and spent an hour looking at their selection."

"I didn't realize you were such a connoisseur."

"I'm not. The only thing I know about wine is that it's made from grapes, and I guess even that's not an absolute."

"So did you select your bottles on the basis of the wine scoring?"

"Is that what those numbers mean?"

Lisbet looked at me skeptically, not sure if I was kidding her or not. "The scores are typically based on a hundred-point scale," she said, "and you're usually safe if you pick anything above an eighty-five from some respectable source like *Wine Spectator*."

"I think my way is superior."

"The cheaper, the better?"

"That's my usual methodology, but in this case I made my selections based on the wine labels."

"I've never heard an oenophile recommend that method."

"I would hate to be known as an oenophile. That sounds like something unsavory."

"*In vino veritas*," Lisbet said.

I did my W.C. Fields imitation, and recited his line: "'I cook with wine, and sometimes I even add it to the food.'"

"Why don't you open one of the bottles?" Lisbet asked. "Or did the label you choose come on a box?"

"You wound me. And here I didn't even consider picking up a bottle of The Bitch."

"That really wasn't a choice, was it?"

"It was. They also had Fat Bastard."

"How could you have possibly passed that one up?"

"I think my mistake was not getting a bottle of The Ball Buster."

"I think you showed uncommon wisdom not getting it."

"A clerk saw me stalking the wine aisles and asked if he could help me pick out the right bottle of wine. I told him I was more interested in the right label. And he said they were all out of Pinot Evil, which was one of his favorite labels. He said it shows a monkey covering its eyes."

"Monkey see, monkey do," said Lisbet. "What did monkey buy?"

"I almost went with Rocket Science."

"Why didn't you?"

"It made me think of drones."

"I'm glad you didn't get it then."

"As you can see, I ended up with a bottle of red and a bottle of white, both from Napa Valley."

I turned the labels toward her and she read from them: "Conundrum and The Prisoner."

"They spoke to my state of mind," I said.

"Let's hope they speak to our palates as well."

"Which would you like to try first?"

"Let's storm the Bastille," she said, and then squinted slightly, looking a little closer at the label. "I think that's Goya," she said, referring to the drawing on the bottle The Prisoner.

On the label was an etching of a bearded and bent prisoner snared in leg irons. Lisbet makes her living as a graphic artist, and in her spare time she loves to go to museums and galleries. She is probably the only person in Los Angeles who could have identified the artist whose work was featured on a wine label.

"Goya," I agreed. "That's exactly what I thought when I saw the drawing on the label."

"I would snort, except that I'd rather have a snort."

"You doubt me?"

"It's too bad you didn't pick up a bottle of Big Fat Liar."

"I didn't see that one; otherwise I might have."

As I applied a corkscrew to one of the bottles I said, "It's time I freed the prisoner."

While I poured our glasses, Lisbet was busy cutting up some red potatoes. She tossed them in a skillet bubbling with butter and olive oil. Between sips of wine, she added garlic and rosemary. As the aromatics filled the room, I sniffed appreciatively. While the potatoes cooked, she composed the Caesar salad, complete with shavings taken from a wedge of Parmesan cheese. Everything looked wonderful until I noticed the anchovies.

"Really?" I said. "Hairy little fish?"

"It's not a real Caesar salad without anchovies."

"I appreciate hairy dogs; I don't appreciate hairy fish."

"Those aren't hairs. They are bones."

I reached for one of the hairy fish and examined it. Doubting Lisbet is always a mistake. What appeared to be hairs were actually thin, little bones.

"Dem bones, dem bones, dem dry bones," I sang.

Lisbet ruined my song by not only singing it on-key but getting in the last word. "Hear the word of the poured," she sang. And then she waved an empty wine glass my way.

I filled her glass while she checked the broiler, which was apparently hot enough. Lisbet had told me she was going to the butcher's shop to pick out something special.

She removed the butcher paper and said, "Voila! Someone here has certainly earned his dry-aged Black Angus T-bone steak."

Then she leaned down and patted the only one of us with a tail.

"I hope you're going to throw me a bone?"

"If you're lucky."

It wasn't what she said, but the way she said it. The evening was looking very promising.

"Did you make it to the dry cleaners on time?" she asked.

When we'd talked earlier, I had been hurrying to make it there before they closed. "I did," I said, "but I'm hoping I'll just be window dressing to the Chief while he's window dressing to the mayor."

The ceremony for the Reluctant Hero was being held in the morning.

"All the media agreed not to use the Hero's name?"

When we'd talked, I had explained to Lisbet how I had uncovered the identity of the Reluctant Hero and had been working on his behalf to maintain his privacy.

"His continued anonymity is part of the package."

"All's well that ends well," she said.

It wasn't exactly the ending the Ranger might have hoped for, but I didn't say anything. I had kept my promise to Pullman. Even Lisbet hadn't heard his story. No one ever would, at least not from me. If Pullman was lucky, the secret of his forbidden love and biological son would never come out.

I watched Lisbet working a pepper mill over the steaks. She had brought the pepper mill, knowing I didn't have one. To her thinking it's a travesty to use ground pepper as opposed to fresh cracked pepper. She also sprinkled a pinch of kosher salt (something else she had brought with her) on each of the steaks before sticking them under the broiler.

For the two-legged, it was a ten-minute wait, five minutes on each side. The four-legged one of us took his steak rare, two minutes per side. Before we even began to eat, Sirius was done and licking his chops.

The meal was wonderful, even the hairy fish salad. And then Lisbet plated up some pound cake with raspberries and whipped cream. Sirius wasn't totally denied; he got a serving of raspberries with just a hint of the cream.

"It was a banquet fit for a king," I told Lisbet. "I really can't thank you enough."

"Open that second bottle of wine, and maybe I'll call it even," she said.

I did battle with another cork, won my joust, and poured.

"Conundrum," said Lisbet.

"A wine that I chose not so much as an accompaniment to the meal," I explained, "but more as a commentary on the state of my case."

Lisbet raised her wineglass. "Here's to you solving your conundrums."

We clinked glasses.

"I thought wine was supposed to loosen tongues," said Lisbet. "But you've yet to talk of your conundrums."

"My tongue is loose," I said, "but I didn't want to burden your ears."

"Wine is great for opening up ear canals."

"In that case I'll open the floodgates."

With her encouragement, I began talking about my professional conundrums.

"One of the stumpers is the man on the scooter," I said. "Who is he, and who was he working for? And did he set me up for the kill, or was he setting Novak up? If I'm to believe Corde, Novak wasn't murdered by the scooter guy. If that's true, then who brought down the fire on him?"

"Do your suspects have alibis?" asked Lisbet.

"Every one of them," I said, "and they're all airtight. The conspiracy theorists might say the CIA took Novak out to shut him up. If I'd had the chance to arrest Novak for the murder of Wrong Pauley, and it was proven he was involved in other nefarious activities, he would have proved an embarrassment to the Agency despite being retired from it. Novak's death also conveniently prevented him from having to answer questions about how he had procured the kind of high-tech equipment no civilian should be able to possess."

"But you're not a conspiracy theorist?" said Lisbet.

"In the words of Ben Franklin, 'Three may keep a secret if two of them are dead.'"

"I wish I could offer insights into your conundrums, but I'm not even good at Clue."

"It was easier when Colonel Mustard had a candlestick for a murder weapon. Now he has a drone."

"I always guess Miss Scarlet did it with the knife. And I'm always wrong."

"I know the feeling. I kept getting it wrong with this case. I was late putting Novak into the equation, and then he was murdered before I had a chance to talk to him. Just when I'm thinking I'm making some headway, everything goes to hell. Or everyone goes to hell."

"Doesn't it stand to reason that Novak was the fall guy for Corde?"

"It makes sense," I said, "but I'm not sure if it's right. With his longtime hunting partner gone, Corde doesn't have anyone to do his dirty work. And he offered up a not-so-veiled hint that any potential incriminating evidence against him is now gone. But I'm holding out hope for a silver lining."

"You think there's evidence that Corde doesn't know about?"

"I think it's more of a case that he does know about it. Just before I was attacked, I met with Elle Barrett Browning. I suspect the only reason she's with Corde is because he has something on her. And if his blackmail was illegally obtained, then it's likely he has now disposed of it for fear of being prosecuted if it was found in his possession. If that's the case, and there's no longer a sword hanging over her head, Elle might be freed up to supply dirt on Corde."

"Have you talked with her since your meeting?"

I shook my head. "She hasn't returned my calls or texts, but I'm guessing, with recent events, her handlers have her in lock-down mode. Rule number one in Hollywood is to protect the gravy train."

"What I don't understand is why Corde would tell you that he's destroyed evidence."

"He wanted to make it clear he was still holding the trump card and that he wasn't giving it up without extorting a price."

"What trump card is that?"

"He's willing to throw me the identity of the man on the scooter, but he knows that's not a big enough hook to snare me."

"So what else does he have?"

"He says he'll tell me about the angel," I said. "He says the only way I'll ever learn anything is by going through him."

"Do you believe him?"

"I believe he got rid of any and all evidence that might pertain to angels, or what was believed to be an angel. And I'm afraid I'll never get answers to my questions without his cooperation."

"What does Corde want in return for his information?"

"He says my investigating his use of UAVs outside of the workplace is not good for his business."

"So if you back off, he'll tell you about angels."

"That's what he's selling."

"You don't make a deal with the devil," Lisbet said, "to learn about angels."

It was what I was thinking, but I couldn't have said it better.

Together we finished the bottle of Conundrum. I didn't get any insight into the too many conundrums perplexing me, but I did get to spend unhurried time with Lisbet, and I counted that as a very good thing indeed.

CHAPTER 25:

THE LONE RANGER

The Peter Gunn theme started playing in the darkness of my bedroom. Next to me I could feel Lisbet stirring. I looked at the clock and saw that it was three thirty.

Not again, I thought, remembering the middle-of-the-night call the last time Lisbet and I had been together. For a moment I was afraid if I answered the phone, I'd again hear a replay of our lovemaking. I still hadn't told Lisbet about that intrusion; it was yet something else in our relationship I kept putting off.

I answered the phone without checking caller ID, intent on silencing the song before it really got into its pounding beat: "Gideon," I said.

"Well at least I don't have to apologize for waking *you* up," said the caller.

His voice sounded familiar. "Who is this?"

"It's Holt from RHD."

Dave Holt worked Robbery-Homicide and was the lead detective in the Rick Novak homicide. He had made it clear my help was neither wanted nor needed in that investigation, even though I had argued that our cases dovetailed. Holt had done what cops call a Bigfoot, taking over anything having to do with the case and moving me aside.

"What do you want?"

"You and Drew Corde had a fairly lengthy conversation a few hours ago. I need to know what you talked about."

"You're calling me in the middle of the night to ask that?"

"I'm calling the people Corde talked to on his cell phone yesterday, and you happen to be among that number."

"He died?"

"You catch on quick, Gideon."

I bit off a reply that might have made me feel good and would have put into question Holt's matriarchal line, but wouldn't have gotten me the information I needed. "What happened?"

"According to Elle Barrett Browning, who was an eyewitness, he shot himself after a night of drinking."

"Did she make a statement?"

"She did, and without a lawyer present."

"I'd like to talk to her."

"Maybe that can be arranged, but right now I need to know about your tête-à-tête with Corde."

His words held out promise, but I knew if I didn't get time with Elle right now, it wasn't going to happen.

"I need five minutes with her."

Holt decided to dash my hopes. "It will have to be worked out another time, Gideon. We got a three-ring circus going on, what with Brownie's being a part of this."

Brownie, I thought. That's what Elle's good friends supposedly called her. Holt's familiarity was annoying, but what was worse was being frozen out. I didn't have an invitation to a party I wanted to attend.

"So why did Corde call you?" he asked.

"He wanted to offer me a full confession before he killed himself," I said.

"The clock is ticking, Gideon. There's no time for you to be sulking in the corner."

Holt was an asshole, but he was also right. "Corde was trying to make a deal. He was dangling the possibility of giving us something for getting something."

"And what was he going to give us?"

"He said he knew who was driving the scooter. And he also said the scooter driver didn't kill Novak."

"How would you characterize his mood?" he asked.

"Do you mean did he sound like someone ready to off himself?"

"That wasn't the question I asked. I'll repeat my question."

"You don't need to."

I answered his question while chewing the inside of my cheek, and did more chewing while answering a few dozen more of his questions. After about fifteen minutes Holt thanked me for my help and said he would call me if he had any more questions.

I didn't let him hang up without hearing my thoughts: "Corde said if we didn't work out a deal in the next forty-eight hours, then it was off the table. That doesn't sound like someone who's about to kill himself."

"Moods are known to change with the amount of liquor being sucked down."

"Narcissists don't kill themselves."

"You speaking from experience?"

"Sounds like you got the case solved already, Holt. That's good work from an investigator everyone says couldn't find his own ass with two hands and a flashlight."

Holt had two words for me that weren't "good night," and then he hung up. I was glad our conversation ended when it did.

Although Holt and I had gone over most of what Corde and I had discussed, the subject of angels had for some reason not come up.

Lisbet propped herself up with a few pillows. "What happened?" she asked.

"Drew Corde supposedly committed suicide."

I leaned over and kissed her cheek. "I'm sorry I woke you up."

"Don't worry about me. I've got a ringside seat."

"And I'm punch drunk."

"You don't think Corde killed himself, do you?"

"When a guy loves himself as much as Corde did, it's a lot easier for me to imagine him throwing others under the bus than throwing himself."

"Maybe he was so egotistical he couldn't endure the possibility of a fall from grace."

"Maybe," I conceded, while thinking about Sister Marie Bernadette. Lisbet's comment about a fall from grace had been one of Sister Bernie's favorite topics in Catholic school. "You don't want to get on the wrong side of God," she had always warned.

Anyone that hunted angels, or even pretended to, had to be on the wrong side of God.

"What are you going to do?" asked Lisbet.

"I'm frozen out by the detectives working the case, so I'm going to have to work it from my own Siberia. But Pullman's ceremony this morning comes first."

"No," said Lisbet, reaching for me. "This comes first."

Suddenly I didn't feel so frozen out.

* * *

The centerpiece of the LAPD police badge is the Los Angeles City Hall Building. I am biased, but I think no police force has a more attractive badge. The art deco look works well as a building and as a badge. The tower was based on the Mausoleum of Mausolus, which was said to be one of the Seven Wonders of the Ancient World. While plenty of figurative bodies were buried at City Hall, I wasn't aware of any actual ones.

In the past I'd visited City Hall for purposes of both business and pleasure. If you want one of the best views in LA., you need go no further than the observation deck on the building's twenty-seventh floor. Best of all, there's no charge, unless you include the extortionate price for nearby parking.

Normally, I'm leery of spending too much time in one of L.A.'s skyscrapers. Just because earthquakes are a part of life for Angelenos doesn't mean I am comfortable with shaking buildings, but politicians being the survivalists they are, there is probably no safer place to be in L.A. during an earthquake than in the thirty-two-story City Hall building. A huge amount of money had been spent retrofitting the 1928 edifice so that it exceeded all earthquake standards. It wasn't an expenditure put before the citizenry, because protecting politicians has never been high on anyone's list of priorities except the lists of politicians themselves.

Partly to stretch my legs, and partly because I didn't want to be bothered putting in for validated parking, I parked a few blocks away in Little Tokyo and walked over. Sirius was lucky; he got snooze time in the car. The mayor's office was housed in City Hall, and the Reluctant Hero press conference was taking place in one of its meeting rooms.

When I entered the building, security was tight. I thought it ironic that once I was inside City Hall I had to show my badge displaying City Hall. One of the guards scrutinized it for what seemed overly long.

"Look familiar?" I asked.

He grunted, and I was allowed to bypass the metal detectors. I took the elevator up to the twenty-second floor, and then had to switch to a second elevator in order to continue my ascent.

When Pullman saw me enter the meeting room, he untangled himself from Sergeant Maureen Kinsman of LAPD Media Relations and made a beeline for my side. I felt a bit of déjà vu. Maureen had been my handler when the Chief had presented me with a Medal of Valor, and Sirius had received a Liberty Award. At the time I felt as uncomfortable as Pullman now looked.

"I thought you told me this was going to take no more than fifteen minutes," he said.

"Once it starts, it will be short and sweet," I promised.

Pullman was wearing his dress Ranger uniform, complete with beret, which he kept twisting and turning on his head.

"Where's your better half?" he asked.

"Sirius begged off. He said to send you his regards and hopes you don't mind his not being here, but there's something about politicians that brings out the rabid dog in him."

"Me too," said Pullman. "You should have brought him. Even if he put the bite on a politician, there's not a jury in the land that would convict him."

"I hope you're not thinking of doing the same."

"Don't tempt me. After this ceremony is over, I'm flying out of L.A., and a few days after that I'll be deploying. It's going to be a relief to return to fighting."

He meant every word he was saying.

"This time I'm the one who's got your six," I said.

"Your PR lady said my name won't be released, and my face won't be shown."

"All the media has agreed to that and more."

He gave a nervous glance at all the news cameras, and looked back at me.

"After I heard the news this morning, I was afraid you weren't going to be here," said Pullman. "It sounds like the shit hit the fan with your case."

"That pretty much describes it."

"I hate to say this, but I'm glad of the timing. With all that shitstorm going on, I'm just yesterday's news."

"If you hadn't been there," I said, "no matter what the circumstances for your being there, I hate to think what might have happened. You deserve the thanks of this city."

He shrugged, uncomfortable hearing what I felt necessary to say. Pullman's eyes scanned the room again.

"Will she be here?" I asked.

He shook his head. "They don't know anything about the ceremony. And I'm pretty sure they won't be tuning into the news today, which means they won't be able to make a connection between me and the Reluctant Hero."

"And why won't they be watching the news?"

"Kelley was having contractions yesterday. Today her water broke. I think she and D.C. are going to be preoccupied."

"You're not going to stay for the birth?"

"I'm going to get the hell out of Dodge," he said. "I told my brother that I'd been recalled early."

"You won't be able to avoid them the rest of your life."

He shrugged. The way he did it seemed far too fatalistic for my comfort.

"And I might need you for more backup."

That got a little smile out of him.

"You got a good woman, Gideon?"

"I do."

"So you got a good woman and a war dog. A man can't ask for more than that, can he?"

"No, he can't."

Maureen was signaling to Pullman. The mayor and Chief Ehrlich were both moving toward the stage. The ceremony was about to begin.

"It's time for you to go and get your key to the city," I said.

Pullman took a deep breath, once more looked for a face that wasn't there and never would be, and then went to join Maureen.

CHAPTER 26:

A BRISKET, A BASKET

There was something about the notion of Caine Pullman's forbidden love that kept playing in my head like the refrain of an unwanted song. From experience I knew that trying to ignore the thought would just increase its percolation, and the only way to damper the jack-in-the-box was to acknowledge it. I took out a notebook and on a clean page of paper wrote the words "Forbidden love." That sufficiently silenced the "Pop Goes the Weasel" music and allowed me to get on with my work.

On another fresh piece of paper I wrote, "Drew Corde." I had read the media reports, but I needed more than that. I called Dave Holt's cell number and was pleasantly surprised when he picked up.

"I'm surprised a celebrity like you would talk to a nobody like me," I said.

Holt and the other Robbery-Homicide detectives working Corde's death had been featured on the news plenty, even if it was only to say, "No comment."

"Call me a glutton for punishment," he said.

"The media still camped out there?"

There had been any number of news reports from in front of the Police Administration Building.

"They were around earlier," Holt said. "We can't open the windows and that means we can't use the media as target practice."

RHD was located on the seventh floor. Maybe the suits had been worried about water balloons.

"I am trying to close the Wrong Pauley case," I said. "As you know, it had a potential tie-in with Corde."

It wouldn't do for Holt to know I was investigating his own case.

"And I was wondering what kind of weapons you found at Corde's house," I said.

"There was nothing exotic if that's what you mean," Holt said. "There were three handguns, including the popgun that killed him, the Beretta Tomcat .32."

"Did he have a California Concealed Carry Permit?"

"All the guns were registered. Friends say he often carried the Beretta in an ankle holster."

"I'm not buying those reports about his drinking heavily that night. He sure didn't sound lit when he called me. He struck me as a guy who always liked being in control."

"You call a blood alcohol level of 1.7 in control?"

That information wasn't public knowledge. "That high?" I said.

"He and Brownie were having themselves quite a party."

There was a prurient note to his words.

"I heard they had sex," I said. Actually I hadn't heard that, as it hadn't been in the news.

"It looked like he went out riding a bucking bronco," Holt said.

"But why would anyone kill himself after having sex with Elle Barrett Browning?"

Holt felt the need to educate the masses. "A shrink we consulted with said that kind of depression is common, especially when combined with alcohol. She said lots of men have PCT, which stands for post-coital something or other. The doc even quoted some Latin phrase she said has been around for thousands of years. It was something like 'All animals are sad after sex.'"

"That sounds like psychobabble," I said, trying to keep him talking. "Singing the blues is one thing; shooting yourself is another."

"According to Brownie and others, he was despondent about the fallout from Novak and blamed himself for the hit his company had taken by letting bad things happen on his watch."

"If he was so despondent, how was he able to party like a rock star and have sex?"

"He got all maudlin afterward. Brownie said he got into this bad funk. She tried to talk him out of it, but she'd also been hitting the sauce and ended up falling asleep. When she woke up, it was to him holding a gun to his head. She tried to pull it away from him, but he fought her off."

"And you're attributing that to PCT?"

"Among ourselves we got another name for it," said Holt. "We're calling it 'bangst.'"

* * *

Holt pretty much clammed up after that. He must have figured out that I wasn't only calling up about my case. As much as I didn't like being frozen out, working from Siberia had its advantages. I worked the case mostly from my home, filling notebooks with my questions and observations and putting my case notes in order. I called other detectives in RHD and found out what I could. I referenced Holt's "bucking bronco" remark and heard about the scratches on Corde's arms and hands. It wasn't clear if those scratches had been sustained during lovemaking or the struggle for his gun. Although it hadn't been released to the public, I was told traces of Corde's skin and DNA had been found under Elle's nails.

There was nothing in the evidence—not in the blood splatter, the angle of bullet entry, ballistics, or the preliminary forensic pathology results—that contradicted Elle's story. After giving her statement, Elle had submitted to a physical examination, which corroborated that she and Corde had engaged in sex shortly before his death.

After cooperating with the initial investigation, Elle Barrett Browning had gone into seclusion. Her manager said she was "grief-stricken." In the three days since Corde's death, the tragic love story of Elle Barrett Browning and Drew Corde had begun taking on epic proportions. The story being spun was that they were the ultimate power couple said to have an equally powerful love. Around the world there was an outpouring of support for Elle.

I was too busy to send her flowers, but hundreds of others did.

* * *

A Porsche Boxster can go from zero to sixty miles an hour in a little more than five seconds, but despite the inequity of our respective automobile engines it wasn't hard tailing Neal Bass. The El Segundo traffic reined him in, and the fire-engine red color of his car allowed me to easily keep him in sight. His driving hadn't improved since I had last talked to him, and I watched him not yield to a pedestrian stepping into the crosswalk. What he did stop for was lunch at Britt's BBQ, a hole in the wall on Main Street.

It took me a minute to find a parking space; by then Bass had already put in his order. He didn't notice me enter the restaurant or place my own order. I waited until my food was ready before joining him. He was already halfway through his brisket and mac and cheese. I found room at his table for my barbecue tacos and iced tea.

His face fell at the sight of me. I guess he thought Corde's death meant he would never see me again. Bass had been eating his lunch with apparent pleasure, but at my appearance he dropped his fork and looked like he had lost his appetite.

"I brought you a DMV handbook," I said, waving the booklet before finding a place for it next to his tray. "You're going to need to study the part about pedestrians in a crosswalk. Five minutes ago you neglected to yield. I'm afraid you're looking at another moving violation."

"This is harassment," he said. "You're violating my rights. It's clear you are trying to blackmail me. As such, there's no way any ticket you might give me would stand up in court."

Country music was playing in the background. I took a bite of one of my tacos. It was a fusion combination I hadn't tried before and was as tasty as I had hoped it might be.

"You have a great way of sounding aggrieved," I said, "but facts are ugly things when you're on the wrong side of them. It's your smokescreen that wouldn't stand up in court, but I do think your lament has potential as a country song."

I tried on some lyrics for him: "A tisket, a tasket, brisket in my basket."

Ella Fitzgerald had made similar lyrics work, but I was no Ella Fitzgerald.

"What do you want?" asked Bass.

I reached for Bass's side order of sweet potato fries and took a handful. At least he had picked out a winning dining spot. Bass put a protective hand over his beignet.

"We need to talk about the one who didn't get away," I said. "And now that Corde is dead, I'd like to revisit the subject of angels."

CHAPTER 27:

PHILADELPHIA STORY

When you want to clear your mind, few things work better than a walk. Sirius and I were on our second walk of the day at the Van Nuys Sherman Oaks Park. It was quieter than usual; normally, kids are running around the baseball and soccer fields, but for the moment those fields were empty. There were some people playing tennis, and one older man was shooting hoops. The most popular area in the complex is usually the pool, but even that seemed unusually quiet.

Sirius and I stayed on the outskirts of the park, traveling along a trail that goes around it. We practiced drills as we walked; the handler probably needed the work more than his charge.

As we went through our exercises, I spoke to Sirius about the case. Luckily he knows the difference between my command voice and conversational chatter.

"Let's say Corde didn't kill himself," I said. "That means Elle was complicit in his murder. But why would she wait until now to be involved in his murder? And what would make her do something as drastic as that?"

With my hand I motioned for Sirius to stop and wait.

"You know what W.C. Fields once said? 'Show me a great actress and you've seen the devil.' We've been looking for an angel, but maybe we should have been hunting down a devil."

I gestured for Sirius to come to me and then motioned for him to sit. He was flawless; I couldn't say the same thing about me.

"Elle knows about choreography. She knows about staging. She could have given a lot of thought to how to murder Corde. She could have encouraged him to get drunk, and seduced him, and made sure the sex was rough so that she could claim they later struggled. She could have practiced her lines to the police and known just what to say.

"Is she a great actress?" I asked aloud.

"Is she the devil?" I whispered.

Sirius sat and waited.

I wondered what had prompted Fields to make his observation that great actresses were the devil. Certainly he had worked with some great actresses, including Sarah Bernhardt, Mae West, and Dorothy Lamour.

"Fields was probably just being funny," I said.

I gestured for Sirius to circle around me, had him do it a second time, and then motioned for him to lie down. With a little grunt he did.

"Fields was known for his one-liners. That's reason enough for anyone not to read into them. When he was asked what he wanted for his epitaph on his tombstone, Fields said, 'On the whole, I'd rather be in Philadelphia.'"

There are a lot of crazy people who talk to themselves. That's why it's good I have a dog. Most people don't think you're crazy if you talk to your dog. I'm not sure if that speaks more to those judging your mental state or to the person talking to a dog. In my case, it helps when I say things aloud. It's the "open sesame" effect that doesn't always happen with the written word. Sometimes doors unexpectedly open. Sometimes logjams clear.

"Philadelphia," I said.

I took off at a run, Sirius at my side.

* * *

Elle Barrett Browning agreed to meet with me without legal representation. Through her intermediaries I had advised her that an "off-the-record meeting" would be in her best interests. As I specified, she met me without her lawyer, but that didn't mean she wasn't well coached.

I wanted her to be comfortable, so we met at a place of her choosing, the office of her business manager. I was the first to arrive there and was shown to a meeting room. While I waited for Elle to arrive, I emptied my briefcase and arranged the items I had brought on a table.

She arrived almost half an hour late and came into the meeting room without fanfare or apology. Elle was wearing black, her color of choice since Corde's death. She had come out of mourning to finish the shoot of her movie but had remained out of the public's eye. Despite that, or because of it, her so-called tragedy had added extra juice to her star power.

"Thank you for meeting with me," I said.

Elle nodded. Grief seemed to become her. She had undeniable physical beauty.

When she was seated and looking at me, I said, "Today I wanted to meet with you for the purpose of having you confess to the murder of Drew Corde."

Her eyes widened in surprise. Whatever she was expecting, this wasn't it. It seemed to be the accepted opinion of everyone and everything, including law enforcement, that Drew Corde had killed himself.

"Is this a joke?" she asked.

"It is anything but a joke. If you confess to the murder, I am sure you and your lawyer can come up with some heart-wrenching explanation as to what drove you to such an act. You'll serve time, but among your fan base I am sure your sympathy quotient will go through the roof. It's even possible you'll be out of prison in time to resurrect your film career.

"In the court of public opinion, something you care very much about, you could potentially end up in good standing. Should you not choose to confess, I will have to charge you with other crimes, and I fear those subsequent revelations would forever turn that court of public opinion against you."

"What are these imaginary crimes?"

I ignored her question. It had taken me ten days of nonstop work to get to this point. Most homicide investigations proceed at a glacial pace. I had gone for light speed, but I was gambling on this meeting, and this moment.

"During the last two weeks I've learned everything I can about your life. I am sure even your most ardent fans don't know more about you than I do."

"I am honored," she said, her words laced with sarcasm.

"You never did a remake of *The Philadelphia Story*," I said.

"I don't remember ever saying that I did."

Her reply was measured, and it was pitch-perfect, but as much as she tried to hide her sudden fear, I could sense its presence.

"Your former fiancé said it, though. That's how your manager and publicist now refer to Corde, don't they? He said it in response to your chiding him about what went on in the Bunker. Corde always liked to have the upper hand when it came to your relationship, so his rejoinder to your remark was that the

Bunker was a perfect place to watch a screening of you in *The Philadelphia Story*."

"You must have misheard."

I shook my head. "That's what he said. But why would he say such a thing?"

"He must have been mistaken."

"I don't think so. Corde was speaking in code to you, but I didn't get his reference at the time. 'The Philadelphia Story' is how the two of you cryptically referred to the film Corde was holding over you, wasn't it?"

She opened her mouth, but I didn't give her time to deny or to lie.

"The nickname for Philadelphia is 'the City of Brotherly Love.' I guess it would have been too obvious for the two of you to refer to your private film as 'Chinatown.'"

Elle got my incest reference. In all the magazine articles on Elle that I had gleaned, in all the interviews, her beautiful indigo-colored eyes were always mentioned. No one had ever written how cold they could also look.

"I suppose I should have known something was up when I quoted my favorite Hepburn line from *The Philadelphia Story*, and you didn't react. That's because you didn't know the movie, or at least that screen version of it. You had your own version.

"You and your brother had a miserable upbringing. Your father abandoned the two of you when you were young. Your father had demons of his own, but they didn't compare to your mother's. I sympathize for Elle Browning, the girl. I know your mother's schizophrenia made your life a living hell.

"I was abandoned by my own mother when I was a newborn. That was never easy for me to accept, but over time I've come to realize I was lucky. I was raised by a loving family. It's possible your mother loved you—somehow she did keep you and your brother together—but I'm sure the two of you would have been better served by being removed from that household. In interviews you've only hinted at how difficult it was, and you've tried to put a positive spin on your circumstances, saying you learned at a very young age how to be an actress. It was your coping mechanism for a mother who terrorized you and your brother. There was little stability in your life and scant comfort from the nightmare who was your mother. You and your brother feared for your lives.

"Everyone always hears the saying that misery loves company. You lived that. Your brother, Robert, was only a year older than you. But he took his older brother role seriously. He protected you as best he could, and each of you comforted the other. There came a time when the two of you crossed a line, but your upbringing was so neglectful and haphazard, the two of you probably didn't even know it."

"How dare you imply—"

I spoke over her false umbrage. "When I went to talk to you at St. Vincent's, I got a look at your brother, but I didn't know it at the time. Others were similarly misled. In interviews you always said your brother was an accountant living a quiet life and had no interest in the limelight. I saw a man bringing you tea and just assumed he was your personal assistant. As it turns out, that's what everyone believed, even your closest companions. Later that day, I saw him opening doors for you. That's what personal assistants do, isn't it? But there was something about his protectiveness that should have made it clear to me that it wasn't just a job for him. He didn't like me because I was making you upset. No one ever suspected that your personal assistant, Joe Valentine, was really Robert Browning. I saw him looking out for you as an older and protective brother might, but it was even more than that, wasn't it?"

I hadn't understood why there was something about Caine Pullman's forbidden love that kept tugging at me. Some loves are the most forbidden of all.

"Corde and Novak uncovered the story behind your relationship with Robert. My guess is that Corde was fixated on you before the two of you ever met, and he had the resources to be a most unusual stalker. With Novak's help, the two of them used one of their flying toys to spy on you. I imagine you weren't the first star they targeted. Corde was twisted. It doesn't surprise me that he was a pervert and a Peeping Tom. Maybe he and Novak had that in common. I suppose they considered their actions just another form of hunting. The two of them used a UAV to spy on you at your Malibu house and were able to shoot intimate footage. I'm sure Corde didn't know at first that your personal assistant was actually your brother. Novak probably did a search on your lover and discovered his background. And with his Philadelphia story, Corde blackmailed you.

"From what I know of Corde, he didn't have a conscience. He always just took what he wanted. But ultimately he wasn't the only one doing the using. Corde got his beautiful star, and you got your Tony Stark boyfriend. It was a mutual lie, but then it was a relationship built on lies."

I didn't think it possible, but Elle's face had turned ugly. "It's your vile conjecture that has been built on lies," she hissed. "You haven't a shred of evidence to back up your disgusting stories."

"I have your brother," I said. "He's the mysterious man on the scooter. My eyewitness saw him, even though we didn't make the connection at the time. My eyewitness identified his scooter. Robert disabled my car. He was part of the conspiracy to try and have me killed. He communicated with the hired assassin who was supposed to run me down; he gave him the all-clear signal.

"Corde was going to give Robert up to me for a price. I suspect he told you his plan and tried to convince you that your brother would ultimately walk and that you needn't worry. But just as Robert is protective of you, so you are of him. You were afraid of the consequences of him being arrested because you knew your brother would be the primary suspect in Novak's murder."

"Bobby had nothing to do with that!"

"Who did?"

"I swear Bobby is innocent. You don't know him. He's gentle. He's compassionate. He only agreed to be involved in this because of me. But he would never murder."

"Even if your brother didn't fry Novak, he's still a coconspirator."

"He only did what Novak ordered him to do."

"Is that your excuse?" I asked. "You helped set me up. From the first you made me think Corde and his drones were omnipresent. When we had our silent interview at the hospital, you blamed the situation on the paparazzi, but at the same time you made me think Corde had surveillance everywhere. I think the real truth is you didn't want your brother overhearing us talk.

"You played me like a pro. When I asked you questions about angels, you knew it was personal to me and pretended you knew things. I'm pretty sure that's one thing that Corde didn't share with you. When you mentioned hearing him say something about a 'seraph's last tariff,' you made that up. Corde wasn't poetic that way. It was Corde's and Novak's secret. Maybe even they knew there were limits to a hunt, even if it doesn't seem that way.

"You strung me along with that story about the friendly cop protecting you from your mother. And when you pretended that I was the kind of good man you were always hoping to find, I couldn't help but be flattered. I'm glad I didn't get caught up in the fantasy you were offering. I'm lucky I have a girlfriend who I didn't want to disappoint any more than I already do. I'd certainly be dead if I had paid attention to your charms. I suspect that was Corde's mistake in the end. On his last night alive, I think you convinced him that you really loved him."

She shook her head back and forth. "All of your wild theories add up to nothing. Everything you've said is guesswork."

"And here's a little more of that guesswork: Novak's death played perfectly into your hands. Novak was Corde's hunting partner, and he carried out all his dirty work. With Novak gone, Corde panicked. I'm sure you spurred his fears. Corde told me, off the record, that he had destroyed all evidence that could implicate him. I'm certain he even got rid of your Philadelphia story. After all, that videotape had been obtained illegally, and was a piece of evidence that could help take him down. I'm sure that is what concerned him much more than the content of the tape. His consideration wasn't that the tape could destroy your career, but that it could hurt him. In Corde's world he was the only thing that mattered.

"Where he miscalculated was in how you would respond to his plans. If he hadn't threatened your brother, I doubt you would have acted as you did, but I'm sure you saw your opportunity as well. Novak was already dead, and Corde had destroyed your blackmail tape. You knew Corde's death would spare your brother from being investigated. And maybe there was a part of you that wanted revenge on him for what he had done and for all of his manipulations."

"Did I miss something in the coroner's report?" Elle asked. "Has your Scientific Investigative Division found any physical evidence that contradicts my story of Drew's suicide? Because my lawyer told me today that your department's forensics supports everything I said."

"It was a good story," I admitted. "It stayed very close to the truth. I'm sure you practiced the part for days. You choreographed where Corde would be, how he would be holding his gun, and the angle of the bullet. By factoring in the struggle, you were able to account for how the blood splatter would strike you. Your crime scene was staged pretty much to perfection."

"So you're admitting there is no evidence to convict me?"

"I thought I made that clear at the onset of our meeting. That's the reason I'm going to need you to confess to murdering Corde."

She was smiling now, although a bit incredulously. "You have just told me a good story, Detective. But you had better never even hint at your wild theories outside of this room. If you do, you will be in litigation hell for the rest of your life."

"You still don't understand," I said. "I have no interest in telling the sordid story behind Corde's death. My only interest is in your confessing to his murder. And I really don't even care how you and your lawyer spin that story. What I'm doing here is giving you a window of opportunity to confess. If you don't, you will end up facing that which you most fear—the court of public opinion."

Her face was chalky white, from fear or anger, or both. "I won't submit to your blackmail. If you try to slander me regarding my relationship with my brother, I will bring every resource at my disposal to crush you."

"I am not Drew Corde. Your privacy should never have been violated and exploited. I will not use your relationship as a bargaining chip."

Elle's face showed her confusion. "But what?" she asked. "I don't understand any of this."

"I can't let you get away with murder."

"But you just said you weren't charging me."

"If you don't confess to the shooting, I will see that you're arrested for another crime."

Elle closed her eyes, and it was a second before she opened them again. In the space of that long blink I could see the realization had come over her.

"The first time I met Corde, he took me to his trophy room and told me that hunting was in his DNA. He was proud of all those dead animals. It didn't matter to him that some of them were endangered. That's why I became convinced that, given the opportunity, he was the kind of man who would hunt down and kill an angel with no qualms. For him, the sport of it would trump any ethical concerns. I don't know if he ever did that. I'm beginning to doubt I will ever know. But given the opportunity, it's something he would have done.

"In college I took a humanities course on nineteenth-century colonialism. I remember very little about that class other than one quote that stayed with me. My professor said Cecil Rhodes and others of his ilk could be summed up in something Rhodes said.

"'If I could annex the planets,' Rhodes said, 'I would.' That's how much Rhodes believed in British colonialism, and that's how Corde was when it came to hunting. There was nothing he didn't want to take for his own. I was slow to make the connection, but I finally did. I should have seen why Corde was trying to make a deal with me and put an end to my investigation. It should have been clear to me there was an ulterior motive for his willingness to give up your brother. Corde knew I was still hunting him, and he knew I already had him dead to rights even if I didn't know it at the time."

The truth had come out in my cryptic dreams, and in the echoes I could not quite hear, and in my thoughts, but it was a matter of my connecting everything and finally seeing it.

I laid down the photo so that Elle could get a good look at it.

"I'm sure either you or Corde destroyed the copy of this picture in the trophy room," I said. "RHD tells me that when they went through Corde's house, all the pictures were gone. But this particular photo was different from most of the others. There's no dead animal on display and no sign of a triumphant hunt."

The picture showed Corde's yacht, the *Wizard of OZ*, out on the open sea. Three men were staring into a monitor. Corde, Novak, and Neal Bass were watching what was happening. Elle was away from the others, sitting by herself.

"Corde gave Neal Bass a picture from that night," I said. "It was Corde's way of making Bass a secret sharer. Their mutual guilt had each of them watching the other's back. Bass said the outing had been planned for weeks. Special work had been done on the yacht in preparation for the trip. It needed a particular kind of launching pad that wouldn't destroy the yacht. I was able to obtain some of the work invoices."

I placed the paperwork in front of Elle, but she didn't look at it. She was staring at the meeting room wall, but looking far beyond it.

"I have the signed statement of Neal Bass. It details how everyone knew the purpose of the voyage, including you."

Elle didn't look at that paperwork either.

"I have also compiled documentation that shows the night the yacht sailed and the morning that it returned. There are statements, pictures, and fueling records that corroborate the time frame."

I gave Elle a chance to speak, but when she didn't, I said, "Bass said everything was documented in video taken by the UAV. He said a few days after your voyage Corde showed all of you the footage in the Bunker. All of you understood the need for secrecy.

"On the night it happened, Bass said champagne was uncorked and fireworks were shot. If you look closely at the picture, you can actually see a few of those opened bottles on the deck. Bass said you were drinking along with everyone else."

"Wouldn't you?" she asked, finally breaking her silence. "I just wanted to dull my mind."

"The ship traveled some fifteen miles offshore. According to Bass, there were no other ships visible in any direction and nothing on the radar. But you weren't alone by any means. All around you were blue whales.

"They are called living monuments, you know. They are the largest animals to have ever lived on our planet. Their majesty is unparalleled. We are lucky to have them still swimming our oceans. Somehow, someway, we had enough restraint not to kill off their species. The entire world now recognizes the magnificence of blue whales, and because their numbers have been so reduced, everyone knows they are sacrosanct and untouchable. They are living treasures beyond measure.

"But one man didn't recognize this. Corde had to get his leviathan. Once he heard about blue whales being off the coast, he felt compelled to act. He was more obsessed than Ahab. He had this compulsion to kill something that was bigger than twenty elephants combined. The nighttime was perfect for his purposes. That's when blue whales come up to feed. Apparently it didn't matter to Corde that these gentle giants only eat krill, sea life smaller than shrimp.

"Bass thinks the missile strike killed the blue whale instantly. He said the videotape all of you watched made it look that way. I hope he's right in that. Blue whales are known for their vocalizations. Their songs aren't as haunting as those of the humpback whales, but they communicate with one another from incredibly long distances. I hope this one died before he had a chance to voice his anguish.

"It was a male, by the way. Corde was probably counting on all its remains disappearing into the ocean. Before the hunting of blue whales was banned, whalers used to inflate them with air so they wouldn't sink. But some evidence lingered on the surface, and it was gathered. And the crime for killing a blue whale is severe."

"I was just a passenger," she said.

"What will your court of public opinion say about that?" I asked. "And what will they say about you watching fireworks and drinking champagne and viewing home movies of the carnage that occurred?"

"I had no choice."

"That's not going to fly. Take Bambi syndrome and multiply it by about a million times. You will be reviled. I am giving you a chance to pick your poison. I am sure you and your mouthpiece will come up with some hanky-waving tearjerker as to why you killed Corde. And in the end, you'll probably spend about the same time in prison for either crime. But in one scenario you'll no doubt appear sympathetic to many, whereas in the other you'll always be the villain."

It was something I didn't need to say. Elle already knew that. And she knew if news of her involvement in the whale hunt got out, it would kill her career and reputation.

Her sigh was faint, but there was a world of hurt and pain in the sound. I was certain she wasn't acting, and despite what W.C. Fields said I didn't think I had seen the devil.

"You won't prosecute Robert?"

"If I can determine he didn't have anything to do with the death of Novak, there will be no arrest."

"And you'll make sure I'm never implicated in the whale hunt?"

"I made the same promise to Bass I'll make to you: if you cooperate I will bury all the evidence that ties you into what happened off the coast."

"I'll talk to my lawyer," she said. "We'll be releasing a statement. If you keep my private life private, I'll admit to shooting Drew."

CHAPTER 28:

ASHES TO ASHES

The reminder had come in the mail: the month of September had been torn out of a calendar.

There was no return address on the envelope, and there was no note or explanation. The postmark showed the envelope had been mailed in Larkspur. The only ink applied by a human hand was the circled date of September 23rd. The significance of that date became clear when I read the notation supplied by the calendar: *First Day of Autumn.*

It didn't take a genius to figure out who had sent me the page from the calendar.

A week after receiving the mailer, I found myself behind the walls of San Quentin, being escorted to see Ellis Haines.

Nine months had passed since my last visit to the penitentiary. Absence hadn't made my heart grow fonder. The claustrophobia of closing walls, and the dampness of San Francisco Bay, was like a cold vise on my chest. Whenever I visit San Quentin, I can't help but feel as if I am the prisoner there. It's a sensation that stays with me long after I escape its walls.

Haines was housed in the Adjustment Center, a segregated section with six cells that was the most closely monitored prison block in San Quentin. His eight-foot-by-six-foot cell was too small to meet in; we always had our talks in a larger cell known as the lawyer's room.

I arrived at our meeting spot before Haines, and took a seat. Before being checked through security, I'd signed my personal possessions into temporary storage. Because pens were considered potential weapons, I had a felt marker to write with. Along with that I had a micro-recorder. I hit "Record" and then stated my name, the date of my visit, where the recording was being made, and the reason I was there. Then I played it back to make sure everything was working. I didn't like the uncertain sound of my voice. I'd heard war correspondents dodging bullets who sounded less shaky. I took a deep breath and made a second recording. What I heard wasn't Edward R. Murrow, but at least I now sounded post-adolescent.

A few minutes later the Weatherman made his approach. A quiet entrance was not his style. He was crooning à la Al Jolson, and his song echoed in the hallways. Hearing a joyous voice raised in prison is usually as unexpected as hearing a songbird trilling in a barren landscape, but this was Ellis Haines after all. He made you listen. Haines seemed oblivious of his surroundings, as insouciant as a poker player holding pocket aces. His song sounded familiar, even if I couldn't be sure if I had ever heard it before.

Boy began to sigh, looked up at the sky,
And told the moon his little tale of woe.
Oh, shine on, shine on, harvest moon
Up in the sky;
I ain't had no lovin'

Since April, January, June or July,
Snow time ain't no time to stay
Outdoors and spoon;
So shine on, shine on, harvest moon.

My visit had coincided with a full moon, I realized. Haines the meteorologist would know it was the harvest moon.

Inmates are not usually kind critics, but at the conclusion of Haines's song there was cheering and a round of applause. I didn't join in. The song talked about kissing under the harvest moon; Haines would want to kill under it.

He came with an escort of three correctional officers, and everyone knew the drill. Haines entered the cell, and then the door closed behind him and the two of us were locked in. Facing me, he put his hands through a slot and waited to be unfettered.

I turned on the tape recorder and said, "The inmate Ellis Haines is now in the room. It is approximately eleven in the morning. Mr. Haines has agreed that I may record our conversation. Is this acceptable to you, Mr. Haines?"

"It is," he said, and then pretending excitement said, "Hi, Mom!"

Haines spoke to me while a correctional officer worked on his cuffs. "The fall is my favorite time of year, Detective. What about you?"

"I think I prefer spring."

"You're not serious, are you? The spring is like some harlot feigning sensuality. It is not until the fall when the year gets down to its real business. I always await the Harvest Moon with enormous anticipation."

"Next time I see the Great Pumpkin I'll give him your regards."

"Please don't *squash* my hopes and forget."

Two of the correctional officers groaned. I didn't want Haines to have even that satisfaction and didn't react. Finally freed of his cuffs, Haines took his place across from me at the table where I was sitting. All the guards took their leave except for one; he positioned himself outside the cell.

"How nice of you to join me at the start of fall," he said. "I even love the name of my favorite season. You don't want to be a *fall* guy, and no one wants to *fall* to pieces. People are afraid of *falling* under a spell. You *fall* in the gutter, and you *fall* into disgrace. And in your case, you've always worried about a *fall* from grace, haven't you Detective?"

"Right now I'm more worried about falling asleep."

"And then there's the biggest fall of all, to fall in love. Did you fall in love with that woman in your life?"

"If you cross that line again," I said, "I will take my leave of you right now and never come back."

"Excuse me, Detective; I wouldn't want to *fall* out of your favor."

"You've never been in my favor."

"I doubt that," said Haines in an insinuating tone that I tried to ignore.

"Your recent visit to L.A. piqued the interest of the Feds," I said. "Most of the questions they wanted me to ask stemmed from your court appearance."

"It was a tour de force, if I do say so myself."

"Tour de farce," I said, pretending to write that down.

"I was hoping you might visit with me again during my visit in L.A., but you were being a *busy bee* weren't you?"

I wasn't drawn in by his Dumbledore reference.

Referring to my notes, I said, "When you were under oath in court, you expressed your disdain at how victim number nine was strangled."

"How could I not have? To use a Texas idiom, the murderer was all hat and no cattle. His premise of using fishnet stockings wasn't bad, mind you, even if it did seem derivative of some desperate Hollywood screenwriter. The stockings would have made an effective garrote if used properly, but our bumbler clearly botched it. That's why he resorted to bludgeoning her. I could respect the work of a copycat, but only if the imitation was artfully done."

"And yet you said it took you some time to become proficient in dispatching your own victims."

"I believe you're taking that statement out of context. I said that the more you practice your craft, the better you get. I was not specific as to what I was practicing."

"But you were referring to the women you killed, were you not?"

"Everyone interprets art differently."

I referred back to the questions the FBI's Behavioral Sciences Unit (BSU) wanted answered.

"You've never addressed how you chose your victims, but judging from what you said in court, you indicated that you were looking for a certain 'type.'"

"It was more a case of knowing it when I saw it."

"And what was 'it'?"

"I call it the *Danse Macabre*."

He said it with a French accent, but that didn't make it sound romantic.

"Can you elaborate?"

"'Vanity of vanities, saith the Preacher, vanity of vanities; all is vanity.'"

His quoting from the Bible surprised me, and he looked pleased at that.

"My actions were designed to expose the vain glories of our everyday existence," he said. "Mine was a call to the *Danse Macabre*."

"You said that victim number nine's—and I'm quoting here—'mousy brown hair, styled like a cross between a flapper and Princess Leia, would have kept her safe from me.' Were specific looks a part of your selection process?"

"Most victims of homicides are prostitutes and the disadvantaged," said Haines. "The dispossessed have always been expedient victims, and their deaths have gone largely unnoticed. I tried to take an evenhanded—excuse the pun—approach and made sure my selections were based on suitability rather than mere opportunity."

I continued with my questions, and Haines surprised me by keeping his word and playing a minimal amount of games. Among our topics were the amount of premeditation he practiced, his ability to compartmentalize, how he maintained the appearance of normality to friends and family, and whether anger was a motivation in his murders.

He balked a few times, playing around with his answers. He was coy about whether he used a machete before settling on a garrote as his weapon of choice, telling me, "One must keep handy a bargaining chip—or bargaining knife."

And he took exception when I asked questions that tried to determine his various personality disorders.

"Don't waste our precious time," he said. "I know the headshrinkers like their labels. I have seen how they've slotted me into the personality disorder categories of being antisocial, borderline, and narcissistic. But with each of those generalizations, they've done their best to fit a square peg into a round hole."

I made a few notes while Haines was talking, and he seemed to find that amusing.

"Are you playing at being my shrink?" he asked.

"That's about the last job in the world I would want."

"Then why are you scribbling? You're already taping everything I'm saying."

"In case BSU asks me about context, I'll have my notes."

"Then perhaps I should be the one making notes. That is, if anyone has cause to ask about you."

"What does that mean?"

"I'll leave it as an open-ended observation. But I wish I had been a fly on the wall when shrinks asked you about the experience we had together. Everyone wants me to be honest, but what about you? I suspect that for all concerned it was better that you lied."

"The next time I visit I'll leave time for you to ask your questions of me," I said, "but right now I have a flight to L.A. I need to catch."

I closed with the five W's on the tape, but as I reached to click off the recorder, Haines said, "That's all, folks!"

"Couldn't resist?" I said.

"Oh, I could," he said, "and I did."

"Am I catching some undercurrent?"

"I think it's more like a rip current."

He leaned close to me and whispered, "Your secret is safe with me."

"Thank God. When the Colonel trusted me with the secret of his eleven herbs and spices, I wasn't sure what to do with it."

Haines said, "Ashes to ashes, dust to dust."

"I think I'm missing something here."

"I was just doing a little musing. I find it interesting that our journey through fire continues."

"I'll let you take the scenic tour of hell by yourself, if you don't mind."

"I hope you're not mired in guilt," he whispered. "After all, it was a case of self-defense."

"What I'm mired in is trying to make sense of whatever the hell you're saying."

"The Chinese say the fire you kindle for your enemy often burns you more than it burns your enemy. But I am glad to say that you weren't the one that burned, were you?"

And then I realized what he was saying, but wished I didn't. "No," I said.

"That's right," whispered Haines encouragingly. "Cryptic words are best. We'll call him 'No' for short, won't we? There's something very classical about that, much like Odysseus telling the Cyclops that his name was Noman."

I opened my mouth, but no words came out. The Novak homicide was still open. Elle's brother Robert had been able to prove to me he wasn't responsible. For the past month I had been looking for a killer that Haines was saying was me.

"And when Odysseus blinded the Cyclops," said Haines, "and he and his men escaped, the Cyclops screamed for revenge, but his desires were foiled by his own words, for he yelled out, 'Noman did this to me.'"

"You," I said.

"I was hoping you would at least send me a thank-you card, but I understood the need for you to be circumspect."

"I didn't," I said. "I wouldn't."

"What you wouldn't have done is tell me about the fire, and the drone, if you hadn't wanted protection. From that starting point, it was just a matter of following the man that was following you."

"It was never—I never—"

"You're beginning to sound like Lady Macbeth. Don't go there, for my sake and for yours. You need not dwell on this conversation with all its hypothetical suppositions. But if you do, remember that had not certain actions been taken, you would be dead.

"And in the fiery landscapes that we both continue to walk, remember it was fire that saved your life."

My words and my breath kept catching, but finally I was able to yell, "Guard! Let me out."

CHAPTER 29:

COMING HOME FROM WAR

On the flight home I kept trying to get a handle on what Haines had said and my role in what had occurred. It was like trying to navigate through a fog—no, more like killer smog. It hurt to breathe, and my eyes stung because I kept forgetting to blink. I was trying to arrive at a truth, even if I couldn't see it.

I wondered if my blind spot could explain my having missed the obvious or if it was wishful thinking that protected me. In the not too distant past, three men had tried to kill me. At the time I had blamed Haines for sending out a hit squad, but he had distanced himself from those followers and claimed they acted of their own accord. The threesome had subsequently turned up dead. The investigators working the case were convinced Haines had ordered the executions from prison. No one knew if Haines had acted to protect himself or to exact revenge, but no one doubted that he had committed murder from behind bars.

I knew what he was capable of doing, so how was it that I had speculated in Haines's presence? Had I thrown out the bait to him? Had I purposely enticed him to look into who had set fire to my house? I had even introduced drones into our conversation. Or he had drawn me out and made me try to look smarter than I really was. He had quoted from the Shocking Blue song "Venus," and I had tried to be cute, tried to show him that I was cleverer than he was, and I had said, 'It was Mars, not Venus.' My martial comment was clue enough for him, especially when I added a drone to the equation. As it turned out, most of my suppositions proved to be wrong, but I had been right enough for Haines's purposes.

During my visit to L.A. County Jail, Haines had wanted me to whisper a name to him. He had asked me to sanction a hit. At the time, I'd refused. But had I? Had I whispered just enough to condemn Novak?

When I confronted Elle Barrett Browning, I'd told her that I couldn't let her get away with murder. Was I holding myself to that same standard?

In my fog/smog I drove home. Sirius was waiting for me, and he could tell right away how much I was hurting. I went into my dark bedroom, and I didn't turn on a light. It wouldn't help penetrate my gloom, I knew. I was sure nothing could. And that's when Sirius brought me a ball. I tried to ignore him, but it's hard to ignore a hairy muzzle breathing hot air just inches from your face. He dropped the ball, and it rolled into me. When I refused to respond, he retrieved the ball and dropped it again. And when I still didn't react, he grabbed the ball and rolled it toward me for a third time.

I broke my silence and said, "I don't want to play, Sirius."

My words drove him off, but only for a minute. He returned with Mr. Alligator, one of his prized stuffed animals. My big, bad wolf has four stuffed animals. He likes to cuddle with them and carry them around the house. Sometimes I chide him for being a baby, but we both know I'm the enabler. They were Christmas presents to him from me.

I ignored Mr. Alligator, so Sirius left the room and came back with Vincent, a bunny rabbit with a missing—well, chewed-off—ear. In answer, I turned over. That didn't stop Sirius from going to get Mrs. Roo. I learned of the stuffed kangaroo's presence when I felt it drop on my back.

"Go away," I told Sirius, and he did, but not for long.

When he came back to the room I could hear him breathing. I did my best to try not to acknowledge him. For five minutes, or maybe ten, he sat there and waited. Finally I opened an eye. In his mouth was Kong the gorilla. Kong is Sirius's favorite. When he saw me looking at Kong, Sirius gave me his prized possession. He pushed it at me, insisting I take his baby, and as bad as I was feeling, I couldn't suppress the tickle in my stomach.

I laughed, and I wiped a tear, and I cradled Kong, and I hugged my partner.

* * *

Sirius's concern over my welfare managed to get me up and moving at zombie speed. That was about as good as I could do, since I didn't feel quite alive. I took Sirius for a walk, and then I fed him. Then I had to take care of myself, which wasn't as easy. I did a few tasks that didn't require thought, before settling in front of my computer to check the day's email.

There was one piece of unusual correspondence. I couldn't remember having ever received an email with an address ending in *@us.army.mil*. The Reluctant Hero had dropped me a note. The subject line read *Sua Sponte*, and it took me a minute to remember the Ranger motto.

'*Of my own accord,*' I thought, and clicked on the mail and started reading.

Never thanked you for the dinner, man. It sure was one hell of an evening. You always that much fun?

Afghanistan is about 10,000 clicks from Hollyweird, like a universe and then some apart, but we still get our Pony Express reports here. It sounds like your case took some weird turns. Maybe you'll write back sometime and tell me what happened. BTW, if a movie is going to happen I'm thinking Brad Pitt should play my part.

Sorry we didn't get to talk after the ceremony. All I could think about was making my escape from L.A. I know I owe you big time for helping to make things right for me. Anyway, next time I'll buy drinks. You can choose the place as long as it's not the Chateau Marmont. It's a good thing I'm getting combat pay, so I can take care of that tab. Drinking there was part of my bucket list. I guess it doesn't take an Einstein to figure out why I was trying to make some headway on my list.

Now that I'm here, things seem clearer. I know that must sound strange, but I guess I needed the distance. For a long time I convinced myself that my life could never come to any good end. I think I needed a world of conflict because that's all I felt inside. But for the first time since forever, I think I'm finally ready to come home from war. I never imagined the possibility of any kind of life awaiting me, but maybe I'll actually be able to join the living.

Kelley emailed me a picture of her little girl. She's beautiful like her mother. She also sent a picture of Matthew holding his little sister. In the pic he was wearing a Lakers jersey that came down to about his knees. I don't know why, but seeing those pictures sort of freed me up, and I got this notion in my head that one day I might be able to be a real father, not a ghost father, and have a real wife, not some fantasy woman I could never have.

Didn't mean to get all heavy here, but like I said, it's easier for me to think better from a distance. And guardians of the night got to stick together, right?

Give your hellhound a hug from me.

More than 'nuff for now,

Caine

I read his note three times, and then I called Lisbet and asked her if I could come over.

* * *

We settled down on Lisbet's coach. I probably looked like hell because she extended her hand toward me and started kneading my arm.

"There's a lot I need to tell you," I said, "but I'm afraid to start because I don't know where it's going to lead, and that's kind of scary."

Her face suddenly looked about as drawn as mine. "What's the matter?"

"I'm the matter. It wasn't that long ago—even though it now seems forever—when both of us were listening to 'Angel of the Morning,' and you told me that it almost felt as if our relationship was an affair. And then I got caught up in my cases, and it seems we've hardly seen each other since, and all this time we both kind of left that door closed."

"I know you've had a crushing workload."

"That's been my excuse," I said. "But I also think that I've been avoiding you."

In little more than a whisper she asked, "Why is that?"

"I thought that by keeping my distance, I could also keep bad things away from you."

"I don't understand."

"I was afraid that you might be—tainted—by my world. I didn't want you to be dirtied by me."

"And that's why you've been keeping me at arms length?"

"That's not what I wanted. But I was sure it was the right thing to do. After the fire I was assigned this one headshrinker who liked to talk about everyone having their shadow side. He said there was darkness in all of us, and that what happened to me could make me potentially vulnerable to that darkness. But I acted like that wasn't an issue, and I made a joke of the whole thing. I did my Obi-Wan imitation for that shrink, and I said, 'Beware the dark side, Luke,' and all the while I pretended like everything was fine. I fooled everyone in my life except for maybe Seth, and I tried to fool myself. But all this time I've been looking for my way out of that fire. And all this time I've been burning. And the only thing I was sure of was that if I was going to combust, I didn't want you burning with me."

"I wish you'd allowed me a say in that."

"I've been as dishonest with you as I was with the shrinks."

"Maybe you're not as good at hiding who you are as you think."

"Do you remember when I stayed over at your place, and Sirius kept interrupting our lovemaking? The reason he was going ballistic is because of what was happening outside. Novak was recording us. I found out that night, but I didn't tell you how our private time together became an object of amusement for Corde and his friends. And since then I've been afraid to tell you what happened. I felt guilty for bringing that evil into your world. And I've been afraid of what else I might bring."

"Do you think there aren't ugly things in my world, Michael?"

"When my house was on fire, one of the first things I thought was how glad I was that you weren't there."

"And when you told me what happened, the first thing I thought was that I wish I had been there to help you fight those flames."

"Everything in these cases I've been working might come back to bite me. Every time I crossed the line, I told myself I was doing the right thing. I brought in a civilian to help me, and the cover story was that he was there as part of another case. I manipulated events, and because of that people died. And when I couldn't find the evidence to solve a case, I compromised others and put them in impossible situations, essentially blackmailing them into compliance.

"And right now I can't even be sure in my own mind if I'm complicit in a murder or not. Ellis Haines took some cues from what I said and then must have had one of his followers trail me. That brought them to Novak. It was a Haines disciple that fire-bombed him in his car. Haines was careful to not come right out and say that, but that's what happened."

"And you think you're at fault?"

"I know I'm a long way from being above reproach."

"Let me play in your blame game then. Novak was trying to kill you. And he wasn't alone. You were lured to a spot where the intent was to run you down in what was supposed to look like a tragic accident. How is all of that on you?"

"I'm supposed to be better than the people I'm investigating. The fire changed me. It started me on a slippery slope. When Haines was on trial and I was on the stand, I lied under oath. I never read him his Miranda rights, even though that's my sworn testimony. And I threatened to murder him while the two of us were burning, which is something else I denied under oath. And now Haines and I have more deaths and more fires we've experienced together. I don't want any of that to touch you."

"Do you think you're the only one who is protective, Michael? Don't make the mistake of thinking that it's nobler for you to retreat than to reach out."

"Do you still think I'm on the side of the angels?"

"More than ever."

"I guess we'll never know. My search for angels has reached a dead end. I thought Bass might be able to provide me with answers. I sweated him, and he said he knew that Corde and Novak were up to something, but they kept it between them. He was sure it must have been some kind of hunting game. Bass said that Corde was a proponent of holographic gaming and had invested substantial research and development money on that front. He was sure it would revolutionize video games, and perhaps war games. So it's likely I was chasing a ghost, and not an angel. But why the secrecy? And why would Corde have made that announcement about judging angels?

"Bass also said he overheard Novak talking to Corde about something he recollects was called 'Project Revelations.' And when Novak realized that Bass was within earshot, he suddenly clammed up. There are all these whispers out there, but that's all they are.

"Corde told me I'd never find out about the angels unless I played ball with him. He said the only way to the truth was to go through him. I guess he was right about that. He got rid of all the evidence. All his hard drives were wiped clean. And anything that had to do with his illegal hunts—whether or not they involved angels—was burned, deleted, or destroyed."

Lisbet nodded and smiled, and that surprised me. "What's so funny?"

"Did you really think you could find your way to angels through Corde? That's not how it works. And neither should you expect to find angels through police work."

I found myself smiling too. That surprised me even more. "I had hoped Wrong Pauley's autopsy would supply answers, but it's not even clear if he was murdered. It's possible his body went into shock because of his cold turkey and his decision to stop drinking. He died of respiratory failure. His system showed elevated levels of epinephrine, but it's unclear whether he was injected with it or he had some extreme fight or flight event that resulted in his death."

"Flight," said Lisbet. "I choose to believe he departed with angels."

"I hope you're right. I came over here to try and convince you that we shouldn't be together and that you didn't need or want my kind of toxicity in your life, but at the same time I was praying you wouldn't listen to me."

"Consider your prayers answered."

I thought about Caine Pullman's note to me and how he was now able to envision a future. I looked at Lisbet and I saw my own future.

And I finally knew it was time for me to come home from the war as well.

THE END

ACKNOWLEDGMENTS

Like Blanche DuBois, I have always depended on the kindness of strangers—and friends. For many years Bob Connely trained dogs, and I appreciate his encouraging me to ask him any and all canine question I might have. Since the publication of *Burning Man*, Bob and other readers have been sending me interesting articles, cartoons, and trivia that have to do with the world of dogs (I can be reached at my website of www.alanrussell.net or on Facebook at www.facebook.com/AlanRussellMysteryAuthor). It was one of those stories sent by Paul Dover that found its way into the plot of this book. Paul is one of my international readers, and is trying to convert me into a Nottingham Forest booster.

I would also like to thank Kevin Smith for his work in helping me improve this book. I suppose it's funny, if not surprising, that in our conversations Kevin and I spent ten percent of the time talking about this book, and ninety percent of the time talking college hoops. And speaking of hoops, here's a tip of the hat to fellow basketball junkie Andy Kurz for doing his lawyerly best to answer some legal questions I had that pertained to the plot.

As always, my thanks and gratitude goes out to Laura and Cynthia. Writing a book is like running a marathon, and I'm glad to not have to run it alone.

And finally, I wish to thank the entire crew at Thomas & Mercer. Since making my home at T&M I have always been encouraged to write the novel that I most want to write. I have worked with many publishers, and I truly believe that T&M is the best. My thanks to Alison, Alan, Jacque, Gracie, Tiffany, and everyone else on the T&M team that helped with the publication and marketing of this novel.

ABOUT THE AUTHOR

Photo © 2012 Stathis Orphanos

Alan Russell is the bestselling author of ten novels, including *Burning Man, St. Nick, Shame, Multiple Wounds, The Hotel Detective,* and *Political Suicide.* His books have been nominated for most of the major awards in crime fiction, and he has won a Lefty award for best comedic mystery, a USA Today Critics' Choice Award, two San Diego Book Awards for best mystery novel, and the Odin Award for Lifetime Achievement from the San Diego Writers/Editor Guild. He lives with his wife and children in Encinitas, California.